UPRISING

FIRES OF PROVIDENCE SERIES

A NOVEL BY

DAWN JAYNE

Time and Tide Books

www.timeandtidepublishing.com

Time and Tide Publishing, LLC
7040 Seminole Pratt Whitney Rd. Suite 25-109
Loxahatchee, FL 33470

Second Edition 2012
www.timeandtidepublishing.com

Cover by Tincar Creations.
Eagle stock photo credit AlaskaStock (deviantart)

ISBN-13: 978-0-9856576-2-8

10 0 9 8 5 6 5 7 6 2 6

Acknowledgements

Writing a book isn't easy, but finding people who are willing to help you write a better book is considerably harder. I'm truly blessed to have friends who gave up time to read and offer invaluable feedback.

Tina, you are the best of the best! Busy with your own writing, you still took time for mine. Your honesty and encouragement kept me going and I couldn't have done this without your support. Great Karma awaits you!

Jodi, your eagle-eye edits are the stuff of legend. My story and skills improved, thanks to your hard work and advice. I'll never look at an em dash the same again. You rock!

I'd like to thank my beta readers, and all those who read my unpublished stories over the years. So many of you offered kind words and encouragement, and I don't think I would've found the courage to write this book without you. You're a fantastic and supportive group!

Finally, I have to mention Time and Tide Publishing. The confidence of knowing my story is in capable hands is a wonderful feeling, and allows the muse to run free. That's perhaps the greatest gift a writer can receive, and any words of gratitude pale in comparison. From my heart and soul, thank you!

Dedication

To my family: You are my greatest inspiration. There are no others I'd rather have by my side during this remarkable journey. I love you!

Chapter One
Tyre

Tyre suspected the young woman would hold a grudge against him. Not because he was going to kill her—she'd thank him for that later—but because of the sex. He knew he took things a bit too far this time, but curiosity got the better of him. With any luck, the inevitable reprimand would be light, but it was hard to tell these days. Being an angel was getting tricky.

The girl, Katie Theresa Connors, had an Irish name and features to match, with pale skin and a mop of red hair. The Catholic School uniform completed the look, though it was currently in a state of disarray.

"I'm never going to get all these wrinkles out," she said. Her attempts to smooth the knee-length plaid skirt bunching around her waist were proving troublesome in the confines of the car. She finally gave up and started to work on the white blouse.

"I hope my roommate's asleep when I get back." She buttoned up, then readjusted her little cross necklace. "She has such a big mouth; the whole senior class will know." Katie re-wrapped a blue scarf around her neck, arranging it with practiced hands until it was a fluffy bow. She looked around, felt under her bottom, and patted around on the floorboard. Tyre picked up the small handbag from where it had fallen between his feet, and held it up by the strap.

"Thanks." She pulled out a tube of lipstick, dotted on some color and blended it with her finger before adding a touch of gloss. Tyre knew it was bubblegum flavored; the taste still lingered on his lips. He couldn't say he cared for it.

Katie made a few last adjustments to her hair and looked with satisfaction at her reflection in the little mirror before flipping up the visor. She favored Tyre with a brilliant smile.

"So, do I still look like a girl who snuck out of a hotel to have sex with a complete stranger?" She stretched across the seat and kissed him.

"Yes, you do," Tyre said. She giggled, but he wasn't joking. "And all things considered, we're hardly strangers." He winked. She blushed and bit her bottom lip, probably thinking he was being flirtatious instead of literal.

Tyre chuckled. He was getting tremendous amusement at her expense tonight, in several ways. Though Katie had tried to put on a show of innocence, he knew their tryst hadn't been the girl's first. He was aware of her history and it was nothing short of scandalous. With a recently deceased mother and a father working two jobs to keep his children in private school, Katie had tried to find respite from grief and loneliness. She'd discovered the allure of cads, and there had been quite a few. Tyre couldn't begrudge her the small comfort, especially since her desperate need for intimacy—even the illusion—had served him quite well. He turned the keys in the ignition and adjusted the rearview mirror which had been knocked out of place during the somewhat awkward liaison.

"You were right about the monuments," Katie said. "They were amazing at night. I'm glad you invited me."

"I'm glad you accepted. Though I admit, I was surprised; I tend to intimidate. The scars didn't frighten you?"

"Not much," Katie said with a shrug. "I kind of like the one around your eye. I had fun tonight. I hope you did, too."

Tyre knew she wasn't talking about the Washington D.C. scenery. "It was a unique experience, one I may remember with fondness." He didn't mention he had other feelings as well, ones not as noble. The girl had given him problems in the past, and he considered his motivations held a touch of malevolence. Why he was risking himself to save her again was vexing. It had been quite a hassle this time, too, which reminded him...

"Why didn't you leave the hotel last night?" he asked, switching on the headlights and maneuvering through the darkened parking lot.

"What are you talking about?"

Tyre pulled into sparse traffic and headed for the interstate. "Last night, at nine fifteen, you were going to leave the hotel and start walking North on the highway, toward the entertainment plaza. You dressed in an ill-fitting purple skirt, applied far too much make-up, and styled your hair in a way you thought appeared exotic, but simply looked unkempt. Then, after such woeful efforts, you failed to depart. Why is that?"

Katie puffed out an angry breath. Tyre knew she was taken aback by his recitation of private moments, and perhaps his opinion on her fashion sense.

"How did you know that?" she demanded, but then leaned closer. "Are you psychic?" Her eyes lit at the idea, any offense apparently forgotten.

"Not by your definition of the word, but I am a good listener. You must've mentioned it at some point." Tyre shrugged as if the answer were of no consequence, though he wanted to wring the truth from the girl. "I was just curious as to why your plans changed." He presented her with an endearing smile. He could be charming when he wished.

Katie slapped a hand over her face and looked out the window at the passing trees. "I swear, I don't remember saying any of that. I can't believe I told you about the hair! I ramble sometimes."

Tyre agreed, but didn't say so. There was no need for rudeness, after all.

"Sister Bernard was on patrol," Katie said. "She pulled a chair out of her room and sat at the end of the hall all night, reading. She wouldn't let anyone get by, not even to get a snack from the vending machine. The other chaperones trusted us, but Sister B is insane."

"Afraid one of her girls would sneak out and engage in sinful acts? You're right. Insanity."

Katie giggled, and Tyre shook his head. He should've guessed one of the clergy caused all the trouble. He did appreciate the irony, though. He pulled up the sleeve on his jacket and glanced at the thick, metal bracelet on his wrist, often mistaken for a timepiece. It glowed brightly and Tyre frowned. He'd been out too long and needed to hurry things up.

"Cool watch," Katie commented, leaning over to get a better look. "That's a Yin-Yang symbol on the face, right? Where did you get it?"

"It's called a *taijitu*," Tyre said, explaining the black and white symmetrical pattern of the design. "It was issued at work."

Katie turned in the seat and curled one leg up so she could fully face him. "Where do you work?"

"That's a complicated question. Let's just say it's a large organization, and I'm part of a rather select group."

"What do you do?"

Tyre pinched the bridge of his nose and squeezed his eyes shut. He had no desire to engage in the infamous post-coital chitchat, but since she'd been accommodating earlier, he decided to indulge her.

"I travel," he said. "I've done a little of everything, but on this trip I'm in Collections."

"I bet you get to go all over the world. I'm jealous. I've never even been on a plane. I think flying would be amazing."

"It is." Tyre was pleased to say something truthful. He merged onto the interstate and picked up speed. There wasn't much traffic at this late hour, as was his plan; he didn't want or need an audience tonight. He accelerated further, and the engine of the car struggled to keep up. He should've stolen one with more power, but he'd been in a time crunch.

"Hey, I think you missed the exit." Katie pointed as they passed by a ramp.

"So I did. We appear to have something in common now."

"You're going too fast." Katie turned back around and buckled her seat belt.

Tyre knew she was beginning to realize something was out of place. He was a little relieved; she'd been far too trusting until this point, and though it had been useful to him, he still found her casual acceptance a curious thing. He normally encountered fear, or at least suspicion, and employed unique, even brutal, methods to gain compliance. He decided to think on the matter later, put the girl's odd behavior from his mind, and pushed on the gas again.

Katie tensed, grabbing hold of the dash for security. "You need to slow down. I mean it, Dominik, I'm getting scared."

Tyre forgot about that particular deception; there were so many tonight it was hard to keep up. "That's not my name, by the way." He reached across the seat and shook her hand. "Tyre. Pleased to meet you."

"What?" She lost some color. "You lied to me?"

He knew this would soon be the least of her issues with him.

"So, your name is...Tyre?" Her voice held a touch of anger. "Like a teardrop?"

"Like the Phoenician city, if you must make a comparison. I thought you might prefer the name Dominik." He didn't tell her why; she'd get the joke soon enough. "But, you're right to be upset, and I'm going to make it up to you. Watch me."

Tyre made sure Katie's eyes were on him, and called upon one of his more theatrical abilities. He shivered; within seconds, his black hair turned to blonde, his green eyes to brown, and he altered his height to give himself more length. He added a full beard, but it was too itchy; he removed it and flashed a grin at his passenger.

Katie's eyes went wide, her mouth fell open and she screamed in terror.

Tyre placed a finger to his ear and cringed. The girl had impressive volume. With his increased height, his knees pressed against the dash under the steering wheel, so he reached to the lever underneath the seat and slammed it back as far as it would go. Katie continued testing her lung capacity, and in such confined quarters, it needed to cease.

"You don't like blondes?" Tyre asked. "Neither do I. How about this one, then?" He shivered again, changing his hairstyle to a long, reddish-brown. He switched up his skin tone and swapped his eye color to a bright blue. He peeked in the rearview mirror to make sure he'd gotten the costume correct and grunted in satisfaction. He thought Katie would, under different circumstances, appreciate the look. Most women did.

The terrified girl grabbed her silver cross necklace and pushed her back against the door, getting as far away from him as she could. Her trembling shook the seats.

"What are you?" she demanded. "What do you want?"

Tyre considered the questions. There was no reason he had to lie to her at this point, and he'd grown tired of the charade anyway. He cocked an eyebrow. "I'm the angel who's going to save your soul. Again."

"You're insane," Katie whispered and started rummaging through the glove box, her hands shaking as she dumped paperwork and other items all over. Tyre guessed she was looking for something to use as a weapon, so he allowed her to continue; it would earn him a few moments of quiet and nothing in the car could harm him.

He hit the accelerator and tested the steering capabilities. It was almost time for the big finish, and he wanted no mistakes. Tyre started weaving from one lane to another, relishing the adrenaline rush. He laughed until a pair of taillights came up fast on the right. "There might be witnesses." He turned to Katie. "This could be a problem. Try to act natural, will you?"

"Witnesses?" Katie repeated, looking back and forth between Tyre and the road. The broken yellow lines whipped by so fast they appeared almost solid. She started to cry, but then she, too, spotted the other vehicle. She seized the manual handle controlling the windows and cranked as fast as she could, calling out for assistance.

"Brilliant." He cast a sideways look to the girl. "Well, there's no way to avoid them now, is there?" He reached over and grabbed her hand. "Wave. Be polite." He waggled her wrist, making her hand dance. "Say farewell."

"No," Katie screamed, "please!" She tried to pull her arm free as they passed a station wagon with brown side panels. The driver and the woman beside him shot angry glances at the speeding car, but a boy with big dark eyes pressed his face to the window and waved back.

Tyre kept up the assault on the car's engine. He realized he hadn't switched his appearance since the last wardrobe change, and breathed in relief as he regained his familiar form. He turned his attention back to his terrified passenger. "I know you're upset now, but you'll thank me for this later." He patted her knee.

Katie grabbed the cross around her neck again, clutching it like an anchor in a storm. She started to rock back and forth in the seat, praying. She rattled off words without a breath. "Our father who art in heaven hallowed be thy name thy kingdom come thy will be done…"

"The Lord's prayer," Tyre said. "Excellent choice. Very popular."

"…on earth as it is in heaven…" She stopped, sobs catching in her throat as the car switched lanes, coming dangerously close to the guardrail.

Tyre stole a peek at her. "Keep going, you were doing so well. *Give us this day…*" He waved his hand as though helping a child with the alphabet. The car was almost at maximum speed now.

Katie's chin quivered, and she could barely squeak out the words. "Give us this day our daily bread, and forgive us our trespasses as we forgive those who trespass against us…"

"That would be me, right?" The little arrow on the speedometer bounced around, having reached its limit.

"…and lead us not into temptation…"

"But deliver us from evil!" Tyre roared the last words along with her, then twisted the steering wheel hard to the right. Katie wailed as the car lurched, slammed into the guardrail and flipped end over end. Metal twisted and cracked, tires catapulted into the air, and glass shattered with the multiple impacts before the car came to rest, upside down, against an enormous oak.

The crash was devastating, as intended, and Tyre was pleased with his work. He stood a short distance away, having vacated the doomed vehicle before things got too ugly. His massive black wings, the mark of his elite choir, the Heralds, were now in full array. It was a tremendous relief; keeping wings tucked for too long was uncomfortable. They'd started to cramp.

He watched as the only remaining tire still attached to the car continued to spin. The final blow of the crash had been delivered with such force it split the trunk of an ancient tree, and Tyre shook his head in regret. He hated destruction of the environment.

Chapter Two
Great Moment

Tyre was impressed at the speed emergency services mobilized, but more so with the news agencies. He watched an attractive woman in a two-piece purple suit wave a microphone across the barricade that had been set up around the accident scene. On occasion, a uniform would walk too close and she'd call out questions. All but once she was ignored, and the one time she wasn't, the answer was well outside the bounds of civility.

Tyre stood in the middle of the chaos, watching the events he'd set in motion. No one saw him, because he didn't wish it, so he was able to move about the area and observe. He checked the bracelet again and frowned. He was pushing his luck now, but didn't want to leave until he saw the mission complete. He scanned the area, looking for any signs of the ones who hunted his kind, but saw nothing. He kept his guard up, nonetheless.

Police officers walked through the darkness, shining flashlights on the road and in the woods, while others worked on accident reconstruction. A few had taken up position near the barricades to hold back the crowd of on-lookers gathering to watch, some of which were snapping photos.

Tyre saw a mother in a car with four children, the youngest throwing a mighty tantrum. He regarded the woman, looking into her soul. It burned red, the color of wrath. That was always a hard challenge, and being stuck behind an accident on the interstate probably wasn't helping.

Most intriguing was the frenzied activity near the overturned car. Several emergency personnel worked on Katie, while others attempted to extricate her from the mangled mess of steel. It irked him the girl still clung to life; he intended death to be quick. He decided to blame it on the car.

Tyre turned his attention to the family huddled together by their station wagon; the unlucky witnesses who had been in the wrong place at the very wrong time. There were four—a man, woman, and two boys. A police officer stood with them, along with a man holding a sketchpad.

Tyre recognized the older boy as the one who waved through the window. The child was trying to give a description of what he saw, but it was a difficult process as English wasn't his native language. Tourists, Tyre assumed, and had a brief pang of empathy; he hated when his vacations were interrupted.

The little boy, his smooth face anguished, waved his hand and chattered up to the patriarch of the family.

"Apology," the man said in a thick accent. "My nephew is upset. He keeps asking if the girl he saw is going to die."

"Tell him the doctors will do everything they can to help her." The officer smiled down at the child.

"Hope springs eternal," Tyre mused. He stopped listening as he sensed another presence nearby, one of his own kind, and one he recognized even before she shimmered into view. Shay. He scowled.

"What are you doing here?" he asked. "It's not safe for you."

Shay moved closer, her lithe form in contrast to the enormous purple feathery wings springing from her shoulders. "I was coming to tell you the same thing. You've been gone too long and I was sent to find out the problem. The minions have surely noticed your light by now." She raised her eyebrows. "You might not be so fortunate as last time."

Tyre laughed. "They landed a few strikes before I killed them, nothing more. I'm almost done. One more moment I think." He nodded to the girl being loaded onto a stretcher. "Look. Here comes the wayward soul now."

At that moment, a shining gold light enveloped Katie, then pulled away and coalesced into a luminous ball hovering above her body. The light paused, shimmered, then bounced around and came to rest near the two angels.

"Come on," Tyre said to the light bundle, and spun his hand in a 'hurry up' gesture. "Let's go."

The light grew brighter, larger, and finally morphed into an enormous man with wavy auburn hair falling past his shoulders, and eyes like sapphires. Shay did everything but swoon.

"Dominik!" She gathered the tall man into her arms and kissed his cheeks, having to stretch on her toes to do so. "Welcome back. We've missed you."

"Speak for yourself," Tyre whispered, and watched Dominik lift the angel from the ground. She burst into joyous laughter and the hug went on and on.

Tyre rolled his eyes skyward. He knew this man held appeal to females, both human and angel alike, but he never understood why. To his eyes, Dominik looked like a great wooly mammoth on two legs, a prehistoric barbarian—all muscle and mane. Even so, Tyre borrowed the look on occasions when it served his purpose, most recently in the car during his demonstration. He looked close and realized he'd forgotten the little stubble on the cheeks and chin. He shrugged. He'd remember it next time.

Dominik finally placed Shay back on her feet, noticing Tyre as he did so. He stiffened. "Was there a problem that required a Herald?"

"It was nothing," Shay said. "You missed your final marker, that's all."

"By what margin?"

"Only a single day, by human time." She patted his arm. "Everything else went as planned. You'll remember it all, as soon as you return to our realm."

He looked to Tyre. "And you intercepted, I assume?"

"That's three times, if you care to keep count. I'm sure there will be more. You never seem to know when to quit."

Dominik stood tall and his jaw clenched. "Then I owe you my…gratitude." He looked like it killed him to speak the words.

Tyre turned away to conceal his smile. Dominik would be far less grateful later, when he regained memory of his recent lifetime. He would review the events soon, with the support of one of the Red angels. Tyre hoped whichever one volunteered for the duty would counsel the man toward viewing the little romp in the car as entertainment. He doubted it, though. In his experience, most of the Red choir lacked a sense of humor.

Dominik turned toward the body on the stretcher; the body he'd just vacated. The paramedics still attempted to revive Katie, using all manner of devices. "They work to save the flesh." His voice was detached. "Was death not instant?"

"No, though it should've been, I assure you. I recreated the original, charted incident as best I could. I went as fast as that car would allow. It flipped several times before hitting that tree over there, on the passenger side, no less!" Tyre waved a hand in annoyance. "If it were anyone else, the soul would've released instantly. Truly Dominik, it's not my fault you couldn't even manage to die properly."

"I grow weary of your taunts, and your misplaced wit." He moved close to Tyre. "My concern is with other souls who will be affected by this incident. My journey was one of sacrifice; the benefits were not for my sake, but for others. I don't wish my error to hinder their advancement."

"There will be far fewer disruptions now. Had I done nothing, it would've been far worse, for them and for you."

Shay placed hands between the two. "I won't have you arguing again. Tyre, we all know you take great pride in your interceptions. Dominik, you're here now and that's what matters. After today, neither of you will ever have to see one another again—not in this capacity." She beamed up at Dominik.

"I'm to receive my wings?" His eyes grew wide. "So soon?"

"Yes," Shay squealed in delight. "You're going to be asked to join the Blue choir right after your life review. Please act surprised; I wasn't supposed to tell." She placed a hand to her mouth and giggled.

"You're joking," Tyre said, shocked. "Dominik's to be an angel?"

"I petitioned just before I took this journey," he said. "I had no idea I would be accepted so quickly. My understanding was the process took far longer."

"It does, for most," Shay said, "but everyone has been waiting for you to take this step, and they would've been utter fools to delay. It's wonderful."

"It's madness." Tyre glanced up as a brilliant light descended from the sky. "That's your ride, Dominik." He flicked his hands, shooing the human away in disgust. "Get out of here before I become ill."

A statuesque angel appeared and fluttered on the air, her golden wings on full display. Her long dress sparkled with energy as it wafted around her ankles. A soft glow, warm and inviting, emanated from her and illuminated a small area below her feet. Her expression was one of serenity as she gazed at Dominik. She beckoned him, raising her arms slowly as if awaiting an embrace.

"Must the Gold do everything with such overly dramatic ceremony?" Tyre spoke so only Shay could hear the words. She twitched her wings in a way only described as curt.

"This is a great moment for Dominik," she said. "He will never again require the assistance of the Gold. Once he has wings, he'll be able to make this transition on his own."

"And he gives up favored position as human to do so. A decision surpassing all understanding."

"I believe he will make a tremendous angel."

"I'm sure you do." Tyre gave her a knowing look. "And once he has wings, you will be free to pursue his affections, though I'm sure that has *nothing* to do with your excitement."

Shay didn't answer. She watched Dominik step into the angel's radiating glow, and raised her hand in farewell. Dominik returned the gesture and disappeared into the nether. Her face took on a dreamy appearance, one that evaporated when she looked back at Tyre.

"Can we go now?" Her purple wings rippled with anxious tension. "I was instructed by my elders to make sure you returned."

"I'm not under authority to your elders."

"But I am. I can't return without you. Please, Tyre. It's a risk to stay in this realm."

"I do love it when you beg. There's one more thing I want to do here." He strolled over to the woman he observed earlier, the one stuck in a car with her children. The little one was still screaming and kicking, throwing quite a fit. The mother had turned off the engine and rolled down the windows. Small beads of sweat trickled down her face. She clamped her eyes shut and kept a furious grip on the steering wheel. The red light of her soul was much brighter.

Tyre leaned through the open window of the backseat, unseen to the vehicle occupants. He looked the child in the face. "Stop complaining about your life," he said. "You had plenty of free will before you got here. It's not your mother's fault you have buyer's remorse." He pointed a finger. "Now, you're going to stop throwing that bottle, you're going to sit in that car-seat, and you're going to shut up for the rest of the night!"

Tyre stepped back, satisfied when the child became quiet. After a moment, the mother's light started to dim.

"Casting influence over a toddler," Shay said. "Have you no shame?"

"Not a drop, and I don't like children anyway." He took one, final look at the devastating scene. Medical personnel still worked on Katie as they loaded her into an ambulance. He admired the dedication, despite the futility.

"We're losing her," one of the paramedics yelled.

"You've already lost her," Tyre whispered. He watched until the ambulance disappeared from view, spread his great black wings and launched into the air with the Purple angel right on his heels.

Chapter Three
Cruel Punishment

Six minions appeared at the scene of a traffic accident. One of them, Gianna, knew immediately their prey had escaped. The only thing left of the Herald was the lingering trace his presence had left in the air.

"We missed him," one of the other female minions said. She turned to her companions, her face outraged. "A Herald, so close, and we missed him!" She looked at one of the others. "You delayed us, Jose. You swore you could find him and you took us the wrong way twice. That caused our failure!"

"The fault is not mine," Jose said. "We took too long trying to gather, at Abel's insistence! I told you it was a mistake to follow him!"

"Feel free to challenge me for position, or leave." Abel waved his hand toward the group. "And take some of these fools with you. None of them have any more skill in tracking than you."

Gianna closed her eyes and fell to her knees. She knew it was a mistake to align with a group so large. It never worked out. There were too many wanting to be in charge, and too few willing to follow. The only reason she agreed was because she knew Abel well, and he was kinder than most.

"Very well." Jose turned to the group, his arms wide. "Who else is with me?" He smiled as other minions came to stand by his side, then looked down at Gianna, still on the ground. "You wish to stay with him?"

She didn't answer. Her disappointment in losing the Herald was almost as agonizing as the pain that was her constant companion. She placed her hands over her head and tried to block the whispers tickling her mind, and the searing heat scorching her from the inside out. A tear escaped when she shook her head.

Jose grunted. "As you wish." He stepped back, tossed his arms into the air and evaporated like smoke. The others standing with him did the same.

Once they'd gone, Abel closed his eyes and moved about the area, his hands outstretched, like a blind man in an unfamiliar setting. "He wasn't alone. I pick up trace of a Purple angel, and a Gold, I think."

"There were seven of us." Gianna's voice shook with rage and anguish. "We could've made an attempt."

"And we would've lost. If it was Tyre - and I have no doubt it was - he could've bested three or more of us alone. The other choirs are not without skill and would sacrifice themselves to save a Herald. Tyre would've escaped, and we would've been killed. No matter the reason, the delay has worked in our favor."

"I can't take this suffering!" Gianna howled. She slammed her fists onto the ground, over and over, until they bled. "I'm going mad."

"I do think that's the point, my dear." He patted her head like a father. "But the Herald has grown reckless. Another opportunity will present. In the meantime, we have duties."

"We have *commands*."

"Ones that must be obeyed." Abel held out his hand. "Come. Many souls are here to choose from." He gestured to the police and emergency personnel still clearing away the accident.

"How can you be so calm?" she asked. "Does the pain not reach you?"

"It does, but I've learned to keep it hidden from my face. You will, too, after a century or so."

Gianna whimpered, but took Abel's hand. She started to move about the area, her presence unseen by human eyes. She looked at them, looked into their souls, one by one, trying to decide. "There's a red one over there," she said, pointing to a car with a mother and several children.

"Her glow is too dim. Let's find a brighter one; we've had too much disappointment tonight. There." Abel pointed to an officer walking alone in the woods, shining his flashlight on the ground. "Look at his color."

"He glows yellow, the color of greed. That's always an easy one in these self-proclaimed civilized countries." Despite the pain, she almost smiled. "And he's as bright as I've ever seen."

"He craves a challenge," Abel said. "Let's give it to him."

The police officer didn't detect Gianna's presence as she walked up behind him. He stopped when he spotted a small handbag. He knelt, opened it and sorted through various items: lipstick, hairbrush, and hotel keycard. He located a wallet and flipped it open, revealing a driver's license for the red-haired girl from the accident. He started to turn away, but then saw several large bills poking out.

"Take it," Gianna whispered in his ear. "It's yours." The words were pulled from her, agonizing, like a disembowelment.

The man took the cash from the wallet and counted it.

Gianna placed her hand on the officer's shoulder, though he couldn't feel the touch. "You need it," she breathed, the words scorching her tongue like flames. "No one will know."

The officer looked around, and then focused on the money in his hand.

"You aren't paid enough." A tear escaped, she clenched her teeth, and her hands became fists. "You deserve more."

The officer started to stuff the money into his breast pocket, but then stopped.

"Take it," she hissed in fury. "Take it now!"

The officer shook his head, shoved the cash back into the wallet and closed up the purse. He clicked on the radio at his belt and spoke into a microphone at his shoulder.

"I've got something," he said

"Dammit!" Gianna stamped her foot and banged her fists against her legs as the officer walked from the woods. "I never have trouble with the yellow ones!"

"He has an unusually strong soul." Abel placed a hand on her shoulder. "Let's try another one. Perhaps we can find a blue. Those are always great fun."

Gianna wiped another tear from her face, feeling the aching pull deep in her gut. She followed Abel into the lights, knowing nothing but agony awaited her. Even more horrifying was the reason why. It was the cruelest of punishments, being doomed to an eternity of inflicting on others what had been done to her.

Chapter Four
Head on a Stake

The transition between realms was a simple matter of altering energy and adjusting vibrations a bit. Tyre had done it many times. There was always a moment, right after the return to the spiritual realm, when he wondered why he ever chose to leave. Shay stood beside him, and apparently held the same view. She closed her eyes, her wings fluttering in contentment.

"I was a prisoner once," she said. "I remember walking into freedom after many long years. It was as though all the weight of the world had been lifted. It feels that way after a return, don't you think?"

Tyre didn't answer. He strode down the cobbled path stretching out before him, heading toward the great river. He could fly if he wanted, but there was no hurry. He adjusted the heavy, spiked mace hanging at his hip, more for display than necessity, as he rarely needed to use it; he had other skills in his arsenal, far more dangerous. The weapon did give a brutal accent to his armor, and he appreciated the wary distance his appearance inspired.

He checked the bracelet on his arm to acclimate himself. Time was far different here than in the human realm. He glanced at Shay. "I didn't know you were ever held captive. Were you a prisoner of war?"

"Prisoner of the Bagne de Cayenne."

"Truly?" He was almost interested. "Were you deserving of the sentence?"

"I was. Unlike you, Herald, I wasn't always an angel, and some of my lives were more successful than others." She looked away, her expression one of distress. "But I guess you know that."

Tyre smiled. The Purple angel was no fan of his, for several reasons.

He slowed as the great river Lethe, the boundary between the temporary and eternal, came into view. It bubbled and sparkled in the pure light, the water so clear it was nearly transparent. Glorious white bridges arched over the river at various locations and the two angels started to cross. As they approached the opposite side, Tyre saw several figures standing at the shoreline. He made no move to stop and Shay grabbed his arm.

"We should let them finish before we pass," she said. "Out of respect; it's tradition."

"Ridiculous." He didn't have anywhere to be, so he decided to tolerate the delay. He crossed his arms over his chest and turned to the ceremony already in progress.

A human soul was preparing to depart for his journey. He wore traditional garb for the event; a long, white robe signifying the clean slate he would bring to the lifetime, and a rope around his waist representing the eternal bond to his spiritual home. His path was already mapped before him, as much or as little as he chose, his challenges literally set in stone.

One of the river guardians, delicately attired in a flowing gown, knelt on the shoreline. She held a Cup of Forgetting, a goblet, golden and ancient. She dipped the chalice into the flow of the river until it was full, then stood and offered it to the soul with both hands.

"Will you drink from the cup, or let it pass away?" Her voice was reverent as she repeated words said countless times.

The man took the cup with as much ceremony as it was given.

"I will drink from the cup," he said and touched it to his lips. Within moments, he became unsteady, his eyes clouding with confusion. It was then a Gold angel, who had been watching in silence, intervened. She took the man by the arm and escorted him across the bridge.

"Beautiful," Shay breathed.

"Yes, lovely. Can we go now?" Tyre was already moving and Shay hurried to catch up with him.

"If you were human, you would probably drive a vehicle right through the middle of a funeral procession." She twitched her wings.

"If I were a human, I'd hope to be in the hearse."

"Did you see the color of that soul when he passed? He'll be focusing on envy; that's a tricky one to master."

"Perhaps he'll even succeed," Tyre said as he made his way to the end of the bridge. He walked down another path that ended in a large, round room, filled with dozens of gateways shimmering in various colors. Each one led to different areas within the Expanse, and most of the time, Tyre chose the one that resonated with a black hue. However, he still had time before he was scheduled to report for his regular duties, so he headed toward the shimmering green one instead.

"You're going to the Weave?" Shay asked. "Have you developed an interest in life charting?"

"Such a suspicious tone," Tyre said. "So you know, I go to the Weave regularly. I like to keep track of souls, observe their charts and review their progress."

"Why?"

"So I can determine which ones are worthy of my time." He gave her a meaningful look. "And which are a better sacrifice, when a choice needs to be made."

Shay's eyes went wide. "All souls are worthy, Tyre. It's not for you to decide such things."

"It is when I'm taking the risks."

"You volunteer for those risks," she snapped. "This attitude you and the rest of the Heralds maintain is disgusting. At least the others stay here and don't interfere in…"

Tyre didn't hear any more. He entered the green gateway and emerged on the other side within moments. Shay was right behind him.

"Are you following me?" he asked.

"I want to keep an eye on you."

He chuckled. "Feel free to tag along when I report to the castle later, as well. You can observe duties of Heralds and perhaps learn something of use."

She went stiff. "I have no interest in the Light Bringer's castle, or anything that happens within."

"I'm sure you don't." Tyre was glad he'd aggravated her. "The Weave is busy today."

He took in the activity around him. It was lively, just short of chaotic. Every seat was filled, each lifepath screen and reflection pool occupied. Angels bustled about, the wings of every choir represented—Blue, Green, Red, Purple and Gold. Mixed in with the angels were humans, some having returned from their most recent journeys, others preparing to go. Tyre looked at the faces as he moved about, wondering how many would fall from their path. From the way things had been going, he estimated the number high.

Tyre, with Shay still trailing him, passed one of the large fountains peppering the Expanse, and saw Libra playing one of her favorite games, dancing on her tiptoes across the narrow ledges above the water. A gathering of humans watched, clapping and laughing in enjoyment while Libra leaped and whirled.

"She has perfect balance, doesn't she?" Shay watched the performance in awe. "And such a beauty!"

"She's a show off," Tyre said, "and far too vain for my taste."

Shay waved to a friend flying by overhead, then caught sight of another angel across the fountain. "One of the senior members of my choir is summoning me. Try not to offend or kill anyone while I'm gone."

Tyre ignored her and continued his exploration, aware of the mistrustful eyes watching him. He glanced at a few lifecharts, but found none of great interest. He saw the twins, Miri and Piri, each with a hand on the hilt of a large kirpan. Tyre was respectful when he needed to be; he placed his palms together and bowed as they passed. The twins repeated the gesture and moved on, their weapons swinging in unison from the waistbands of the traditional garb they wore.

Tyre weaved through a cluster of reflection pools—the things reminded him of ornate birdbaths—and took a moment to observe a review. A human woman stood, shaking her head and wincing as events from her recent life floated across the water. A Red angel stood at her shoulder, whispering in her ear and sometimes placing his finger into the pool, creating little ripples, moving events forward and backward. After a short time, the woman's face relaxed and she nodded in understanding. Tyre knew this was the reason human souls didn't regain memory of their lifetimes right away. They were often hard on themselves and unable to see the greater picture. Red angels, despite their haughty nature, were skilled at helping them gain perspective.

The sound of an argument caught Tyre's attention, and he turned to see a Green angel scanning a lifechart. It was one of the mobile charts, a little larger than a notebook. Three-dimensional images sprung up from the device, displaying the life the soul had chosen. The angel was shaking her head while the human beside her looked on. Tyre stayed out of their line of sight, and listened in on the conversation.

"...and things will go better if you add more exit points, Liam," the Green angel was saying. "You don't have any scheduled until your thirty-fifth year. I think it's a mistake."

"But I don't want to risk leaving any earlier," Liam said. "I'm already behind. I want to get as much advancement as possible."

"It's your choice. Perhaps you would at least consider allowing for a few interventions. You remember what those are, don't you?"

The man look confused, but then lit with understanding. "That's when an angel can come to my aid if something beyond my control is going to happen, something that might alter my chart. Is that right?"

The Green angel nodded. "Now, keep in mind that interventions are tricky. It's a risk for the angel—"

"Because of the minions."

"Exactly. And only angels of great power and authority can correct a life that has already gone off course."

"Those would be the Heralds, right?"

The Green angel fluffed her wings. "Yes, the Heralds, but they rarely venture outside the realm, so most of the angels assisting you will be from other choirs. The clues you're given can be subtle—you'll have to look for them. And sometimes angels will help you with one problem, but create another. It can be bothersome."

"Yes, I read about interventions in the scrolls," Liam said, becoming animated. "If something uncharted is going to happen, such as...I'll be attacked by a python if I leave for work on time...an angel might do something that will cause me to be delayed. He might hide my vehicle keys, or change the time on my alarm clock, or steal something I need, like a sock!"

"Yes, and the Blue choir loves to steal socks." The Green angel laughed, then noticed Tyre watching. She placed a protective hand on the man's arm.

"I've never seen a Herald." Liam looked at the black wings with a guarded interest. "Are you the one called Tyre?"

"I am. Is this your first journey?"

"Yes," Liam said, bowing reverently from the neck.

"Would you like to examine his chart?" The Green angel offered it to Tyre and her chin rose a fraction. "If you had any suggestions for success, we would be…honored to hear them, of course."

Tyre checked his timepiece, then flipped through the chart. Images and words hovered in the air, and he used a finger to whip through the information, reading it with a practiced eye.

"What's your primary challenge?" he asked the man.

"Gluttony."

Tyre grunted, scanned a bit longer, and paused. "It says here you've chosen to live in an area riddled by drought and famine, and you chose gluttony?" He looked Liam in the eye. "That's not a challenge, it's cheating. Try Italy if you want advancement. Do you have a secondary?"

The man flinched. "I was considering wrath."

"That's more like it," Tyre said. "Although, I see nothing here that will attract much attention in any area. This is simplistic; average intelligence, appearance, no physical ailments or disabilities, no extreme poverty or financial windfall. You've even chosen to die in your sleep. How dull."

"He wanted to be conservative," the Green said. "It's his first time."

"I don't want to fall to the temptations of the minions," Liam said. "I don't want to become one of them."

"No one ever does." Tyre slapped the lifechart into Liam's chest. "You'll do fine if you have any strength at all, but listen to your Green angel and give yourself more exit points. You're in for some rude awakenings in battle, and young souls often retreat under fire. You'll end up trying to find a shortcut back home and that always makes a big mess."

He left without another word, heading toward the viewing rooms in hope events in the human realm might offer something approaching interest.

As he neared the area, Tyre heard the sound of a loud, muffled voice. A cluster of humans and angels gathered around a closed door leading to one of the private viewing chambers. Such rooms were throughout the Expanse, but this one seemed to be of particular interest. As Tyre moved closer, he heard loud banging along with the yells. Those gathered around were chuckling and whispering, some covering their mouths in an attempt to be discreet.

"Not another one!" a deep voice boomed from behind the door. *"Have you lost your wits entirely?"*

The words elicited another round of laughter and Tyre stepped forward. "What's going on here?"

The humans regarded him with fearful eyes and the angels' wings twitched with tension, but then there was another great crash and the amusement resumed.

"It's Leo," one of the angels told him. "He's been at it for a while."

"At what?"

"His British Prime Minister is out at a drinking establishment, getting quite intoxicated." There was another bellow from the room and it set the angel to giggles. "Leo is taking it personally."

Tyre's wings shifted in surprise, and his eyebrows rose. "The Prime Minister of Great Britain…is on a bender?" He kept well versed in current human vernaculars.

"Well, he's not the Prime Minister *yet*," another angel said, "but he will be in another twenty years or so."

"Maybe," a woman snickered.

"I can't believe what I'm seeing! We went over this and over this! Put the bloody glass down this instant!"

"Leo has been so proud," the angel continued. "He told everyone who would listen how this soul was destined to do great things, and all would be due to his powerful influence."

There was another crash, more chuckling.

"Let me pass." The group parted and Tyre maneuvered his way forward. He placed one finger over his lips and pushed open the door, using great care to be quiet. The men and women pressed around his back to get a glimpse inside. The angels fluttered up to see over the heads of the humans.

Leo, a literal giant of a man with a mane of golden hair, paced the floor with clenched fists, watching an event taking place in the human realm. An enormous viewing screen filling an entire wall displayed a man, perhaps in his thirtieth year of life, with a bourbon glass in his hand. He was spouting insults, swaying on his feet and stabbing a finger into the chest of a much larger man. Tyre watched as the encounter became heated, and then turned physical as the man tossed his drink to the floor and threw a punch.

"Oh, now we're going to get in a brawl?" Leo picked up a chair and tossed it across the room. It slammed into a far wall and shattered into pieces. "Walk away!" Leo shook his fist at the screen. "Walk away! And don't you even think about driving, sir!"

This put the group by the door over the edge and they burst out in laughter.

"Problems?" Tyre asked politely when Leo whirled around.

"Look at this!" Leo pointed to where the two men were now shoving and punching one another. "He's drinking and fighting like some Yankee cowboy!"

"You know he can't hear you?"

"Of course I know!" Leo watched the drunken fellow take a solid hit to the chin and go flying into a table. Drinks spilled, enraging two other men who then joined in the battle. A woman came into view, laughing as she used a video device to record the incident.

"Oh, look here. This will end up on the news one day." Leo overturned a small table, and pointed a finger at the screen. "Don't make me come down there!"

Tyre watched a few moments longer, and considered he might schedule an intervention with the would-be politician, if things continued. He would look at the chart later, and see if any intervention points were charted. Most souls allowed for at least a few, and Tyre had always liked Leo.

He was still considering the matter when an enormous form blocked his path. A strong hand landed on the center of his chest and Tyre looked up to see Dominik glaring at him with steely blue eyes. A female angel with blood red wings stood at his flank and looked ready to pluck Tyre's feathers out by the roots, one by one.

"I see you've finished your reflection," Tyre said. "I trust it went well."

"You seduced me," Dominik said, biting off the words. "You seduced me *using my own name!*" He looked ready to explode.

"You did what?" Shay asked as she returned.

"It was hardly a seduction," Tyre said. "The word implies a certain amount of effort was brought to bear, and that was far from the case." He looked to the Red angel. "I hope you didn't give him too much credit in lust this time. Truth be told, I believe he may have taken a backward step in that area."

"The Scriptures will hear of this," the Red stated, livid, "and the Light Bringer. I will make report of it, I promise you."

"I have no doubt," Tyre said. "Give them my regards."

"You find this amusing, do you?"

"It's an abomination," Shay interjected. "A violation of every sacred oath we—"

"Please," Dominik interrupted with a motion of his hand. "Allow me to speak with Tyre alone."

Shay fell silent, and nodded. She floated into the air until she was respectfully out of earshot, but still within view. She kept her eyes focused on Tyre.

The Red angel touched Dominik's arm. "I'll wait for you near the fountain. Don't be too long, your wing ceremony is set to begin shortly. The whole Blue choir will be in attendance, as will many others, myself included."

He patted her hand. "I'll only be a few moments"

Tyre watched the Red angel stride away and disappear around the corner. "I think she wants my head on a stake," he said, "but I suppose you'd prefer other parts be severed. Tell me, did you truly not notice the wings, even when we—"

"Stop your taunts." Dominik waited until a small group of angels passed by before continuing. "I asked that your actions not be reported. The Red angel wouldn't hear it. She finds the offense too great to remain silent."

"It's within her rights, but what of you? You wished to have words. I'm prepared to hear them."

"I want to know what you were thinking," Dominik said, each word deliberate. "What drove you to such a violation?"

"Curiosity and opportunity," he replied. "I'm surprised the act has caused you so much distress. If you'll be taking position in the choir, you'll need to gain a more...open perspective on things."

"Don't speak down to me, Tyre. I've had many lifetimes, male and female both. The physical act gives me no distress. Indeed, if I thought some carnal curiosity was your only motivation, I would view the entire incident as a sacrifice to your growth."

"Spoken as one who already bears the Blue wings. Impressive." He clicked his tongue. "Boring, but impressive."

"It is the intent behind your action that concerns me," Dominik said. "You're an angel, a Herald! I'm human, and was lost in the Forgetting. You overstepped."

"And I will answer for it."

"What of the other matters; the casual cruelty, the needless infliction of fear and obscene displays of power? These things don't reach me, but could cause lasting misery to others. Do you hold no respect for the journey, or the souls on them?"

Tyre moved close and his wings spread. "If I held human souls in no regard, I would be as others in my choir and only take on duties required." He shoved a gloved finger into Dominik's chest. "I put myself at risk when I come for you, for all humans who miss the marks and go off the path. I set things right." He stepped back. "A fact you appear to have forgotten."

"Is it truly the advancement of the souls that drive you? Or is it your own need to exercise your power?"

"You watch your step." Tyre's eyes turned black with fury. "You have neither the position nor the right to question me. I'm within a breath of losing my patience. I could have you stripped to your skin and lashed within an inch of your life!"

"I don't fear you," Dominik said. "What pain or indignity can you possibly inflict, greater than your actions today? Not to mention events in the past. I'm the one whose patience is nearing the end!"

"I should've left you in that realm to rot." Tyre's voice turned to ice. "I saw potential in you at one time. You could've continued on, perfecting your soul and achieving greatness. Instead, you turn your back on your humanity and petition for wings. You spit in the face of a Herald!" He balled his fist and whipped his hand up, coming just short of landing a strike. Dominik didn't flinch.

Tyre considered him. "You're not without bravery. It will earn you clemency. " He lowered his hand.

"You place the Black choir apart," Dominik said, "and hold other angels in even lower standing than men. You see no honor in their sacrifice."

Tyre was tiring of the conversation. "When you have been given your wings, when you have faced down minion blades, and given advice and guardianship to souls only to see them fall into the fire…maybe then we can revisit this discussion. For now, I have nothing more to say." He turned and walked away.

Dominik called after him. "Do you know why I'm giving up my humanity?"

Tyre stopped, but didn't turn back. Despite his anger with the man, he was curious. "No, I do not."

"On one of my first journeys I took on too many challenges, despite the wise counsel of the Green angel assisting me. I came close to failure, but you intervened and placed me back on course. You survived a minion attack in the process."

"I recall. It was long ago."

"I couldn't deny the impact your actions made on my life, the advancement I achieved. My hope is that one day I can assist another in the same way."

Tyre turned to him, laughing. "Touching. You have gall, to compare yourself to a Herald. You take up wings of your own choice." He tapped his chest a few times. "I was never human. I am a pure angel; my very nature is beyond your comprehension. I have been granted powers and knowledge you will never possess. Make no mistake on this, with wings or not, you will always be a lesser creature. You will *never* be as I am."

"That is a comforting truth." Dominik stretched out his arms. "One that leaves me awash in gratitude." He turned and strode from the hall.

Tyre watched him go, shaking his head. Shay drifted down and planted herself in his path.

"You're doing that following thing again." He pushed her out of the way.

"Dominik has great courage to confront a Herald so boldly." She looked off to where the man had disappeared.

"He lectures me like a father, without regard for the fact he wouldn't even be here were it not for my actions."

"He demands answers to questions others wouldn't dare ask." Shay kept pace with Tyre's strides as he moved through the crowd. "Most are content to tolerate your sins, in exchange for the service you render. It's a far greater friend, one who speaks the truth despite risk of retribution."

"Dominik is no friend."

"I'm sure he would agree. Even so, he has great strength. Why do you treat him so?" She gestured to the Weave. "And not only Dominik, but all of us. Your disdain is well known. How many times have you stood before the throne to answer for your offenses?"

"A few."

"Did I ever tell you about my time in Egypt?"

The change of subject was so abrupt, Tyre stopped mid-step. "No, I don't think so."

"It was a long while ago, when I was still human."

Tyre didn't care, but the Purple angel seemed determined to engage him in conversation. He crossed his arms over his chest.

"I lived in this little village," she said, "and there was a girl, beautiful, kind." Shay waved her hand. "I'd taken on the male form that time, I couldn't have been more than ten, and I was hopelessly enamored with the girl. She went to the river every morning to fetch water and I'd hide off the path and wait for her, then I'd jump out and hit her with sticks."

"Charming. I'm sure you won her heart."

"I never harmed her. I simply desired her attention. In my innocence, I was unable to find words to give voice to feeling. It's a curious thing—this memory often comes to mind when I see you."

Tyre raised an eyebrow. "You would mark me as innocent?"

"I would mark you as an arrogant ass," Shay said. "Tell me, are you even capable of holding anyone close?"

"I'm more than capable, and I do hold others very close, as often as time allows." He stepped back and inspected her from all angles. "Are you making an offer? I prefer the company of females in my own choir, but you're not an entirely revolting specimen."

Shay stood speechless and Tyre thought the situation had improved.

"You know precisely what I meant," she huffed, "and I'd rather be put to the fires than share my chamber with a Herald!"

"You say that because you've never had one." He winked and enjoyed the outrage on her face. "I suppose you're saving your intimacies for Dominik. Well, he'll have his wings this very day, perhaps you can convince him to flutter off for a celebration." He grunted. "You'll probably find yourself standing in line for that, and unless you're made of parchment, I doubt he'll even notice you." He considered a moment. "Though, he did make for quite a wanton girl. Would you like to hear the details?"

She glared at him with disgust. "You are a despicable creature."

"Then why are you still trailing after me like an attention-starved child?" He looked hard at her. "If you have something to say, I suggest you speak your mind. I've already been lenient one too many times this day. You're close to scrubbing the floors in the castle for the next fortnight, just for boring me."

"You would use your power of command in such a manner?"

"Yes, and that's a far lighter sentence than many Heralds would impose. Do you know Ikizo? He's fond of—"

"I've heard." She shuddered.

Tyre enjoyed her reaction. "Get on with the reason behind your intrusive visit. It must be something urgent, or you wouldn't be here. I imagine you want a front row seat for Dominik's ceremony."

"I'm here to give you a warning. I feel I owe you, for the interception today." She wrinkled her nose. "Many believe you've forgotten your position."

"I forget nothing."

"Then you willingly choose to ignore it—a greater offense." She hesitated, judging his reaction. "You spent too long in the human realm tonight. Your light was shining like a beacon and it's only by luck the minions didn't track you. They would love nothing more than to see your wings ripped from your shoulders and mounted as decoration, not to mention the Free Spirits who would do far worse."

"Little good it would do any of them, without the words of surrender," Tyre said, "and that is something I will never give."

"If they capture you, they'll be merciless. The surrender of a Herald would be the greatest prize. They could hold you and torture you for an eternity, trying to force you to speak the words. Anyone can be broken—even you. You should stay here and stop putting yourself at risk."

"You weren't so quick to say that when I decided to retrieve your precious Dominik. Such a little hypocrite, like all the rest." His eyes became slits. "Tell me, what has spurred this sudden burst of concern for my well-being? There's something more here than your appreciation at having that oversized bastion of knowledge back in the realm."

She looked away and Tyre grabbed her face with one hand, forcing her to look at him.

"Shay of the Purple choir, I command you to tell me your purpose." He squeezed her cheeks until her lips puckered.

She started to shake and a tear slid down her cheek. She fought his words, but it was useless. "An elder of my choir saw us walking together. He asked me to speak with you, to get information."

"You were sent to charm me?" Tyre laughed, and tossed her away. "The elders are becoming more duplicitous by the century. This should be interesting. What information are you trying to glean from me?"

"Three from our choir have fallen in the past month, including my mentor, Elizabeth, killed only a day past."

"I'm aware of the situation."

"Five of them came for her."

That gave Tyre pause. "Are you certain of this?"

"It was just discovered. You've been attacked many times. Have you ever encountered such a large group?"

"Not often. They turn on one another when more than two or three band together."

"Do you know what's happening?" She shook, the words forced from her throat by an unseen power. "There's suspicion someone is leading them, someone other than Lucifer."

Tyre played with a piece of the Purple angel's hair. "You go back and tell your elder I have no idea why the minions are gathering." He allowed his influence to fade away.

Shay stepped back, breathing heavily. She glared at the Herald. "Do you have any idea what that feels like? To be compelled?"

"No, but I imagine it's not pleasant." He clicked his tongue. "Heralds do not respond well to lies or deception. However, since you were ordered into this pitiful ruse by higher authority, I won't take it personally."

"Take it any way you like." Shay wiped away a tear, enraged, her face almost matching the color of her wings. "I hope you and the rest of your choir are all banished to the nether!"

Tyre chuckled, then a distinctive sound caught his attention. Another Herald, black wings expanded in flight, descended from above and planted herself in front of him. She was dressed like Tyre in the traditional armor of their choir, and her high boots struck the ground with a sound like hammer on stone. Nearby angels and humans stopped what they were doing to watch. Heralds knew how to make an entrance.

"You've been summoned," she said.

"That was faster than I expected." Tyre looked down at Shay. "If you change your mind on the other matter we discussed, I'll be in my chambers later. It's been a while since I've had one of the Purple choir." He smiled at her horrified face. "Don't worry, my dear. That wasn't a command this time.

Chapter Five
The Light Bringer

Tyre regarded his escort, called Alira, as they flew together toward one of the portals that served as quick transport around the Expanse. In many ways, she was similar to all of their choir; black wings, scars, and the same emerald eyes granted all Heralds. But her long limbs and blonde hair gave her a uniqueness Tyre admired. He'd shared intimate moments with her, from time to time.

"Tell me—is he angry?"

"He's annoyed," Alira said, "but when is Lucifer, or anyone else, *not* annoyed with you? Is it true you seduced a human?"

"That word is being tossed around with abandon today."

"Then it is true!" Alira laughed. "Was it remarkable, as legend says?"

Tyre smirked. "Perhaps you'll find out on your own one day. But that would require you to leave this realm, wouldn't it?"

"I value my wings." She cast her eyes over his body. "And other things."

Tyre grinned. "Have you been back since you completed your trials? Much has changed."

"I'll return when Heralds are called upon to fulfill our ultimate purpose."

"We've been waiting a long time, and it could be much longer. Are you content to remain here, immersed in trivial tasks unworthy of your station?"

Alira shrugged. "I tolerate things. On the day we're called up, our choir unites, and the full weight of our power is brought to bear, it will be glorious. I intend to be here to see it."

Tyre only smiled, then flew through one of the large gateways high above that resonated with a dark power. Within a breath, the white light of the yang turned into black radiance of the yin, every bit as magnificent, but in stark contrast. Tyre cast his eyes downward as he soared, impressed at the sight, even after so long. He knew both sides of the Expanse served a purpose, but he felt at home in the Black City in a way he never experienced on the other side of the great Taijitu. And in the middle of the sparkling darkness, standing as a beacon, was the shining white fortress of the Light Bringer.

Lucifer was nothing if not dramatic. His castle, and it was very much a castle, was as intricate as it was intimidating. A massive entryway flanked by spiraling columns greeted visitors. Heralds serving duty as the Outer Guard stood at the ready. As Tyre approached, they each took hold of a thick, polished clamp and pulled open the massive doors.

Tyre, with Alira beside him, moved through an actual labyrinth of halls and stairs that finally spilled into a large room, octagonal and bare, except a round pit in the center. Smoke and dust wafted up from the chasm, and the smell of sulfur permeated the air. Tyre looked down into what appeared an endless abyss, but was simply another gateway. This one, however, was far more foreboding.

Two other angels from his choir approached, their black wings catching light from torches lining the walls. A short human walked between them, barefoot and wearing ill-fitting garments with scorch marks around the edges. His face was dark, blackened unnaturally from ash, and his fear-filled eyes fixed on the chasm.

The two Heralds gave a nod, then lifted the man and tossed him without ceremony into the smoking pit.

"Impressive," Alira said. "He never made a sound."

"Not his first trip into the fires, I suspect."

Tyre continued on, advancing down a long corridor on the other side of the chasm. Stone tablets, more than could be counted, were mounted on the walls. Each one was unique, holding words carved by the hand of every human soul who was now on a journey. Each tablet would be safeguarded until the lifetime was complete—an eternal reminder of the challenges the soul agreed to undertake, and the consequences that awaited if they failed.

The hall spilled into a grandiose wonder of a room with high ceilings, pillars, and flooring that caused footfalls to echo. Men holding positions of power had copied the design of Lucifer's castle, in one way or another, for ages upon ages in countless civilizations. All had believed their designs unique and marveled at their own creativity. But Tyre knew it was like most things in the human realm; the souls retained a spark of their spiritual home within their heart, even when their mind was lost in the Forgetting. Indeed, there was nothing created by humanity that wasn't already in existence.

Tyre saw his reflection flickering in the polished floor, and heard the telltale ruffling of wings above. He knew his brother and sister Heralds were watching, and he tossed up an arm in greeting.

A woman, her hair singed and wearing garments covered in grime, staggered past. Her eyes misted, her face a picture of disbelief when she glanced at the two angels. Her chin quivered and she smiled a tiny bit before continuing on her way. A Gold angel would be waiting for the woman when she left the castle, to escort her to the Scriptures for final judgment.

"She's free of chains," he said. "Perhaps he's feeling merciful today."

"For your sake, I hope so." Alira lofted into the air and disappeared.

Mighty doors stood at the far end of the great room, guarded by six enormous men clad in leather, with shields on their arms and broadswords on their backs. The Valhallans were the most loyal and trusted of Lucifer's guards, but Tyre had never held them in much favor. He suspected the feeling was mutual. He approached, and one of the brutes held up a gloved hand.

"Wait here."

Off to his right, a long line of humans, men and women both, stood against a far wall. They were chained hand and foot with heavy black metal, and shackled together at the waist, one behind another. They were haggard in appearance, their garments little more than filthy rags, tattered and torn. None of them wore shoes, and most kept their eyes downcast.

He moved closer, casting his gaze down the row of minions—the lost souls awaiting audience with Lucifer. The smell on them was one of death, pungent and foul. Tyre smiled. A few times the distinctive stench had saved him, as he smelled his attackers before he ever saw them.

He approached the one in the front, a man his own height with crude features and stringy hair falling into his eyes.

"You," Tyre demanded. "What is your name?"

"Marcus." He had a thick accent, and teeth, rotted and stained. He looked the Herald up and down with open disgust.

"How long have you been in servitude?"

"Six hundred and three years," Marcus growled. His eyes fixed on the black wings, filled with hatred and longing.

"That's a long while," Tyre said. "Is this your first time to come before the throne?"

"Fifth," the man said. "It won't be my last, either."

"You seem certain."

"My people still offer words for the dead. Little good it's done."

"Invocations can only grant you a review. You still must prove yourself worthy of freedom. Perhaps this time, he'll award it to you."

"He won't," Marcus rumbled. "He never does. I'm too good at my job."

"Is that so? And what is your job?"

"Whatever he commands," Marcus said, regarding the others in chains, "the same as everyone else." His eyes became slits and he leaned in close. "But you know what else I do, Herald?" He spit the last word.

"Tell me."

"I hunt angels." He grinned, showing mangled teeth.

"Do you?"

"Aye, I've killed lots—Greens, Reds, Purples, Blues. I even got a Gold, once. Oh, now he was a prize, that one. Took him all by myself, too." He started to breath in rasps, like his own words excited him.

"But have you ever caught a Herald?" Tyre already knew the answer.

Marcus hesitated, then laughed and jerked his head toward his companions. "If I had, none of us would be standing here."

Tyre grunted and started to move down the line.

"They're funny things," Marcus called out, grabbing Tyre's attention once more. "Angels. They don't die quickly, you know. Even with our blades, we can stab them or cut them, over and over—"

"You can cut them a hundred times," another minion interjected from his place down the row.

"Aye," Marcus agreed, "you can cut them a hundred times, a thousand times, and they'll bleed. Oh, angel blood is thick nasty stuff and it keeps coming—never-ending, it is. And angels don't bleed out, like a man. Angels won't die, you know, until you take a wing!" His eyes went wild, and he spoke as though revealing a great secret. "It's no easy task to sever an angel wing. You have to work at it; you have to saw it off with the blade. It takes some effort, you have to put your back into the job, and at the end, the last bit, you have to rip it out with your own hands!"

He tossed his head back, laughing. "That sound, when the flesh and bone tear, is a horrible, dreadful thing." His lip curled back and he leaned close. "But sometimes you can miss it, on account of all the screaming."

Tyre stared at Marcus, committing his face to memory, then confronted the minion who had spoken out of turn. This one kept his eyes on the floor. "So, you're an angel hunter, too, then?"

The man shook his head, and didn't look up. "I used to be, but no longer."

"Why is that?"

"I lost all taste for it. I've accepted my fate. I obey commands as I must, but nothing more."

Something in the man's words, in his tone, intrigued Tyre. He stepped closer. "What was your failing that led you into chains?"

"War crimes," the man said. "I committed acts of barbarism, against the innocent."

"I hear shame in your voice. Is it genuine?"

The man nodded once.

"When you stand before the throne, he'll be able to see into your heart," Tyre warned. "If you attempt to deceive him with words, he'll grant you no mercy."

"I no longer desire mercy, or even freedom," the man stated, and his head hung even lower. "I don't deserve it."

"Spoken as a man who may have earned both," Tyre said, and then turned at the sound of screams.

The throne room doors opened, and two Heralds emerged, dragging a woman between them. She wailed, kicked, and pulled against the angels' hold, her arms nearly snapping from the strain. She pleaded with them, her tears creating thin trails against her soot-blackened face.

"Please, I beg you!" She collapsed, but they snatched her up with such force her feet left the ground. "I can't go back there! I can't! Have mercy! Please, no!"

The two Heralds ignored the woman's desperate pleas, and performed their duty with impassive expressions. They continued down the hall and were soon out of sight, though the screams continued for a while longer.

One of the Valhallan's pointed to Tyre.

"He'll see you now."

Tyre walked between the guards and into the throne room. He took position at the bottom of the stairs that led to the dais of the Light Bringer. Lucifer stood on the balcony behind his throne, his back toward Tyre. The Herald marveled, as he always did, at the sight of him. The Light Bringer struck an impressive figure—long and lean, with massive wings the color of melted silver, and hair to match, rippling down his back like lava. Tyre knew the eyes were the same, though he couldn't see them.

"You have an eclectic group out there today," he said. "A few might have potential, but most are a rather nasty lot."

"I understand there was a problem with an interception." Lucifer's voice was like steel, hard and cold.

"There was no problem," Tyre answered. "The soul was extricated successfully. There were witnesses, but it was unavoidable, a matter of little consequence."

Lucifer didn't move or speak. He simply waited.

"There was a breach of law," Tyre said. "One that won't be repeated, I assure you. I accept whatever punishment is deemed appropriate."

"Breach?" Lucifer whispered the word, then turned to face the black winged angel, his silvery gaze firm. "The seduction of a human soul in your charge is no mere breach, Herald."

"Again with the seduction." Tyre ran a hand through his hair in exasperation. "I admit my judgment flawed, but the incident caused no harm. The soul in question is being awarded wings as we speak, any offense forgotten in happy celebration."

Lucifer descended the dais in tightly controlled moves, his wings expanding with each step. Tyre had a moment of uncertainty. The Light Bringer was slow to anger, but when his tolerance was pressed, he could be dangerous.

"Human souls are not for sport," Lucifer said. "You have grown bold in testing the oath and the patience of those above you. We've been lenient in hopes you would heed the warnings you've been given. Your failure today has proven us wrong."

"There was no failure," Tyre said. "The girl died, the soul ascended, all was set right. My actions caused no consequence."

"Didn't they? They have forced my hand." He looked Tyre in the eyes. "You are to be dismissed from the choir."

Tyre's muscles flexed, and his wings shot out. "You wouldn't dare."

"The decision has been made." Lucifer crossed the room to gaze once more out the balcony. "You will be stripped of your wings and cast out of this realm to wander the nether with others who disgraced the sacred oaths."

"I can't believe you would even consider such a thing." Tyre's anger was rising fast. "If I'm gone, who among the Heralds will take my place?" He motioned toward the doors. "Which of them will risk minion blades to do what I have done? I have saved many souls that would otherwise be burning in the fires, or standing chained in this very castle!"

"The others show caution."

"They show cowardice!" Tyre boomed. "I alone among the nineteen have taken on duties outside this realm, duties not commanded of me, but ones only a Herald can provide."

"Other choirs can perform those tasks," Lucifer said. "The Blues in particular have shown great skill."

"The other choirs are limited, in a way Heralds are not. Why were such abilities granted us, if we were not meant to use them?" Tyre paced the floor, his black boots pounding. He strove to find calm, but it was buried too deep beneath layers of fury. He held out his arms, clenching his fists. "I bear the scars of my trials, as do the others, but I'm the only one who uses the power earned by them!"

"You abused that power," Lucifer said, taking a seat in his throne. "There is no argument you can give that will change your circumstance. A new Herald will be created to replace you. The event has already been set into motion and will not be undone."

"You are not the final arbitrator," Tyre said through clenched teeth. He moved to stand near Lucifer. "There is another authority. I will appeal to it."

"That's within your rights, though I fear the Scriptures are as powerless as I in this matter." He leaned forward, his gaze intense. "There is divine providence at work here."

"This is madness," Tyre said. "The minions have grown in number. They hunt angels for sport and will leap at a chance to capture a Herald, especially a fledgling. They know we're at our most vulnerable when born into flesh to face our trials, and they'll be merciless when they detect his presence."

Lucifer smiled a slight bit. "*Her* presence will be masked, as it was with you."

Tyre paused as the implication of the words struck home. He laughed out loud, placed hands on his hips, and shook his head. "You add salt to the wound, to replace me with a female. And *her* powers won't remain locked away forever. The world of men has changed, Lucifer. Faith in the old ways is being abandoned, and those in the fire don't dare hope for a chance at redemption. They grow impatient and seek another way. This Herald will be hunted like no other."

"We're aware of the challenges," Lucifer said. "She will be given assistance."

"In what form?" Tyre raised his eyebrows. "An advisor? Few angels are worthy, less that would survive the task. How many will be sacrificed before the inevitable? Your new Herald is doomed, and you'll be lucky if it's only the trials she fails. I can't believe you would risk a surrender, simply to see me punished."

"The choice wasn't mine." Lucifer placed a hand on Tyre's shoulder. "Out of respect for your past service, dubious as it has been at times, you'll be allowed three days before you're cast out. Make your appeal to the Scriptures if you wish, but do not dare to hope. Take the time given to bid farewell to those you hold close, if there are any. After that, they will never again see your face."

"I will not allow this." Tyre knocked Lucifer's hand away. "Do you hear me, Light Bringer? I will not allow another to take up my wings. I will fight for what's mine and destroy any that stand in the way!"

"You should not speak such a challenge." Lucifer's voice was coated in warning. "Does your pride run so deep that you would wage battle against this realm?"

"My pride should be the least of your concerns," Tyre said, laughing. "Believe me when I say it's nothing compared to my wrath."

CHAPTER SIX
CIRCLE OF HELL

John Connors had been told many times that Washington, DC had some of the best doctors in the world. So far, none were good enough to help his daughter.

John stood at the foot of Katie's bed, hands pressed into his jeans pockets. He watched the rise and fall of her chest, assisted by the tube running into her lungs. Her face was a mass of bruises and cuts, her legs and one arm were in casts. She reminded him of a beautiful porcelain doll that had been broken and abandoned.

Katie's younger sister, Debbie, had barely moved from the bedside since they arrived. She sat there now, reading aloud.

The call about the accident came in the middle of the night and was almost like a dream. John didn't like that; he wanted to remember every detail. He still didn't know what happened and the questions hurt almost as much as the sight of his daughter's mangled body. He didn't know why his Katie left the hotel, or why she was in a car with the man who fled the scene and left her for dead. He hated the unknowns.

He looked at the paper in his hand, a police artist representation of the man wanted for questioning. Witnesses who saw Katie minutes before described the man as best they could. John gazed at the black and white drawing, into eyes that were dark and hollow on paper. He'd been staring at it for days; it was another thing he wanted to remember.

He shifted in his boots and ran a big, calloused hand across his face. The place was starting to get to him. He hated the antiseptic smell of hospitals and even the footfalls in the hall, quiet as they were, grated on his ears. He'd spent too many days in hospitals, watching his wife waste away. Now he watched his daughter.

"John?" a soft voice said from the doorway.

He turned, surprised to see Monsignor Raphael from his home parish, dressed in his black robes and holding a colorful bag. He held out his hand, and the Priest took it in both of his and squeezed tightly.

"You came a long way," John said. "You didn't have to."

"I wanted to be here earlier, but I couldn't get away." He turned his attention to the girl, sitting in the chair beside Katie's bed. "Hello, Debbie."

The girl didn't look away from her sister.

"John, I'm so sorry," the Priest said. "Sister Bernard told me what happened, as much as she knows anyway. It's a terrible thing, and to happen on the senior trip, well…"

"I'm not planning to sue the archdioceses, if that's what you're worried about." He was ashamed for even attempting a joke. He knew the school, and specifically the chaperones, felt tremendous guilt for what happened, but he didn't blame any of them. "I have three children, and two are teenagers. I know how it is—can't keep eyes on them all the time."

The Priest nodded and moved to Katie's bedside. He touched the silver cross around her neck, neatly arranged and poking out from the blanket covering her. He reached into the bag and pulled out a stuffed doll; an angel all in white, with wings and a halo stitched with gold thread.

"The choir asked me to bring this," he said. "They miss her. They said Katie has the voice of an angel and can't wait to hear her sing again." He started to place the doll on the little table by the bed, but Debbie reached for it. She tucked it beside her sister so it was touching her cheek.

"Would you like to pray together?" the Priest asked her.

Debbie didn't look up. "No."

"Perhaps later, then." He turned back to John. "Has there been any change?"

"None. I think I see her move sometimes, but then I think I might be imagining it. She looks so much like her mother, doesn't she?" He smiled a little and breathed deeply. Father Raphael had performed the funeral mass for his wife.

"She does." The priest pointed to the paper in John's hand. "Is that the man they're trying to locate?"

"Do you recognize him?"

The Priest looked at the picture for a good while before handing it back. "I'm sorry, no."

"I don't know why Katie was in that car," John said. "I don't know—"

"She was kidnapped." Debbie's voice was hard, too hard for a fifteen-year-old. "He kidnapped her and he raped her."

John's heart froze in his chest at the words. "We don't know that."

"Yes, we do." Debbie stood and faced her father. "I heard what the doctors told you and I know what it means."

John looked down. He'd hoped Debbie hadn't heard that part, about signs of recent sexual activity. A young nurse told him later, in private, there was no evidence the act had been by force, no bruising or tears. He knew the nurse was trying to be kind, to give some small comfort to a father whose mind was ravaged by images of his daughter's final hours.

"We can't know for sure what happened," John said. "Maybe when this man is found, we'll get some answers."

"Katie wouldn't have left with a guy to have sex," Debbie insisted, her voice rising. "I know it. She saw me kissing Nathan last year and was furious."

"Nathan Ferrario?" The Priest frowned, clearly familiar with the boy; most likely a student at the school and not one he looked to be particularly fond of.

"Yes. Katie told me he was a jerk and only wanted one thing from me."

"Debbie," John whispered in warning. The door was still open.

"I didn't do anything with him." Debbie started to cry and bit her lip in anger. "Katie told me I should save myself for when I get married. She said sex was a gift!" She looked back and forth between her father and the Priest, and her jaw set. "She's not a slut!" She pushed her way past her father and left the room.

"She's having a hard time," John said, watching her go. "She and Katie have been closer since their mom passed on."

"How is the little one doing?"

"I brought him up here the first day." He rubbed his neck. "I thought I prepared him, but I guess not well enough. He hasn't spoken a word since."

The Priest bowed his head. "The whole congregation is praying for your family."

"I appreciate that." John went to stand by his daughter, and tucked a little piece of hair behind her ear. "Tell me something, Father. Do you think my Katie is even in there anymore?"

"That isn't for us to decide. "

"I'm afraid that's where you're wrong." The doctors had briefed him on his daughter's condition, and though most of the medical words went well over his head, he did understand one thing: There was nothing else they could do. "They told me there might come a time when I'll have to choose. Do I let my little girl stay like this and wait for a miracle? Or do I let her go to heaven? I keep waiting for a sign, but it doesn't come."

"Perhaps we can ask for guidance." The Priest took a black beaded chain from the pocket of his coat.

John looked at the rosary, and an image of his wife flashed in his mind. She had kept a rosary on the night table in the bedroom, in a little ceramic bowl Katie had made as a mother's day present when she was little. It was still there.

"I don't think I will, Father." John bent over, kissed his daughter on her forehead, and smoothed back her hair. "I'd appreciate it if you would say a few words, though. Maybe God will listen to you better than he does me."

He headed for the door to find Debbie, but stopped at a little trashcan on the way. He looked down at the sketch in his hand, and crumpled it in his fist. "I know this doesn't make me a good Christian, but I'm praying there's a special circle of hell for this man."

CHAPTER SEVEN
GODSPEED

Tyre walked in silence, and all eyes watched his every move. The Expanse, usually bustling with activity, was hushed. The only sounds were soft footfalls and the ruffling of wings. Angels and humans alike had gathered to observe the momentous event; every spot was filled. Humans stood, and most angels fluttered above them to get a better view. Everyone had come to see the mighty Herald brought low. Stripped of his wings, his weapons and even his armor, Tyre looked different, though he still retained a regal air.

Dominik stood near the Great Arch, with Shay and many others. Tyre was approaching, dressed in a white gown normally reserved for human souls leaving for a journey. He suspected Tyre hated it and wondered if humiliation was part of the punishment.

"The Scriptures escort him," Shay said. "I heard he appealed to them."

Five angels, an elder from every choir except the Heralds and two human souls of great advancement and wisdom, comprised the revered assemblage. They wore traditional robes, black and long, and walked single file behind Tyre.

"They will see their judgment to completion," Dominik said, "the mark of true authority."

A woman named Miriam bowed her head and began to weep. Two others held her in comfort.

"Don't shed tears for him," one said. "He would not do the same for you."

"I know," Miriam said. "But he saved me once. He came for me when no other would."

"But he took an oath, and knew the consequences if it was broken."

"What will happen to him?"

A Gold angel hovering nearby answered the question. "He'll go into the nether. We don't know what awaits him there; none who have been banished have ever returned. Legend tells us it's a fate worse than the fires."

"Maybe the other Heralds will learn from this," a Red angel said. "Look up there." He nodded to a spot high above where the remaining members of the Black choir were gathered. The eighteen were given a wide berth and their black wings pounded in unison, creating a sound like a mighty drum. "They're in a rage. They see this as an injustice."

"They're always angry when one of their numbers is taken. It's as though they've lost a limb."

"And they'll direct their torment on the rest of us." The Red angel shook his head. "Like wounded animals, they will lash out until their damnable choir is whole again."

Miriam wiped away her final tears, fear taking the place of sadness. "How long will that be?"

"The process has already begun," the Gold angel said. "I heard a rumor the new Herald will be a female this time, only the seventh ever created. She'll soon be born into flesh to face trials, but there's no guarantee of success. Many fail and suffer banishment. If that happens, the process starts again. The last time it took five attempts before one was proven worthy."

"*Worthy*," the Red sneered. "I wish I knew the standard involved in the judging."

"That's a secret known only to the Great Architect," the Gold said. "But this moment serves as a reminder that what is given, or even earned, can also be taken away."

Dominik regarded the heavy ring on his finger, the one presented when he joined the ranks of angels. The center stone was dark blue, the signature mark of his choir. It had been hand-selected, cut and set by artisan gemsmiths. The band itself was equally impressive, made from a dark and precious metal, with delicate etchings representing moments from his human lifetimes. The commonly called 'band of the soul' was a humbling gift, a constant reminder not only of his past, but also of the oath he'd taken. He couldn't imagine what would drive an angel into abandoning his honor. He looked up as the processional came close.

Tyre's gaze was fixed straight ahead, but then he turned his emerald eyes to Dominik and paused. He broke formation and protocol to come stand in front of him.

"The Blue wings are a good fit," Tyre said. "With your preposterous size, you make a rather imposing angel. Minions may run at the very sight of you." His eyes narrowed. "If not, are you prepared to fight them? To kill them?"

"I've taken life before," Dominik said, "and I will do so again, if the need arises and the cause is just."

"A good attitude, I hope you keep it. It would be a shame for you to be killed after all the trouble you've caused me." He stood back and took a good look at the newest Blue angel. "Despite our differences, I've always considered you something of an unruly but favored pet. I'd give you a scratch behind the ears, but I think you might bite my hand."

"Even now you can't resist your taunts," Dominik said. "And standing here on the verge of ultimate punishment, your eyes are without a shred of emotion, even remorse."

"Remorse is a human failing I've never suffered," he said. "But if you look closer, you might be surprised at the emotions to be found in Heralds. Few have ever held courage enough to try; it's a dangerous thing to stare too long into the abyss." His tone was part challenge, part threat. "I can look into your eyes as well, Dominik of the Blue. There's a flame of righteousness in you, bordering on the fanatical. You find me abhorrent, those and others like me. I think you might know of hatred." He shook his head, chuckling. "A terribly unbecoming quality for an angel."

Shay stepped forward, her eyes angry. "Don't you have a pressing engagement elsewhere?"

Dominik held his hand up to keep her in place. "He's trying to provoke me, something I won't allow." He turned back to Tyre, and his voice hardened. "You accuse me of hatred. I won't deny the truth of such a claim, but you will carry it with you into the nether and it will disappear from my life, as will you. Any power you've ever held over me is severed. I won't think on you again after this day."

"Oh, that's where you're wrong," Tyre said. "You will think of me every day for the rest of your existence, as long or as short as that might be. And I'll tell you something else." He leaned close, his voice menacing. "Being an angel is a risky endeavor. Wings can be clipped, just like that!" He snapped his fingers in Dominik's face. "And that bothersome oath you revere tends to get in the way. You'll understand soon."

Tyre stepped back, his casual demeanor returning in an instant. He winked at Shay and then gave a jaunty salute to the Heralds above. "Well, the nether awaits. Farewell, Dominik. You try to be a good dog."

Dominik placed his hand on the fallen angel's shoulder. "Godspeed."

Tyre tossed his head back and laughed loud and hearty. He continued on his way and didn't look back. Once he disappeared from view, a deep silence fell, as though the entire Expanse was holding its breath. At some unspoken cue, the Heralds above began to chant. Their voices brought forth a tidal wave of sound that echoed through the halls. The hymn was ancient, the words in a language long ago abandoned, but the significance behind it was unmistakable.

The stained glass shook and the water in the fountains began to bubble and overflow. Every note pummeled at the hearts of those who heard, every word an accusing shard, terrifying and awesome.

"They haven't lifted their voice in song in over two thousand years," Shay whispered. "Are they mourning the loss? Or celebrating creation of the new one?"

"Maybe both," Dominik said, "or maybe neither. I wouldn't dare guess at the intentions of Heralds. Perhaps they just want to remind us they're still here."

The final note hung in the air and the Great Arch began to tremble. It cracked, splitting cleanly at its apex. Large pieces began to fall, crashing into the stone floor like an avalanche. There were screams and frantic scrambling as men and women fled, trying to avoid being crushed. Angels swooped in to help and pulled some to safety. No souls were lost, but many lay wounded. The Heralds dispersed, leaving the Expanse in chaos and fear.

Dominik helped a man injured by a glancing blow from a piece of the Arch. The angel sloshed through water pooled on the floor from the fountains and steadied the man on a bench. A healer arrived, medicine pouch in hand. He took out a pinch of crushed herbs, applied it to the man's wound and offered prayers. The injury repaired itself within moments.

"This is insanity." The man looked up at Dominik. "How can Heralds be allowed such power? And why would they raze the Great Arch?"

"I don't know." The angel surveyed the scene, disgusted by the destruction. He strove for calm, knowing part of an angel's duty was offering a comforting presence during times of tribulation. He sighed heavily, and grinned. "But, they might want to stay in the castle for awhile. This mess will take weeks to repair. The master masons are going to be enraged. Have you ever seen what they can do with a well-hewn chisel?"

The man laughed, some tension leaving his face. "They might use Herald blood for mortar." He touched his bloody shoulder. "I want to thank you, for your quick action. I believe you kept my head from being severed."

"No gratitude required." Dominik moved his gaze over the crowd. Many were still prone, but angels were everywhere. Shay knelt beside a woman with a broken arm and waved to get the attention of a healer. "It looks like everyone is being tended. I'll assist in the clean-up. Perhaps I should find a mop."

He ended up hauling pieces of stone into piles so the artisans could determine which were salvageable. The masons were already on top of things. They were fit to be tied, but worked efficiently. By the time most of the Expanse had gone back to regular duties, they had set up scaffolds around the Arch and began work on the reconstruction.

Dominik and many others labored deep into the night. Once the situation was in hand, he was dismissed with thanks by one of his elders. He was exhausted, covered in dust from the stones and his uniform breeches soaked to the knees. He longed for a warm shower, both to cleanse the grime and soothe his emotions.

He knew the actions of the Heralds, with the destruction of Great Arch, was the beginning of a nightmare that would only get worse in the years to come. He felt a gnawing sense of responsibility for his unwilling part in the events that had led to the fracture of the Black choir. That Tyre had selected *him,* out of all the souls in the realm, to be the target of his lust was more troubling than he cared to admit.

He was halfway back to his chamber when he was approached by Nikiti of the Purple. She was every bit as disheveled as he, but she made it look good.

"Dominik," she said, "I was on duty and didn't get to come to your wing ceremony. I've been meaning to congratulate you."

He smiled, the first real one of the dreadful night. "Thank you."

"I was wondering if you might like to meet me in the Astronomy wing in a little while. I've heard you're an expert in that area and I've always wanted to gain more knowledge of the stars. Plus, I think we could both use a little break after this disaster."

There was a flirtatious tone in her voice and Dominik hesitated, not because he didn't want to accept, but because he did. It was a strange sensation. As human, there had been an invisible barrier in place, something instinctive keeping him from getting too close to angels. He grimaced inwardly; at least he'd never gotten too close *knowingly*, when he wasn't lost in the Forgetting. He pushed the memory aside, realizing he was being rude.

"I'd be honored." He took her hand, raised it to his lips, and kissed it lightly; a gesture he learned many lifetimes before and decided to keep. Most females found it chivalrous, he found most females appealing, so it worked out well all around. And Nikiti was a lovely creature. He checked his timepiece. "Shall we meet at the upper level, say at the midnight hour?"

"That would be perfect. I'll put on something nice for you!" She lofted, her wings marked with excitement.

Dominik watched her go, his mood much improved.

He found a small scroll outside his chamber door, an invitation from one of the angels in his choir, inviting him to a musical performance on the artisan level the following night. He tossed it on his resting pallet, trying to decide how to best decline since the time was in conflict with his scheduled combat training. He started to disrobe, but then another scroll arrived via messenger—one from a Red angel who was quite direct in her desires. That offer was marked as standing.

Dominik was flattered by the sudden attention, but also confused. Since his wing ceremony three days past, angels had come out of the rafters—sometimes literally—with similar requests. He asked one of the elders if this was usual behavior for angels. She'd only smiled, patted him on the shoulder and told him he would understand soon enough.

Dominik arrived at the astronomy wing with time to spare and discovered an unusual amount of activity. The lower levels contained graphs and plotting devices where human souls could make decisions on future starcharts. Most of those were in use, even at the late hour.

Out of habit, Dominik headed toward one of the spiraling stairways but changed direction and took a flightpath instead. He flew to the highest level serving as an observatory. Enormous balconies scattered throughout, offering perfect views of the heavens. Small groups clustered all around, with couples using the stars as an aphrodisiac. Some walked hand-in-hand and spoke in soft voices. He saw two Green angels share a kiss, and then touch their foreheads together, smiling in unabashed adoration.

A few of the Magi huddled together making notes on various alignments and activity. Dominik spoke to them briefly, continued on, and was surprised to see the Scriptures, the entire council, gathered in one of the balconies. They were in deep discussion, pointing to the sky and referring to charts spread out on giant easels. More startling was the group on the terrace opposite the Scriptures; Lucifer stood there, surrounded by his Valhallan guards. Dominik was fascinated, curious to why these powerful figures convened.

Nikiti found him, looking resplendent in a short dress matching her violet wings. She wore a unique headpiece with little trails of jewels dangling around her face. They sparkled against her ebony skin, and her wings flared out from her back, picking up light from the stars.

"You are exquisite," Dominik said, and meant every word.

She smiled beautifully and took his hand. "And you look magnificent. I love the tunic; it echoes the influence of China. I spent a lifetime there."

"You told me that once."

She cocked her head. "I did, didn't I? That was years ago, how do you remember?"

"I would never forget words spoken by the lips of a lovely angel."

"Are you trying to impress me, Dominik of the Blue?"

"Only if it's working." He winked and she laughed.

"So what's the big occasion?" she asked. "I saw Pisces and Gemini on the lower level, and someone said the Light Bringer is here. He never leaves the Black City."

"Well, he did tonight," Dominik said, pointing. "He's over there. The Scriptures are down the way, as well." He peered over her head. "Turn around, look who else has been invited to the party."

"That's Aries!" Her wings shot out and she lifted from the ground for a moment. "I've always wanted to meet him!"

The strapping man moved with fiery purpose. He gave the two angels a brief nod as he passed, and Nikita almost swooned. "He's so handsome. He was ruler of the sun during two of my journeys."

"I never chose him," Dominik said. "How did it go for you?"

She shrugged. "It wasn't bad. I hit all my markers ahead of schedule, but my planets were all over the place so some of his influence was diluted. I was always an astrological mutt. How about you?"

"I was created under the Libra sun and I've tended to stick with her, almost exclusively."

"You're one of the Scales?" Nikiti started to ask something else, but then raised her eyebrows. "Do you realize we're standing here on our first evening out, asking one another about our signs? We're horrible!"

Dominik laughed. It felt good, but even better was the feel of the Purple angel's fingers entwined in his. He was starting to suspect angels were naturally forward in the area of romance and affection; Nikiti had already managed to wiggle her way close to his side. He didn't mind at all.

"Let's get closer to the Scriptures," he said. "Maybe we can find out what celestial activity has them out here so late."

"You want to spy on them?" She looked exited by the idea.

"Absolutely not," Dominik said, feigning offense. "Spying would be underhanded. We'll remain in plain sight, but there's no dishonesty in having well-attuned hearing."

The two walked around, finding a little table a few lengths away from where the council was standing. Aries was with them now, looking skyward and waving his arms. The stars and planets moved, manipulated by his hand.

Nikiti leaned across the table and lowered her voice. "How is he doing that?"

"It's an illusion." Dominik watched in fascination. "From the looks of things, they're trying to chart something, playing around with configurations."

"There we go," Aries said. He used one finger in a nudging motion and the moon inched to the left. "A little closer, almost there and…stop!" He breathed as though he exerted great effort, and looked with satisfaction at his work. "So, what do you think?"

The Speaker of the Scriptures, a human woman called Chi, stepped forward. She tapped her fingers on the rail of the balcony and studied the constellations for a long while. "Neptune is a little off. And the placement of Venus might cause an issue."

"You won't get a better alignment than this," Aries said, "not in the timeframe you require."

"We appreciate your efforts," Chi said "We'll take everything under advisement and let you know of our decision."

Aries looked offended, like an artist whose work had been impugned. "There's no reason to even waste time with the other potentials. They'll try to make a case, but none have my level of experience. Don't forget that more Heralds have been born into flesh under my sign than any other."

Chi looked at him, her eyes firm. "Including Tyre. Believe me, we haven't forgotten."

Aries looked ready to argue some more, but placed his hand to his chest and bowed. He walked away and within moments, Taurus arrived. She greeted the Scriptures and got to work without delay. She moved her hands with confidence and efficiency, adjusting the planets and stars to her preferences.

Dominik and Nikiti looked at one another, understanding.

"They're talking about the new Herald," she whispered. "They're trying to decide on the starchart!"

"And apparently taking bids on who will have influence." Dominik sat back, all contentment disappearing. His promise to not think about Tyre was already proving difficult. "Perhaps it's best we leave them to their work."

"Don't you want to stay and watch? I know you have a special place in your heart for this sort of thing, and this is an extraordinary event."

"That's true, but I've had my fill of Heralds and anything to do with them." He stood, reaching out his hand. "I'm sure we can find other amusements."

Her face brightened, and he pulled her to his side. They left the observatory and wandered the Expanse for a long time, talking. Dominik enjoyed the companionship after such a trying day, and Nikiti had an easygoing manner he appreciated. She told him of a time she was so excited about starting a journey that she'd stumbled and fallen headfirst into the river Lethe.

"It was horrible," she said. "Everyone was laughing and there I stood, soaking wet! My hair curled up and puffed out to here. And that white gown did not hold up well in water. It was nearly transparent!"

Dominik enjoyed the image that brought to mind. "Terrible for you, but a blessing for everyone else."

She became quiet for a moment. "I do miss it sometimes, taking the journeys. The part I remember most is when the Cup of Forgetting would touch my lips and I'd taste the water…"

"And knew there was no turning back?" Dominik smiled. He understood exactly what she meant. It was thrilling every time, even knowing the risk. "It's a leap of faith."

"What was your favorite part?"

He considered. "I think it was the review."

"Oh, I found those frightening. I always ended up humiliated or in tears, horrified at some of the decisions I'd made."

"We all did. I suppose that's part of the lesson. But there's also the sense of amazement, when you see the ripples your life created. When you realize how even the smallest, most seemingly insignificant moment made a profound impact. I think I'll miss that the most. I knew it was the right path for me, to become an angel—" He stopped, not wanting to put a damper on the evening by his introspection.

"But you feel sadness for what you've given up?" She squeezed his hand in understanding. "Our souls will never reach enlightenment, but there are still ways we can learn and grow. And we can watch as others rise up, and feel joy knowing we helped. That's our purpose now."

"It's strange we're the ones with the wings," he mused, "when others are destined to ascend far higher."

They walked into one of the garden areas and paused in an easy silence beneath a canopy of green vines. Dominik smiled when she tucked her head into his chest, her hair smelling of scented oil. He ran his fingertips along her arm, loving the soft feel of her skin.

She peeked up at him. "You're close with Shay of the Purple. I've seen you speaking with her many times."

"We took a journey together once," he said. "She's dear to me."

"Were you family? Lovers? Both?" She giggled.

"None of those, but we're bound far tighter. It's a long story." He didn't elaborate. It was a private burden, and the specifics would touch too closely on subjects he was trying to put from his mind.

"Do you have intentions toward her?" Nikiti asked. "Or she for you?"

He was surprised by the questions. He and Shay shared a history, a deep pain neither of them had spoken of in many years. Dominik knew her devotion to him was absolute, and in turn he felt tremendous obligation toward her. But as far as he knew, that was the full extent of their relationship.

"I've never looked upon her in such a way," he said, "and if she's taken interest in me, she's been true to her oath and never mentioned her desire. Why do you ask?"

"Because she's a choirmate." Nikiti wrapped her arms around his waist. "I don't want to cause trouble within the ranks." She lowered her voice, running a hand along his chest. The purple stone in her ring glittered. "There are many things lost to us now, but angels have been rewarded for those sacrifices. If you're willing, I'd like you to come to my chamber so I can be the first to show you one of the gifts."

Dominik knew what she was offering. He pulled her closer, enjoying the feel of her body against his. "I'd like nothing more." He touched one of the sparkling jewels in her hair. "I hope you won't be disappointed. I've only been an angel for a short time." He chuckled a little. "Truth be told, I'm not even sure how to manage the wings."

"Trust me," she said, smiling into his eyes. "Everything finds a place."

Chapter Eight
Final Taunt

Dominik sat in the library with a collection of scrolls strewn atop one of the heavy tables. He'd gotten into a routine the past many months, and each morning he had a study session with one of the elders. Today's lesson concerned residual memory, a complicated subject Dominik found particularly fascinating.

He was paired this time with Hermias of the Blue, a stately angel with a full beard and bald head. He was a jovial fellow, quick of wit and sharp of mind. Dominik liked him very much. The elder sat across the table, reclining in a narrow-backed chair designed to accommodate wings. The area they chose was isolated, surrounded by towering shelves filled with rolled parchments. Dominik tapped his fingers as he read.

"There are two possible answers here and both are viable," he said. "I thought when I became an angel things would change, but there are still no absolutes." He gazed into the endless rows of knowledge. "I have much to learn."

Hermias smiled. "These scrolls are an invaluable resource, but you will find experience is still the best teacher. That's something else that doesn't change." He shifted a little, adjusted his wings and whipped out a cigar. He held it over one of the large candles illuminating the table, took a few puffs and blew out a long stream of smoke. "I hope you don't mind. This is something I enjoyed when I was human, and it gives me pleasure even now. The smell and the taste reminds me of fond times and companionship."

"Feel free," Dominik said. "I maintain small tokens from my lives, as well."

"There's a question I've been wanting to ask, if you will indulge me." He inhaled again and looked at the cigar with appreciation. "Why did you choose the Blue? I understand you were approached by elders of every choir, all of them trying to lure you into their ranks." He pointed a finger. "I know it's not because of the incentives we offered, because you turned down every one."

Dominik leaned back and stretched his legs. "It wasn't my intention to appear ungrateful in declining. All of the choirs were generous, none moreso than the Blue."

"Bah! You're too diplomatic," Hermias said. "Don't worry about protocols with me. I have one standing rule; for everyone to speak freely in my presence."

"Very well." Dominik smiled and rolled up the scroll while he spoke. "I believe the Blue is where I can do the most good. I made my choice after careful consideration and reflection. I admit, I see no benefit in offers of enticement. If such things succeed in swaying a decision, it's a disservice to all parties involved."

"I can't say I disagree with you," Hermias said. "I've become frustrated with the competition between choirs. It's bordering on political and there should be no place for that here. This realm has festering dens of vipers, ready to strike." He waved the cigar, sighing. "But we'll leave the extermination to others. I think I can speak for all the elders when I say we're glad to have you with us. There's been nothing but praise for your aptitude. I hope you're finding the choir to your liking."

"I'm impressed. The Blue perform the most interventions while still maintaining the highest success rate; a difficult thing."

"We also hold another title," the Elder said. "The minions have taken more of our wings than any other. You were attacked once already."

Dominik frowned. The incident occurred the week before during what should've been a routine intervention. He'd taken care of the problem and came away unscathed, but it still grated on his mind. He thought he'd done everything right; he entered the realm in a secure location, monitored his time and was well within the bounds of safety. At least he'd been able to complete his task. That was the important thing.

"Don't beat yourself up," Hermias said. "We reviewed the encounter and can't find any fault in your actions. Sometimes those minions are just in the right place at the right time, or we're in the wrong one. It happens and you can expect more of that." He leaned forward. "I saw you training in the arena last night and I know your ability. Don't let it falter." He motioned toward the towers of scrolls. "It's easy to get wrapped up in all this; there's so much wisdom to be found here, more than anyone can ever hope to learn. But all the knowledge in the realm will be of no use if you're dead, and there are no second chances for angels."

"Are you Dominik of the Blue?" a voice asked.

He rose, nodding at the Purple angel hovering nearby. She handed him a rolled page tied with a black ribbon.

"You've been summoned by the Scriptures," she said.

"What in the realm do they want with you?" Hermias asked with a chuckle. "Have you done something wrong?"

"I'm sure I have, but nothing worth a trip to the sanctuary." He unwrapped the summons and frowned. "It says here I'm to report at the top of the next hour, but it doesn't say why."

The elder looked at the timepiece on his arm. "I'd take to the air if I were you. You don't want to keep them waiting." He started gathering up the parchments. "You go on. I'll return these to the proper place."

Dominik departed and only by energetic flying was he able to arrive at the sanctuary of the Scriptures by the designated time. Two women, both tall and dark, dressed in leather tunics and high boots, met him at the entrance. They opened the mighty black doors and Dominik moved forward.

The throne room was large and round, and the seven members of the Scriptures sat in a semi-circle. He tried to discern what they wanted with him by their expressions, but they allowed nothing to show. Dominik positioned himself in front of Chi, the speaker of the group. He kept a respectful distance and took note of the lifechart on her lap.

Chi held up her hands in greeting.

"Welcome, Dominik," she said. "We have an issue of time, so we're going to get to the heart of our summons. You're aware of the recent events within the realm, regarding Tyre. What are your views on the matter?"

Dominik shifted on his feet. Whatever he'd been expecting, it wasn't this. He had many views on the fallen angel, most left unspoken in polite company.

"Tyre had much courage and skill." He chose his words with care. They left a sour taste on his tongue, but he pressed on. "His loss was great, but the reasons for it were just. I would not question the decision of the Scriptures, or the Light Bringer."

Chi exchanged glances with the rest of the group, and her lips curved up in a tiny smile. "That's good to hear. As you know, a new Herald is being created. The process is well underway and her birth into flesh is imminent." She crossed her ankles and smoothed her gown. "We are in search of an angel to assist her when she comes of age."

Dominik's wings spread a little. He tucked them away and tried to remove all other signs of shock from his appearance. He couldn't imagine why he was being considered for such a position. He had no desire to accept for many reasons, including his personal distaste for the Black choir. That was another thing best left unspoken.

"I'm new to the wings," Dominik said. "There are others with far more experience, better suited for such a duty."

"It's true we usually choose angels with more time in their choirs, but we also consider other factors." She looked closely at Dominik, studying him with interest. "Before Tyre departed, he made a final request, one we found most curious. He asked that *you* be given to his replacement."

Dominik's wings popped out again and he jerked them back in frustration. "Why would Tyre name me?" His voice was heavy with suspicion.

"We wondered the same thing." Chi picked up the chart on her lap, touched the screen, and a three-dimensional image sprang forth and hovered. "So, we pulled your lifechart and what we found was fascinating." She used her finger to scroll through the images. "You had many lifetimes; your history is quite extensive. Aside from your more notable exploits, you also spent time as a Hamarabic scribe, a mason in France, a Conquistador, a slave, a Vintner in Greece..."

Dominik watched as image after image of his human lives flashed by. He had no idea what Tyre had been up to, dropping his name to the Scriptures, but he suspected it was one, final taunt from the Herald. He looked away, bit his tongue and tried to keep his mounting anger in check while Chi continued her analysis.

"...Roman centurion, a barrister, you were even a tribal medicine man at one point. And most recently..." She let the image of Katie Connors flicker for a while. "A schoolgirl in America." She flipped off the lifechart and placed it back on her lap. "In most cases, especially with an older soul, we see patterns develop. But you always chose great diversity, and struck an uncommon balance between the various challenges. Your advancement was extraordinary."

"I had help," Dominik said. "I was given wise council before and after my journeys. I was fortunate to have angels intervene at times, and I was even intercepted on several occasions...by Tyre, in fact." He hated to admit, but the infuriating Herald had probably saved him from the fires. At the moment, he thought damnation might've been preferable.

"Humility is a fine quality," Chi said, "but your successes and failures are still yours alone. We are impressed by your accomplishments and have decided you will be given the task as advisor to the new Herald."

Dominik struggled to remain calm. He became an angel to assist human souls, not to waste time grooming a creature that would one day come to despise them. He searched for an appropriate response. "I'm honored you think I'm worthy," he said, "but I don't think I should have the responsibility."

"We disagree."

He started to grow agitated. He wondered if Tyre was laughing at him from the nether. "There's too much at stake. I believe my strengths lie in other areas. It would be a disservice for me to take on this particular duty."

"The decision is made. There is nothing—"

"I don't like Heralds!" Dominik clutched his fists, furious with himself for the breach of etiquette.

Chi's eyes went wide at the outburst and she sat straight. After a protracted silence, she placed a hand to her mouth and her shoulders shook. Within moments, the Scriptures all began to chuckle and exchange knowing glances.

Dominik took a calming breath. "Apologies for my disrespect."

"Your hesitation is understandable," Chi said, "but I would remind you of the words you spoke when first entering this sanctuary. You said you trusted our judgment. We will hold you to those words, and your oath."

Dominik nodded, trying to keep the discontent from his face. "Certainly. I will perform to the best of my abilities." He wanted to pick up the nearest object and toss it against a wall. "How would you like me to proceed?"

Chi stood, and the rest of the Scriptures followed her lead. "All necessary information will be written up and delivered to you. Strict rules are in place to govern advisors, and all will be explained. Until then, you should spend time in research. There is a wealth of knowledge in the scrolls concerning the Black choir. It will be of use to you."

"How much time will I have to prepare?" He didn't think any amount would be sufficient.

"The new Herald must first reach the age of maturity, in human years, before we'll call upon your services." She held out her hands, and the Scriptures began to file from the room.

Dominik waited for them to go, but Chi stayed behind and approached him.

"I want you to know that I'm here, should you have any questions or need to speak with someone."

"I appreciate that." He couldn't believe he found himself in this predicament, but he'd made sacred vows, obedience to lawful authority among them.

"I'll be gone for a short while," Chi said, "but otherwise, I'll make myself available for you."

"You're taking on a journey?" He was surprised. The human members of the Scriptures were the most advanced of souls, invaluable to the realm.

Chi smiled. "A gesture for a dear friend. It's still years away, even by our time, and I'll be back quickly, barring any missteps on the charted course. Go in peace, Dominik."

He bowed and made his way from the sanctuary. He wished for a moment that Tyre were still around, so he could choke the life out of him.

Chapter Nine
Gift from God

Kim Mendez didn't like the couple sitting across from her.

James Hawke was a little man, but substantial around the middle. He sat in one of the client chairs on the opposite side of the antique desk, watching Kim's every move. His expression and body language—he had his arms crossed over his chest in a haughty way—made it seem like he was giving up valuable time to be there. He made a show of brushing off the seat before he sat down, and made sure to mention the crack in the window, just in case someone hadn't noticed.

Kim had been a lawyer for a long time and was pretty good at sizing people up. She'd pegged Mr. Hawke as a sanctimonious prick the moment she met him and he'd done nothing so far to alter that assessment.

Lynnette Hawke wasn't much better. She sat straight, wringing her hands, and wearing a dress that might've been in style thirty years ago. Her thin lips, coated in some horrid shade of orange, remained pursed. She'd asked a few questions but was silent now, ever since her husband had tossed her a scowl. That the woman was quick to do as her husband commanded didn't sit well with Kim, but she buried her concerns. It wasn't her job to pass judgment on these people; someone else had already done that. She only needed to make sure everything was in order, legally.

"Have you decided on a name yet?" Kim asked. That information was, oddly, missing on the paperwork.

"Yes, we have." Mrs. Hawke beamed at her husband, but her happiness died quickly under his gaze and she cast her eyes down.

"Jalynn," Mr. Hawke said.

"Oh, that's lovely," Kim said as she filled in the blank spot on the form. "Like James and Lynn."

Mr. Hawke looked supremely satisfied. The name must've been his idea and he was proud of his own cleverness. Kim shuffled a few more papers, hoping her face wasn't giving anything away. She didn't know what it was with people who adopted children, but they often picked names that were a combination of their own. Since they couldn't make a baby together, they could at least make a name.

"Middle name?" she asked.

"Rise."

Kim looked up, not certain she heard him correctly.

James Hawke repeated the name and then spelled it slowly, as if speaking to a person of limited intelligence. Kim wanted to stab him with her pen.

"She was born near Easter," Mrs. Hawke said, looking apologetic for daring to speak. "It reminds us of our Lord rising from the grave."

Kim sighed and filled in the last blank. She found the choice odd, but knew the couple must be religious fanatics considering the adoption agency they used.

"Is there anything else you failed to properly complete?" James Hawke asked.

Kim bit her tongue and forced herself to smile as she slid a paper across her desk. "No, I think we're all done now. If you could both sign at the bottom, please."

Mr. Hawke signed first. Mrs. Hawke had to stretch to reach the pen when he was finished.

Kim gathered up all the papers and handed Mr. Hawke an envelope, his copies of all the important documents. Kim stood and offered her hand. "Congratulations."

Mrs. Hawke thanked her and shook her hand briefly. Mr. Hawke did the same, only with less enthusiasm and without the thank you.

Kim opened the door to an adjoining room and motioned to Mae, one of the workers from the adoption agency. A woman with red-framed glasses came in with a small bundle in her arms. The new mother smiled, but the father grunted, looking the worker up and down with open disdain.

"She's sleeping now," Mae said. "Poor thing cried all the way here, wore her little-self right out." She kissed the baby on the forehead before handing her to the new mother.

Kim had heard the baby crying earlier. After meeting the Hawke's, she decided the tiny girl was probably psychic and terrified of her fate. Kim felt a pang of conscious, but then remembered the Hawke's had written some large checks over the past few months, checks that had gone a long way in greasing the proverbial wheels of the adoption. Those checks also paid Kim's fee and she had kids, too. Life was a bitch.

Lynn Hawke cooed at the baby in her arms and moved the blanket to get a better look at her daughter. Mr. Hawke stood behind his wife, inspecting the infant in a clinical manner.

"You're sure she doesn't have any problems?" he asked. "She's small."

"As you know, she was born early after a stressful pregnancy, but she's been examined several times and pronounced in perfect health ."

"She's beautiful," Mrs. Hawke exclaimed as the baby opened her eyes. "Oh, James, look! She has green eyes, as bright as emeralds!"

"I thought white babies were born with blue eyes." Mr. Hawke peered at Kim as though she'd been the cause of the abnormality.

"It is unusual. But they're lovely, aren't they?"

"Oh, yes," Mrs. Hawke said. "It's a sign that she's our gift. Jalynn Rise, our gift from God!"

Kim watched the new family with a terrible feeling of unease. She was pretty sure God had nothing to do with this.

CHAPTER TEN
ROLLING AWAY THE STONE

Jalynn Rise Hawke tore through her room, dumping out drawers and emptying her closet, throwing everything she owned onto the floor. There wasn't much left after the recent blowout with her family, but she didn't care. It meant less packing, and she was already running late. Her parents and younger sister had gone to Easter mass, but Jalynn had swallowed half a bottle of ipecac to feign illness so she'd have an excuse to stay home. The less-than-brilliant plan worked, but it took longer than expected for the vomiting to subside.

She moved fast, stuffing clothes and other small things into a backpack. She picked up a sweater, examined it, then tossed it into the growing pile of items she never wanted to see again.

She reached for a belt and froze. Doorbell. Her heart pounded and she held her breath, then realized her family would hardly be ringing the bell. It must be her ride.

She jogged through the house and checked the peephole. It was indeed Danny—the only person in the world who knew what she was doing. She flung open the door without a word, and was back to work before he had both feet inside.

"Hello to you, too," Danny said as he joined her. "And Happy Birthday."

"Thanks." She couldn't remember where she'd gotten a pair of shoes, so off they went into the big heap.

Danny looked around her room. "Where's all your stuff?"

Jalynn grabbed her purse from the bed and smirked. "Some if it's broken. Most of it's bagged up for the trash." She moved past him and flipped on the light in the little bathroom across the hall.

"What happened this time?" he asked.

"Don't ask if you don't want to know. My father tried to do a virginity check on me again."

"Oh, hell," Danny groaned. "He's still making you do that?"

"Every year around my birthday."

"He's twisted."

"You're just now figuring that out? I told him I'd shove a crucifix up his ass if he touched me. That's when he started breaking things. He said I must be *guilty* or I wouldn't be arguing." She grabbed a few items from the medicine cabinet—toothbrush, deodorant, razor—and shoved them into her purse. "Then my mother got involved. She started crying and being dramatic, saying I was in league with Lucifer. I mean, really? Who talks like that?" Her hair was in rough shape, so she pulled the whole mess into a sloppy ponytail.

"These things in the big stack going?"

"Nope," Jalynn answered as she snatched up the backpack and slung it over her shoulder. "I'm only taking the stuff I bought myself. I don't want anything from those people."

"By 'those people' you mean your parents?" Danny gave her an amused look.

"Yep. They can sell it, give it away or burn it all. I don't care."

"You going to leave a note for your sister?"

"Why would I?"

Danny looked at her like she'd lost her mind. "Because she's your *sister,* and now she's going to be stuck here by herself. Don't you think she'll miss you?"

"She'll miss not having someone around to blame for everything."

He shook his head and Jalynn made a dismissive motion with her hand. "You see anything missing from her room? No. That little follower learned the art of blind obedience a long time ago."

"Jealous?"

She barked a laugh. Danny knew better, but he was trying to rile her. She took the bait anyway. "If doing every single thing you're told without question is the standard for approval, I don't mind being hated. Some things are worth fighting for." She snapped her fingers as she remembered something. "I'm going to take the computer Aunt Missy gave me."

Jalynn made a beeline to the attached garage. Several big trash bags lined the wall, and she ripped one open. Books, CD's, trinkets and more clothes spilled out. She rummaged through, choosing things she still considered hers.

She nodded to the far corner. "The computer's over there." She moved to the next bag, grateful trash pick-up wasn't coming until the next day. By then, she'd been long gone.

"Didn't this belong to your cousin?" Danny asked as he hefted the computer into his arms. "The one killed in Iraq?"

"That's right. I hope it works. My mom didn't want it in the house. She said it was a bad omen or cursed or whatever. She's such a freak."

"It looks okay. Emory can probably get it going. He's out in the car, by the way. He was in town to visit his parents and decided to come along. Hope you don't mind."

"I don't care." Jalynn ripped open the final bag. "I haven't seen Emory since last summer."

"He invited you to his Christmas party, but you didn't show," Danny said. "And he was at my New Year's party, but you ditched that, too."

"I know, I suck." She found a few more little items, and began going through a mental checklist, making sure she hadn't forgotten anything important.

Danny left with the computer and returned for the monitor. He wasn't wearing a jacket today and Jalynn was a little taken aback at the muscles flexing in his arms. She wondered when that had happened.

"You ready?" he asked. "You have all the clothes you want, books, your ID—"

"ID! I can't believe I forgot that." She checked the clock. Mass would be ending in about ten minutes and the church was only a few miles away. She had to move fast.

She sprinted down the hall and into her parent's bedroom. She always felt strange in this room; it had been off limits her whole life. She went for the closet where she knew her father kept the little silver lockbox. She saw him hiding the keys once, so she knew where to look.

"You better hurry," Danny said from the doorway.

"I'm trying. My birth certificate and social security card are in here. I'm going to need those when I start work tomorrow." She rummaged through papers and found the items she needed, along with a sealed envelope with her full name on the front. Whatever it was, it belonged to her now.

"We should go," Danny said. "I don't want to be here when your parents get back."

"Neither do I." She shoved everything into her purse, and put the lockbox and keys back where she found them. "I need one more minute to make sure I have everything this time."

Jalynn made one final pass through the house, and took a moment to stare at the enormous dining room table her parents adored. It was old and heavy, with intricate designs carved around the edges, and Jalynn had sat there every night for family dinner. She clamped her eyes shut, fighting unwelcome memories. The sound of forks and knives scraping against plates played through her head in an endless loop. It made her sick.

Rage churned up and she allowed it to boil over. She picked up one of the matching chairs, the one that had been her assigned seat. She slammed it into the table, over and over, destroying the thing as best she could until Danny grabbed her from behind and pulled her away.

"What are you doing?" He let her go when she struggled against his hold. "Isn't that an antique?"

"It belonged to my Grandmother." Jalynn's voice shook with fury. "You know how many times my father came around this table at me? Because I wasn't eating enough, or I didn't answer a question fast enough, or I wasn't sitting up straight like a *lady*?"

She swung the chair one more time, then tossed it down. "I hate this thing, and even when I leave, I'll still have to see it every single day when I look in the mirror." She traced the crescent-shaped scar framing her right eye, a perfect replica of one of the designs around the table edge. She'd gotten the injury on her thirteenth birthday, her gift for struggling when her parents held her down for her first 'intactness' check. She could still remember the way her mother had grabbed her shoulders and pressed her back into the table while her father forced her legs open. She remembered the cross necklace her mother wore, and could still picture it dangling above her face while she kicked and screamed.

Danny shifted on his feet. He only knew a fraction of what had happened in this house, and Jalynn knew if she'd ever told him everything, he'd have come over with a shotgun. It was part of the reason she never told him. She didn't need him fighting her battles, and if anyone was getting the satisfaction of vengeance, it was going to be her. She stared at the destruction she'd inflicted, thinking it was a damn good start.

Danny touched her back, but didn't say anything. He wasn't comfortable with emotional entanglements. It was one of the things Jalynn liked about him.

"I remember the first day I met you, in that First Communion class," she said. "The night before, right here, my father beat me until I peed myself. It got on the floor and he rubbed my face in it, and told me I was a dog. The carpet scratched up my nose and chin and I told you I got hurt playing football—remember that?" She looked up at him. "You tried to give me that purple sucker you'd already had in your mouth. So disgusting."

"I was trying to make you feel better." He grinned down at her. "I knew you were lying. You were way too skinny to be playing football. I figured you were trying to impress me because I was wearing that Colts jacket."

Jalynn made a face. "I was not trying to impress you, trust me.

"Hey, I was already good-looking when I was eight. And I know you wanted my sucker, you just didn't like grape." He nudged her with his shoulder. "Come on, killer. Let's get out of here."

Danny had propped open the door with one of the large, decorative boulders Lynette Hawke kept on the front porch. Jalynn pushed it away with her foot and the door started to close, but then a burst of wind tossed it back. She let it swing. The house could use some airing out.

She hopped in the backseat. Emory turned around and tossed her a chocolate egg.

"Happy Birthday, Miss Jalynn. And Happy Easter."

"I guess Danny didn't tell you; I'm changing my name legally. Do *not* call me Jalynn ever again, please and thank you."

He chuckled. "What am I supposed to call you, then?"

She took one last look at the front door; it was still swinging freely and she started to laugh.

"Call me Rise."

Chapter Eleven
Master Plan

Emory brought along an audio book for the hour-long drive from Nineveh to Indianapolis. Rise was bored with it before they even got to the interstate. A little beep sounded on her watch and she rummaged in her purse.

"Can I have a drink of that water?" She took the bottle handed to her. "It's crazy pill time."

"You still take that stuff?" Danny didn't look happy.

"Every day, never miss a dose."

"What the hell are crazy pills?" Emory asked.

"I'm unruly," Rise said with heavy sarcasm. She popped one capsule and took a swig of water. "My parents decided I had an attention disorder because I wouldn't obey without question. I'm going to quit those, but I can't stop cold. I tried once and the withdrawal about killed me." She shrugged. "Plus, I have another one I take for anxiety. It's a sedative and it rocks."

"Maybe now you won't need those, either." Danny smiled at her in the rear-view mirror.

Emory changed the subject. "You going to graduation?"

"I already graduated mid-term."

"I know, but you can still go. You can do the cap and gown thing. See everyone again for the last time."

Rise barked a laugh. "I haven't talked to anyone from High School since December, except Danny, and I have zero interest in the ceremony. Besides, I'll probably be working.

My Aunt Missy found me a job at the vet clinic where she takes her dogs. I start tomorrow, full-time."

"I remember your Aunt Missy." Emory twisted around in the seat to look at her. "She drove down to Nineveh last summer for the Fourth of July festival, had two little fuzzy things with her."

"Pomeranians."

"Right. She still single?"

"Yes."

"Is she dating?" Emory flashed a huge grin.

"Really?" Rise cocked her head. "Sorry, you're not her type."

"She doesn't like blind guys?"

"You're nowhere near being blind yet, but no, that's not it."

"Am I too debonair?" He brushed a non-existent piece of lint from his colorful shirt.

"No."

"She doesn't like dreadlocks?"

"She doesn't like twenty-year-olds, Emory," Rise said in exasperation, and Danny laughed.

Emory winked. "I turn twenty-one next week."

"That's right, we're both Aries; probably why I don't completely hate you right now. You having a party?"

He snorted. "Like you'd show up if I was? I'm going to keep it low key; maybe hit some bars near campus with a few guys. I'd invite you two, but it's *real* adults only. Hey, where are we going anyway, Miss *Rise*?"

"Piccadilly Place Apartments. It's over near 42d and—"

"I know where it is." His dark eyes peered from underneath thick glasses, unbelieving. "You sure you aren't taking anything besides those crazy pills?"

"Why?"

Emory laughed hard, shook his head and his hair bounced around. "My cousin had her car stolen over there a few months ago. Your dad would have a stroke if he knew where you were moving."

Danny grinned. "I think that's part of her master plan."

"Bite me," Rise said, not because her friend wasn't on the right track in his assessment, but because he was. She'd gotten good at being the mysterious, emotionally distant loner, but Danny had gotten into the irritating habit of seeing her a little too clearly. She'd have to work on that.

She turned her attention fully back to Emory. "My father has no idea where I'm moving and I'm not planning to tell him or anyone else in that family. I've been waiting eighteen years to get away." She looked out the window and saw the Indianapolis skyline coming into view. "The only thing that keeps me sane is knowing I'm not blood-related to any of them."

Emory whistled. "Harsh. Hope I never get on your bad side."

"You won't." She chuckled. "Not today anyway. And about the apartment—it's cheap, and right on a bus line that'll take me four blocks away from the clinic."

"Now, that's good." Emory cocked a finger in the air. "Public transportation in this city is terrible. When it gets to the point when I can't drive at all anymore, I'm going to have to move."

"Exactly," Rise said. "The only thing that sucks is I had to pay two months in advance, plus a deposit. I don't even have enough cash left to buy a bed." It wasn't a complaint. Sleeping on the floor in her own home was better than sleeping on a bed at her parent's.

The guys exchanged a look Rise couldn't identify. She ignored them for the rest of the trip and listened to the sleep-inducing audio book.

Danny remembered the way to the apartments, going slow on the ragged roads weaving through the complex. He popped the trunk and grabbed the computer.

"Hurry up," Emory said, hefting the monitor. "If anyone sees us with this stuff, you might not have it tomorrow."

"Knock it off." Danny looked at her. "He's just trying to scare you."

"I know." Rise put her game-face on to mask the escalating apprehension. She tried to be inconspicuous while she glanced around. The upper-level apartments had small balconies, and a few folks sat in folding chairs, watching the new arrivals. Most windows had mini blinds, but some looked to have sheets tacked up on the inside.

The main door to her building was solid, but the latch was broken. Her apartment was on the top floor, and she navigated around a group of children sitting on the stairs, unwrapping candies from Easter baskets. They all went quiet and watched the newcomers with big eyes. One little boy offered Rise a jellybean that looked like it'd been in his palm for a good while. She made a face.

Rise unlocked the door, dropped her bag on the discolored beige carpet and watched Danny and Emory look the place over. There wasn't much to see.

"Kind of small." Danny stood in the kitchen, which was little more than a sink and refrigerator jammed together under a few cabinets.

"I don't need much space." She headed into the bathroom; it only took a few steps. She flipped the light switch, but nothing happened. No bulb in the fixture. She turned the knob on the sink and water came out in halting spurts.

"Bedroom's not bad," Emory said from behind her.

Danny peeked out the window, then smiled. "He's here."

"Who's here?" Rise tugged the cord to lift the blinds, and the entire fixture pulled away from the wall and tumbled to the floor in a heap. Danny's father, Phillip Daly, stood by his truck, loosening up tie down straps.

"Why is your dad here?" Rise asked in astonishment.

"Birthday presents," he answered, grinning.

She ran outside and couldn't stop a little squeal when she saw her gifts. She wouldn't be sleeping on the floor, after all. She hugged Mr. Daly and he went stiff.

"Don't get too excited." He patted Rise on the back a few times, then adjusted the cap on his salt-and-peppering head. "It's not new, just some extra stuff that's been taking up space out in the shed. From what Dan told me, you can probably use it."

That was an understatement. Rise held open the door while the men moved large items upstairs. She caught sight of a shiny object, half-buried in the dirt beside the crumbling steps. She picked it up, surprised to find a palm-sized Star of David medallion on a chain with a broken clasp. She inspected it with interest as she headed upstairs.

"Look what I found." Rise turned the jewelry in her hand and yelped when it cut into her fingers. The edges were razor sharp. "Good thing I found it before those kids."

"I didn't think you liked kids," Danny said.

"I don't. Being called 'scar face' every day in middle school will do that, but doesn't mean I want them bleeding out on the front steps."

"Let me see that thing." Emory took the medallion and held it toward the light. "Someone made this into a weapon. Pretty cool, actually." He handed it back to her. "You might want to fix the chain and keep this on you."

"I'm not Jewish."

"I don't think anyone out to rob you at knifepoint will care."

Rise just rolled her eyes

As it turned out, Danny's father presented not only a twin bed and mattress, but also a small desk, mismatched sheets and towels and a host of other things. It looked like Mr. Daly went on a scavenger hunt through his house, even giving her a half-used box of laundry detergent. Each item was something Rise would use, and most were things she wouldn't have thought about until she needed them.

Emory set up the computer, while Mr. Daly grabbed his toolbox and busied himself going room-to-room, tightening knobs and checking plumbing. He fixed the blinds, and was especially concerned with the door locks.

"We'll need to get you a deadbolt," he said. It sounded exactly like the kind of thing a dad would say. One with normal, protective instincts, anyway.

Mr. Daly wiggled the handle back and forth a few times, then opened the door to check the outer lock. A man passed by, wearing a nice suit and a fedora with a little red feather. Maybe in his sixties, with skin the color of oak, he carried a cane with unusual carvings. Rise thought he looked remarkable.

He glanced into the apartment. "You folks moving in?"

"Just my friend, Rise," Emory told him.

The gentleman looked her up and down and grunted. "You alone, young lady?"

"Yes, sir."

"Hmmm. Not sure this is the best place for a little girl, but if any of these punks around here give you trouble, let me know." He tapped his cane a few times. "My name's Elijah Crawford. I live down the hall there with my wife. She had a stroke a few years back, so you probably won't see her out too much. Our granddaughter lives with us." He beckoned to one of the children on the stairs. She had pigtails, a pink basket, and scuffs on her shoes from play.

"Vanessa, this lady is going to be our new neighbor," he said. "Her name is Rise, that right?"

She nodded, hoping her smile passed for sincere.

The little girl opened a piece of chocolate from her basket. "What happened to your face?"

"Vanessa," her grandfather reprimanded.

Rise glanced at Danny and raised her eyebrows. Some things never changed.

She gave her standard lie. "I fell into a table." One day she'll start telling the truth and say a man three times her size slammed her face-first into the thing, and see how that goes over.

"Must've big a big one," Vanessa said.

Rise adjusted her hair, trying to pull a piece over her eye. The scar had gotten a little better over time, but it was raised in a peculiar way and impossible not to notice. A few years back, a strange guy at the mall asked if the mark was intentional; he swore it looked like a ritual burn from a tribal ceremony.

"Well, we should be going." Mr. Crawford looked down at his watch. "We're off to church, aren't we?"

The little girl nodded and popped another jellybean in her mouth.

The men shook hands and Mr. Crawford tipped his hat to Rise. Mr. Daly took that as a cue. "I reckon I should be getting on back, too," he said. "You get settled in here and I'll come by tomorrow with a deadbolt. Oh, I almost forget." He opened his toolbox and pulled out something that looked like a black handle. He flipped his wrist, and a silver baton extended to about an arms length.

"This is just like the police carry." Mr. Daly used his palm to push the metal part back into the handle, then whipped it open again. "You want to try to hit these spots." He demonstrated on Danny, lightly tapping his neck, knees and a few other areas, then handed it to Rise.

"Won't do much good against a gun," Emory pointed out, and everyone gave him various expressions of annoyance. He held up his hands. "Just saying."

"He's right, though," Mr. Daly said. "The best way to avoid danger is to stay out of its way, but if it ever comes looking for you, well, I'll feel better knowing you have this."

It took her a few times to make it work, but finally Rise was able to extend and retract the baton with ease.

"You need anything, give Danny a call." Mr. Daly gathered up his tools. "After next month, I guess you can call me if you need to." He turned to go, paused, and his face suddenly appeared decades older. He spoke into the floor. "Wish I'd known before what was going on with you. Wish I would've...." He let the words hang as he removed his hat and put it back again. "Well, just get settled."

"What did he mean after next month?" Rise asked after Danny's father had left.

Danny jammed his hands into his pockets and leaned against the wall. "I'm going to boot camp two days after graduation."

She crossed her arms and glared. "I thought you weren't leaving until end of summer."

Emory looked back and forth between his friends, mumbled something about using the bathroom and disappeared.

"The recruiter called last week and asked if I'd be interested in going earlier." Danny pushed himself off the wall. "I'm signed up for linguistics, but I don't get to choose which language. The Sergeant said he could almost guarantee I'd get into Arabic school if I left next month. If I wait, I'll probably get funneled into Mandarin."

"You need to learn English first, Dan!" Emory called from another room. The walls were thin.

"Shut up, Emory!"

"When were you planning to tell me?" Rise demanded.

"Don't give me that righteous anger look," he said. "I was *planning* to tell you weeks ago, but every time we saw each other I was driving you to fill out applications, or you were looking at apartment guides—"

"I had to…" She was losing steam.

"I just didn't want to pile anything else on you." He stuck a finger in her face. "You know, I would've told you if you would've asked. Don't get mad at me because you didn't."

Rise bit the inside of her cheek and tried to formulate a defense. She didn't have one. Danny was right; she'd been consumed with her own problems for months. Years, to be more accurate.

"Tell her about the car!" Emory was still eavesdropping.

Rise tilted her head. "Car?"

Danny grinned. "I was going to ask you to take care of it when I leave."

She brightened. It would be a while before she could afford a vehicle and she liked Danny's, except the horrible burnt orange color.

"Only until I get out of boot camp," he said, "so don't get too attached, and definitely don't crash. And no, you can't paint it, either."

Rise hugged him with a little squeal. She was excited about the car, less so about Danny leaving. She didn't like many people and the feeling was mutual in most cases, which suited her just fine.

She walked her friends out a few hours later, waved goodbye, and took a seat on the steps, getting a feel for her new neighborhood. Mr. Crawford came out and took a seat beside her. A sickly-thin man with scraggly blonde hair came down the walk, singing Jingle Bells. He passed by as if in another world.

"Is he getting his holidays confused?" Rise asked.

Mr. Crawford sighed. "I doubt the poor man even knows what year it is. That's Scotty. He's been hanging around here for a few months. He lives in his head, fixated on Christmas. He'll sing those carols to you all day long."

She watched the strange fellow turn a corner. "Is he dangerous?" She didn't have much experience with mentally disturbed people, unless she counted herself, and most of the time she didn't trust her own reactions. She fluctuated between apathy and rage, and sometimes that pendulum swung fast.

"I've never seen the man violent," Mr. Crawford said. "He does have a tendency for sticky fingers, though." He grunted. "We have a few others around here with the same condition, except they don't have the excuse, like Scotty, in saying God didn't give them the sense to know better. I'd stay tight to anything you want to keep. Neighborhood watch does a good job, but they can't be everywhere all the time."

Rise promised to keep that in mind, and excused herself to finish unpacking. She headed back upstairs to find a few kids huddled around, antagonizing a huge cat sitting right in front of her door. The orange tiger clearly wasn't in the mood for games. He bared impressive fangs and swatted at his tormentors with claws that looked razor sharp. Rise liked him immediately.

She turned to the kids. "Leave the cat alone, and go work on a sugar coma."

After a few smart remarks, they dispersed. She knelt down, and her new friend purred against her hand. He didn't have a collar, and looked like he'd been on his own for quite a while. She considered letting him stay. She always wanted a pet, but her parents hadn't allowed it. They hated cats, said dogs were filthy, and would've been horrified by the idea of taking in a stray. That alone made her decision.

Rise picked up her new roommate, determined he was indeed a male, and decided to name him Oliver. He explored while she grabbed a pair of scissors and headed to the bathroom.

She stared into the mirror and let her hair fall loose. She'd never liked the unruly mop, except the unusual jet-black color. It was heavy, cumbersome and so thick it snapped hairbands. She begged to get it cut often, but was always refused.

Women should have long hair, her father insisted.

It would help cover the scar, her mother said.

Rise took enormous pleasure in chopping it all off.

Chapter Twelve
Artificial Bliss

The spring and summer months churned into a kaleidoscope of trials and errors, but by the beginning of September, Rise had found her rhythm.

She worked almost every day and enjoyed her job, menial though the work was. She'd gotten used to the poop, the smell of urine and the sight of blood. The money wasn't great, but allowed her to pay bills on time and get a few things for the apartment.

She got ready for work, donning scrubs which made her look more like a nurse than *the kennel girl*—her unofficial title at the clinic. Oliver rubbed against her legs while she arranged her hair. The style was super short now, professionally cut, and she loved it. It was thick as always, but with help from gooey styling products, she was able to get little pieces to stick up in different ways.

She took one last look in the mirror, satisfied. Spending time on her appearance had never been a priority before, mostly because she thought of herself as a lost cause in that area, but the better Rise felt on the inside, the more she found she wanted the outside to match. It surprised her that it did. She wasn't oblivious to the looks she'd been receiving from men.

She popped her crazy pills, vowing once again to stop taking them when her prescription expired, and headed out the door for another day of responsible adulthood.

She was halfway down the stairs when she saw her neighbor, Mrs. Hernandez, loading boxes into the trunk of her car. Rise cringed and tried to be invisible. She'd forgotten she promised to donate something for the community sale. Mrs. Hernandez hadn't.

"Ah, Rise! There you are!" The little woman had a thick accent, thick body, and never forgot anyone's name. "I was looking for you earlier."

"Hola, Mrs. H." It was the only Spanish word she knew. "Sorry, I was probably in the shower." She'd actually ignored the knocks on the door.

"Do you have things ready for the sale?" Mrs. Hernandez wasn't one for chitchat, and most days Rise appreciated her directness.

"I sure do, let me run back up and get it."

She sprinted back into the apartment, grabbed a paper grocery sack and searched cabinets and closets, cursing under her breath. Oliver jumped onto the kitchen counter and watched.

"Don't look at me like that." Rise knew what she was doing; she'd learned the word *anthropomorphic* at work, which meant giving her pet human attributes. She wasn't convinced there wasn't some truth to the phenomenon; she was certain Oliver found her panic amusing.

Rise tossed three little jar candles into the bag, but then removed one. She hated giving away anything, but proceeds from the sale were going to a family who lost their house in a fire, and she didn't want the neighborhood to find out she really didn't give a damn. She spied the green and pink umbrella she bought a few weeks back. The forecast looked wet for the next few days so she'd probably need the thing, but she dropped it into the bag anyway.

"Here it is," she said when she was back outside. "It's not much."

"No, this is wonderful!" Mrs. Hernandez' face turned into a wrinkle mosaic when she smiled. "It's not what you give, but the *spirit* in which you give. That's what's important."

Rise was on the fast track to hell, if that was the standard. Her neighbor had trouble with a heavy box, so she reached to help, thinking it might slow her descent into the fiery pit of eternal damnation.

"Let me get that for you." It felt like she was lifting a bag of feathers instead of a box of books. Her workout routine was starting to pay off. The veterinarian who owned the clinic, Dr. Mark, was a fitness fanatic. He kept exercise machines on-site and *encouraged* the staff to keep in shape. He hung bodybuilding photos in the break room, and tacked a height-weight chart on the refrigerator. Rise only started using the equipment to score points with the boss, but found the changes in her body addictive. She had small, defined muscles now.

"Look how strong you are," Mrs. Hernandez said. "I never would've guessed; you're so skinny." She poked Rise in the ribs a few times. "You come by if you get a chance," she said as she slammed the trunk. "The sale is today, tomorrow and Saturday. We have tents, so even if we get the rain, we'll still be there, okay? You tell your friends to come, and your boyfriend."

Rise snorted. "I don't have a boyfriend."

Mrs. Hernandez patted her cheek. "I know. But if you find one before Saturday, you tell him to come, okay?"

There was zero chance of that, but Rise gave a smile anyway, wished her neighbor luck with the sale, and headed to work in the temporary car she'd come to love.

Eastside Animal Care had a full parking lot. Dr. Mark was in the lobby, wearing his usual attire; blue scrubs custom fit to accommodate his biceps and a red stethoscope draped around his neck. He'd colored his hair again, and looked like he'd been hitting a tanning salon.

Rise gave a little wave, but her boss didn't notice. He stood, chatting up a client and potential next ex-wife, one wearing a short skirt and holding her Shih-Tzu like a fashion accessory. Dr. Mark was almost striking a pose, grinning while he explained the finer points of urinary infections. The only thing missing was a little sparkle of light to glint off his teeth. He'd been a devil with the flirting since his divorce, but according to office scuttlebutt, he hadn't exactly been an angel beforehand.

Rise clocked-in on the computer and got to work. The trashcans were already full, so either everyone was too busy to deal with the mess or—more likely— they were waiting for Rise to show up. Not that she minded the laziness; she figured it meant job security.

She crushed down the trash, recognizing a shrill voice coming from one of the exam rooms. It was one of the clinic regulars; a woman with an obnoxious accent, red spikes for fingernails, and a menagerie of pets. *Rescued* pets, as she constantly reminded everyone. Rise made a little gagging sound, and one of the nearby assistants chuckled.

"If you think just listening to her is bad," she said, "try being stuck in a room with her." She lowered her voice. "She brought her new dog today—adopted from a rescue, big surprise—and swears he's crazy because he barks at the rain. She's talking about putting him down."

Rise glanced at the exam room door. "That woman is a walking reminder of why I'd rather deal with dog shit than people." She tied up the bag and headed to the kennel area, ready to make good on those words.

She cleaned up a few accidents, then continued her daily routine of dispensing medication and rationing food and water. She grabbed a leash to begin daily walks, but was intercepted by Tammy, a Veterinary Technician with a long string of initials after her name from various specialty degrees. Common Courtesy 101 was not part of the curriculum.

She thrust a heavy plastic body bag at Rise. "Euthanasia in exam one," she snapped and kept walking.

Rise cursed, trudged to the exam room where everyone's favorite client had just been, and cursed again. A sweet-looking dog, barely a year old, lay dead on the table. In her opinion, the wrong life had been juiced.

"I guess barking at the rain is a death sentence in this state," she whispered, giving him a scratch behind the ears. "That sucks, but if it's any consolation, my *rescue* didn't go so great, either."

Rise shook the body into the heavy plastic bag and pressed out the air, stunned she didn't despise the duty. That was a first. Preparing pets for group cremation was the one part of her job she hated, and not because the task disgusted her. It didn't, but she always thought she should feel something for the dead creatures, and she never had, until now. The knot of emotion in her gut relieved her in a small way.

Tammy stuck her head in the door. "Hurry up, we need this room." She snapped her fingers and disappeared. The tech had mastered drive-by rudeness.

Rise hauled the bag onto her shoulder, carrying it like a Santa of Death back to the big freezer. Tammy was already there, adjusting the remains of other pets so the new one could fit.

"Was the dog really crazy?" Rise asked as she placed the limp body in the freezer.

"No idea," Tammy said. "The owner was, though. Dr. Mark wanted to try some meds, but she said twenty bucks a month was too expensive."

Rise rolled her eyes. The bitch probably spent twice that much on her nails. "You still want me to come in early tomorrow? You said something about it yester—"

"Yeah. We're going to be shorthanded for a while and might need extra help in the rooms. Be here a little before we open so I can give you the crash course in what to do."

Rise washed her hands and splashed some cool water on her face, trying to shake off the feelings about the euthanasia. She took a few bags of garbage out to the dumpster and caught sight of the dog's former owner pulling out of the parking lot. She was on her cell phone, driving a big white Suburban that looked brand new. A sticker in the back window read 'Adopt a Pet'.

The sky turned dark, and Rise looked up as a few raindrops hit her face. She closed her eyes and then, just for fun, started barking as loud as she could. She went back inside, popped one of her anxiety pills and welcomed the warm rush of artificial bliss. She went back to work and forgot about the dog.

Chapter Thirteen
Spark of the Divine

"That's the new Herald?" Shay looked down at the sleeping form in the bed, then over to Dominik. "I'm surprised."

"What were you expecting?"

"I thought she'd be bigger. It's odd how human she appears on the outside."

"It's the power inside her that's important," he said. "Or perhaps I should say the *lack* of power. Her abilities should've begun to manifest months ago. The Scriptures are confused and so am I."

"It's been a long time since a new Herald was created." Shay snickered. "Maybe the Great Architect has finally made a mistake and her design is faulty."

"I have a suspicion." Dominik started searching the nightstand and then the closet. He knew the Herald wouldn't wake. He could subdue the area around him, one of the many talents afforded angels, and one he'd perfected.

Shay followed him as he poked around in the bathroom. He opened the medicine cabinet, checked the floors and pulled back the shower curtain, then moved to the next room. "What are you looking for?"

"The thing inhibiting her growth."

"Are you in such a hurry to deal with her?"

"Absolutely not," Dominik said, "but the sooner she begins to learn, the faster I can be rid of her and turn my attention to those who would value my assistance." Oliver circled his legs. He knelt and stroked the cat. "You remember me, don't you? Is she taking good care of you? If not, I hope you're biting her toes."

The cat mewed and scurried away. Dominik continued his search, grunting in satisfaction when he located a small bottle of pills in a handbag. "This is the problem. The spark of the divine, once again mistaken for insanity."

Shay's eyes went wide. "You think that's the cause? Advances in medicine are one of humanity's greatest achievements."

"She uses this for self-indulgent comfort, not healing." Dominik headed for the kitchen. "I've done extensive research; Heralds of the past turned to strong drink and herbs. This one's not going to get away with such abuse, not on my watch. She can suffer her trials without sedation." He dumped the medicine into the sink.

"Are you permitted to do that?"

"Angels are allowed to perform interventions, are we not?" Dominik turned on the water, flushing away the pills. "As her advisor, I have considerable leeway and intend to make the most of my position."

He took inventory of the apartment, rifling through cabinets and drawers. "She has no sense of quality." He picked up a book, flipped through a few pages, then tossed it down. "Vampires and werewolves. Her frivolity will cease, I'll see to that."

"You have to stay within the bounds of the edict."

"I have no intention of breaking the laws," Dominik said. "She's not worth a breech to my honor or the oath. I'll only give her information as allowed, but I can make things very hard if she doesn't listen."

"That sounds suspiciously like a threat." Shay smiled. "Are you still harboring a grudge against Heralds?"

"I hold a grudge against one, for placing me in this situation."

"I'm not making an accusation, you know my opinion on the creatures," Shay said. "Their cruelty has increased tenfold since Tyre's departure, and if this one fails, it will get far worse. They're still angry one of their own was taken, and hold you responsible. I imagine they're watching your every move. They'll pounce on any misstep in a heartbeat and enjoy nothing more than seeing you stand before the throne for reprimand."

"They can observe me until their emerald eyes bleed. The only Herald that concerns me is the one I'm under obligation to tolerate." He glanced toward the bedroom where the fledgling still slept. "Thankfully, there's nothing in the mandate saying I have to like her."

He picked up a little jar candle and took a whiff. "Her taste in fragrance equals her taste in books. I'll have to replace these with something suitable. I have no desire to reek of," –he looked at the label with disgust—"Vanilla Explosion. I'm heading back. Would you like to join me?"

"Are you returning to the library, the arena, or meditation? That's all you ever do anymore." She gave him a sly smile. "When was the last time we celebrated?" She slid into his arms.

Dominik smiled and pulled her close. "What's the occasion?"

"Does there have to be one?" She touched the glowing pendant hanging around his neck. "Now that her abilities will start to flourish, you'll be stuck here more and more. It took so long for me to get your attention. Can't we have one more night together before a Herald starts to interfere?"

"I've been neglectful, haven't I? After your sacrifices, I shouldn't treat you in such a way." He kissed the top of her head. "Tonight there will be nothing else, but you. I promise."

Dominik motioned with his hand, removing the invisible veil he'd drawn over the apartment. He felt certain he was right about the Herald's problem and wondered how long it would be until her abilities started to flow. There were variations in the process. Sometimes power would burst forth in a rush, like a dam breaking. Other times it was stop and go, like a sputtering faucet. He'd have to keep careful watch on her from now on. He dreaded the notion.

Chapter Fourteen
Road Rage

The next day brought more rain. Rise had the wipers flying, but it wasn't much help. She kept a two-handed grip on the wheel and cursed the downpour. Streets on the Eastside of Indianapolis were questionable on good days, and when it rained hard, the potholes created a series of little ponds. Rise saw ducks using one as a bath.

She squinted, leaned forward, and tried to see past sheets of water. Her shoulder muscles were tight. She could feel a headache coming on and headlights from passing cars were painfully bright. Rise recognized the symptoms; she forgot to take her morning dose of sanity. She cursed. Withdrawal effects were kicking in much faster lately, and she didn't know why.

Rise heard an alert on the radio; a little girl abducted from a bus stop. The location was nearby.

"…ten-year old female, pink raincoat, braided hair…" That was the only part of the description she caught.

"I hate people," she muttered and moved to switch the station to something more uplifting. She only took her eyes off the road for a second, but she looked up to find a figure directly in her path. Scotty, the mentally disturbed man who wandered the area, was walking in the road, oblivious to the cars.

Rise swerved, avoided Scotty, but came within a breath of hitting a white van coming in the opposite direction. She screamed; it felt like her heart was going to explode. The driver of the van laid on his horn. Rise checked her rearview mirror, saw the guy make a quick U-turn, and in the next instant he was on her bumper, honking like a madman. She got a murky glimpse of his face. He was infuriated.

"Oh, holy hell." Rise switched between watching the road in front and the guy behind. She sped up, and the van driver kept pace. She made a fast right into a neighborhood, scanning for anyone who might be able to help if the road-raging idiot had a homicidal streak. Not a soul was outside, except kids huddled together on porches waiting on school busses. No help there.

Rise switched to panic mode. She didn't want to speed in a residential area, but she also wanted *to* speed because a crazy person was on her tail. At least he'd stopped with the horn. Her nerves were like sparklers.

She reached for her cellphone, but the van took a hard left, tires squealing and the whole bit. At first, Rise assumed he tired of his let's-scare-the-dumb-girl game, but then she saw the school bus coming in the opposite direction.

"Thank God." She pulled over, leaned back and closed her eyes in relief. Her arms and legs felt like cooked spaghetti, her muscles ached. She fumbled in her purse and whipped out her little bottle of anxiety medicine. She shook it and heard nothing. "Where the hell are my pills?"

She dumped the contents of her purse, frantic. She was positive she had a week's worth left. She flopped back into the seat, tossed the useless bottle and watched it roll around on the floorboard. She couldn't afford a refill until her next payday and wondered how she'd make it that long. The rain on the window sounded like explosions and it was going to get worse.

She pulled herself together enough to get moving, only to realize in her panic she'd managed to get lost in a maze of unfamiliar streets. She drove around, hoping to pop out in a place she'd recognize, but it only got worse; she ended up on a barren road.

She stopped and squinted, trying to see the street signs through the rain, but then a bright light consumed her vision. She looked up, at first thinking the sun had come through the clouds. But all she saw was a truck passing by, right in front of her. In the passenger seat was a little girl, her head resting against the window, as if asleep. She had braids in her hair, wore a bright pink rain jacket...and she was glowing. Radiating was more accurate.

She squeezed her eyes shut, recognizing a weird symptom she sometimes experienced after missing a dose of her medication. Doctors called it the *halo effect*, and Rise called it annoying. Then time stopped as she was hit by a memory: the alert from the radio.

"That's her," Rise said aloud, as though speaking the words would make them real. "That's the girl!" The truck kept going down the alley and she turned to follow. Her leg shook as she hit the gas, and a powerful feeling swept over her, telling her to stop. She ignored it and grabbed her phone.

"Emergency services, what is your emergency?" A calm voice asked.

"I think I found her," Rise said. "The little girl from the bus stop. I think I see her in a truck!"

"Ma'am, where are you?"

"I don't know; I'm lost! He's getting away!" The truck sped up; the driver probably realized he was being followed. Rise kept pace, going dangerously fast through narrow streets. She ignored the instinct to brake.

"Ma'am, do not chase him," the voice said. "Look for a sign and tell me your location."

Rise passed one she could read, repeated the information, but didn't call off the pursuit. The truck made all sorts of wild turns, but couldn't shake her. She was going to be late to work, and wondered why she was even thinking about that.

Police sirens were getting louder, and it must've spooked the truck driver because he made a bad move. He drove onto a street flooded from the rain and started to skid. He was going fast when he hit and ended up sliding down a hill and into a retention pond. The heavy truck started to sink headfirst. Rise parked her car and ran down the embankment, leaving her door standing wide open. Her seat was going to be soaked. She was almost to the pond when she realized she'd left her phone in the car, but spied a tall man not far away. She waved at him with both arms.

"Help me!" She took a few steps toward him and pointed to the van. "There's a girl in there!" Surely the man had witnessed the incident, but he didn't move, didn't even flinch. His face was locked up, maybe even angry, but Rise didn't care about that. She was more concerned with his not coming to help and a righteous fury flared in her. "Don't just stand there! Come help me!" Still the man did nothing, and she stomped her foot in fury. "Call the police, you idiot! Tell them where we are!"

A resident from one of the nearby houses came outside on his back porch, clad only in long sleeping pants. "What's all the screaming about?" he demanded.

Rise pointed. "That's the man who took the little girl!" She realized the words wouldn't make sense to anyone who hadn't been listening to the news, but she was panicked and pissed off. Coherency wasn't her main concern.

Regardless, the man on the porch sized things up fast. He reacted in a normal, helpful way, and Rise breathed in relief there was still someone left in the crap world with a Good Samaritan complex. The guy hollered for someone to call the police, then he was tearing from his porch at a dead run. He wasn't even wearing shoes, but he caught up to Rise and the two of them bounded into the water at full speed.

The front of the truck had already submerged and the driver was trying to escape. Rise saw a small hand pressed against the window. She pounded on the side door and tried to pull it open, but it wouldn't budge. The neighbor was a big guy and able to break a window with his shoulder. The truck continued to sink, but sirens were louder. Within minutes-that felt more like hours - police were running to help, some with guns drawn. They pushed Rise out of the way, ordering her out of the water.

She stood near the pond, soaking from head to toe, her scrubs clinging to her body and her shoes heavy as bricks. Fortunately, she'd worn her good bra, because every curve she had, few as they were, were on full display. She watched the little girl pulled limp from the tuck. She looked sleepy, but she was moving. Her little arms clung around the neck of burly officer as he carried her to safety.

The driver was also pulled out, but treated with far less consideration. When he passed close, he looked over at Rise and smiled, but not in a nice way. He had jagged teeth, almost demonic, and a face riddled with pockmarks. A diverse crowd had gathered near the lake and every single one of them stood united, wishing the vile criminal a quick death. They screamed at the cops to shoot the guy, a few offering to do the deed themselves.

Rise dropped to the ground in utter exhaustion. An officer asked her something, but she didn't answer. She *couldn't* answer. Everything was chaos—the crowd, the cops, the media who was starting to arrive. Her mind felt like a giant spiderweb, trapping the barrage of information and refusing to let it go. She shook her head and tried to focus, then caught sight of the man she'd seen earlier, the one who refused to help. The big jerk was still there, just standing in the rain, glaring at her. His long jacket was drenched and his hair clung to his face. Rise hoped he got pneumonia. She gave him her best scowl.

"I need your name," the officer said, and this time she acknowledged him. She'd never talked to a cop before and though she'd done nothing wrong, she still felt guilty.

An ambulance arrived and Rise begrudgingly agreed to a quick check. Getting to work on time was out of the question, but if helping save a child from a psycho wasn't a good enough excuse, then Tammy could bite her butt.

Chapter Fifteen
Shenanigans

People love happy endings. Rise had been elevated to hero status after a local news station dropped her name during one of the reports on the 'abduction of ten-year-old girl, Keisha Williams, by registered sex offender, Kevin Nichols.'

She hadn't gotten in trouble at work for being late, and Dr. Mark even bought her lunch. He'd actually bought pizza for the entire staff, but made sure everyone knew it was because of Rise. Neighbors she'd never spoken to, or even seen, had been coming up and thanking her, some even offering hugs. It was odd, as she usually tried to keep a low profile. But after she got past the initial shock of instant celebrity, she found the attention wasn't bad. She was starting to buy into the consensus of others, and was feeling proud of herself.

The little girl, Keisha, was fine. She'd been knocked out by some kind of inhalant and spent a day in the hospital. Her mother had been on the news briefly, hugging her daughter and thanking everyone involved that helped in the rescue. But, as was usually the case when something bad happened to kids, there are those who find a way to blame the parents. Mrs. Natalie Williams had become a prime target.

"It's a shame," Mr. Crawford said. He was sitting outside on the steps, reading the late paper on Saturday. Rise was there, too, and some young kids had gathered. "These people saying it was this woman's fault what happened. Just a shame." He shook his head in disgust.

Rise remained silent. She'd been at work most of the day and wanted a shower, but Mr. Crawford asked her to 'sit for a spell' and she couldn't refuse. He caught two teens trying to break-in her apartment a few weeks back, and chased them out of the building, yelling and swinging his cane. She'd owed him for that. They were even now.

"That man should never have been let out of prison," Mr. Crawford went on. That was the sentiment of most everyone. "And here some folks are saying this woman was neglectful, to let her child wait outside by herself. What kind of world we living in that a child can't be safe outside her own house?"

"Keisha's in my class," one of the little boys said. He sat on the cracked sidewalk exchanging some sort of trading cards with a friend. "My mom knows her mom. They were talking on the phone last night."

"Is that so?" Mr. Crawford asked. "She doing okay?

"Yeah. Keisha's mom always makes her wait in the house until the bus comes, because they live way back on that street. But Keisha got a new umbrella at that big sale, and wanted to see if it worked." The boy had gone back to his cards. "That's how her mom knew she was gone. She saw it on the driveway. Keisha shoulda hit that man with it, but she was probably scared to, because she's a girl."

Rise felt like her head had drifted away.

"What color was it?" she asked. "The umbrella?" She knew already; she could feel it in her gut.

"It was pink and green," a little girl said, looking up from a book. "I was there, too, and my dad bought me a lamp for my room. I saw Keisha get it."

Rise couldn't speak a word. She stood slowly, but once on her feet, she bounded upstairs and into her apartment, breathing like she'd run a mile. She went to the bathroom and splashed cool water on her face, wishing once again she could take a sedative. She felt like she was going to have a panic attack or hurt someone.

"It was mine," she said, though no one could hear her but Oliver. The cat was more interested in lapping up little drops of water that splashed on the floor.

Rise leaned back onto the wall and slid to the floor. She didn't know what to think. Sure, she'd saved Keisha from a terrible thing, but that terrible thing wouldn't have happened if Rise hadn't donated the umbrella. She hadn't even wanted to give it away in the first place and decided the bottom line was she'd been too nice. She should've told Mrs. Hernandez she didn't have anything or, even better, told the truth and said she didn't want to participate in the stupid sale. She'd always suspected kindness was overrated.

The knock on the door rescued her from full-blown emotional overload. She didn't move. Whoever it was could go away. But the knocks became insistent, even rude. Whoever was on the other side wasn't getting the hint and Rise was in no mood to play the lets-see-how-many-times-I-can-knock-before-she-answers game.

She gathered her anger in a big ball as she strode to the door. She flung it open without even looking through the peephole, because at that moment, she felt like the scariest person on the planet.

"What the hell is your—" she started to say, but then her mouth fell open in shock.

"Guess who's back, baby?" Danny held out his arms, grinning from ear to ear.

Baby? Her friend was decked out in a Dress Blue Marine Corps uniform, and posture so perfect he seemed a foot taller. She couldn't say a word.

"Move it," he said, and walked right past her.

"I forgot you were coming in today." She cringed inside. Her first words to him in months and this was the best she could do?

His shoulders slumped a little bit. "You forgot. Are you serious?"

"Yeah. Sorry. It's been a crazy few days. Long story."

"I already heard it." He grabbed her up in a solid hug. "Home grown hero right here!" His arms were bigger and he seemed intent on breaking her ribs. He sat her down after a few moments and played with a piece of her hair. "I like it. Kinda short, though."

"Look who's talking!" She pulled off his cover and ran her hand over the close-cropped military cut. It was soft, like new grass. They stood in silence for a moment.

"You can say it," Danny coaxed, "you know you want to."

"What?"

"I look good, right? C'mon."

Rise remained doggedly silent.

"You do, too." From all appearances, he was being truthful.

"I look like crap. I've been at work since seven and I smell horrible."

"Well, you better shake that ass, girl, because we've got to go."

"Go where?"

Danny looked at her like she'd sprouted horns. "To the party my dad is throwing me tonight. My combined boot camp and high school graduation party...the invitation he said was mailed three weeks ago. Any of this ringing a bell?"

It was starting to ring a whole bunch of bells, none of them good. "Give me fifteen minutes to get ready." That was pushing things, but she added in the unspoken female factor which doubled the time allotment.

He looked at his watch. He'd never worn a watch before.

"Okay, you have until 1800. That's 6:00 pm to civilians like you." He grabbed up the remote to the TV, plopped down on the second-hand sofa, and kicked his feet up like he owned the place.

"How did you get here anyway?" she asked as she headed to the bathroom.

"My dad picked me up at the airport. He dropped me off here so I could get my car."

Rise felt her stomach drop. She was going to hate getting back on the bus.

She showered in a flash, and made sure Danny wasn't watching before bolting to her bedroom with a towel wrapped around the important parts. She took longer than usual to find something to wear, but decided on a sleeveless black top and denim. She styled her hair and put on make-up with far more precision than normal. One of the best things about short hair was her earrings would always show; she'd added quite a few more holes over the summer, another private finger-wave to James Hawke, who always said earrings were a whore's calling card. She stepped back and looked at her reflection, satisfied. When she emerged, she had a moment of pure satisfaction when Danny scanned her.

"Whoa, when did you get these?" He lifted her arm and whistled at the muscles. "And that?" he asked, walking behind her and looking down.

She whirled on him. "I told you in that letter I was working out. And stop looking at my butt."

He laughed, a man's kind of laugh. "Where are my keys?"

She dropped them in his palm, trying not to look too disappointed, and they headed out. Danny took a few minutes in the car to adjust the seat and reorganize. He removed the multi-colored lea air freshener she'd hung over the rearview mirror and tossed it in her lap, then spotted the CD case.

"You have *not* been listening to Lady GaGa on my stereo." He tossed that in her lap, too. "You defiled my car. What else do you have in here?" He reached over to open the glove box and she leaned back as much as she could. The proximity had gotten a little too close, mainly because she liked it. But then he pulled away like he'd been burned. "Oh, Christ."

He found the little box of tampons she kept in the car for emergencies.

"I'm going to have to get this thing detailed twice to get the chick stench out," he said. Somehow, the smirk twisting his face made him look even better. She caught herself peeking at him off and on the whole trip.

"Why are you getting off here?" Rise asked, when Danny exited earlier than expected.

"My Uncle Joe is throwing the party at his bar. He closed it down to the public tonight, so we'll have the whole place." He glanced at her. "You didn't even read the invitation, did you?"

"Sure I did." She'd never even opened it; it was still lying on her nightstand. "I just forgot."

Danny grinned at her. "You're just full of shit."

The bar, Shenanigans, was cozy and had an Irish theme, but tonight there were American Flags and red, white and blue streamers crisscrossing all over. Rise had never been in a bar before, and she felt strange walking through the door. She felt even more ridiculous when a cheer erupted and everyone swarmed her. They were coming for Danny, but since he'd somehow maneuvered his arm around her shoulder, she was caught up in it, too.

Rise managed to disentangle herself after a few minutes, and she watched while Danny greeted friends and family. She recognized a few kids from High School, including one girl Danny had dated for a short time. The hug he gave her went on a little bit longer than most of the others and he even gave her a kiss right on her pouting, red lips.

"Jealous?" Emory asked as he came up to stand beside her.

"Not even a little bit," Rise said. "Why are you carrying that cane?"

"I'm trying to get used to it, before I really need it. I'm also networking a bit tonight, trying to get support for the organization." He pulled out a little black case and handed her a business card. "Check that out. I had new ones printed up."

Rise took the card, impressed at the quality. Emory's eye disease was rare, with a long name she'd never been able to pronounce. Choroideremia. He and others were raising funds for clinical trials. That kind of testing came with a hefty price-tag, and government funding was out of the question. Emory and others like him were on their own. "You asking for donations?"

"Nah, this is Dan's party so I'm not asking for money tonight." Emory tapped the cane a few times. "But if someone sees this and asks me about my disease, and I just *happen* to mention the organization..." He shrugged.

Rise grinned, hoping it worked. She couldn't imagine what it must be like, to lose sight a trickle at a time. She thought being born blind was merciful in comparison, at least then you didn't know what you were losing. "Good luck." She tucked the card in her purse and Emory left to get a drink.

The bar filled up fast. Rise found a comfortable spot against the wall and sipped on a soda while Danny continued to mix and mingle with his admirers. Uncle Joe hopped up on the bar - he could do that since he was the owner – and whistled. He held two glasses of beer; he handed one down to Danny.

"Look here," Uncle Joe announced. "I don't want to hear anything about this Marine not being twenty-one. This is my bar, and in my bar any man old enough to put on a uniform for his country is old enough to have a beer." There were claps and cheers, then laughter when Joe spotted one of the county police officers. "As long as that's alright with you, Sheriff."

"I'm off duty!" Sheriff Scott said and he took a big swig of his own drink.

"Well, all right then!" Uncle Joe was enthusiastic. "Raise your glasses now, y'all. My brother wants to make a toast."

Phillip Daly put an arm around his son's shoulder. "Danny has been a fine son. He's given me trouble, but I reckon' that's what sons are supposed to do. A lot of you have been coming up to me, and congratulating me, and I appreciate that. But Danny here is his own man, and he's a good one. Now, if I had a little something to do with that, then I'm humbled. I'm truly humbled." Mr. Daly bobbed his head a few times and lifted his beer. "To Danny!"

"To Danny!" the crowd repeated and there was another round of cheers. Two women came out from the back on cue, carrying a jumbo-sized cake on an enormous platter.

Rise winced when she saw the plates and forks were real. She knew she wouldn't be eating, and it was a shame; she was getting a little hungry. She only used paper and plastic at home. She knew it wasn't good for the environment, but it was great for her mental stability. Danny found her little quirk funny, and for Christmas the previous year, he'd given her two huge boxes of assorted plastic dinnerware.

After a while, someone turned on the jukebox and people started to dance. The music wasn't terribly loud, but it still propelled Rise into another headache. A couple men pushed tables out of the way to make more room, and the sound of the hard wood scraping on the floor almost brought her to her knees. A few times she had to blink when flashes of light appeared in her vision. It reminded her of what happened with little Keisha, only more colorful. She rubbed her temples.

"Why are you still over here being anti-social?" Emory asked as he found her again.

"I'm de-toxing." She tried to smile. "I ditched my crazy pills. It's getting ugly." She didn't mention it was only because she couldn't afford the refills.

Emory laughed and held up his beer. "Congratulations on your sobriety. You having withdrawal?"

"I think so. Everything is too loud, and I swear I'm seeing lights in my vision." She knew she must sound like a mental patient. "I've never been off my meds before."

"It's hard," he said. "My cousin had a problem with pain pills a while back. Work through it, you'll be all right. Go eat something, you might feel better."

"I'll be fine."

Within a few hours, as the party got livelier, Rise was reconsidering her answer. People were eating, drinking and having a blast while she was spiraling into misery. She tried to keep a smile, but wanted to curl up on the floor in a dark, soundproof room. She slipped outside, thinking some fresh air might help.

She leaned against the brick wall outside, closed her eyes and tried to relax. She could still hear the ruckus inside, the voices and the plates and forks scraping together. She breathed rhythmically, and focused her attention on a stray dog sniffing around some litter. He wandered over, his bushy tail wagging, but then his fur stood on end he took off running.

Rise wondered what spooked him, then spotted a stumpy figure strolling down the middle of the street in her direction. She couldn't see his face, but the warning tingle on the back of her neck said the dog had the right idea. She scurried back into the bar.

The outside air had taken the edge off her headache, but the sappy song booming from the jukebox brought on a wave of nausea. Danny swayed to the music, his arms around a redhead sticking her chest out so far, it looked like her spine would snap. Rise wanted to gag, but then Emory came over and grabbed her hand. He didn't say a word, just pulled her to the makeshift dance floor and whipped her into his arms.

"Thanks for asking first." She glared at him, but he stared over her head with a mysterious smile.

"Shut up and let me do my thing." He spun her around a few times, positioning them right next to Danny and his bendy-straw partner. Emory was a strong lead; he maneuvered Rise into a few moves that almost made her blush, but she kept up and before long she was dancing like she'd been doing it her whole life. At the end of the song, he tossed her backward into an arch so extreme the top of her head nearly touched the floor.

Rise laughed as Emory pulled her back up, and everyone in the bar whistled and cheered at the performance. Almost everyone. Danny just stared, his face flicking between his two friends with an unreadable expression.

"You're welcome," Emory whispered into her ear. He retrieved the collapsible cane from the cargo pocket of his pants, leaving Rise biting her lip to keep from smiling.

Chapter Sixteen
Hog Board

"That was a good party," Danny said when the last of the guests had gone.

"Lots of people here," Rise stood on a chair, taking down decorations. She hopped down with a pile of streamers in her arms and tossed them in a trashcan. "You were sure Mr. Popular tonight. How many girls gave you their numbers, anyway?" She tried to sound casual.

"Two," Danny said. "Well, one gave her E-mail. Does that count?"

"That counts," Rise said as she cleared off a table. "Three is a pretty good haul, even for a Marine."

"I've still got the touch."

"Leave that stuff," Uncle Joe said as he emerged from the stock room. "It's late. Danny, you okay to drive, right? If not, you hand your keys over to the young lady."

Danny assured his uncle he was fine, and made an attempt at arguing about leaving before the work was done, but it was futile.

"You driving her all the way back tonight?" Mr. Daly asked, looking at his watch. "Rise, why don't you come on over to the house. You can bunk in Emily's room and we'll get you back home in the morning."

Danny was quick to agree; he'd been slowing down the past few hours after the alcohol had burned off. Rise was having a little trouble staying awake, too, and wasn't going to argue.

The drive was silent, except for the radio. Danny patted around in his pockets when they got to the front door. "I didn't get the house keys back from my dad. Maybe the back door is unlocked."

It wasn't, so they sat on the concrete steps to wait.

"How was boot camp?" she asked. "You haven't mentioned it at all."

"You haven't *asked* at all," Danny said. "We got yelled at a lot. It was a good time."

"You seem different."

"How so?"

Rise shrugged. "You're more confident."

"And?"

"What else do you want me to say? Cocky? That's not exactly new."

"I am different, though." He played with his cover while he spoke. "I realized it tonight. All those people from school were there, still talking about the same things, dealing with the same drama." He looked off into the darkness. "I couldn't understand it anymore."

"I never understood it to begin with," Rise said with a little smirk. "But I know what you mean. I'm working, paying my own bills." She shrugged. "We've moved on and they haven't. Screw 'em."

Danny smiled and shook his head, then became quiet again. "Did you hear what that guy said, the one who came with my cousin?"

She almost growled. "I heard." The guy in question was a grad student with some extreme, and loud, opinions on the military. At one point, he asked Danny right to his face if he joined up because colleges wouldn't take him.

"I wanted to slap the hell out of him," Rise said, angry she hadn't done exactly that. "You handled it much better than I would've. You didn't even tell him you were on the honor roll every year."

"He was drunk." Danny blew out a breath. "I've heard it before, anyway. You know, during World War II some men committed suicide because the military wouldn't take them. Now if you join up, people think there must be something wrong with you."

"I don't think anything is wrong with you."

"I know you don't." He gave her a gentle smile. "Hey, why didn't you send me a picture? I asked you in every letter."

"I didn't have one to send," Rise said. "Besides, why did you want a photo? You've been looking at me for over ten years."

"For the hog board, baby!"

"The what?" She noted it was the second time he'd called her 'baby'.

Danny laughed from his belly. "It's a wall where the guys could tack up photos of their girlfriends, or just hot girls from back home."

"And you called this a *hog board*?" She was offended on behalf of all the women in the world, but also a little flattered Danny had wanted her photo. "I don't think those guys wanted to see my ugly mug up there."

"You need to get over that crap. You're beautiful." He looked her right in the eye when he said the words.

Rise forced herself not to flinch. She hoped her make-up wasn't smeared.

"I'm going to break our rules against sentiment here, so prepare yourself." Danny turned so he faced her. "I thought about you every night while I was away. If anyone did something wrong, the whole platoon got thrashed, and some nights I'd lay in my rack and feel like the biggest screw up on the planet. Then I'd think about you."

"And realized you were only the second biggest screw up on the planet?"

"Not exactly." He did that smirk thing he'd done in the car. "There was so much going on, and they were throwing so much at us so fast, everything else disappeared after a while. My family, the guys from the team, and the girls I dated; I didn't have time to think about them." He caught her eyes again. "But I always made time for you. And I'm wondering what that means."

Rise knew her eyes must have looked like big, green pool balls sticking out of her head. She was acutely aware of the darkness around her, and Danny's closeness. She could smell his aftershave, and hoped her deodorant was holding up. He bent close, and she wanted to run screaming. Instead, she grabbed his shoulders, holding him away.

"What's wrong?" He smiled and moved even closer. "C'mon, you've kissed me before."

"We were in the seventh grade and it was a dare."

He sat back, but held her gaze. "Are you attracted to me? Tell the truth."

"You're okay." She wanted to retract the words as soon as she said them. She had no idea what was wrong with her. Many women would love to be in her position.

"Are you not into guys?" He laughed at the outrage on her face. "It's a legitimate question. You've never dated anyone that I know of. I just want to know where I stand. I'm spilling my guts here and you're looking at me like you want to sprout wings and fly away." He raised an eyebrow. "You're making me wonder."

Rise shifted. She didn't know how to explain, and didn't want to try. It wasn't that she didn't have natural urges; she did, and when they hit she took care of things on her own. She didn't want the bullshit that came with a relationship, or the risk of a casual encounter. Plus, her parent's behavior had left its mark, in more ways than one. The idea of sex made her sick to her stomach, but there was no way she was going to mention that. She tried to come up with a better answer.

"I'm not gay." She didn't think so, anyway. "I value our friendship. I don't want to…corrupt it." She wanted to hit her head on the nearest tree. Her word choices were getting worse.

"Friends are supposed to make the best lovers." He moved close again and placed his hand on her neck. "Maybe we can find out why."

A pair of bobbing headlights came up the drive and Rise released the breath she'd been holding. "Your dad's here." She headed around to the front door and heard Danny curse under his breath.

"Locked out," he said before his dad could ask what was happening.

"You could've used the spare key," Mr. Daly said. "It's in the same place it's always been."

Even in the dark, Rise thought Danny's face turned a little pink.

"I forgot." He didn't look at her.

"I'm sure you did," she whispered as she walked past him into the house.

Once settled in Emily's little twin bed with Hello Kitty sheets, Rise had time to consider the day. She passed by the Keisha drama from earlier, skimmed through the party and let her thoughts settle on Danny.

She understood what he meant when he talked about being too busy to think about anyone. She'd been in much the same situation; a new apartment, new job, new responsibilities. She'd barely thought about anything from what she now called her 'old life'.

Danny was the first person who ever called her beautiful. He supported her when she moved, listened to her when she had bad days. He was smart, had nice arms and a handsome face, but she hadn't thought about him at all while he was gone.

She stared at the ceiling and wondered what *that* meant.

Chapter Seventeen
Intrusion

Rise was the last one up the next day. She trudged to the kitchen, surprised to find Emory sitting at the table. Danny leaned against the counter, and she wished him a good morning. He didn't even acknowledge her presence. She poured a glass of juice and took a seat, hating the awkward tension in the air.

"The pervert got killed in jail yesterday." Emory pushed a newspaper across the table. "Front page news."

"No way." Rise looked at the police photo of Kevin Nichols, the stumpy pedophile who abducted little Keisha. She skimmed the article. "A guard did it?"

"Necessary force—that's the story."

"Yeah, right." She wasn't naïve enough to believe that, but hoped they gave the guy a medal. "Great loss to society," she muttered and shoved the paper away. "What are you doing over here so early?"

"It's not so early," Emory said, "and I'm here because I'm taking you home."

"You are?" She looked to Danny, but he didn't say anything. She didn't appreciate the silent-treatment. It was one thing for her to avoid *him*, quite another for him to avoid *her*.

"I'm heading back to Indy anyway," Emory said. "No reason for Dan to drive all that way. You ready?"

"Now?"

"I'm going to church in a little while," Danny said. "I knew you wouldn't want to go."

He was right. "You want to get together later?"

"Won't have time. My dad is going to help me replace the brake pads on the car, then I'm taking everyone out to dinner at the Inn." He shrugged. "I feel like I need to hang out with my family today."

"The Inn has great cheese fries." Rise knew something was wrong, and assumed it was her reaction to his advances. "I hope you all have a good day of bonding."

"Yeah. Be careful driving, Emory."

"I still do okay in the daytime," Emory said as he grabbed his jacket. Once they were in the car, he turned to Rise. "What was up with him? He seemed a little quiet."

She shrugged. "No idea." None she was going to talk about, anyway.

Emory popped in another audio book. Rise suspected it was a very important classic, which translated to boredom. "How'd the cane work out for you last night?"

"I got a few bites. Danny's uncle was generous. He's going to have a fund-raiser night next month."

"He's a good guy," she said. "Did you notice how much all the men in that family look alike? Same build, same eyes..."

"Amazing how that happens when people share a genetic code."

"Smart ass. Maybe it's strange for me, because I'm adopted. I've never looked like anyone."

"I thought you were going to check into that. Do a search for your birth family?"

She shrugged. "I was considering it at one point. I still might, one of these days. Indiana has strict privacy laws, so it'll be a hassle."

"If you decide to do it, give me a call and I'll try to help. I've gotten good at tracking people down for the organization. I'd bet money you have a little soul in you." He grinned over at her. "You were keeping up with me pretty good on the dance floor last night."

"Speaking of that, what were you thinking, dragging me out there?"

"You know exactly what I was thinking," Emory said. "You and Dan need to knock off the sexual tension thing and move on to the next level. I know when people are trying to hide things. Is this the right exit?"

"Yes. And believe me—if there's any sexual tension, it's one-sided."

"Bullshit. I saw the way you were looking at him last night. I thought you were going to stab that redhead with a fork."

Rise didn't answer.

Emory pulled into the apartments and parked beside a red convertible with the top down. The driver wore sunglasses, a black tank top and bobbed his head to music so loud it shook the car. Emory cranked up the volume on his stereo and starting bobbing his head along to the audio book.

Rise slapped a hand over her face, but the guy in the convertible was a good sport and laughed hard. She thanked Emory for the ride and headed upstairs.

The rest of her day was one big attempt at keeping her mind off Danny. She read a few chapters in a book about a sexy vampire cop, one that had all the women at work raving. She watched TV and played with Oliver, but nothing worked. She kept thinking back to their conversation the night before, and his odd behavior this morning.

Around dinnertime, Rise decided to bite the bullet and send him a text. If a ten-year friendship had been destroyed over some bullshit, she wanted to know. She held her breath, typed up a quick message and hit send. Her phone rang less than a minute later.

"You're a crap driver," Danny said. "I checked those brake pads right before I left for boot camp and they were fine. You wore them out in three months."

Rise had to regroup. This wasn't the conversation she expected. "What do brake pads have to do with my driving?"

"You're also very female," he said, "but that explains the driving problems, right? Look, I'll call you later. My dad and Emily are waiting downstairs to leave for the restaurant."

She clicked off her phone and spent the next ten minutes analyzing the brief conversation. He was talking to her again, a good sign. He also insulted her, a better sign.

Rise started painting her nails to pass the time, choosing a dark silvery-black color that matched her mood. She considered the possibility Danny lied, and was out on a date. She went through a list of potential candidates in Nineveh. It was a long one, but she didn't know why she cared. Jealousy? Possessiveness? She didn't have a right to be either.

She finished with her fingers and started on her toes, but then a strange sensation overwhelmed her—a feeling she wasn't alone. She scanned the room, attuned her hearing, then glanced at Oliver. The cat was a fantastic alarm system, and went into a frenzy whenever a stranger was around. The way he lounged on the bed told Rise nothing was amiss. She positioned the little polish brush on her nail, but the odd feeling became stronger. Her hand trembled, and a tingle flew up her spine.

"Hello, Rise," a voice said.

It wasn't words, not spoken anyway, but she heard them loud and clear and directly in her head. She froze.

"Not going to greet me?" The voice was masculine, powerful. Intimidating.

Rise held her breath, and watched as the black polish pooled on her toenail and overflowed onto the carpet. She was afraid to move a muscle, not sure what was happening. If this was another side effect from her withdrawal, she was going to beg, borrow or steal enough money for a refill. Seeing lights was bad enough, hearing voices was on a whole different level of crazy.

"You think you're going mad, don't you?" the voice asked, sounding amused.

"I'm considering that possibility." Rise wondered if she just proved the point by answering. "Are you real?"

"As real as you are." This time, there was a definite tone of mocking humor. "Consider that and we'll chat later."

The voice and tingly feeling faded, slipping away like a master thief. Rise pulled her knees to her chest and hid her face in crossed arms. She breathed rhythmically, trying to convince herself what happened was some sort of auditory delusion, brought on by stress and withdrawal. Maybe the ability to realize her insanity was a sign she wasn't too far gone.

Her head snapped up when her phone rang. She grinned. Danny's call was much earlier than expected. He didn't speak, but she could hear him breathing.

"Danny?"

"My dad died," he said.

Chapter Eighteen
Free Spirit

Phillip Daly knew the Gold angel was getting impatient. He stood in what had been his home, staring at the body he'd owned for fifty-one years, until about an hour ago. He examined it with a detached interest.

"Do you think I carried too much weight around the middle?"

Claire shook her golden wings and turned her eyes skyward. She sat on the floor, one hand against her pale cheek. "I don't think so. Was that supposed to be one of your challenges?"

"No, I was working on sloth. You said I hit all my markers, right?"

"From what I know, yes. If we leave, you can get a Red angel and start your review. Then you'll remember everything and won't need to ask questions I can't answer. I don't like lingering here. We should go."

"Just a few more moments," Phillip said. The coroner had arrived. He watched Danny, speaking with the emergency workers. He was proud of the young man's strength in this situation.

"He found me," Phillip said. "He tried to revive me, but I'd already released. He'll have a hard time." He looked at his daughter, sitting in a chair with her face wet from tears. "So will she."

"Yes. But they will both gain strength and advancement from the challenge." She looked at the bracelet on her wrist. "Phillip, please...."

"I'm ready now."

Claire sighed in relief and stood, and held out her hand. "This is my favorite part of being a Gold angel." She smiled as Phillip approached, but then a wave of darkness flooded the room, and a stench of decay filled the air. Her eyes went wide.

"Minions!" She whirled when three dark figures came at her, brandishing blades glowing with eerie power. It was something every angel feared, and Claire retreated in horror. She spread her wings and leapt into the air, spinning like a top. She kicked, striking the tallest of the minions in his face. He flew backwards into the wall.

Phillip grabbed one of the remaining two figures, one with red hair, but he was no match for the dark entity's strength. The minion tossed Phillip aside, and stood over him.

"Don't interfere," the minion said. "This is not your fight."

"Claire!" Phillip screamed. "Go!"

She glanced at him. "I won't leave you!" She threw her arm up, barely blocking an attack.

The angel continued to fight, but she was out-numbered and her strength started to ebb. The tall minion was back up, and he was swinging at the angel with his blade. The strikes were hard and frenzied, but none landed. Claire moved with skilled grace, dodging and darting away, the air her ally. She ducked a brutal swing aimed at her face, but lost focus in the process. Another minion, far shorter than the others, took advantage of the distraction. He attacked from her flank, stabbing her cleanly between two ribs. She screamed in pain and fell to her knees. Blood like liquid gold spilled from the wound.

"Claire!" Phillip ran toward her, but the minions blocked his advance.

The one who struck the final blow stood over the fallen angel, pushed her face into the floor, and grinned at his accomplices.

"A Gold!" he said. "I'll be revered for such a prize."

The tall one scoffed. "You weren't alone in this. I took a Blue by myself four years ago."

"Blue angels," the short one said with disgust. "They're everywhere, intervening all the time. We've collected too many of those already. But a Gold is a rarity."

Without another word, he placed his booted foot against Claire's head and grabbed one of her wings. He ignored her sobs and screams as he cut into her, using his blade as a saw until the glorious wing was barely hanging on. Then he grabbed it with both hands and ripped it the rest of the way until it was a bloodied stump in his hand. He held it up and the minions cheered.

"What have you done," Phillip whispered. He watched as Claire quieted, and finally lay still. He knew angels were hunted like this, but he never conceived of the brutality in the act. He pulled against the minion holding him, and was released, flicked away like a fly.

"We should thank you," the tall minion said. "For delaying her, as you did. We've been trying to collect a Gold for a long time, but most are smart enough to leave before we can track them down."

Phillip's face turned to outrage. "Cowards! You had no strength in life and you have no honor now!"

"That's exactly why we do this," the short minion said and shook the wing in his hand. The golden blood dripped onto his pants and pooled on the floor at his feet. "We're no longer given the opportunity to prove ourselves, so we have no choice left, except to take by force what we've been denied."

The tall one patted Phillip on the back and leaned in to his ear.

"Enjoy your stay.

Phillip stumbled back, as understanding of his predicament became clear. The Gold angel had been his passage back home, bonded to his soul, and now she was gone. He ignoring the laughter of the minions as they departed the same way they'd arrived. He fell to his knees by the fallen angel and held her in his arms. Her body was limp and light. Phillip brushed the hair from her face and kissed her forehead.

"I'm so sorry," he whispered.

A few moments later the beautiful angel turned to glass and shattered into tiny, golden shards. Phillip bowed his head and leaned against a wall for a long while.

He was a Free Spirit now, the light forever out of his reach. He wondered when the madness would claim him.

Chapter Nineteen
Dominik

The funeral was four days later and Rise sat in a pew in the middle of the church. Sheriff Scott's wife was next to her on the left. She and her husband were acting as bookends for their three kids and several times during the service they had to administer stern looks and admonishments for various misdeeds.

Emory, who had been kind enough to come pick her up that morning, sat on her other side. He looked nice in his olive green suit and hadn't removed his jacket as most of the other men had done. He used a handkerchief to dab a bead of sweat from his brow now and then.

Danny was in the front row, wearing his dress blue Marine Corps uniform. Rise hadn't talked to him much since the night his father had died. Her friend looked especially handsome, and he was being strong again, as he'd been the night before at the showing. Rise hadn't seen him cry once. His sister, on the other hand, hadn't stopped. Emily sat beside her brother, and kept her eyes on the casket in front of her. It was draped with an American flag and surrounded by sprays of flowers.

The service was traditional, complete with the Eucharist celebration. Rise could still taste the wine on her lips. Now it was time for the final hymn and she hoped it was a short one.

She watched as a tall man came forward. His appearance elicited some whispering from two girls directly behind her, and she could see why. He was a little older than she'd normally find appealing, but striking. He had reddish brown hair falling in a natural curl past his shoulders, and eyes the color of deep ocean waters, set off by bronzed skin. He stood at the podium, looking regal with flawless posture and a commanding presence. He wore a knee-length jacket over a dark blue suit, and though it looked good on him, Rise couldn't help but wonder if he was going to have a heatstroke.

The organ started playing and the man started singing. From the first note, Rise was blown away by the voice. It was strong and rich, and the words flowed over her like warm water. Her skin puckered up, and the hair on her arms stood on end. She found herself leaning forward, drawn to the sound in a way she'd never before experienced.

"You shall speak your words in foreign lands...and all will understand...be not afraid..."

Mrs. Scott leaned toward her husband. "Who is that?" she whispered.

Rise listened for the answer.

"I think his name is Dominik," the sheriff replied and flicked his hand, shushing his wife. The kids found that quite funny.

Halfway through the second verse, the singer glanced at Rise. It was only for a moment, but something in his eyes triggered a memory and she felt the sensation of falling. This man with the voice, Dominik, was at the pond the day she saved Keisha; the same guy who stood and watched the whole incident and didn't assist. Rise wanted to smack herself for not recognizing him earlier, and wanted to smack him even harder.

"Oh, my God," she whispered.

"Yes, he's amazing," Emory said. "And check out that accent. I bet he's from South America."

Rise sat back and didn't respond. She stared hard at Dominik, didn't even blink, and tried to fight the emotions his voice was pulling from her. She didn't want to like the song anymore, but found she had no choice. She felt raw, as though she'd been sliced open, and Dominik's voice was a soothing balm. Then he looked at her again, looked her right in the eyes, and held them as he sang.

"If you pass through raging water in the sea, you shall not drown....if you walk amid the burning flames, you shall not be harmed..."

She couldn't have looked away if she wanted. His voice was becoming stronger with every word, building to a crescendo that was almost frightening in its power.

"If you stand before the power of hell, and death is at your side...know that I am with you, through it all..."

Rise was relieved when the song was over. She saw Danny wipe a tear from his eyes, the first she'd seen him shed. She started to tremble.

"You okay?" Emory touched her leg.

"I'm fine. The song got to me, I guess." It was almost the truth. She spent the rest of her time trying to get a glimpse of Dominik, but he'd disappeared somewhere. She decided she'd ask around about him, inconspicuously, since she didn't want to come off as one of his adoring fans. The two girls behind her were still talking about him.

"Did you know that singer?" she asked Emory on the way out. She played with her fingernails, trying to act bored.

"No, but the guy had some serious talent." He looked over at her with a gleam in his eye. "Handsome, too, don't you think?"

Rise shrugged. She agreed on both counts, but wished she didn't.

"He's visiting from another parish," Sheriff Scott told her. He was standing close enough to hear Rise make the inquiry. "He's in a choir back home and he's also prior military. He was moved to offer his services."

"Oh, what a lovely gesture," another woman said, placing her hand over her heart. "I'm sure it meant so much to the family."

"He did a fine job," a tall man agreed. "Phillip would've liked that. It was his favorite hymn."

After that, the conversation turned into a big Dominik love festival. Rise wiggled away to think by herself for a moment, having doubts about her recognition. She'd been in a rough state of mind that day at the pond and, by all appearances, Dominik was a genuinely religious man—certainly not the type who would stand by and do nothing while a child drowned.

Everyone gathered outside to wait for the casket to be loaded into the hearse, and Rise saw Dominik kneeling in front of Emily. He touched her on the shoulder, wiped a tear from her cheek, then stood and shook Danny's hand with both of his. He said a few words Rise couldn't hear, but ones that relaxed her friend's grief-filled face.

She convinced herself she was wrong about him, and smiled when he turned her way. He didn't return the gesture; he stared at her with the same hard expression he'd worn at the pond. It sent a chill up her spine.

She could tell herself it was just a coincidence, but wasn't sure she believed in them anymore.

CHAPTER TWENTY
BROKEN

Rise had more or less composed herself by the end of the short graveside service. Dominik hadn't come to this part and she was trying to put the unnerving situation from her mind.

A long stretch of cars were trying to leave the cemetery, so Emory wandered off with his parents to look at headstones until things cleared out. Rise didn't join them. She stayed in a chair under the small tent. Everyone left, except Danny. He stood by his father's casket, holding the carefully folded flag he'd been presented.

Rise wasn't sure if she was being rude; maybe Danny wanted to be alone. She got up to leave, but he stopped her.

"I have three of these," he said, regarding the flag. "My dad had my grandfather's, and my great-grandfather's, so those are mine now, plus this one. I'll need to get another one of those display cases." He looked away. "Three generations of men in my family have served their country."

"Four, including you," Rise said. "You look nice today, and did a good job when you spoke."

"Uncle Joe did better; he added those funny stories. I couldn't think of any when I was standing up there, but now I could rattle off a hundred." He shook his head.

"Your dad was proud of you, especially for joining the Marines. He bragged on you to everyone." She hated dealing with emotional events; she never knew how to act or what to say. "Are they going to give you some extra time? Bereavement leave?" Emory had mentioned that term.

Danny shifted his stance. "I'm not going back. I'm getting a discharge for hardship, that's what they call it. It will still say honorable on my service papers. I guess I haven't been in long enough to do anything dishonorable."

Rise was shocked. "What are you going to do then? You've never talked about anything else."

"Uncle Joe knows a guy who will give me a job for a few years until I turn twenty one, then I can help run the bar if I want. I might take some classes online. I haven't got that far yet."

"Maybe you should take some time to think."

"Nothing to think about," Danny said. "I can't drag Emily all over the world, and if I get deployed...."

"She could go live with your Uncle Joe and his wife, couldn't she?"

"Emily is my sister. She's my responsibility."

"You're going to take care of a twelve-year-old girl and yourself?" Her tone was harsh, but she couldn't believe what she hearing. She thought it was insane.

"That's exactly what I'm going to do." Danny sounded angry, too.

"You've been talking about being a Marine your whole life," she said. "You can't give that up now."

"Not everyone is like you, Rise." He stepped close. "I can't write people off and walk away."

"I'm not telling you to." Her voice was rising now. "I work every day and barely make enough to pay bills and eat, and I don't even eat that much. You won't find a job around here that pays as much as the military. Maybe you can send money back or something. I'm sure Emily will understand—"

"Understand what?" Danny demanded. "Her mom is dead, her dad is dead and her brother is ditching out on her?"

Rise put a hand to her forehead. "This is your entire future. Your dad wouldn't want you to throw it away!"

"He'd rather I throw my sister under a bus?" He backed down a little when Rise flinched. "Let me ask you something—did you even talk to your parents or sister today? They were sitting three rows behind you, so don't try to say you didn't see them."

"What does that have to do with anything?"

"That's what I thought," Danny said. "You had a crap life, I get it. You want to take off and not look back, great. I know you don't give a damn about anyone and I've never given you a hard time over it. Do me the same favor and don't try to talk me out of this."

Rise was taken aback at the harsh words. Danny had never raised his voice to her like this, and she wasn't the type to back down.

"I do give a damn about people," she said, looking him up and down. "You, for one."

He laughed and walked away a few steps, shaking his head. "You know how many letters you sent me while I was at boot camp? Two. In three months. I wrote you almost every week. Hell, my bunkmate got more mail from his ten-year-old second cousin than I got from you."

"I was busy with the new job—" Rise began, but then froze. She knew Danny was right. She would've had time, if she'd wanted to.

"You were always busy," Danny said. "In school, when people would invite you anywhere, you always had an excuse. You never even called me, unless you wanted something."

"That is not true!" She wasn't as convinced of her words as she tried to sound.

"You're broken," Danny said. "I don't know if it was your traumatic childhood or maybe that blow to the head, but something is not right with you. I don't think you're even capable of caring about anything, or anyone."

"What the....?" Rise was conscious of her surroundings and refrained from using the words poised on her tongue. She took an angry step forward and lowered her voice. "Is this because I wouldn't have sex with you? Are you trying to guilt me into it?"

Danny had started to walk away, but stopped and turned back, his eyes livid.

"You're kidding, right?" His voice was harsh, his words clipped, and he wasn't even making an attempt to keep his volume in check. "Rise, I hate to break it to you, but I can get laid anytime I want, and I sure as hell don't need a...brat...like you to help."

Rise felt her face crumble in shock. She recovered quickly and stood as straight as she could, hoping her eyes reflected the rage she felt.

Danny stared her down for many long moments, but then closed his eyes and huffed in frustration. He reached into his pocket and pulled out a small keychain. He removed one of the keys and tossed it to her. She caught it, though barely.

"You can have my car," he said.

Rise had a moment of actual excitement, but then tossed the key to the ground in spite.

"I don't want your car."

"Yes, you do." His stance and tone was combative, but he regained composure and lowered his voice. "I've got my dad's truck now. I can't afford to keep both. Insurance." He glanced at the coffin. "My dad would want you to have it; he always hated you taking the bus. It's parked in back at the church." He walked away, and didn't look back.

"He's grieving," Emory said.

Rise jumped. She hadn't heard him approach and wondered how much of that shouting match he'd heard. "Do you think I'm wrong, too?"

"I see what you're saying. I can't see Danny being happy doing anything else, either. Life's too short to try to be something you're not." He stared at the casket for a long moment. "But family is important, too. He's going to have to make that call on his own."

"Whatever."

Emory retrieved the key she'd thrown, having to feel around a little bit to find it. He held it out to her, but she wasn't willing to back down on her display of independence.

"Danny was right about one thing, though. You're a hard bitch sometimes." Emory shoved the key into the side pocket of her purse. "Come on. I'll drive you to the church to get the car."

CHAPTER TWENTY-ONE
MIRI AND PIRI

Rise spent the next week waiting to hear from Danny. She felt bad about their fight, though not nearly as bad as she should. Maybe she really was broken.

She walked in a funk down the street to get her mail. She had quite a few pieces, since she hadn't bothered to check the box all week. Most of the time she only got advertisements or a bill, but today there was a small black envelope addressed to her in elegant handwriting using some sort of white ink that sparkled. It was on the bottom of the stack, so it had probably been delivered days ago. She opened it while she headed back inside.

It was a party invitation. The front had only one word, in big blocked letters: OUT. There was a date, time, location and a handwritten note that said 'Hope to see you'. It was from Emory.

Rise's mouth popped open. "He's gay?"

She said it too loud and a man getting into his car looked at her and raised his eyebrows.

"Not you," she whispered, and stood for a few minutes in confusion. She couldn't believe Emory hadn't told her, but then again it looked like he hadn't told anyone. She tried to figure out if something should've clued her in and wondered if she was the last to know.

The party was set for tonight, at eight. Rise was dead tired from working a nine hour day, but ditching out was not an option. Emory helped her move, so she would support him now. Plus, she'd never been to a coming out party and was curious.

Rise showered and decided on her best jeans, dark and tight, and a shirt that fit like second skin. She arranged her hair in a funky style, with little chunks going this way and that. She used some gel to pull a piece down so it more or less camouflaged the scar. She used great care with her make-up; she was getting better at making her eyes look dramatic. She switched out her work purse for a smaller one with a long, thin strap that she could wear across her body. She headed out, hoping she didn't get lost. She hated navigating downtown Indianapolis; the one-way streets always got her turned around.

As it turned out, Rise found the tall apartment building with ease, though she had to park down the street. It was past eight when she arrived and the party was in full swing. An unfamiliar woman answered the door, but Emory found her quickly and greeted her with a huge smile.

"Look at you," he said, and scanned her from top to bottom.

Rise gave him a sly wink. "Look at *you*."

Emory was dressed to impress, as usual. He was wearing his glasses with the red, wire frames tonight. They matched the design in his silky shirt, and his shoes. He pulled her close to his side. "Appreciate you coming," he whispered in her ear.

"I guess I can tell Aunt Missy the date's cancelled?"

Emory burst into laughter and squeezed her even tighter before going off to greeting someone else with a handshake and slap on the shoulder.

Rise didn't recognize most of the people at the party; they looked to be Emory's family and friends and from college. There was a big metal bucket in the floor of the kitchen, filled with ice and loaded down with bottles of beer, bottled water and other things. Rise grabbed a diet soda and was relieved the plates and silverware were plastic. She nibbled at her food, stayed against the wall, and tried to ignore the little flashes of lights popping up every once in a while. She didn't see Emory's parents and wondered if they weren't invited because it was a younger crowd, or if they had been invited and didn't want to attend.

The crowd parted once, and she spotted Danny. He'd obviously been one of the first to arrive, since he had a coveted seat on the couch. He had a bottle of beer, and looked nice in a dark green shirt she'd never seen him wear. He sat, talking to a young woman with straight, blonde hair. She kept flipping it around when she giggled, which she was doing quite a bit.

Danny glanced her way once, and nodded. She considered going over, but then thought better of it. He was engaged in his flirting, and besides that, he was the one angry with her, not the other way around. She'd already reached out to him with unanswered texts. It was *his* turn.

The party was no different from most others. If Rise hadn't known the theme for the night, she wouldn't have ever guessed. It shouldn't have surprised her; she knew better than to expect rainbows and dancers in chaps. This was Emory's style and he was being himself, in more ways than one now.

Rise took a moment to walk to the window. The building was tall, and the apartment was on one of the middle floors. The view would've been amazing if not for the equally tall and abandoned building right across the alley. The area was in an older part of the city, and pretty haggard, even a little bit spooky. Rise watched a few people come and go down the alley. There wasn't much foot traffic, so it wasn't hard to spot Dominik when he came to stand right below the window.

Rise recognized him immediately this time and almost dropped her cake. It was getting ridiculous, the way he kept showing up. She was going to put a stop to his crazy behavior. She dumped her plate in the trash and headed for the door. She didn't know what she'd say to him, but it wasn't going to be polite.

Rise made it to the street in time to see Dominik disappear around a corner. She followed him. She knew it probably wasn't the wisest thing, for a woman to confront a man she didn't know by herself, nor to wander down an unfamiliar and unlit alley, but that's exactly what she did. Her ears picked up sounds of an argument coming from one of the apartments and muted pounding music from another. Her footing went out from under her once when she failed to see a stack of wood, broken branches and other trash discarded in a heap beside a green dumpster that bore a sign reading 'No Dumping'. She came to the end of the alley and looked right and left, but Dominik had disappeared. Her heart leapt in her chest when a strong hand grabbed her arm.

"What are you doing?" Danny demanded. "You just took off."

"I thought I saw someone I knew. The guy that sang at the church, the tall one with long hair and—"

"I remember my dad's funeral." He looked around and relaxed a little. "He's gone now, if he was here. You have zero sense of self-preservation. This isn't the safest area to go wandering around, you know."

She couldn't argue that.

Danny pulled out a lighter. Rise recognized it as having belonged to his father, the kind that always stayed lit with the USMC emblem on the side. Danny used it to light up a short cigarette. The movement was casual and practiced.

"Since when do you smoke?" Rise asked.

"Since now." Danny took a long drag, then his shoulders slouched a bit. "I've been doing it, off and on, for a few years. I was going to stop after boot camp, but now I figure what the hell." He tapped off some ashes. "Not like I have to worry about staying in great shape anymore, right?"

Rise turned away, not sure what to say. This wasn't exactly the reconciliation chat she'd been hoping for. She wondered why Danny even came looking for her if all he wanted to do was argue.

"How's Emily?" She figured it was a neutral question.

"She's better. She's spending the weekend with Aunt Lydia and Uncle Joe. They have a pool. I had to take her to buy a new swimsuit last night." He looked disgusted. "Every place we went, all they had were these little bikini-looking things."

"That's pretty normal."

"She's twelve!" Danny sounded very much like a protective older brother. "My sister doesn't need to be wearing that stuff."

"What did you end up getting?"

"I got her a damn bikini-looking thing." He tossed the cigarette butt down. "It's all they had." He took out his lighter again and flipped it on, staring at the flame like it held the answer to all the universe's questions.

Rise was trying to come up with another question, when the attack came. Without warning, a dark figure sped from the shadows like a bullet. He slammed into Danny from behind, knocking him flat. The lighter, still lit, flew from his hand and bounced away. Danny tried to push himself up from his belly but the dark figure brought his foot down hard, catching Danny in the shoulder. His head smacked into the pavement with a terrible crack and he went limp.

The moment was surreal, like something from a movie. Rise took a step backward as the dark figure turned on her.

"I don't have any money." The dark figure was close enough for her to see his face, even in the low light. His cheeks were sunken and pale, and the smell on him reminded her of death. His teeth were perfect and white, in contrast to the filth covering his face.

"I can't believe it," the man said in a wondering voice. "You certainly aren't what we expected; we were tracking another." He shook his head. "Fortune has finally smiled on us."

Every instinct Rise possessed warned her to flee, but as she turned to run, a second man blocked her path, grabbing her by her upper arms and shoving her back against the metal of the dumpster.

The second man had the same obscene odor about him as the first, but all similarity ended there. This one was short, broad in the shoulders and clean-shaven, including his head. His eyes were level with hers, and his large hands encircled her arms. If he tightened his grip much further, Rise thought it would cut off circulation. He terrified her, but she refused to let it show.

"What do you want?" she demanded.

"Your surrender," the man said. "Give it to us and we'll make things easy on you. Maybe." He gave her a shove, and her head hit the dumpster with a thump.

"Come now, Marcus," the taller man said. "This is a night for celebration, there's no need for rudeness."

He looked at Rise and rolled his eyes. His hands loosened a fraction. "He's a slave to etiquette, that one. As he said, I'm Marcus. That's Zebadiah—"

"Call me Zeb."

"Stop interrupting," Marcus said. "Herald, we're both exponentially sorry to meet under these circumstances, but we will be requiring your immediate surrender. Your inconvenience in the matter is deeply regrettable." His tone belied any sincerity and he turned back to his partner with an annoyed expression. "Can we get on with it now?"

Rise was panicked and confused. Her breathing became shallow and her thoughts turned dark when she considered what these men might want from her. There were worse things than death for women, things she could hardly bring herself to consider. Zeb came to stand behind Marcus and, between the two of them, the stench was almost overwhelming. Rise nearly gagged. She turned her head as far as she could and saw Danny was still lying where he'd fallen. The lighter had bounced into the pile of trash and a slight trail of smoke began to form.

Rise pushed against her attacker. He only smiled and moved one hand downward, toward his belt. She tried to scream, but the man grabbed her by the throat and held her up so only her toes were touching the ground. She struggled, but it only made it harder to breath. She heard the sound of a buckle sliding loose and her eyes went wild. She clawed at the hand encircling her throat and bucked, attempting to kick as best she could. But then a knife, longer than a dagger but short of a sword, flashed in her face. She froze as cold metal touched her cheek.

"Surrender," the man said. "Say the words, Herald." He released the hand on her throat enough for Rise to speak.

"My name's not Harold." She could smell the smoke now, even over the decaying scent of the men.

"Your name's not...." Marcus started to laugh. "Oh, we've got a funny one here, don't we?"

"I don't think she's joking." Zeb raised a dark eyebrow. "I don't think she even knows what she is. Not yet, anyway."

"Oh, she knows," Marcus said and moved his face closer. "Somewhere in there she knows. Don't you?"

Rise didn't have time to consider the cryptic words, nor did she want to. Her only thought was escape. She moved her eyes when she saw a flicker of light. The wood had caught the flame from the lighter and was burning, not a meter from where Danny still lay.

"Surrender!" Marcus thundered, spit flying when he spoke. "You do not want to live with what is coming if you refuse." He pressed the blade more firmly to her skin.

"You might want to do as he says," Zeb said in a calm, almost apologetic, fashion. "He can be a nasty bugger."

"No!" she screamed, grabbing the knife blade with one hand and slamming the other one up with all her strength, making contact with Marcus's nose. It broke with a horrid crunch, and Rise was both proud of herself and stunned at her own strength. She had no idea where the surge of power had come from, but it was appreciated. Marcus cursed and swung the blade up again, and Rise tossed her hand up and felt another cut. The momentary distraction was enough for her to get away and put some distance between her and the two men. She felt blood between her fingers and she looked down. The wounds were bad, two deep cuts on her palm.

Zeb actually laughed; a real laugh this time directed toward Marcus. Rise poised to run but heard Danny say her name. He was groggy and attempted to stand, but the movement was awkward. Rise was torn; she could leave her friend and run for help, or stay and hope for something else. She realized the hesitation made the decision for her.

Marcus wiped away the blood trickling from his nose. He hit Danny hard with the hilt of his knife, made sure the young man was unconscious, and lunged at Rise in fury, only to have his move intercepted.

"Find your senses," Zeb told him. "We haven't spent all this time waiting for a Herald to have it gutted without reward." He peered at Rise and his eyes became curious. "It's almost a shame. I rather like you. In another life, I suspect we would get on well. But in this one," —he made a clicking sound with his tongue—"not as much."

"Go to hell," Rise spat and the two men shared an amused chuckle.

Zeb smiled and moved toward Rise, all semblance of civility gone from his face. "Maybe you should come along with us for a while."

Rise stood straight, her brain working furiously to decide if any fighting moves she'd seen in movies would be useful. She moved into a loose stance and raised her arms. When Zeb was close enough, she swung at his face with all her might. He dodged the blow easily, and stepped away, smiling. He reached into a pocket on the leg of his pants and pulled out a knife, the same kind as Marcus. He made some teasing, stabbing motions at Rise, and she danced backward. Both men were now advancing toward her. The situation was not good.

Danny made another sound, and Marcus growled in annoyance. He walked over and grabbed Danny by the hair, and placed the knife at his neck.

"No!" Rise and Zeb yelled at the same time.

"He's an innocent!" Zeb said. "We can't break that law!"

"We have her now," Marcus said, nodding to Rise. "Why should we care about the laws?" He moved his arm to make the killing strike, but then an explosion, like a burst of compressed air, filled the night.

A boy and a girl, not even teenagers, appeared. They wore unusual clothing, loose fitting breeches and sleeveless tunics, and held magnificent curved swords. The two wielded the weapons as skilled warriors, the blades flashing and spinning in a series of intricate moves. Marcus was terrified. He stumbled backward, fell, and swung his knife into a defensive position.

"Oh, he's in a lot of trouble." Zeb glanced down at Rise. "We did warn him, didn't we?"

Rise wasn't sure what to make of the situation, but was acutely aware she was the only one without a weapon. She ran to Danny, who was moving a little bit. The fire was now at a full burn, and with the additional light, she saw her friend had blood covering his head and face. He was in no condition to run. He outweighed her by a good amount, so trying to carry him was out of the question.

Rise heard the sound of fighting and turned to see Marcus trying to fend off the two children who were attacking him together, moving fluidly, as one unit. They disarmed him, literally. Marcus screamed as his arm was severed above the elbow. The children nodded at one another, then brought their swords up high. In a move that looked choreographed in its perfection, they swung their blades down in unison and sliced through Marcus's midsection. The body fell in two even pieces.

Rise stared at the gruesome thing with wide eyes, and watched as it started to change. The pieces of Marcus turned hard, smooth and black. In the next instant, it shattered into countless tiny pieces, the remains littering the ground like a broken bottle. The children turned to Zeb.

"It wasn't me, I never touch the innocent." He raised his hands in a gesture of peace and jerked his head toward Rise. "I only want this one. She's new, but still fair game."

Rise pleaded with her eyes, hoping the two strange kids would help her out. Instead, they whipped their swords down and sheathed them at their waist. Another burst sounded, the two warrior children evaporated, and that left Rise alone with Zeb. He grinned victoriously as he approached.

Rise worked to formulate a plan for defense. She whipped her head around, spotted a long piece of wood lying in the fire and snatched it up. One end burned like a torch as she swung it around in front of her. Zeb stopped in his tracks.

"Stay back," she warned.

Zeb stared at the fire, not Rise, and his expression turned fearful.

"Well played, Herald." He stepped backwards, away from the flames. He pointed the knife at her face as he retreated. "There will be another time, I promise you."

He turned to go, but then Dominik showed up again. He was even bigger up close than he looked in the church, towering over Zeb, who wasn't short.

Zeb's face filled with recognition. He swung his knife in a move intended to eviscerate, but Dominik moved with impossible speed and spun away, his long jacket billowing around him. Zeb readjusted his grip on the weapon and held it up. "It's been a while. A pity; I do hate to kill a hound of the Lord!" He charged forward in another attack.

Dominik waited until the last possible instant, then tossed out his arm and hit Zeb in the throat. The man fell flat to his back and lost his hold on the knife. Dominik picked it up, found the one Marcus had wielded and tossed them both into the fire. He looked at Rise with hard eyes.

She pointed the burning stick at him. "Stay away from me." She took a step forward, fully prepared to light him up.

"The difference between friend and foe confounds you, doesn't it?" Dominik pointed at her face. "Do not move from that spot. You and I are going to have words." He turned his back on her, took hold of Zeb and hauled him to his feet. "How did you find her? Speak!"

"Why would I tell you?"

"He wasn't looking for me," Rise interrupted and both men turned to her. "He said he was trying to find someone else. He said he got lucky."

"You have a big mouth, girl," Zeb said. "It's going to get you into trouble one day."

"It already has," Rise retorted, then squawked. The fire had burned down the stick and was close to her hands. She dropped it and stepped away. The knife cuts were still bleeding and she tried to use the end of her shirt to stop the flow. She cursed; it was her favorite top.

Dominik peered down at Zeb and raised his eyebrows. "Looking for someone else, were you?"

"We were ordered to track a Blue." Zeb looked him up and down. "I guess it's been found. You going to kill me, old friend?"

"Do the others know of her?"

Zeb remained silent until Dominik gave him a good shake. "No. I didn't even know she existed until tonight. There've been rumors, but there are always rumors. I didn't believe them."

"Who ordered you to track me?"

"I don't know his name, but he's powerful. He spoke in my mind like the Light Bringer. Now I know why."

Rise perked up at those words. It sounded like Zeb was describing the experience she'd had with the mysterious voice in her head a few days back, the one she'd dismissed as being a hallucination.

Zeb glanced at Rise. "She won't stay hidden for long, and they'll all come for her. Patience has waned. A legion will band together, if that's what it will take. That's all I know, I swear."

Dominik placed his hands on Zeb's face, one on each side. "Thank you."

"You'll release me, then? I give you my word I'll stop hunting. At least give me a chance."

"You had your chance." Dominik twisted his hands in a sharp motion. Zeb's neck broke with a horrible crack and he fell to the ground. As with Marcus, the body soon turned hard and black and shattered into shiny shards.

Rise watched in stunned silence as Dominik knelt by Danny. He inspected the injuries with a practiced eye.

"He requires attention," he stated.

"You think?" Rise said. Her voice was high-pitched from stress. She reached into her little handbag to get her phone. Her hands were slippery from the blood, and shaking from the adrenaline. She fumbled and the few contents of her bag spilled out onto the ground. "I'm calling the police."

"And you will tell them what?" Dominik asked. "That you were attacked by glass?" He nodded toward the remains of the two men. The sound of a siren could be heard in the distance, getting louder. "It appears someone has already reported the incident. We should go." He grabbed her car keys from the ground.

"I'm not going anywhere with you!" Rise said. "Give me back my keys!"

"We have no time for foolishness," Dominik said. He reached down and ripped off a big piece of Danny's shirt and handed it to Rise. "Wrap your wound. I'll take him."

Dominik scooped Danny up and tossed him over his shoulder in a fireman's carry. He moved swiftly down the alley despite the extra weight and Rise had to run a few steps to catch up.

"Where are you taking him?" she asked. She was trying to wrap her hand and keep up with Dominik at the same time. She turned back and saw lights from a fire truck appear at the opposite end of the street. "Who were those guys?"

"Minions," Dominik said. "Why were you in that alleyway?"

"I was following you!" Rise answered as she struggled to keep pace with the long strides. Dominik scowled down at her and she gave him an incredulous stare. "You started it!"

Dominik rounded the corner and went straight to Rise's car. He opened the back door with one hand and tossed

Danny into the back seat, eliciting a slight groan from the injured young man.

"See to him," Dominik instructed. He strode around to the drivers side and took position behind the wheel.

Rise stood dumbfounded on the curb. Too much happened in the past few minutes; she felt as though her brain and emotions were out of sync. Dominik seemed to be helping, but that was small comfort after she'd watched him kill someone.

"You're kidding, right? You think I'm going to just do what you say?"

"That's exactly what I think." He started the car, placed a hand on the wheel, and tapped his fingers, waiting. He looked certain she would comply, which only made Rise determined to stay rooted in place. She didn't budge for several long moments. It was a standoff, but they both knew he had the upper hand and Rise cursed under her breath. It might be taking the proverbial leap into fire, but she slid into the back seat. The car moved before she even slammed the door.

Streetlights allowed a better view of Danny's injuries. Rise touched the angry gash above his hairline, trying to ascertain the extent of the damage. The blood was in the sticky stage; she thought that was a good sign. Her own wounds were still bleeding, soaking through the makeshift bandage. She caught Dominik's eyes in the rearview mirror. He was watching her instead of the road, and driving fast.

"Who are you?" she asked.

"Dominik."

"You know damn well what I mean." She placed her hand on the seat in front of her and leaned forward. "I saw you at the pond that day and again at the church. Why are you trailing me?"

He didn't answer. Rise recognized the area enough to know the turn for the nearest hospital was several streets past.

"Where are we going?"

"Your friend needs care." He glanced at her hand. "As do you."

"The hospital is back that way!"

"Do you have funds for such a place? Or did you assume my assistance included financial support?"

Rise hadn't considered that. She didn't have insurance, and had no idea about Danny. Her hand was going to require stitches and he could have a concussion, or worse. Both sounded expensive.

"I know of a man who can help," Dominik said.

"I think we should go to a hospital." She pushed back Danny's hair and winced. "It looks bad."

"It's not fatal. Miri and Piri would've intervened sooner if the blow was life-threatening."

"Who? You mean those kids with the swords?"

"Those were not children."

"That's what they looked like."

"You shouldn't trust everything you see," Dominik said. "Miri and Piri are powerful entities, guardians of the temporal and the spiritual realm. When an innocent is attacked, it sparks their ire."

"Okay," Rise said, forcing a semi-polite tone. "I appreciate your help, but if you're some kind of religious freak, I should warn you that I don't even go to a church anymore. And I'm not in the market for a cult, either."

Danny made a sound and started moving.

"The boy is waking," Dominik said. "Do you care for him at all?"

"Danny? Yeah, he's my friend."

"Then you will not speak a word of what happened in that alleyway tonight," Dominik said. "You were attacked by bandits and I happened across your path and offered assistance. That is what you will tell him. Do you understand?"

"You want me to lie? And you want me to use the word 'bandits'?"

Dominik stopped at a red light and twisted in the seat to face her.

"Rise, your questions—and I know there are many—will be answered in time. Until then, tend to your friend, follow my lead and keep your mouth shut."

Rise sat back heavily in the seat and crossed her arms over her chest.

"Do I have a choice?" she asked.

"Not anymore."

CHAPTER TWENTY-TWO
Taijitu

Dominik drove them to a large ranch house, surrounded by fields. The driveway was long and winding, and the enormous yard was manicured to perfection. The porch was covered with potted plants and flowers in hanging baskets. Rise followed Dominik from the car, keeping one arm around Danny's waist; he was conscious, but still a little wobbly on his feet. The front door of the house was arched at the top. Rise had never seen one like it and thought it was beautiful.

Dominik rang the bell several times, in what appeared to be a deliberate pattern, as though tapping out a secret code. The door opened, held back by a security chain. A young woman peeked out with dark eyes, a bright red scarf wrapped around her head and neck. She smiled at Dominik, but when she looked past him, her eyes widened.

"Have no fear of them, Saba," Dominik said. "I apologize for the lateness of the hour. Your brother, is he home?"

Saba nodded and unhooked the chain, then stood back while the group filed inside. She locked the door behind them and flipped on the light. Her hand went to her chest and she gasped. Rise knew they must've been quite a sight; all three of them were bloodied.

"Saba!" a male voice called from another room. "Why are you answering the door?"

A man, perhaps thirty or so, entered the room, drying his hands with a small towel. He stopped short at the sight of the ragged bunch intruding upon his living room. A huge Persian strolled behind him.

"Kafi," Dominik said, "these two are injured."

"I'll get my bag." He looked to his sister. "See them to my office."

Rise followed behind Saba, who kept peeking back and biting her lip, as though trying not to smile. The house was spotless, the décor unlike any Rise had ever seen with bright colors, ornate rugs and short tables. Stacks of mailing boxes were scattered around, and one room held an enormous television playing an old black and white kung-fu movie.

Kafi's office looked like one belonging to a doctor, complete with an examining table and rolling chair. Danny took a seat on the table and Rise stood back, trying not to touch anything. A futon was available, but she didn't want to sit down and risk getting it dirty. The office was as pristine as the rest of the house. Several framed documents lined the wall, including a large medical school diploma. Rise hoped it was real.

Kafi returned with a large, black bag in tow and placed items on a metal table with wheels. He took a quick look at Danny's head wound, flashed a tiny light into his eyes and frowned.

"What happened," he asked.

"No idea," Danny said. "Last thing I remember was talking to Rise and then I'm waking up in the backseat of the car. I guess we got jumped, but Dominik showed up and scared them off."

Rise looked down, feeling a little guilty about the lie she'd told. But even without Dominik's insistence she keep quiet, she wasn't sure she'd be able to explain what happened in that alley. Danny, remembering Dominik from the funeral, had been quick to trust the man. Rise thought her friend might have brain damage, and wondered if she did, too. All things considered, she ought to be freaking out by this point. She felt odd, almost subdued.

Rise watched Saba hand her brother a sponge. The girl looked at her again, and bit her lip. Kafi poured some antiseptic from a large bottle, and wiped at the wound on Danny's head. The cat wandered into the room, immediately went for Rise and began winding around her legs. She considered petting it, but bloodstains would clash with the white fur.

Rise peered over at Dominik who had taken up position near the lone window. He stood in a wide stance, his arms crossed over his chest. His sheer size was intimidating, and his clothes only added to the effect. He wore a long, brown leather jacket that hit his knees, heavy boots and dark denim jeans. His hair was tied back in a leather strap and Rise couldn't decide if he reminded her more of a cowboy or a biker. He caught her eyes on him, and she switched back to watching Kafi.

"How bad is it?" she asked. The maybe-doctor was picking small pieces of dirt from Danny's wound with tweezers.

"I've seen worse." Kafi glanced at his sister.

"I'm fine," Danny said.

"You will be." Kafi pushed back in the rolling chair and placed his hands on his knees. "But you're going to stay here tonight, so I can watch you, in case I'm wrong." He turned to his sister. "We can move him to the great room to rest. Give him one of my shirts. An old one."

"You don't have to do that," Danny said as he slid off the table.

"Yes, I do. You're filthy and my sister keeps a clean home."

"Come with me." Saba lead Danny from the room.

"Give him one of those horrid things Aunt Mura sent last month!" Kafi turned his attention to Rise. He unwrapped the makeshift bandage, studied the injuries and looked up. "Minion weapon?"

Dominik nodded.

"Strange. This larger wound looks like she grabbed the blade."

"I did," Rise said.

Kafi grunted. "You're brave, but not too bright. Go wash up, right through that door. Towels are in the drawer on the left."

Rise did as instructed. There was a half-bath connected to the exam room, with a sliding wood door. She pulled it closed, leaving it open a small crack. She turned on the water, but instead of washing off the blood, she pressed her ear to the door and listened to the conversation between the two men.

"Is that who I think it is?" Kafi asked.

"Yes."

Kafi laughed. "Saba will be thrilled. She's been getting impatient. Does the girl know?"

"Not yet," Dominik said. "The situation tonight has sped up the timeline. How are you holding up?"

"Same as always. Take that any way you like."

Rise strained to hear more, and pressed heavily against the door. It flew open a moment later and she lost her balance, falling forward into Dominik's chest. She felt her face reddening.

"Problems?" He took hold of her upper arms to move her away. "Kafi is doing you a favor. You shouldn't keep him waiting."

Rise backed away, wanting to retort, but knowing Dominik had a point about the doctor's generosity. She cleaned up quickly and hopped up to the exam table. She held her breath while Kafi injected what she hoped was anesthesia into her hand in several places. She could hear the television coming from the adjacent room, and she tried to concentrate on the dialogue while Kafi began suturing. He had a delicate touch and she was grateful. Her eyes wandered and she spied a flag on the wall. She recognized the crescent moon and star as being an Islamic symbol, but couldn't place the country.

"Where are you from?" she asked.

"Pakistan. I came to the United States many years ago for school and never left." He looked up and grinned. "Yes, I'm a real doctor."

"Like you'd tell me if you weren't? And I wasn't going to ask."

Kafi chuckled and continued stitching.

"Okay," Rise blurted out after a couple minutes of silence. "Who wants to tell me what's going on? What's a minion?"

"Excellent question," Kafi said as he dabbed some cream onto Rise's palm. He stood and slapped a roll of bandages into Dominik's hand. "You can answer that one. I'm going to check on my other patient." He left, closing the door behind him.

Dominik picked up her hand and studied the wounds. "Kafi did a good job; the stitches are even. Does it cause you pain?"

"Not much." Her hand looked tiny in Dominik's grasp. He had a solid-looking ring on one finger with a huge blue stone set into dark metal. She stared at it for a long moment until realizing he was watching her closely. She turned her attention back to her injury. A long cut ran from her index finger to the heel of her palm and a smaller one bisected the first. They made a cross shape and were deep. She frowned. "It looks bad, doesn't it?"

"There will be a scar." Dominik brushed away a small piece of hair that had fallen over her eye. "One to add to your collection." Rise batted his hand away. His lip curled and he wrapped the soft bandage around her injury while he spoke. "The word 'minion' is a common term, used for those suffering the burden of servitude."

"Servitude to whom?"

Dominik looked into her eyes. "Lucifer."

Rise broke out in laughter. "Lucifer? You mean—"

"The name means 'Light Bringer,' and he is no laughing matter." Dominik finished with the bandage and let her hand drop. "He has power over the minions and serves as their protector."

Rise decided the guy was definitely in a cult, maybe even the leader. He looked like he actually believed what he was saying, but she wasn't about to start drinking the kool-aid. She shook her head and moved on. "One of those *minions* knew you. He was going to kill you."

"He was going to try," Dominik said. "Zeb was a fine man before he lost his way. I always hoped peace would find him again."

"Not likely now, since he's dead." Rise let the edge in her voice dull. "Not that I'm complaining; better him than me. What happened to him and the other one? Why did they…fall apart like that?" She suspected the answer though it seemed impossible. "They weren't human, were they?"

"They were once," Dominik said, "as was I, for many years."

"You're not human?" He looked normal, except for being ridiculously tall and maybe more attractive than most men. He smelled a little strange, but not in a bad way. It reminded her of incense from church; nothing like the death scent on the minions. "What are you, then?"

He regarded her a while. "I'm an angel."

Rise snickered as she slipped off the exam table. "Of course you are." She tilted her head. "Sorry, but I don't believe in angels."

Dominik leaned back, half-sitting on the edge of the desk. His long legs stretched in front of him. "You saw Miri and Piri arrive and depart on a breath of air, you saw two men turn to glass and shatter before your eyes, but you refuse to believe in angels?"

"Fair enough." Rise placed her hands on her hips. "Let me rephrase; I don't believe that *you* are an angel."

"And why is that?"

She gave him a glare. "First of all, an angel wouldn't stand around while a little girl was drowning."

"This is your problem?" He pushed himself from the desk and shrugged off his jacket.

"That's part of it," she said. "Plus, you don't look like an angel."

"Enlighten me."

Rise laughed. "Oh, where to begin on this one?" She waved a hand up and down in his direction. "You have chest hair and look like you haven't shaved in days." She snapped her fingers. "Ah, probably no razors in the hereafter. We'll skip that. Where are your wings? Where's your halo? Did you leave them in Heaven, or maybe you traded them in for that Clint Eastwood coat and those—"

Her words skidded to a halt as blue-silvery feathers appeared at Dominik's back. They grew larger, increased in length and width and became enormous wings that nearly touched the ceiling at the highest point and fell to the floor in a gentle arc. Rise reminded herself to breath.

"Please, continue what you were saying," Dominik said. "I find it fascinating."

Rise held up a finger. "Give me a minute here." She kept her distance, circling him like a cat, and trying to discern any sign of a ruse. The wings were comprised of countless feathers in various sizes, and created a soothing, ruffling sound. She moved closer and saw they emerged from long slits in his shirt. She stood captivated, reached out a tentative hand, but then jumped back as the wings flared out and shook violently.

"Do not touch those," Dominik said. "Not tonight, nor in the future."

Rise noticed the spark of victory in his eyes. She forced her face to relax, and lifted her chin. "Where's the halo?"

He ignored the question. "Do you now believe that I'm an angel?"

There wasn't much use in trying to deny the obvious. "Okay, yes. I believe you."

"Excellent. Now we can move on to other matters." His shoulders flexed and the wings disappeared from view.

"Where'd they go?" She walked behind him, captivated. Now that the initial shock was over, Rise found herself consumed by curiosity. She saw the wings were still there, but almost flush with the angel's back. The feathers were collapsed, one on top of the other, and tucked in tight. It reminded her of a slinky toy she had when she was little. "How did you do that?"

"How do you turn your hand into a fist?"

Rise inspected the long slits in his shirt; they weren't tears. They had defined edges, complete with elegant embroidery.

"You must spend a fortune on tailoring," she said. "Can you fly?"

"Put ridiculous questions aside." Dominik checked his watch. "I have information to impart and time is an issue. The minion attack on you tonight will not be the last. You must be prepared."

"Why?" She looked down at the bandage on her hand. "What do they want?

"They want your surrender."

Her eyes went wide. "That's what they kept saying. Why do servants of the devil want me?"

"I never said anything about a devil." Dominik brought his hand up fast, and held his wrist to her face. "What do you see?"

Rise flinched. "A hairy arm," she said, but then decided it might not be the best idea to get smart with an angel. She sighed. "A big, glowing bracelet with a Yin-Yang symbol. What does that have to do with anything?"

"This symbol, the taijitu, represents the spiritual realm," Dominik said. He pointed to a tiny white dot within the black swirl. "This denotes Lucifer, the bringer of light within the darkness."

Rise's face twisted with confusion and she pointed to the other dot, the black one inside the white swirl. "Then who is that? God?"

"That denotes the Scriptures, the balance to Lucifer, the dark within the light. Do you understand?"

"Is there going to be pop quiz?"

Dominik dropped his arm and looked down at Rise with a firm gaze. "Do you understand?" he repeated.

"I don't remember this from catechism class." She waved her hands in an erase gesture. "But, yes—light, dark, balance. I get it. You tell me minions are going to attack me, and then you go off on a tangent about your bracelet. I know you're an angel, but I think we need to have a talk about priorities." She pointed to his wrist. "That's all fascinating, but not on my important list right now."

"It is important," Dominik said. He took her by the shoulders and bent down so his eyes were level with hers, unblinking and intense. "This concept is the foundation, the cornerstone of everything you will learn. If you want to succeed, you must take the information I offer with a serious mind and open heart. Do you—"

"Understand?" Rise was tired of hearing that, even if it was coming from an angel. "Yes."

Dominik removed the bracelet and dropped it into her palm. "Keep this. Consider it a gift, and don't lose it."

"It's heavy." It was some sort of metal, dark and polished, with an odd clasp. She placed it against her wrist, thinking it would be far too large, but it snapped tight against her skin like it was made for her. The odd glow had dimmed; it was almost non-existent. "I think I broke it already."

"As your understanding increases, and your power, the glow will return," Dominik said. "When that happens, you need to worry about the minions. They were tracking me tonight, not you."

One word caught her attention. "Power?"

Dominik's eyes went cold. Rise noticed they were the same color as his wings and wondered if that was by design or chance.

"Concentrate on the 'understanding' portion," he said, "that is where your strength will lie."

"Right," she said, but then a memory surfaced, the strange experience with the voice in her head. Her eyes went wide and her voice turned accusing. "Hey, was that you talking to me a few nights ago? It was, wasn't it? Don't do that again, you gave me a headache."

Dominik's expression was genuinely puzzled. "Someone spoke to you?"

Rise shuddered at the recollection. "Yeah, it was weird. He was in my head—"

"Who was it and what did he say?"

"Obviously, if I knew who it was, I wouldn't need to ask you. And he didn't say much of anything. It was like he just wanted to mess with my head." She didn't admit how well it worked. "If it wasn't you…" She sucked in a breath. "Do you think it was one of those minions?"

"Minions don't have the ability to invade the mind. Nor do angels such as myself."

"But Lucifer does," Rise said. "I heard that guy Zeb say so."

Dominik almost smirked. "The Light Bringer has far greater concerns than you, and he does not waste time engaging in trivial chat and mind games"

"Then who was it?"

"There are other entities, many with rare talents not always documented. You will tell me if this occurs again."

"*Other entities?*" Rise closed her eyes and shook her head hard. "I can't believe this. In one night, I've found out there are minions and angels, and what did you call those two with the swords?"

"Guardians. The weapons they wield are kirpans."

"I don't know why I'm not curled up on the floor having a breakdown."

"Because somewhere in here," Dominik jabbed a finger into her forehead, "and in here," he poked her breastbone, "you've always known these things existed. You've spent a great deal of energy trying to convince yourself otherwise."

"Why am I so important?" She bit her lip in anticipation. "Do I have a…divine purpose?" The thought intrigued her.

"Everyone has a purpose," Dominik said, "including you." He didn't seem especially pleased with the last part. "You've also been tasked with certain responsibilities, the first of which is heeding my words, so you might as well get used to that. As for the rest, I'll relay information at the appropriate time, when I've been given leave to do so."

Rise held out her hands. "By whom?"

"By those with far greater wisdom than you will ever possess," Dominik said. "That's all you need to know for the time being."

"Oh, come *on*! You can't show up and drop this on me without any explanation!"

"I assure you, I can."

"This is such bull—" She wasn't getting anywhere with this angel through logic, so she switched tactics. "Can you at least give me a hint of what's going on?" She looked away and clenched her fists. "Please," she said as politely as her pride would allow.

Dominik considered her. "That hurt you to say, didn't it?" He headed for the door.

"You're leaving?" Rise was astounded.

"For now. I have work to do, and so do you."

"What work? What am I supposed to do?" The situation was becoming more infuriating by the second.

"I suggest you put effort into improving yourself," he said. "Spend time in study and meditation. You've become dedicated to a physical regimen, but balance that with other activities."

"How do you know I've been working out?"

"Learn a new language," he said, ignoring her inquiry. "You might find Latin to be useful. Take up an art—"

"Art?" Rise made a face. She wasn't exactly the right-brain type.

Dominik continued, "These are all pathways to growth— utilize them. But more than these things, observe. There are clues, signs to the great mysteries all around you. Open your mind to them."

That sounded like a lot of work, especially when she didn't know the reason why. She looked down at the bracelet on her wrist. "Okay, so then what? Stare at this thing until it starts glowing? What do I do if the minions come back?"

Dominik waved a hand. "If it will ease your mind, know you won't be confronted when you're in the presence of innocents. The two that attacked you tonight were foolish to disregard the law, and you saw the result. Plus, you have a protector in your home."

"I live by myself."

"Is that so?" His tone held a hint of amusement, but then he flipped the serious switch again. "Before I depart, I'll offer my first piece of advice and you can consider it a warning, one to heed. Sever your relationship with that young man."

"Danny?" She slapped a hand to her head. "I can't believe I forgot about him, I should go see how he's doing. I won't say anything about..." She had no clue how to sum up everything that was happening. "All of this. Why can't I be his friend?"

"It would be for the best," Dominik said. "I suspect the loss won't be great, for you. You don't truly value him."

Rise stood straight and bit her cheek, fury welling up at the implication. She could almost hear Danny's words from the funeral, telling her she was broken. She was determined to prove that wrong.

"And what if I just say 'no' to all of this?" Rise challenged him. "What are you going to do? I might not be a Bible beater, but I know how this works. I still have free will."

"Do you?"

Rise opened her mouth to argue, but there was something in the angel's simple question that gave her pause. A few hours ago, she wouldn't have believed any of the night's events to be possible. She admitted there was a good chance she didn't know as much as she thought. But, at least she didn't have to admit it out loud.

"I need to go check on Danny," she mumbled.

"I gave him a sedative," Kafi said from the doorway. He had a bundle in his arms, a few blankets, a small pillow, and a nightgown. "It already took effect; he's resting. I'll stay up to keep an eye on him. Rise, you can sleep on the daybed, or the floor if you prefer."

"I don't know how much sleep I'll manage." Rise took the bedding from Kafi.

"Understandable, but try. Do you need something for the pain?"

"She does not," Dominik stated.

Rise didn't appreciate the angel answering for her, but she shook her head. "I'm fine." In truth, her hand ached terribly, but she wasn't about to appear weak.

Kafi retrieved a small bottle from his pocket, dropped two tablets into his palm and placed them on the desk. "If you change your mind."

"Thanks for everything."

Kafi nodded. "Toss your clothes outside the door. Saba will put them in the laundry for you." He left and Dominik did the same, shutting the door behind him without looking back.

Rise changed. The nightgown hit her at the ankles, had long sleeves and a high neck. She hated it. She started preparing the daybed until a soft knock interrupted her. She opened the door to see Saba with a big smile and dancing dark eyes.

"I couldn't wait any longer!" She grabbed Rise into a big hug. "I'm so glad you're a girl!"

Rise stood in the embrace, unsure what to do. She patted the girl's back a few times and then Saba pulled away, but kept her hands on Rise's arms.

"We can go to the movies! Or maybe we can go shopping!" Her eyes went wide. "Will you take me to a mall? I've always wanted to go to a mall in America!"

Rise wasn't sure how to respond. She tried to smile, but it was a feeble attempt.

"Oh, I'm being so rude, aren't I?" Saba said. "I'm supposed to be serving you, and here I am making demands. I'm so sorry. Is there anything I can do for you? Is there anything I can get for you? Anything at all?"

"No, I'm fine," Rise said. "I'm going to go to bed. Oh, wait!"

"Yes?" Saba pressed her hands to her chest like she was waiting for a birthday present.

"Do you have a Bible I can borrow? I want to—" Rise stopped, horrified at her error. She focused on the headscarf. "I guess you don't, do you?"

Saba's face broke into an even bigger grin. "Wait here." She was back in less than a minute and handed a Bible to Rise. "You can keep it, I've already read it." She leaned in close with a gleam in her eye. "I know what you're going to do. You're going to poke around in that book and try to find clues about angels and minions and all the rest, aren't you?"

"That's exactly what I was going to do. I guess you know about Dominik?"

Saba tilted her head. "Absolutely. Did he show you his wings? Aren't they amazing? And he's so handsome. I always thought angels were androgynous, didn't you?"

"I never thought about angels at all until tonight. I guess he looks okay, but he's kind of an ass." An understatement on both points.

Saba pointed to the Bible. "I did the same thing after I met him. I read the Qur'an over and over, then the Bible and the Talmud, and everything else I could get my hands on. I have quite a library if you want to borrow anything, most is in English."

"I think I'll just start with this." Rise flipped through the pages.

"Have you ever read it?" Saba didn't wait for an answer. "Leviticus is so interesting." She lowered her voice. "Did you know women used to be put away in menstrual tents?"

"I've heard about that. Crazy, isn't it?"

"It is. Such a shame it's been done away with. Wouldn't it be lovely to have an excuse to get away from men for a week every month?"

"Saba," Kafi called from another room. He said something more in a language Rise didn't recognize and Saba responded the same.

Saba pouted. "He says I have to leave you alone so you can rest, but we'll talk more in the morning." She doled out another hug and squealed as she shut the door.

Rise shook her head at the excitement her presence inspired, and wondered if Saba was one of those women she'd read about, the ones who were forced to stay isolated. The thought riled her, but she put it out of her head and opened up the Bible. There were bookmarks in a few places, and some highlighted passages. She decided to start at the beginning, repeating some of the words aloud.

"In the beginning, the earth was void, and darkness was on the face of the deep…and God said 'let there be light' and there was light…"

Rise looked down at the bracelet on her wrist, focusing on the black swirl and the tiny white dot. She felt a tickle in her brain, the kind she got when working on a crossword puzzle and knew the answer was in her head, but just out of reach.

She read a little more until the pain in her hand refused to be ignored any longer. She placed the Bible on the floor, popped one of the pain pills, and choked it down without water. She didn't mind acting like a wimp in private.

She lay down and stared at the ceiling for a long time. The room was black as pitch; there were heavy blinds on the windows so not even the streetlights intruded on her. She pulled the blanket up around her chin and rolled onto her side, feeling vulnerable and alone in the big room. She hadn't prayed in many years; she'd given up on the endeavor by the time she was twelve. But tonight, she figured it was worth a shot.

"Lord?" she said, but then stopped. "God?" She stopped again. She felt foolish, and even a little embarrassed. She hadn't used either word in years, except in conjunction with others, most of them not particularly respectful. She shut her eyes and decided to just pray for sleep. She didn't know if it was the Almighty or the drugs, but one of them answered.

Chapter Twenty-Three
Do No Harm

Rise awoke after a fitful night. Everything had felt like a dream for a few blissful moments, then memories had come back, bringing pain along for the ride. At one point during the night, she fell off the little daybed and, in retrospect, she should've stayed there. Her back was stiff, her neck ached and her hand was throbbing. She kicked off the blankets, fumbled to find the light switch, and slammed her toe into a table. Her curse was a little too loud.

Saba knocked on the door and cracked it just enough so her whispered voice was audible. "Rise? Are you awake?" Her excitement from the night before hadn't faded.

She rubbed a hand over her face. "Yeah, come in."

Saba wore a two-piece outfit and bright red scarf, and looked as though she'd been awake for hours. "I have your clothes." She placed the neatly folded stack on the chair. "I have breakfast, too. Do you like bagels?"

"I do." It'd been a while since she'd had such a treat. Her breakfast was usually a bowl of whatever cereal was on sale, or a pop tart. "I don't want to eat with morning breath, though."

"Towels are ready for you in the guest bathroom right down the hall, and there's a bunch of new toothbrushes in the vanity—pick whichever one you like. Anything else is probably in one of the drawers under the sink. We've been expecting you, so I've had everything ready for months. I'll be in the great room. Hurry!"

Rise found everything as described, and the hot shower relieved most of the aches she had accumulated overnight. When she was dressed and presentable, she came out and wandered around, trying to navigate the house. Danny was still asleep on a couch in the adjoining room. He had one arm tossed over his eyes and was lightly snoring. Saba found her seconds later.

"This way," she whispered and tiptoed off to the room with the big television. Another karate movie was playing, with sub-titles. Saba took a seat on the floor in front of a short table and motioned for Rise to sit with her. A glass of orange juice and several bagels were already on the table. Rise picked a cinnamon one.

"You have a beautiful home," Rise said.

"Thank you. I re-decorate every few months. It drives Kafi crazy; he says he can't find anything. Oh! Look what I got yesterday." She reached for a purple and gold headscarf sitting atop a mailing box. She removed the red one, and Rise was shocked to see a mound of curly, dark hair spill out. Saba wrapped it up in the new scarf and beamed. "Isn't it fantastic?"

"I love it," Rise said, "but you have such gorgeous hair. Do you always keep it covered?" It was probably rude to ask, but Saba didn't seem to mind.

"I usually wear it down when I'm at home, but we have a guest now." She grinned, and jerked her head toward the room where Danny was sleeping. "Is he your boyfriend?"

"Best friend." She hoped that was still the case, anyway. Further discussion was interrupted when the big Persian jumped into her lap. Rise stroked the thick fur, smiling. "She's a sweetie."

"I hate that cat," Saba said. "I clean up hair twenty times a day, and she got her claws into my favorite hijab and ripped it to shreds. Infuriating creature, but how do you turn down a gift from an angel without appearing ungrateful?"

"Dominik gave you a cat?" She pushed the tail away as it swiped under her nose.

"He thought I was lonely. I'd rather have a bird." She brightened. "But now I have you to keep me busy. What are we going to do first?"

"I'm not sure." Rise took a long drink of her juice, stalling. She wasn't in the market for friendship, but the young woman was determined. She tried to deflect the conversation. "I like your accent. Kafi's isn't as strong."

"I've only lived here for two years, four months and six days. Kafi has been here since he was a boy."

"You didn't grow up together?" Rise asked. "Sorry if I'm being intrusive."

"Not at all! We should get to know each other." Saba leaned forward, putting her chin on her hands. "Our father died when I was a baby. Kafi was older—eight or nine. We had family here, and they offered to take him so he could continue his schooling. He was a promising student, and as you see, he's a doctor now." She looked proud.

"Are you here for school, too?"

"The angel didn't tell you?" Saba was openly shocked.

"Dominik didn't tell me much of anything," Rise said. "He popped up last night, flashed his wings, rattled off something about balance and gave me this." She held out her wrist.

"Oh, that's lovely," Saba said, touching the bracelet. "I wish I'd gotten one of those instead of the cat. And I know what you mean about Dominik; he's confusing sometimes. I don't know if I'm supposed to tell you this..." She leaned across the table and lowered her voice. "He's new."

"New at what?"

"He's a new angel," She said. "He hasn't had his wings long, from what Kafi tells me. I think you and I are—what's the term? Lab rats?"

"Guinea pigs?"

"That's it! But wait, you mean he didn't tell you *anything* about me?"

"He didn't," Rise said, shaking her head. "Sorry."

"Oh, no." Saba covered her face. "You must think I'm insane then, don't you?"

"Not at all." That wasn't the whole truth. "Hold up—are you an angel, too?"

Saba laughed, the sound like wind chimes. "No. I'm a Returner."

"A what?"

Saba reached over and grabbed her hand. "A Returner. I don't know if that's the official term, but it's the best translation I can come up with. I died, you see."

Rise stared, not sure she heard that correctly. "You're dead? Are you a ghost?"

"No." Saba laughed harder. "I'm not dead anymore. I was sent back to help you!"

"Me?" Rise was astounded.

Saba shrugged. "I think I'm on loan."

"I can't believe... I mean... Why me? What happened?" She leaned forward, too many questions fighting for dominance. "How did you die?"

Saba cringed. "It's a long story, and Kafi might come out looking bad. I'll tell you, but you must promise not to hold it against him."

"Okay."

Saba leaned back on her hands and took a deep breath. "I can't believe Dominik didn't explain this already. If he wasn't an angel, I'd strangle him! You remember I told you Kafi came here for school and I stayed home in Pakistan?"

"Right."

"After my father died, my mother and I went to live with her brother in a tribal area. Kafi came to visit many times, and he wrote almost every month. He'd tell me stories about America, and promised he'd bring me here one day."

Rise nodded.

"On his last visit, he told me I could come back with him for a short vacation, before I had to get married." She made a face. "My Uncle had promised me to an ugly old man. But the day we were supposed to leave, I made a terrible mistake." She bit one of her knuckle. "This is where the story gets unpleasant. Are you sure you want to hear it?"

"Go ahead."

"I was in love with a boy and I still saw him in secret. I snuck away, to tell him good-bye before I left, and we were caught together. The leaders of my village decided to make an example of me. I was dragged back and stoned to death."

Rise almost choked on her juice. Saba could've been reciting a recipe for casserole, as nonchalant as she sounded. "You're kidding?" Maybe she'd misunderstood. "You were stoned? With rocks?"

"Is there another way?" She wasn't being sarcastic; she looked intrigued. "Kafi was told that since he was my brother, he should be the one to cast the first stone. And he did." Saba shrugged. "I don't know if his rock killed me or just knocked me out, but it's the only one I remember." She waggled a finger at Rise. "I told you Kafi might look bad."

"Saba…he looks *really* bad."

"No, no," she said. "You have to understand, he did it out of mercy. He knew he couldn't stop it from happening, but thought if he struck me hard enough, I wouldn't have to suffer. There were stories of women pelted a hundred times, for an hour or more, before they died."

"What happened?' In a terrible way, she was fascinated.

Saba's eyes danced. "Kafi was permitted to take my body away. He put me in the trunk of a car, and at some point I went to…wherever it was. I was greeted on a bridge by a group of angels, and a man and a woman. They asked me if I would go back, that another would need my help and…" She growled in frustration. "I've tried so hard to remember anything else, but I can't. But I must have agreed because"— she tossed her arms in the air— "here I am, ready to do whatever you command of me."

Rise knew her mouth was hanging open. She closed it. "I don't understand that last part."

"That's when Dominik found me," Kafi said from the doorway. He looked as though he hadn't slept much, but his hospital scrubs were clean and crisp. "He asked what I would do to have my sister back, and I said anything." He muttered something in his native language. "The angel agreed to that arrangement. I was instructed to care for Saba, and keep her isolated until the one appeared she was meant to help."

"That's you," Saba said, and squeezed Rise's hand. "I knew it the moment I saw you. Dominik only told me I would be in your service. He didn't even tell me if you would be a man or a woman. Isn't it fun I was able to recognize you right away?"

"Fun," she said, nodding. "I guess so."

"You must be someone of great importance." Saba shook her head back and forth in amazement. "You've been given an angel, and me."

"What, exactly, am I supposed to do?"

Saba made a little sound and shrugged. "I have no idea, and hoped you'd tell me. I guess we'll find out together. This is so exciting, isn't it?"

Rise watched Kafi through new eyes as he went to the kitchen and rummaged through the refrigerator. The phrase 'do no harm' kept repeating in her mind. She was still staring at him when she heard Danny moving around in the other room. She hopped up and ran to him.

"Hey," she said, then remembered they were technically still fighting, unless an evening of getting beat up re-bonded their friendship.

"How's your hand?" he asked.

She shrugged. "How's your head?"

He shrugged and smiled, and Rise knew things were okay between them now. His face was bruised on one side, but his hair obscured the worst of the wounds. He'd removed his shirt at some point, and Rise stared with a little too much interest when he stretched.

"We need to be taking off soon," Danny said. "I have to pick up Emily, and my car is still over at Emory's place." He laughed. "He's probably mad as hell about us leaving his party."

"Shower is ready for you," Kafi told him, "and Saba made bagels, if that's your thing. If not..." He twisted the apple in his hand.

Danny headed down the hall, and Kafi took a small business card from his breast pocket, along with a pen. He bent over the kitchen counter and scribbled some numbers.

Rise was still processing all the new information when Saba grabbed her hand, hard.

"Kafi," Saba said, "I was just telling Rise how I haven't been able to go *anywhere* while I've been waiting for her." She nodded as she spoke, and kept her eyes on Rise. "I explained that if she *commanded* me to do something, then I'd have to obey her, even if it meant *leaving the house*." She bit her lip in anticipation.

Rise took the un-subtle hint. "That's right," she said, "and as it turns out, I need Saba's help. I need her to...get me something." She looked around, and spied a chain around Saba's neck. "I need a necklace. A silver one, I think, and long, very long." It was a terrible lie, but the best she could do on the spot.

Kafi looked up from his writing. "You need a necklace? I can get one for you on my way back from the hospital—"

"No," Saba and Rise said in unison.

"Saba needs to be the one to do it. I...*command* her to do this for me." The words sounded absurd.

"Why?"

"Because..." She cringed inside; that was a good question. "Because...it's a matter of... great spiritual urgency."

"Is that so?" Kafi crossed his arms over his chest and looked between the two women.

"I think we should do what she says." Saba used a solemn voice. "She's important, after all."

"Yes, I am." Rise lifted her chin, tried to appear regal, and decided to go all the way. "And the best place to find this mighty necklace…of destiny…is the mall." She heard Saba squeak in delight.

"The mall?" Kafi repeated.

"That's right," she said, "and I don't want her to grab the first one she sees, either." She made a grand, sweeping gesture. "She must search for the right one in many stores."

"Of course she must." Kafi looked at his sister. "We can go when I get home. I wonder if fate will demand you get a new pair of shoes for yourself." He turned back to Rise, holding the business card between fingers. "Dominik asked me to give this to you. He'll get in touch later. I put my cell phone number on the back, and Saba's, too. If I don't answer, I'm probably in surgery."

"I'll answer for sure," Saba said. "You can call me anytime you want, day or night."

Rise took the card, intrigued. It was dark blue, high quality, and had Dominik's name etched on the front in bold script. There was a paw print in the upper right corner. She'd never have guessed an angel would have a calling card.

Kafi kissed Saba on the forehead, grabbed keys from a little basket on the counter, and covered his eyes with expensive-looking sunglasses.

"Hang on," Rise said. "What else did Dominik say?" She spread her arms. "What are we supposed to be doing?"

"Well, I'm going to work." Kafi made a gesture toward his sister. "Saba is going to stay here until I return, and I assume you'll be going back to…whatever it is you do when you're not dealing with matters of spiritual urgency."

Rise dropped her arms. "I don't get it."

Saba shrugged. "No one gets it."

"But you will get used to it," Kafi said. "Angels keep their own schedule."

After her brother left, Saba pulled Rise into a big hug, bursting with joy. "Oh, thank you," she said. "The mall! I just know we're going to be great friends!"

Dominik stood in a viewing room, glaring at the screen in front of him. Shay's giggles were not helping his mood.

"The necklace of destiny." The Purple angel's wings shook with laughter. "That's a new one, isn't it?"

"It's not funny. She's abusing her power for amusement." He couldn't believe it was starting so soon.

"She's not thinking about her power." Shay wrapped her arms around Dominik's waist, pressed her chin to his chest and gazed up at him. "She doesn't even know her title yet, let alone her abilities."

"She needs to be told before she causes more trouble."

"That's not up to you. You can only give information as allowed, at the designated time."

"I think that's going to be easier said than done. She's resistant to authority, combative, headstrong; a dangerous combination."

"They're dangerous creatures," Shay said, "and every one of them has a wild arrogance. They believe in nothing greater than themselves, and this one will be no different. It's in her nature. Nothing you do will change that."

"I'm aware of their nature," he said, "but I don't understand them."

"Don't try," Shay said. "Follow the protocols—do what you must and nothing more. It will save you frustration."

"Look here at what she's doing now," Dominik said, pointing at the screen. "Thanks to Saba, she has an extensive library at her disposal. She could be acquiring useful knowledge. Instead, she stands there gossiping about celebrities and other nonsense."

"You shouldn't spend too long here," Shay said, her voice easing as she took his hand in hers. "I know you want to keep an eye on her, but in some ways she's like all others on a journey. You have to let go sometimes. If you don't, you'll start to notice every mistake, every fault. You'll become angry with her and angry with yourself. You'll start to believe you're doing something wrong."

Dominik stroked a finger across Shay's cheek. She'd been steadfastly supportive of him in his new position, though he knew it was difficult for her.

"You sound like the elder of my choir," he said. "They counseled me the same."

"Then listen to us," she said with a smile. "Go somewhere else for a while, and I don't mean back to the scrolls for more research. Oh, I don't know how you can spend so many hours in there! Let's take to flight for a while, or go watch a performance on the artisan level."

"Just a little while longer," Dominik turned back to the screen. "I gave her a warning at our first meeting. I'm curious what she'll do with it."

"She's a Herald. Don't take it too hard if she doesn't listen."

CHAPTER TWENTY-FOUR
SIGNS

Rise sat in the passenger seat of her own car, listening in while Danny talked on the phone. Emory called, in the spirit of true friendship, to hassle the two of them about leaving the party without even a thank you for the food. Danny was filling him in on the attack in the alley and Rise could hear Emory's voice on the other end. He was furious.

"I heard there was a fire last night," he said. "Nobody said a word about anyone getting jumped. You sure you two are okay?"

"I'm not bad," Danny said, "but Rise got her hand sliced up and—"

"I'm fine, Emory," Rise said loud enough for him to hear.

Danny clicked off the phone after a few more minutes and tossed it down. "I always try to be aware of my surroundings," he said. "I can't believe I didn't see those guys coming for us last night." He hit the steering wheel with his fist. "I didn't see them at all."

"It's not your fault. Believe me, they came out of nowhere." Danny's guilt over 'allowing' himself to be beaten was getting on her nerves. Rise came close to telling him the truth, but it didn't seem like a good idea to countermand an angel. Not yet, anyway.

"It's messed up," he said. "Two guys cut up a woman in an alley, and the only calls to the police are about a fire."

"It's why women are told to yell 'fire' if they're being attacked," she said. "Us getting jumped didn't affect anyone else, but fire is dangerous to everyone."

"I'm glad Dominik showed up." He glanced at Rise. "God only knows what they would've done to you." His hands clenched on the wheel until his knuckles turned white.

"We're both fine. Let it go."

"The doc was a good guy," Danny said, sounding more relaxed. "We got lucky with that; a hospital bill would've killed both of us. I offered to pay, but he said no. His sister was cool, too. She has a thing for kung fu movies—did you see that collection?" He shook his head and smiled. "Not many girls like her."

"I think you're right on that one." Rise stared out the window, thinking about everything Saba told her, and what she was going to do about Dominik's request. She peered over at her friend, and wondered how, and why, she was supposed to disengage from his life.

Danny pulled into the lot at Emory's building, then put the car in park. "How much longer do you have on the lease at that apartment?" he asked.

She had to think for a minute. "It's up next month. Why?"

"I think you should move back to Nineveh."

"Not gonna happen." She knew he'd never been happy with her decision, but thought he understood her reasons. "Everything there reminds me of things I want to forget."

"It wasn't all bad, was it?" Danny lowered his sunglasses so she could see his eyes. They held a little spark of flirtation.

Rise couldn't help but smile. "Okay, you weren't so bad. But that's a small town and you know I'll run into my parents or my sister, and I want to put that part of my life behind me." She looked away. "Can we drop it? I don't want to start up another argument."

"I'm not going to argue with you." Danny leaned back heavily into the seat. "Look, I was upset that day at the funeral. I didn't mean what I said to you." He smirked. "Not all of it, anyway." He placed his hands on the steering wheel and stared at them, as though trying to make a decision. "You remember when you sent me that text, and I called you back and hassled you about the brake pads?"

"I remember," she said. "What about it?"

Danny kept staring at his hands. "That's when my dad had the heart attack. I found him right after we got off the phone. I tried to save him, but it was too late. I kept thinking I would've found him in time if I wasn't talking to you."

Rise didn't know how to respond to that.

"I don't blame you." He turned to face her. "Not anymore. It was just something I had to work through." He peeked over his sunglasses again. "This is the best apology you're getting, by the way."

She shook her head and smiled.

"Now, back to the Nineveh thing," Danny said, becoming business-like. "We've established you don't despise everything in the city. What's another issue?"

"I can't believe you're making me have this conversation." Rise steeled her nerves for the battle. "Family drama aside, I can't afford to move back there." She held up her hand. "Don't mention that cheap trailer park near the lake. I already know about it and I'm not living in a double-wide. Plus, I work in Indianapolis. I'm not going to commute an hour back and forth every day."

"Get a job in town. You remember Michelle, from school?"

"The cheerleader? The one you dated with huge—"

"That's the one. She's working at the courthouse part-time while she goes to colleges, and told me they're still hiring. I bet she'd give you a reference."

"I didn't know you still talked to her," Rise said. "And Michelle never liked me."

"Bull. *You* never liked *her*. She asked about you just last week."

"Whatever." She waved her hand. "It still doesn't fix the rent problem. Trust me. I'm fine where I am."

"What if..." He stopped until he was sure he had her attention. "What if you didn't have to pay rent?"

She laughed. "Right. I'm sure there's a bunch of free places out there. Maybe I can find a nice bridge and roll out a sleeping bag." Danny just stared at her, a little smile on his face. "You can't be serious," she said as understanding hit her. "You want me to move in with you?"

"And Emily," he said. "Dad had the house paid off. You can have his old room, with your own bathroom and everything." He held up a hand when she started to argue. "I'm not trying to maneuver you into being my girlfriend. We'll be roommates, that's all. I'll take care of the bills, but you can buy the groceries, if it makes you feel better."

"How long have you been plotting this?"

"A few days. Not bad, huh?"

"I walked right into it." She touched her forehead, trying to figure out a way to decline his offer without having to be harsh. "I can't let you do that for me. It's too much."

"This isn't completely for you," Danny said, and wiped a hand over his chin. "What are you doing today?"

"I was planning to go home, sit around and feel sorry for myself about my hand and...observe my surroundings." She laughed at little.

"Follow me out to my house." He unhooked his seat belt and opened the door. "It won't take long. I have to show you something."

"What?"

"I can't explain. You're going to have to see it." He headed for his truck before she even replied.

Rise slid into the driver's seat and pulled out behind Danny. She scanned the sky as she drove, half-expecting a pissed off angel to throw a lightning bolt at her car.

Once they'd arrived, Danny headed upstairs to Emily's room. Rise smiled at the big wooden letter E on the door. She knew Mr. Daly carved it himself.

Danny placed his hand on the knob. "You ready?" He flung open the door and stepped back so she could enter.

Emily's room was as tidy as could be expected from a twelve year old; the bed was made, and the big rug in the middle of the room looked recently swept. Then Rise noticed the walls and gasped.

"Angels." She looked around in awe. On every inch of wall space, Emily had drawn angels, some as big as a ruler, others as small as pencil erasers. "There must be hundreds," Rise said as she reached out and touched the largest one. It was a female in a long dress, with golden wings.

"She started right after our dad died." Danny rubbed his neck with one hand. "At first, there were only a few, but she kept at it every day. She started before school, and after. When she ran out of space in here, she started on the walls in the back room."

One of the angels looked familiar. Rise traced the blue wings with her finger, impressed and concerned Emily had the look of the wings precise; she'd even crafted varying sizes of feathers. "She's quite an artist. Why is she doing this?"

"No idea, and it gets worse." Danny released a long breath. "Emily insists dad has been talking to her, in her dreams."

Rise cringed. She was out of her depth. "That might be a coping mechanism. The past few years have been rough. Your mom was sick for a long time before she died, and now your dad…"

"I know," Danny said. "I've gone to every website I can find about grief, but there's no advice for something like this." He glanced around, looking lost. "I don't know what to do. If she keeps this up, she'll paint the whole house. But, I think you might be able to help her."

Rise was incredulous. "How can I help with this?" A better question was why she'd want to, but kept that to herself. "I don't know anything about child psychology. You said it yourself—I don't even like kids."

"I don't want to freak you out, but you see this one here?" He pointed to an angel above the headboard, the only one with black wings. "Emily said this one is called 'Rise'."

"Maybe it's a coincidence—"

"How many people have that stupid name?" He tried to smile. "I've never been one of those people who look for…"—he waved his hands at the ceiling— "signs, or whatever crazy people think they see, but I'm out of ideas."

Rise froze at the words. "Signs," she whispered. "I'm not sure that's entirely crazy anymore."

Danny brightened. "Does that mean you'll move in?"

"I don't know—" Dominik told her, in clear language, to break off her friendship with Danny. He also told her to be more observant; signs were everywhere. She wavered, not sure what to do.

Danny saw her hesitation and upped his game by pulling out his puppy-dog eyes. "You might be able to help Emily."

"Playing the 'welfare of a child' card is unfair."

"Then you're going to hate the next one in the deck." All trace of humor vanished from his face. "I've never asked you for anything. If it doesn't work out, I'll help you move back to Indy and I swear I won't hold it against you. I'm only asking you to give it a shot."

Rise put her hands on her hips and took a deep breath. She couldn't wiggle out of that argument. Danny helped her out more times than she could count. She had a debt to repay. Agreeing to this would clear it and then some.

"Okay," she said. "I'll put in notice at my apartment, but I'm not quitting my job until I know this is going to work. This does *not* mean we're dating and there will be no wandering into my room without an invitation. I *will* pay half the bills, but I'm not doing your laundry or—"

She had a list of rules to impose, but Danny grabbed her up in a big bear hug and squeezed until she thought her ribs would crack. There was no backing out now.

Rise took another peek at the blue wings on the wall. If she was breaking cosmic law by disobeying an angel, so be it. Dominik barked out a bunch of orders, with no explanation as to why. She wasn't going to follow along until she had more information. In the meantime, she could have secrets, too. Besides, what the angel didn't know wouldn't hurt him.

Shay struggled to keep the smile off her face as she looked up at Dominik. The Blue angel looked ready to jump through the viewing screen and choke the life from the Herald under his charge. Shay warned him to stop watching, but was happy he didn't. She was secretly praying he'd become so enraged he'd ask to step down. That wasn't likely. He took his oath seriously, too much so, in her opinion.

"She ignored my words." Dominik's face locked down, his jaw clenched. "I told her to sever that relationship and what does she do? She agrees to move into his home."

"Don't take it personally," Shay said. "For humans, the appearance of an angel would be taken seriously. You can't expect that from her."

"There must be a way to reach her, or there would be no reason for the Scriptures to enlist my service."

"Oh, there are ways," she said. "She's bound by flesh for the time being and you are not." She cocked her head. "There's a reason advisors are allowed such great latitude. Use it to your advantage." She hoped he was listening.

"In my experience, guidance achieves a better response than shows of strength."

"Your experience is with humans and angels." She didn't understand Dominik's hesitation. There were many, including herself, who would jump at the chance to have the upper hand on a Herald. "That creature is nothing like the rest of us."

"I know that all too well." Dominik's expression turned dark. "I won't let this one get the better of me." He flipped off the viewing screen and paced the room for a while. "And now there's a Free Spirit involved. That's going to complicate things further. What do you know of them?"

"Very little. They're as evil as any creature of legend, and powerful. They can manipulate dreams and can even consume the body of a human, if they wish."

"That's my understanding as well. Do you know if any of them have the ability to communicate telepathically?"

"Mind invasion?" Shay shook her head. "I've never heard of that, but that doesn't mean it's not a possibility. Free Spirits are rare, and not a subject I've studied beyond what was required. I've hoped never to encounter one. They're vile creatures, extremely dangerous."

"It's a tragedy this soul should be condemned to such a fate, through no fault of his own. But he's new, so perhaps he still retains some righteousness."

"They all go mad after a while." Shay remembered her time in prison. She'd earned the sentence, but others had been unjustly accused and suffered twofold. "If a Free Spirit has a chance to gain freedom, he will seize upon it without hesitation."

"And this foolish Herald is going to walk right into his lair." Dominik was almost purple with rage. "Her defiance has created more trouble for herself, and for me." He flung open the door. It smashed against the wall and bounced back.

Shay followed him, concerned. Dominik was normally even-tempered and kept his emotions in tight rein. His increasing volatility was unnatural. She enjoyed those moments when his passion flared, but preferred it channeled in other directions. "Where are you going?"

"Back to the library. I need to research Free Spirits, ascertain their abilities and figure out which laws still bind them." He stopped when an angel flew into his path and handed him a small scroll.

Dominik read quickly. "The Scriptures wish to see me at my earliest convenience. I suspect that means now."

Chapter Twenty-Five
Fifty Grand

Rise was angry and in pain by the time she got home from Danny's house. Her car had a manual transmission and the shifting irritated her injury. It was a gloomy day, but kids in the building weren't letting the lack of sun slow them down. The basketball court was filled with teenagers and music was booming. Rise stared. Some of those 'kids' were her age, but right then she felt decades older. She scurried into the apartment and Oliver was on her immediately, purring and wailing.

"Sorry, honey," she murmured, heading to the kitchen to fill his bowl. He attacked the food while Rise grabbed a bottle of water and downed a few aspirin, hoping it would dull the pain. She plopped down and checked her E-mail and networking page.

She found a friend request waiting from Saba, and clicked to accept. The young woman used an alias and her profile photo was some sort of flower. She had no other 'friends', but liked to play online games. Her page was loaded with announcements of high scores and achievements. Saba needed to get out more, and Rise hoped she visited every store in the mall.

She stood, deciding to get a head-start on packing. She found a box and filled it with things from her closet she wouldn't need. In the process, she discovered the envelope she'd taken from her parent's lockbox many months before. She'd forgotten about the thing.

She sat with her back against the closet door and pulled out a small stack of paperwork with letterhead from an attorney's office. She scanned the pages and caught the name of the adoption agency her parent's had used for both Rise and her sister. Saint Anne's. Her dad gave the organization an annual contribution, and they got Christmas cards from the place every year.

She didn't find anything interesting, just legal forms common in adoptions, but then a small receipt fell out and landed in her lap. Her mouth dropped when she saw the amount. Her parent's were never short on money, but they were far from rich. Even so, James Hawke had given the attorney's office $50,000 dollars.

Her phone buzzed.

"I talked to Michelle," Danny said. "If you change your mind about getting a new job, she can hook you up. So, what are you doing?"

"I just found something strange." She held the receipt and explained her discovery.

"Maybe it was illegal." He sounded intrigued.

"I don't think so. Everything else looks official."

"You can always try to get your adoption records unsealed, if you really want to know."

"True. I just had this conversation with Emory. Weird."

"Maybe it's another sign." Danny laughed. Rise didn't.

They chatted a little longer. The new roommate agreement prompted Danny to start going through his dad's things, and he'd discovered a nice handgun in the closet. He'd been into hunting since he was old enough to hold a license and appreciated a good firearm. He went on about sightlines and grips, and Rise tried to sound like she cared. She welcomed the knock on the door as an excuse to get off the phone.

She found a large box in the hallway outside her door, wrapped in brown paper and tied with narrow string fraying at the edges. Rise took the strange package out to her little balcony, and unwrapped the contents one-by-one. She discovered two books, ancient and well worn. She picked up the heaviest one, flipped through a few pages, and groaned. It was written in Latin, which explained why the second book was a guide to translation.

"You've got to be kidding me." She knew exactly who was behind this even before she found the letter written in elegant script and slightly smudged, as though it had been penned using a brush and a bottle of ink.

Be prepared to discuss the first three chapters at our next meeting.

Dominik

"I hate angels," she said, shoving the books aside. The third item was a boxed craft kit that looked like it came off a shelf in the toy aisle at a drugstore, and was obviously a not-so-subtle prompt for her to take up an art. The kit had colorful plastic beads, thick yarn, and labeled as being for ages five to eight. She leaned over the balcony, turned her face skyward and screamed at the top of her lungs. "Smart ass!"

The final item almost made up for Dominik's jab at her intelligence. Rise found a tall, triangular candle. It was dark blue and glistened in the sunlight like nothing she'd ever seen. The smell was exquisite; a scent she couldn't place and had to be otherworldly. She grinned, ran her fingers along the smooth wax and inhaled. The intoxicating fragrance was even better when she lit the wick. Within minutes, her apartment oozed Heaven.

Rise busied herself the rest of the afternoon, not thrilled with the little tasks the angel tossed her way, but also not willing to fight him too hard until she had a better idea of what he wanted and why. She trudged through a few pages of what she discovered was a book on philosophy. The translating was tedious, but once she got the hang of things, she found she didn't exactly despise the job. She discovered she had a knack for the ancient language, or at least she thought she did. After a few hours she was able to decipher most of the words without help.

With her mood improved, she strung together a necklace from the ridiculous crafting kit and gave it to little Vanessa down the hall who was thrilled by the thing. Rise kept checking the bracelet Dominik gave her, but the glow hadn't changed a bit. She tapped it a few times, annoyed she hadn't progressed after an entire afternoon of spiritual homework.

Her mind kept going back to the amount on that receipt, and the phone conversation with Danny. She hadn't talked about her adoption in years, but the subject had come up twice in as many weeks. It couldn't be a coincidence, and having an angel pop into her life had ignited a curiosity about her heritage. On impulse, she dialed the number for Saint Anne's, forgetting it was a weekend until she heard the voice recording.

Surprisingly, there was an option to press a number if she was an adult adoptee wanting information on his or her birth family. Rise listened to a recording that briefly explained Indiana privacy laws, and the steps needed for information to be released. It sounded like a long process, laced with absurdity. It was *her* life, after all, her information. She shouldn't have to ask permission to take what already belonged to her. She left a brusque message at the end, giving her name, number and what she wanted.

Rise clicked off her phone, still in a huff. She lay back on her bed and Oliver hopped on her stomach. She stroked him, feeling a little better.

"Do you think I'm worth fifty grand?" The cat raised his tail high in the air and kneaded her with his front paws. Rise smiled. "That's what I thought. I don't think so, either."

Chapter Twenty-Six
Urgent Situation

Dominik stood before the Scriptures, his stance wide, his hands laced behind his back under his wings. The revered members of the group were all present, except for one. Chi's throne sat empty and the void was palpable. She never returned from the journey she'd taken. Dominik let his gaze linger, and it fueled the festering rage inside him.

The Scriptures had requested an update on the new Herald. Dominik had given a brief account, and was awaiting a response. The group huddled together, speaking too softly for him to hear, but looked to be in disagreement. Dominik suspected he might be dismissed from the duty he'd been given. Part of him wished for it; he was still furious with Rise for doing the opposite of what he recommended, and was equally angry at his own failure to ensure she complied.

He wondered if she received the package he sent via messenger, and if she'd even bothered to open the books. He assumed not, but hoped she was at least treating them with care; they were from his personal collection. The Scriptures resumed their seats and Dominik brought his thoughts back to the moment, prepared for discipline.

"You did well," Cornelius said. He was serving as speaker now, due to Chi's absence.

Dominik tried to hide his surprise, but knew it didn't work.

"We didn't summon you here for reprimand, Dominik," Cornelius said. "We are in agreement that you don't deserve it—" He paused when the representative from the Red choir flicked his wings. He held up a hand. "*Most* of us are in agreement, and we prefer to leave those unpleasant duties, if needed in the future, to the Light Bringer."

"Then perhaps we should send him to stand before Lucifer's throne." The Red angel glared at Dominik with hard eyes. "He allowed minions to come within a breath of his charge, well before the appointed time."

"But he destroyed them before they could do any harm," the Purple angel said. "The other engagements have been successful. He even discovered the cause of her stifled power, something none of us here were able to discern."

"Successful?" The Red twitched his wings and made a gesture to the vacant throne. "He's already allowed one travesty."

"That event was beyond his control," the Blue angel said, motioning to Dominik. "He doesn't wear the black wings. He can't circumvent free will, or take life on a whim."

"That is exactly my point," The Red angel bellowed. "Heralds will run roughshod over an advisor if given the chance, and wreak havoc on the tapestry." He slammed his fist into the arm of his throne. "Heralds need a firm hand!"

"But tempered with compassion," the Gold angel said. "Dominik, I think you will find a small gesture of kindness now and again will be useful."

"Kindness?" The Green angel laughed. "I wouldn't go that far. Heralds view such things with disdain."

The dispute raged on, much to Dominik's surprise. The Scriptures rarely discussed issues in the presence of others, and they certainly didn't argue. He couldn't imagine what caused the tension, but found the situation intriguing. He was getting an idea of which members he hadn't impressed, and a bit more insight into the group as a whole. He nearly smiled. Though the topic was far different, the debate could've been raging in any great hall throughout the realms.

"This will stop!" Cornelius stood and the group fell silent. "Dominik, what you just witnessed is the reason for our summons." He gestured to the empty throne. "Chi was our most powerful voice of wisdom and reason. Without her, this council is divided. Our decisions have been split many times and I fear it will get worse." He approached, and was tall enough to stand eye-to-eye with the angel. "We need her back. You must convince the Herald to exert her authority and deal with this. You understand what we're asking?"

"I do." Dominik met the eyes of the others, trying to detect a sign of dissent. On this issue, the Scriptures appeared to stand together. "I'll make every attempt to persuade her to this cause, but she refused to listen to me in a much smaller matter."

"Then you will find a way to make her listen." Cornelius placed a hand on Dominik's shoulder. "We know the request is unorthodox, and would never place such a burden on a fledgling Herald if not for the urgency of our situation. We chose you for a reason, and are confident you will guide her with success."

Cornelius cast his gaze to the others. One by one, each member of the Scriptures stood, even the Red angel, though he was the last to do so. Dominik was moved by the show of faith. He hoped to honor the trust placed in him.

"Remember," Cornelius said, "the birth of understanding is never without pain. The Herald will learn from this challenge, and so will you." He stepped closer and lowered his voice. "One more thing—sooner will be better than later." He jerked his head toward the rest of the group. "These angels are about to drive me into the fires. I'm close to resigning. I don't know how Chi managed to handle them for so long."

Dominik bowed from the neck. "I'll deal with the Herald tonight."

The problem was he didn't know how was going to accomplish that. He took to flight for a while, to clear his mind and consider the matter. He'd studied the Herald since the day she was born into flesh; she was not quick to accept demands, nor was she inclined to place stock in appeals for the greater good. She did, however, maintain a curious abhorrence to obligation and went to great lengths to avoid feeling indebted to anyone. That could be useful. Dominik circled the Expanse for a long while before finally touching down near one of the fountains.

A rooster from one of the trines wandered by, crowing at the top of his lungs. The proud creature had been making sure everyone knew the year belonged to him. It gave the angel a moment of amusement amidst his dark thoughts until he saw a woman on a bench nearby. Her face was a picture of anguish. A Green angel knelt by her side whispering soft words, and a man held her hand in comfort. Dominik saw another of his choir, Carmen, not far away.

"What's happened?"

"Her journey has been aborted," Carmen said. "Two hundred years of careful planning, wiped away." He placed his arms over his chest and looked down. "The one that was to be her mother failed to reach a marker." He regarded the woman. "She doesn't weep for herself —"

"But for the one who is lost on the journey," Dominik said. "Was it a new soul?"

"Not at all, but even the most experienced are falling to the challenges these days. We did the best we could, but the problem was too great for even our choir. The elders put in a request to the Heralds for assistance. They refused."

"Of course they did. Tyre was the only one who accepted appeals with any regularity; even then, it was on his particular terms." Dominik shook his head. "After what happened with him, the others have dug their heels in even harder than before."

"I never thought I'd say this, but I almost miss that arrogant black-winged bastard." Carmen raised a finger. "Almost, mind you. How are things going with the new one? Has she driven you to insanity?

"Not yet, but I think that might be her ultimate goal."

"Better you than me." Carmen slapped him on the shoulder and laughed. "You'll survive. Some of the choir is meeting on the combat level in a little while—you should join us. I could use a good sparring partner."

"I have a request from the Scriptures. I'm to convince the Herald to perform a duty I don't believe she's prepared to undertake. If I succeed, I'll meet you."

Carmen chuckled. "Even if you don't, still come. Training is an excellent way to burn off frustration."

Dominik bid farewell to his friend, lofted and enjoyed the feel of air beneath his wings. It was an interesting thing to him, that some angels chose never to fly, or rarely. He couldn't imagine why; he loved the freedom, the ability to see creation from a different perspective. He halted as an idea came to him. Perhaps the Herald would benefit from a different perspective, as well. He switched direction, preparing for transition to the human realm.

Chapter Twenty-Seven
Three Paragraphs

Rise felt an odd sense of familiarity when she pulled into Saint Anne's New Beginnings. She received a message letting her know the information she requested was ready. She was excited, nervous, but tried not to look either as she walked into the main entrance. She gave her name at the desk and waited for her own history to be handed over like a magnanimous gift from on-high.

She looked around. The place was ancient, with crumbling bricks and a choppy parking lot. She knew a little about the agency; it was built back in the 1950's to house girls that were 'in trouble' and whose families were too embarrassed to have them around. After giving birth, the girls went home in shame and the poor little babies were given away to proper families for a proper upbringing. That's what her parent's said, anyway. Rise thought the whole process sucked, especially since she was on the receiving end of the bullshit.

"Are you Jalynn?" A middle-aged woman walked toward her, hand extended. Her headdress marked her as a nun. "I'm Sister Margaret."

Rise forced a smile. She always felt slightly intimidated by the clergy. It was worse now, since she knew they were right all along in a few big areas. "I actually use my middle name now; Rise."

"I see. I have everything ready for you. We can go to my office."

Rise followed, took a seat and reached for the envelope handed her. It felt too light.

"It's very basic," the Sister explained. "I'm afraid we didn't have anything in the file about the alleged father."

Rise bristled at the casual use of the word 'alleged', but didn't think it was meant as an insult. Then again, maybe it was. In her experience, judgmental pricks were rampant in religion.

"I typed up a medical history," Sister Margaret continued, "and there is a general description of the birth mother. There isn't a great deal more I can offer, but I'd like to explain the procedure involved if you would like to know more. We can take your information, contact the other party, and if both sides consent, we can release identifying information."

Rise nodded. "Is there a form I need to fill out to get that started?"

The Sister nodded to the envelope. "It's included." She leaned forward and clasped her hands together on top of the desk. "Have you been thinking about finding your birth family for a long time?"

Rise was taken aback by the question. "Not really. Why?"

Sister Margaret closed her eyes briefly. "Adoptive children that come back to us all have personal reasons for their search. I see many grown men and women starting their own families and concerned with medical issues. Others are merely curious, which is natural, but you are so young..." She shook her head. "Have you considered all the consequences?"

"I don't understand," Rise said. "I just want to know. I think I have a right to know." The question offended her; she didn't want to explain, and it shouldn't be necessary. Many states would've allowed her to have the information when she turned eighteen, but Indiana clung to laws as archaic as they were unfair. Rise had to beg for scraps while the woman right across the desk was keeping all the answers tucked away in a file folder.

"Our rules aren't set up only for the birth families or adoptive parents," Sister Margaret explained. "My responsibility for the babies that come through here doesn't stop when they go to their new homes. If you decide to pursue the search, I will assist you within the bounds of my legal and moral obligation. However, I would recommend you take some time to think about your decision. Consider how you'll feel if the birth family declines the request to release information, or if they agree, and you don't like what you find."

Rise felt her indignation deflate. She hadn't considered those things; her request was spur-of-the-moment, prompted by the receipt for fifty thousand dollars.

"How much do you charge to adopt a baby?" Rise asked.

"This is a charitable institution," Sister Margaret said. "We rely on donations and certainly don't charge our families. Why do you ask?"

"Just curious," Rise said as she was getting up. "Thanks. I might be getting back with you."

It was a nice day, so she took a seat on a long bench under a tree near the parking lot. She braced herself, slid a finger under the flap of the envelope and peeled it open with great care. There were two pages; one was the consent for release of identifying information, the other was a short history, three paragraphs long. Rise felt her heart sink.

She read everything twice, cementing it to memory. Her birth mother—not named—had been seventeen, with European ancestry. The rest was nothing but a physical description and a few tidbits about the birth. The only interesting part was a notation stating the delivery had been medically assisted, which probably meant C-section.

She shoved everything back into the envelope, utterly disappointed. It wasn't much more than she already knew, nothing to help if she decided to search on her own, and not a single clue as to why she had an angel crawling up her ass. The entire endeavor had been a colossal waste of time.

"I need to sit myself down!"

Rise looked up, startled. An old woman, perhaps eighty or better, sat heavily on the opposite end of the bench. She had a green cane she clutched with gnarled hands, a wizened face and short, white hair. She peered at Rise over the top of thick glasses. "You with child, little girl?" she asked.

Rise almost said something smart until she remembered she was sitting outside an adoption agency. It was a legitimate question, under the circumstances. "No. I was adopted through here."

The woman nodded. "Oooh, you were here to see Sister Margaret, then. She's a Godly woman. She get you what you needed?"

Rise looked away, unaccustomed to perfect strangers coming up and talking to her, especially about something so personal.

"Oh, Lord have mercy, I forgot my manners," the woman said. "It's been happening more and more as the years go on by." Her speech was slow and measured, but she laughed robustly. "My name's Maebell Eileen Johnson. Everyone around here calls me Mother Mae Ei." She smiled, showing dentures that would never pass as real teeth.

"Mother? Are you a nun?"

"No, I had a different calling," Mother Mae said. "I married a man, going on sixty years now. We have seven children, thirteen grandchildren and five great-grandchildren." She reached down to pull up one of her stockings that had slipped down to her ankle. "One of them is acting like he's going to give me a great-great grandbaby before I die, running around like a peacock, chasing after girls."

"Do you work here?" Rise had no idea why she asked the question; she was ready to go home and shower.

"I worked here every day for many years," Mother Mae said. "Now I just come in from time to time and do what I can. We have four girls living here now. They want to get lazy, especially at the end. I have to get on them, make sure they keep moving; it's good for them, good for the babies."

She raised her head, and studied Rise's face. "What's your family name, child? I reckon I might remember you."

"I don't think so."

"If I held you, then I remember you. I remember all the babies." She huffed. "Wish I could say the same about my glasses."

Rise decided to humor the old lady. She told her name, and her parent's, too.

"Hawke…" Mother Mae's face crumpled up in thought. "Hawke…" She broke into a big smile. "You come in the springtime, didn't you? Round about eighteen years back, if this old memory is still working."

"Oh, my God, yes!"

"Don't take the Lord's name in vain, girl."

"Sorry," Rise said, cringing. "I just can't believe you know that. I turned eighteen on Easter Sunday this year."

"Easter," Mother Mae exclaimed, "the day our Lord rose from the dead. Oh, that's nice. A fine day to have a birthday. Yes, a real fine day."

"Did you know my…birth mother?" The words were foreign, uncomfortable.

"Now, you know I'm not supposed to tell you about that." Mother Mae peered over her glasses with a stern expression.

Rise looked away, and the old lady chuckled.

"That's okay because I've got nothing to tell. I never met your mama; she didn't live here. You were brought over by a Priest from Holy Trinity. I knew him; he baptized two of my grandchildren."

"Are you sure?" Rise couldn't imagine why she'd been in the custody of a priest.

"Oh, I'm sure on that. Let me think here. He did say your mama was a good student, I recall that." She looked over at Rise and shook a finger. "That's saying something because Holy Trinity keeps to a higher standard than these public schools nowadays."

Rise filed that away in her memory and leaned closer as Mother Mae continued this tale of her life.

"The day you came to us, I carried you right along here."
She pointed to the sidewalk with her cane. "You were a little,
wrinkled, pitiful thing. I think a rat might've been bigger."
She looked Rise up and down. "You're still scrawny, ain't
you?"

Rise shrugged. She'd actually put on a little weight.

"You were healthy, though, and that's all that mattered.
We kept you here in the nursery for two nights until your
parents come to claim you. Your new mama, her eyes lit up
when she saw you. Your daddy, though, Mr. James Hawke,"
she spat the name and grunted. "I come out with you in my
arms and he looked at me like my color was gonna rub right
off on his new baby." She laughed uproariously, and leaned
over close to Rise. "I gave you a kiss on your forehead before
they took you away, just to make him mad."

Rise put her hand over her mouth to stifle a laugh. James
Hawke never kept his views on racial matters a secret, at
least at home. Her arguments with him on the subject earned
Rise more than a few bruises over the years.

"Oh, look at them over there," Mother Mae said. Two
girls, both pregnant, stood on a little path between the main
office building and the dormitory. They were smoking,
scanning the area, clearly trying to hide. "This here is why
they still need me. Help me up." She got on her feet and gave
Rise a pat. "You take care. Maybe I'll see you again, now
that I've seen you again." She started up the walkway. "I see
you over there," she called out and both girls tossed down
their cigarettes. "Don't do that. You're in enough trouble
with me already. Pick up those butts. I already warned you
twice..."

Rise snickered. She enjoyed Mother Mae's spunk and
enjoyed her willingness to talk even more. The old woman
gave up more information than she realized and Rise
intended to make the most of her new clues. She whipped out
her phone and dialed the number for information. Her heart
pounded.

"Holy Trinity Catholic Church, please."

Chapter Twenty-Eight
Walk Fast and Carry a Folder

Rise waited in a middle pew of the church. She found the place easily enough, but the administrative office had already closed when she arrived. A woman saw her peering into the glass on the door and let her know if she needed to speak to someone, Father Paul was hearing confessions in the sanctuary until 7:30. Rise checked the time on her cell phone; she had another ten minutes.

She passed the time watching people as they disappeared into the small confessional. She made a game of trying to figure out which person had the most egregious admissions by noting the time they spent with the Priest, and how long they spent in prayer afterwards. So far, the woman kneeling in the front row was the clear winner. Either she was slow at reciting her Hail Mary's, or she had lots to atone for.

Other than those doing penance, there was one other gentleman. Rise watched as he lit three candles, in front of a statue of Mary. He prayed for a while, then placed a few dollars in the drop box before he left. Rise knew the payment wasn't obligatory, but it was a nice thing to do when offering up prayers. Candles aren't free, after all.

Rise heard movement and took a quick peek. The last man was going into the confessional. She hoped he wasn't going to recount every instance of deadly sinning. She checked the time again, sighed in boredom, and let her eyes wander. The sanctuary had impressive, stained glass windows depicting the Stations of the Cross. Her eyes fell on the resurrection scene, complete with trumpeting angels. They didn't look anything like Dominik; the ones in the glass were feminine, all dressed in white with slender wings. Rise would never have believed she would one day be in a position to critique the inaccuracies of angel renderings.

A little after 7:30, the sinner in the front made the sign of the cross and left. A few moments later, the last man emerged from the confessional and departed without doing his penance. He was probably going to do his praying on the drive home, and Rise didn't blame him; there was nothing wrong with multi-tasking. Finally, a young Priest emerged from the booth.

"Father," Rise said, catching his attention.

He pulled up his sleeve and looked at his watch.

Rise took the hint. "I'm not here for confession. I have a question about a baby."

"Are you a congregant?"

"I go to church down in Nineveh." She felt her face redden.

"I see. What can I do for you?"

"I was over at Saint Anne's today and I was referred to you. There was a student who went to school here about eighteen years ago. She gave a baby up for adoption."

Rise was proud of how casual she sounded. She spent the whole ride to the church figuring out ways she might be able to finagle some information. She had no idea if her birth mother had been a student here, but it was a solid guess, and Mr. Daly once told her if you walked fast and carried a folder, people always assumed you were working.

"Did Sister Margaret send you?" the Priest asked.

"I talked to her this afternoon." Truth, yes. Answering the question, not even close.

Father Paul considered. "I only know of one young woman. Her father is still a member of the parish and—" He froze, looking like he just slammed his car door shut with the keys inside. "You're playing me, aren't you?"

"No," Rise whispered and looked around.

"Yes, you are," he said. "I can't believe I fell for this. They warned us at Seminary about people like you." He raised his eyes skyward and muttered in what Rise now recognized as Latin.

"I'm sorry," she said. "I'll say ten rosaries tonight if I have to. You said the girl's father is a member?"

The Priest stared her down. "Look, I'm missing the Kentucky Indiana game and you…you need to pray." He balled his fists at his sides. "I need to pray, too, but you *really* need to pray, young lady."

Rise watched him leave and ran her hand through her hair in frustration. "Shit," she whispered, then looked at the crucifix mounted above the altar and spread her arms. "Sorry!"

CHAPTER TWENTY-NINE
BIG MISSION

Rise didn't get home until almost nine. She trudged up the stairs and flopped down on the loveseat. She intended to stay there the rest of the night, but as soon as her butt hit the cushions, she heard three loud raps at the door. She groaned.

Oliver bolted from the bedroom, wailing and circling. Rise forced herself to move, checked the peephole, and whipped open the door. Dominik stood there, his huge form almost blocking the whole doorway. She was surprised he knocked. She figured he could walk through walls if he wanted.

"Do I have to invite you in?" she asked.

"Angel," he said. "You're thinking of vampires. Come with me."

"I've had a long day."

"As have I. Come." He stood aside and motioned with his hand.

Rise picked up her keys and followed him from the building. Her legs felt like lead, her hand was hurting again, and the withdrawal symptoms were making her irritable. "I understand you're a Heavenly being," she said, "but can you try to materialize on days when I haven't been up since six in the morning?"

"I could, but I won't." Dominik looked down at her. "I'm not here for your convenience."

"Oh, I figured that out." He was doing his fast walk again and she jogged to catch up. "Why didn't you tell me about Saba?"

"Because I knew she would do so with great haste. I won't waste valuable time telling you things you can learn from another."

Rise didn't like his tone, which was definitely curt. "Then tell me something no one else knows. Like why you're here. Why do I have an angel hanging around all of a sudden?"

"I'm here to give you advice," he said, glaring down at her, "and warnings you choose to ignore."

Rise felt color in her cheeks. He couldn't know about her decision to move in with Danny. Or maybe he could. She peered at him with suspicion. "Are you spying on me?"

"Quite regularly, yes."

Rise wasn't expecting the truth and stood perplexed for a moment, then felt a little sick to her stomach. She tried to think back, and hoped she hadn't done anything potentially embarrassing. "Do you watch me in the bathroom?" She hated to ask, but wanted to know.

"I have no interest in your private moments. My concerns lie elsewhere."

Rise hoped that meant no. She trailed a few paces behind, so she could give her new stalker a thorough scan without him knowing. He sported a different duster tonight, a black one with military style boots that matched. His hair was in a thick braid and he wore a weird necklace with a glowing pendant. He looked very put together and she looked exactly like a person that had been in the same clothes for fifteen hours. Totally unfair.

"Where are we going?" she asked. The angel was taking a circuitous route through the complex and his strides and posture projected urgency.

"A duty has been requested of you."

Rise smiled, excited at getting some more information. "You're saying we're going on a mission for God?"

"For the Scriptures."

Rise looked down at the bracelet on her arm, remembering they were the black dot in the white. "There is a God, though, right?"

"Faith can be a greater asset than certainty."

"I see what you did there." Rise looked up at him "You're side-stepping the question."

"Perceptive."

"I have my moments. So, can you fly? You never answered that."

"You have seen my wings."

Rise laughed. "You just did it again, and I know lots of things with wings that can't fly. An ostrich can't fly, or penguins. Turkeys—"

"Yes, Learned One. I can fly."

She thought he might've smiled for a second. "Can I see?"

"You will very soon; I've decided we won't be taking a vehicle tonight."

Rise wondered about the logistics of traveling with an angel. "What are you going to do with me? Put me on your back?"

Dominik scowled. "I am not a pack mule."

They passed through the little park in the back of the apartments. The slide and swings were in a state of disrepair and rarely used. The benches served as sleeping areas for transients when the weather was warm; a few were strung around, one nearby. The man smelled strongly of alcohol, his clothes were filthy, and Rise turned up her nose and made a gagging sound.

Dominik didn't miss her reaction. "Would you feel differently if you knew the wife who shared his bed for twenty years died a long and painful death? That he gave up a successful career so he could care for her in the final months?"

"Is that what happened to him?" Rise turned back to the man and her expression softened.

Dominik let the moment linger. "Or perhaps he fell to the lure of hard drink and games of chance and abandoned his wife while she was heavy with child." He watched Rise's face. "Your disgust returns. How easily you allow yourself to be led." He continued walking and Rise didn't budge.

"Which is it?" she called after him. "Or were you just trying to make me feel like an ass?"

"It's neither." Dominik looked over his shoulder. "And yes."

She caught up with him. "You don't like me very much, do you?" She wasn't surprised he didn't answer.

They passed two men carrying flashlights; red armbands marked them as neighborhood watch volunteers. They recognized Rise from the news reports, shook her hand and thanked her over and over for her bravery. She offered a civil smile, but didn't say anything. The men took her silence for embarrassment at the attention. They gave a good-natured laugh, thanked her once more, and moved on.

Rise could feel Dominik's eyes on her. She didn't meet them.

"A polite response to their gratitude would've involved speaking," he said.

"I never claimed to be polite. Besides, I'm not sure how to feel about that mess anymore." She started walking again, though she had no idea where to go.

"No longer basking in pride, are you?"

Rise clenched her eyes and fought the urge to punch him in the face. "No, smart-ass, I'm no longer *basking in pride* for helping save that little girl." She looked down. "Not since I figured out the whole thing was my fault."

The angel grunted. "You assume her abduction was prompted by the item you donated to the community sale."

Rise whipped her head up. "How do you know about that?" She slapped her hands together. "Right, because you're watching me every chance you get. Is there anything you *don't* know?"

"There's a great deal I don't know," Dominik admitted, "but one thing I do know is over a dozen umbrellas were donated to that sale by an anonymous party. Had the child not chosen yours, she would've found another, and the results would've been the same." He allowed the words to register before continuing. "The belief that your actions alone orchestrated those events is borne of ignorance, arrogance, and is as misplaced as your previous pride."

Rise stared at the angel with a crazy mix of emotions. Dominik mocked her, insulted her, and still managed to make her feel better. She didn't know whether to thank him or yank out a few feathers. She decided to do both, verbally.

"Well, I guess it's good to know I wasn't responsible for what happened." That was as close to thanks as he was getting. She switched to attack. "You have no right to lecture me. You're an angel and you did nothing, absolutely nothing, when that truck went into the pond. You're still on my list for that."

"In that case, you should know that you are on my 'list' as well." He headed off without another word.

Rise trudged behind him into a dark, secluded area of the park. The angel knelt, removed his jacket and folded it into the backpack. His blue-silver wings tucked tight against his back and Rise was again fascinated. She was dying to know what they felt like. She crept closer, reached out, and when her fingers were within inches of a feather, Dominik stopped her.

"I told you not to touch those. Stop trying."

Rise stuck her tongue out when he turned away. She vowed to get hands on them at some point.

Dominik removed an odd device from his pack; a harness, similar to what a skydiver might wear. He maneuvered the contraption over his shoulder, fastened the buckles, then motioned to Rise.

"Come."

Rise understood what he was planning, and felt a wave of excitement mingled with a healthy dose of terror. "I guess this is a tandem flight?"

In answer, Dominik grabbed her and pulled her close so her back was against his chest. He secured the harness around her. She shivered when he clicked the buckle below her breast.

She twisted her head to look at him. "Do you do this a lot?"

"First time." Dominik gave a quick tug on the straps to check the strength. "I was fortunate to come across this device in a second hand store; easily modified for our purpose."

"It's used?" The contraption did indeed appear well worn. Perhaps a little too well worn.

"The clerk assured me of its safety."

"Oh, well if the sales guy told you…"

A great rush of wind whipped her hair into her eyes as Dominik spread his wings, expanding them to full breadth. He placed one arm firmly around her waist and launched into the night sky. Her heart froze and her stomach flipped like she was on a carnival ride. She clutched the angel's arm with both hands, squeezed her eyes shut, and couldn't stop the little squeak escaping her lips. Her loose work pants fluttered around her ankles. She hoped she didn't lose a shoe.

After a few moments of ascent, it felt like Dominik reached cruising altitude. She opened her eyes one at a time, amazed at how far up they'd flown. Buildings looked like dollhouses, and intersecting streets created a maze far below. The clear night enveloped her, all sounds of vehicles and voices and other worldly distractions disappeared. The only sound was Dominik's wings as they moved against the air in steady, powerful strokes. She concentrated on the rhythm and before long, she loosened the death-grip on his arm. She decided to enjoy the ride, not even caring where they were heading anymore.

"This is amazing," she said.

She pressed the back of her head against the angel's shoulder and looked up. She saw the moon and the stars, and her breathing slowed as she drifted into a sense of freedom she'd never before experienced. She closed her eyes again, this time in bliss, and enjoyed the feel of the air on her face.

"I feel like I could stay like this forever," she said. "Does everyone become an angel when they die?"

"Not everyone." Dominik's voice was right in her ear. His breath on her neck sent a shudder up her spine.

"Do you think you can pull some strings for me?" She turned her face to his, as much as she could. "I definitely want wings." She felt his chest move when he chuckled. Something inside her unraveled and she relaxed into the moment, closing her eyes in euphoric bliss. She'd never felt so free.

"You're at peace," Dominik whispered. "Hold onto that, look down and tell me if the world appears different."

Rise peered beyond her dangling feet, past the buildings, billboards and other fabricated things that now looked obscene in their existence. She wasn't sure what she was supposed to see, but then little spots of color started to pop up and her eyes grew wide.

"Lights," she breathed. Tiny pinpricks of color—blue and green, purple, red and yellow—peppered the ground below her, moving here and there. "Are these coming from people?" Rise pressed the bounds of the harness to attempt a better look. Dominik had chosen quite right in bringing the thing; she would've wiggled out of his arms if he'd been carrying her.

"It's the light within." Dominik spoke with reverence, like he was imparting a great secret. He came to a halt and hovered, his impressive wings moving forward and back, whooshing the air. He spread his hands and made a sweeping gesture. "These souls are all on a journey."

Rise was captivated. "What do the different colors mean?"

"It represents the focus of the journey, the primary challenge to be overcome. You will come to understand, in time."

"How are you doing this to me?"

"I'm not," Dominik said. "You've had the ability to see into the soul for some time now, but your senses were dulled.

You're a little behind, so we have some catch-up work ahead of us."

"Dulled?"

"Science and medicine are extraordinary, but when abused, it can serve to alter a perception that should not be impeded."

Rise thought about that, and the light-switch in her brain flipped on. "My crazy pills?" She made a face. "I mean, my prescriptions?"

"I would warn against taking such things." He took hold of her chin and turned her face so he could look into her eyes. "This time, you will listen to me."

"No problem." Rise flicked her gaze across the lights, astounded at what she'd been missing. "I don't understand. How can I see this?"

"Every creature is bestowed gifts. Some are more flashy than others, but all are designed to assist the soul on their path to ultimate purpose." He bent close her ear. "And before you think to ask what your purpose entails, don't."

She was having too much fun to debate the point. She almost wished she were still on speaking terms with her parents; she would love to tell them they were wrong. Long ago, she mentioned seeing lights, and the next day her mother hauled her off to the doctor who said it was a visual disturbance, even suggesting there might be some brain damage from the 'fall' into the table. Rise never believed that, but her parents did. She argued, they deemed her irrational and combative, and put her on meds to 'control' her defiance. She snickered. The drugs might've killed the lights, but never made a dent in her attitude.

Dominik started flying again, and Rise loved every second. The turns were great fun, but the descent was a little frightening and she grabbed his arm again as he took them down. They landed in the backyard of a residence. A child's swing-set and other toys littered the ground. A good-sized dog on a chain barked a few times until Dominik held up a hand. The dog quieted, tilted his head, and his cropped nub of a tail started to wag furiously.

"Neat trick," Rise said. "I need to learn that one. It would come in handy at the clinic."

Dominik unlatched the harness and placed it back in the knapsack. He headed toward the back door of the house. The backyard pressed up against a row of large trees and no other homes were nearby. Rise watched Dominik insert a little piece of metal into the lock and the door popped open.

"What are you doing?" She looked around, worried. "Does somebody live here?" She had no idea what the angel was up to, but it looked a whole lot like breaking and entering.

"Come." He stepped inside and motioned for her to follow. His tone made it clear it wasn't a request.

Rise stepped inside with tremendous hesitation. The house was dark and silent. She followed Dominik, doing her best to be silent. New toys, big balloons and bags of candy were everywhere. It looked to be the remains of a child's party.

The living room split into two hallways. Dominik took the one to the right and stopped in front of a door with small pink handprints imprinted against the wood. He opened the door, and stood aside so Rise could enter. She hesitated, but remembered they were on some kind of a mission and gathered her courage. She stepped forward and saw a little bundle under a mound of blankets in the canopy bed. She started to back out, but Dominik blocked her path.

"Look at her," he said, pointing to the sleeping girl. "Go."

Rise waved her hands, surprised at his use of a normal voice. "You're going to wake her up."

Dominik placed his hand on Rise's neck and marched her to the bed. He tossed back the blankets, but the girl didn't flinch. Her chest rose and fell in sound sleep. Rise peered down at the little face on the pillow and her eyes went wide with recognition.

"That's Keisha Williams!" She was louder than intended and slapped her hands over her mouth. She wiggled away from Dominik and stood against the wall in panic. "What are we doing here?" She did little more than mouth the words.

"You wanted to know why I didn't assist you the day she was abducted. Examine her light. Tell me what you see."

"It's gold." Rise thought back to the flight. The other glows were different, more colorful.

"That is the sign of a soul that has taken on a journey of sacrifice," Dominik said. "It is a rarity, a mark worthy of great respect. Touch her, and you'll understand."

Rise shook her head, but the angel grabbed her arm and pulled her to her knees beside the bed. She struggled as he forced her hand against Keisha's arm. Now that she was close, she could see the light didn't surround Keisha, but resonated from the inside. It was beautiful.

"Look beyond the flesh," Dominik said. "Concentrate on the light, see into the soul."

Rise bit her lip and stared at the golden glow, not blinking. She thought about movies she'd seen and attempted to mimic the actions of superheroes who could control things with their mind. Nothing happened. She felt like an idiot.

"You have the ability," Dominik said. "Embrace it."

Rise breathed in deeply and tried to regain the feeling she experienced when flying. She recalled the stillness, the wind in her face, and felt a warm rush in her chest, expanding outward. A darkness intruded on her peace, starting at the edge of her vision and tunneling inward until nothing remained except a pinprick of golden light, moving farther and farther away. Every nerve in her body flickered, a sound burst in her ears like a breaking balloon, and everything changed.

Rise knew she was physically still in the bedroom, but also knew part of her was somewhere else. Visions flooded her mind like broken images on an old projector. She saw Mrs. Williams and Keisha as they were perhaps a year before, walking in a park. Others image arrived; Keisha as a toddler with her mother swinging her by the arms in play, Mrs. Williams holding a newborn baby in her arms. Rise understood time was going in reverse, and when she thought she'd come to the end of the mental slideshow, she saw two women sitting on a white bench in front of an enormous fountain. Neither of them looked familiar, but somehow Rise *knew* it was Keisha and her mother.

"I can't ask you to do this, Chi," the woman who would be Natalie Williams said. "It's too much."

"You're ready for this challenge," Chi said. "I want to help you."

"The Scriptures needs you. They won't let you go."

"I'm sure they can manage. It will only be a short time, even in human years."

Mrs. Williams looked away. "What if I fail?"

Chi laughed. "You say that every journey, and every time you advance by leaps and bounds. I wouldn't make the offer if I thought the risk was too great."

"It will be so horrible for you—"

"But it's my choice. It's my gift to you." Chi took the woman's hands. "Allow me to do this. There's only one thing I'd ask. If possible, I'd prefer to coordinate things so I can be born under Virgo's influence." She waved a hand. "Not the scorpion again—that never did work out. Believe me, you won't want the tantrums."

The women shared a hug and the vision faded away. Rise hopped up and looked to Dominik with wide eyes. "Was that real?" She switched between looking at Keisha and the angel.

"It was."

"They knew each other. They planned this whole thing." She looked at Dominik for confirmation and he nodded. "They had other lives?"

"Yes."

She put a hand to her forehead. "I can't believe the Buddhists are right."

"A discussion for another time." He pointed to Keisha. "The soul trapped in that body is the speaker of the Scriptures. They want her back and you will give her to them."

"What do you mean 'want her back'?"

"She was never meant to survive that abduction," Dominik said. "That was her final exit point from life and now she's on an uncharted path. The minions will sense this and attack her without mercy. If she falls to them, the loss will be devastating. Her soul needs to be released."

"Are you saying we're supposed to kill her?" She could barely form the words. "That's the big mission?"

"Not 'we'. You alone must be the one to do this." He reached into the knapsack, pulled out a syringe filled with a clear liquid and held it out.

"No way," Rise said. "If this is so important, you do it. You're the angel."

"I haven't been granted the power to take life and, aside from that, I wasn't the one that took her from her path. *You* did, and *you* will set it right."

"I didn't know!" Rise tried to sound as indignant as she could while still whispering. "I thought I was helping her."

The angel cocked an eyebrow. "Are you familiar with the phrase 'ignorance of the law is not a defense'?"

"Are you familiar with the phrase 'life in prison'? What am I going to say? An angel told me to do it? I'm sure judges never hear that one."

"Your hand in this will not be known." Dominik slapped the syringe into her palm. When he spoke, he enunciated each word. "Give her back to us."

Rise gritted her teeth and looked at the deadly concoction in her hand. She knew how to give an injection, thanks to her job at the clinic. She knelt beside the bed, and looked up at Dominik. "I swear, if I go to hell and become a minion for this, you're the first one I'm coming for!"

Rise tried to control the shaking in her hands, still in disbelief at what she was about to do. She positioned the syringe on Keisha's arm and held her breath while she punctured the skin. The little girl didn't move. She injected the drug, whatever it was, and stood. The moment was surreal.

As Keisha's breathing slowed, the gold light became brighter, larger, and finally burst from her chest and formed a radiant ball hovering in the air. Rise watched in fascination as the light took the form of the woman in the vision. At the same instant, another angel arrived, this one with glorious golden wings. Rise backed into a corner. The little bedroom had become cramped with the supernatural.

The Gold angel waggled a finger and smiled. "You're late, Chi."

"Am I?" Chi glanced around, her eyes falling on the little body in the bed. "Well, I can't be too far off; the age is right." She reached down and touched one of the braids like she was handling a cherished keepsake. "What happened? We charted so carefully, we even had safeguards in place to ensure the event went as planned."

Dominik and the Gold angel both turned to Rise. She held up a tentative hand.

"That was my fault," she said. "Sorry." She wondered if she should curtsey; she didn't know spiritual protocols. Rise fumbled on, trying to explain how she unwittingly tried to damn the woman's soul.

Chi listened in amused silence, placed a hand to her mouth, and looked Rise up and down. "My, how lovely you've become, and already causing some trouble, are you?" She turned to Dominik. "Problems?"

He smiled at her. "Let's just say I've missed your counsel."

"We should go," the Gold angel said. "We went through some trouble to get you back. We wouldn't want you to become a Free Spirit." He held out his hand, Chi took it and they disappeared.

Rise followed Dominik, leaving the house the same way they entered. He started to get the harness from the pack, but she stopped him. "I'm going to walk. I need to think." She felt a desperate need to get away.

"That wouldn't be wise." He pointed to the bracelet on her wrist; the glow had increased a small amount. A buzzing sound interrupted them. Dominik reached into his pack and pulled out a sleek cell phone.

Rise raised her eyebrows. "You have a cell phone?"

"I keep it on vibrate while I'm working." He looked at the number flashing on the screen and slid open the phone with one hand. "Saba," he said and starting talking in another language.

"Tell her I say hi." Rise headed across and down the sidewalk. She only made it about a block before Dominik intercepted her, touching down heavily in her path.

"I thought we agreed you wouldn't walk."

"No," Rise said, "you said it would be unwise for me to walk. That's an opinion, not an agreement." Since the angel showed no signs of moving, Rise went around him.

Dominik took her arm and spun her around until her back was against him. She tried to push away, but he whipped the harness on her and grabbed her around the waist. He bolted into the air before she could figure out the best words to insult him. She was getting tired of being manhandled, even if the handler was a good-looking angel.

"Where are we going?" They were heading in the opposite direction of her apartment, and she could feel the tension in Dominik, even through her clothes. "What's wrong?"

"Kafi requires my aid."

"What happened?" Rise shouted to be heard over the whoosh of the wings; they were pounding away, faster and stronger than before.

"A problem I will deal with." He became quiet for a moment. "You did well tonight, Rise."

She didn't know to respond. It was the first time he'd come close to saying something kind. It might have been a compliment, but she wasn't sure she deserved it.

"I killed someone," she said. "I don't care what the reason was; I still stuck a needle in a girl's arm and killed her."

"It upsets you. Understandable."

"No." Rise leaned her head back, letting it fall against the angel's shoulder. "It upsets me that it doesn't." She was quiet for a long while. "I think I'm broken."

Dominik didn't say anything, but Rise thought he held her a little tighter.

Chapter Thirty
Game On

Saba flung the door open when Dominik and Rise arrived, and it slammed against the stopper on the wall. The sound blended with the ruckus behind her.

"What's going on?" Rise could hear glass breaking and what sounded like furniture being tossed around.

"I'm sorry you have to see him like this," Saba said, then turned her attention to Dominik. "I didn't know what else to do, so I called."

"You were right to do so."

Kafi stumbled from the kitchen looking disheveled. He wore hospital scrub pants and a tee shirt tucked in on one side. He was barefoot and glossy eyed.

Kafi held his arms out in a welcoming gesture. "The angel arrives!" His words were ragged around the edges. "Saba, get our friends a drink. You, the important one, do you like bourbon?"

"I'm not old enough to drink," Rise said.

"And I'm a faithful Muslim. I won't tell if you won't."

Dominik turned to Saba. "This isn't the first time, is it?"

She shook her head, looking apologetic. "No."

Kafi left to the kitchen and started pouring dark liquor into a short glass. The angel took both and dumped everything into the sink. Kafi moaned, watching it disappear.

"We discussed this," Dominik said. "You cannot allow yourself to fall to temptation."

"Or what, I'll go from my path?" Kafi fell against the wall and wavered a finger at the angel. "I already did that, remember?"

"But you're not lost, not yet, and believe me there are those that would see it otherwise. You must remain diligent." Dominik caught him as he started to fall. "What's caused this?"

"Aunt Mura called tonight," Saba answered, then looked at Rise. "She has dementia. She was having a bad day."

"Sorry," Rise whispered.

"Aunt Mura speaks to me like I'm still a child." Kafi's chin lolled to his chest. "She talks about Saba, tells me we should go back to Pakistan to visit her. The only person in the whole world who still speaks to me of my sister." He clenched his eyes. "Aunt Mura wants to see me, and I can't give her that small comfort."

"I told him he should go." Saba looked to her brother. "I'll be fine for a few days. I have my movies, and now I even have a friend." She smiled unabashed at Rise.

"I made a vow to an angel," Kafi said, staring hard at Dominik. "Didn't I? I went from my path. Now I'm cursed."

"Your path was taken from you."

Kafi laughed, pushed Dominik away and slapped his hands against his chest. "Some people might think my life is a blessing. I came from nothing, nothing! I went to school, I excelled." His voice rose, but not in anger. "I got a scholarship to medical school—"

"Pride," Dominik said in a warning tone.

"Don't lecture me of pride." Kafi wandered into the great room and the others followed like a parade. He whirled and held up a hand. "Okay, the last time you talked about pride, you were right. I admit, I shouldn't have posted photos of Betty on the Internet. That was bragging..."

"Who's Betty?" Rise whispered to Saba.

"His Jeep Wrangler."

"...but this is truth!" Kafi continued. "I worked hard! My Uncle, may he rest in peace, and Aunt Mura, they raised me.

They fed me, clothed me...." He went on, listing everything he'd ever been given as a child, right down to a video game system and designer jeans. "...and now I'm a doctor. Some would think this path is pretty good!"

Dominik stood with arms crossed over his chest, not speaking.

"But what do I have?" Kafi asked. "I have an angel asking me favors. Kafi, I need you to go here. Kafi, I need you to go there. Kafi, I need you to patch up this person, or that person. I need you to steal drugs from the hospital where you work, the hospital that pays you so you can support your sister...." He looked at Saba and his voice gentled. "Allah is praised for that." He glared back at Dominik. "Maybe if I lose my license, I'll get my path back. Is that the plan?"

The angel looked like a coiled serpent prepared to strike; even his wings were tense. "I'd like to speak to Kafi in private."

Rise exhaled in relief; she was anxious to get away from the emotional scene. She followed Saba out the back door and onto an impressive wooden deck surrounded by a heart-stopping array of exotic flowers, colorful shrubbery and waves of decorative grasses. Tiny strands of lights in vibrant hues weaved through the foliage, the flickering bursts of color adding a mesmerizing touch to the garden. Rise felt like she had stepped into paradise.

"Saba, this is..." She shook her head, unable to find words to accurately describe the beauty. "I've never seen anything like this."

Saba beamed. "Nature did the hard part, but thank you." She tilted her head. "How did you and Dominik get here so fast? I didn't see a car."

Rise grinned. It was Saba's turn to be amazed. "Check this out. We flew."

"Oh, what was that like?" Saba jumped up and down in excitement. "Tell me!"

"It was...awesome." She looked up at the stars, remembering the feeling. Then she heard Kafi's voice, loud.

He was talking in Arabic and Dominik was answering him in the same language, and volume. Oddly, Rise thought she could understand a few of the words. "What are they fighting about?"

Saba listened for a moment and closed her eyed in frustration. "They're arguing scripture."

"Your brother is arguing scripture? With an angel?"

Saba waved her hand. "It's not the first time. Let me show you my garden." Saba hopped off the deck in between two of the rose bushes. "I have tomatoes now."

Rise followed her, being careful as they got further from the small light on the porch. The ground was uneven and sloped.

"Kafi never used to drink," Saba said. "He's faithful, but the situation with Aunt Mura…it's wearing on him."

Rise understood Saba felt obligated to defend her brother and explain his actions. "I'm not in a position to judge anybody, believe me." She could still see the life draining from little Keisha. She realized she and Kafi had something in common. They were both killers, though neither of the victims seemed to be holding a grudge.

"Kafi says he was never supposed to go to medical school." She adjusted her pink headscarf a little. "According to Dominik, he was supposed to have a different life. I don't understand how that can be. Kafi has talked of nothing but being a doctor for as long as I can remember." She looked at Rise hopefully. "Has the angel told you anything?"

"Nope," Rise said. "I'm definitely on a need-to-know basis."

Saba's face fell. "I was taught that angels would only appear to mankind at the end of times. And those that had not followed Allah would despair the day. I think Kafi believes this is true."

"Do you?"

"I don't know. Oh, here are the tomatoes." She reached down and popped a few from the vine. "Do you want one? I don't spray them with chemicals. I'm trying to go green."

"Me, too," Rise said. "I have a bunch of those reusable bags, but I never remember to bring them from the car into the store, so I end up carrying as much as I can in my purse and my hands. Last week I dropped canned pears all over the parking lot."

Saba laughed and took a bite of the tomato. "I'm happy to have someone to talk to, even when it's not about matters of cosmic importance. That reminds me; I have a necklace for you in the house. It's silver and long, just as you commanded." She winked. "The mall was glorious. Kafi followed me around for hours. We ate at the food court and I had the most wonderful cinnamon roll."

Rise plucked off a tomato and held it up to her face. It was hard to see in the dark and she didn't want to bite into a bug. Then a foul smell hit her, hard.

"Did something die out here?" She winced as the odor became stronger, then her eyes went wide. She knew that smell. "Run!"

It was too late. A pair of females minions came at her, a male heading toward Saba. Rise was assailed from both sides, knocked down, then snatched up and held by her arms and legs. She was astonished at the unnatural strength her enemies possessed.

"You got her?" the red-haired minion asked the blonde.

Rise kicked and pulled and bucked, and managed to disentangle from her attackers. She flailed in the grass, the minions grabbing at her. She risked a glance at Saba. The young woman had trouble running in her flowing pants and tripped. The minion pursuing her brought his foot down toward her face, but Saba grabbed his leg, pulled him off his feet and rolled into a low crouch with one leg out. The move was graceful like a dancer, and when the minion came for her again, Saba dropkicked him in the head, letting out a mighty scream as she did so. He went down, and Saba whacked him a few more times for good measure.

"Run," Rise screamed, still fighting her own battle. "That's a real command this time!" The minions had her again, one holding each of her arms and trying to drag her across the yard. She jerked hard and thought she dislocated something, but succeeded in freeing one arm. She twisted around and scratched the red-haired woman's face. She felt flesh and blood pile under her fingernails. The attack worked; the lost soul, minion, or whatever she was hadn't lost her vanity. She wailed and patted her bloodied face with both hands trying to ascertain the damage.

"Let it go, you look fine," the blonde one said. "Max!" she called into the darkness, but it was no use. He was curled up and moaning. It was clear where at least one of Saba's strikes landed. Blondie cursed and whipped out a knife.

Rise saw the flash of the blade and everything else disappeared. She was still on her back, but rolled right and left, evading the furious slashes coming at her. The minion brought her weapon straight down in a two-handed grip. Rise flung her hands up with all her might and captured the minion's wrists, keeping the blade in place mere inches from her heart. It was a battle of will and strength, and Rise knew she was on the losing end of one of them.

Saba ran, bellowing all the way, and leaped directly onto the blonde's back.

"I meant run the other way!" Rise didn't realize she had to specific with commands, but that didn't matter now. The minion wasn't expecting the attack, her hold on the weapon loosened, and Rise was able to wrest it away.

Even with Saba on her back, the blonde continued to fight and the battle became a tangle of arms and legs with Rise still on the bottom. She didn't want to risk stabbing Saba and wasn't about to allow the minion to regain the blade, so she threw it as far as she could and concentrated on getting to her feet.

Saba grabbed two handfuls of hair and started to shake back and forth until the minion's teeth could be heard clanking around in her mouth. The blonde had to let go of Rise or risk her head being torn off; Saba was in compete battle mode.

Rise stood and faced the enraged redhead who had stopped fretting over her face. She pulled out her own knife, but Rise dodged every blow coming at her. She had no idea where the skill was coming from; she spun and fought like she had been training her whole life. She landed a powerful blow, the minion dropped and she turned back to Saba.

Saba was on her back, the blonde sitting atop her chest. The minion was crazed. She spit and cursed, and her head whipped around like she was in the middle of an exorcism. From the little Rise knew of these minions, she didn't think that was a half-bad idea. The blonde twisted her fingers into Saba's throat.

Rise spotted a large decorative boulder in the garden. She held it with both hands over the minion's head, but hesitated.

"Hit her," Saba choked.

Rise looked at Saba, then at the rock in her hand.

"Hit her." Saba was turning blue.

Rise brought the full weight of the rock onto the blonde head and she fell, not moving. Rise couldn't tell if the minion was knocked out or dead until she shattered. She blew out a long breath. That was the second time she killed in one night.

Saba held her throat and gasped for air. "Why did you wait so long? Crisis of conscious?"

"Crisis of political correctness. I didn't want to traumatize you."

Saba laughed as much as she could. "I'm going to say this once, so we don't have this problem again." She coughed and gagged. "The next time someone is trying to kill me, crush her skull. I have closure on my death."

Rise was drenched in sweat, her muscles trembled, but she was on her feet. The same couldn't be said for the surviving minions; they crawled around, moaning from their wounds. Rise snatched up a discarded blade and bounced it around in her hand, impressed. "This is perfect. The balance is amazing." She didn't have a clue how she knew such a thing; she'd never held a weapon like that in her life.

Saba stared at her with wide eyes. "Does this happen all the time?"

"No, but I'm already sick of this shit."

"What do they want with you?"

"I'm about to find out." Rise saw Dominik destroy a minion without hesitation, so she didn't think it was much of a sin to kill the creatures. It was *game on.* She strode over to the one called Max and plunged the blade through his back, ignoring Saba's shocked scream. That was three now and she wasn't the least bit guilty.

The last minion was on her hands on knees. Rise stood behind her, yanked her head back by the hair and shoved the knife against her throat. "Why are you coming after me?" She pulled the blade across the skin, enough to inflict pain. "Tell me!"

The minion clenched her teeth. "I want my freedom."

"What does that have to do with me?"

The minion struggled to speak. Her lips moved, but no sound escaped, as though an unseen hand was crushing her windpipe. Rise stared into woman's eyes and shook her. "I swear if you don't answer me I'll cut your head off!"

"I can't," the minion whispered. "I…can't…"

Rise quaked with fury. "Bitch!" Keeping a grip on the red hair, she sliced open the minion's neck and watched as black sludge poured from the wound, taking any hope of answers with it.

She heard the back door slide open and the debate team sprinted into the yard. Kafi went straight for his sister and pulled up the sleeves on her shirt, looking for injuries. Dominik headed toward Rise, but stopped short at the sight of her standing over the limp body and holding the blood-soaked knife. He locked eyes with her, his expression somewhere between horror and pride, and didn't move until the minion turned to shards.

The angel surveyed the scene. "How many?"

"Three," Rise said, dropping the weapon. "We didn't have time to get away."

"They were after her," Saba said. "I think they were trying to kidnap her."

"They would've gotten me, but Saba beat one down and jumped on another."

Kafi glanced around in shock, looking like he sobered up fast. "Saba, you did this?"

"But Rise killed them all." Some tension faded from her face and she broke into a grin. "You boys missed a great girl fight."

Rise chuckled. "Complete with hair-pulling and scratching."

"But how?" Kafi demanded, shaking his head.

Saba put her headscarf back in order. "What do you think I do all day at home?" She struck a kung fu pose. "Bruce Lee, disk seven! And you should've seen Rise; she fought like a lioness. It was amazing!"

The girls looked at one another and fell into a hug. They giggled and danced around, each insisting the other was the better fighter. Rise couldn't believe what she was feeling. The battle left her tingling, and it was more than a rush of adrenaline. It was an awakened sense of power, of ultimate conquest. It must've been written all over her face because the angel watched her every move with a troubled expression.

Dominik turned to Kafi. "Take your sister into the house and make sure she's unharmed." He gathered up the minion blades and pulled a small lighter from the pocket of his jeans. He set the weapons ablaze, keeping a respectful distance from Saba's garden. He found a rake and pushed the glass pieces into the fire as well.

Rise didn't move to help. She was still riding the wave of battle victory, and since she did the hard part, Dominik could take care of the clean-up.

"You came through unscathed," he said as he worked. "You appear to have both fortune and skill in your favor."

"That's four by the way, if you're keeping count," she said. "I've killed four people today."

"You released one soul in peril, and destroyed three minions that would've returned and shown you no mercy." He paused a moment. "Though, from what I witnessed, your actions were driven by anger more than defense."

"If they would've come back for me, what difference does it make?"

Dominik stood close, his wings flickered in the firelight. The flames lit up the area and the melting glass created a strange smell wafting upward with the smoke. "Have you been keeping up with your physical regimen?"

She looked away. She'd been blowing off her daily workouts more and more lately, and it was already creating some guilty feelings. Leave it to the angel to poke a stick at that sore spot. "I've been busy. Haven't had time."

"Make time."

"When, exactly, am I supposed to do that? In between my job, and sleep, and taking up an art, and learning a language, and getting attacked?"

The frustration that had been building up came to the fore and Rise didn't even try to keep it contained. She smashed a tomato by her foot, found a few more and did the same, then whirled on the angel and spat words like bullets. "You expect me to do all these things, but you won't even tell me why." She stood right in front of him, challenge in her posture, fury in her eyes. "I am about one more cloak-and-dagger-bullshit-demand away from telling you where you can shove your warnings, your advice, your dusty old books and your stupid candle. *This is not fair!*"

Dominik stared hard at her. "You have no concept of fairness, apart from your desire to have your own way. I suggest you put that notion from your head, because despite what you believe, the realms will not cater to your whims, and neither will I."

She clenched her fists, trembling with anger at his words and lack of control over her own life. "I don't like this one bit. And I don't think I like you, either."

"There is nothing about our duties that necessitates like or dislike. You have your purpose and I have mine. That's the end of the matter. Go inside, and remove your shoes so you don't sully the carpet with stains from your tantrum."

Rise wanted to punch him, but opted to say a few words normally reserved for special occasions. She stomped back to the house, kicked off her shoes on the porch and slammed the door. She stood seething.

Saba was wary. "Are you okay?"

"I hate him," she said. "You'd think he'd be happy we weren't killed, but no. All he wants to do is lecture me."

"Does he think you did wrong?"

"Not exactly. I guess we get a free pass if we kill in self-defense." She went to the bathroom and washed the blood from her hands. It swirled into the drain, dark and disgusting. Saba handed her a towel. "I thought I'd feel guilty, but I don't." She regarded her reflection in the mirror, staring into her own green eyes. "People are supposed to feel bad when they take a life, aren't they? Shouldn't I be crying, or at least upset?" She stared at the bloodstains trailing down the sink. "I don't even know how I managed to fight like that."

"Perhaps you were meant to." Saba placed a hand on Rise's shoulder. "May I show you something?"

Rise nodded and followed Saba to a room built to be a third bedroom, but now served as a library, with comfortable chairs and stacks of books lined up on shelves. Saba moved her fingers across a row of books and flipped one out. She thumbed through pages, many marked with colored ribbons.

"You were raised in Judeo-Christian culture, yes?"

"My parents were Catholic," Rise said. "They made me go to mass every week and I did all the standard crap—first communion, penance, confirmation—but only because I had to. They were total frauds. Half the time my dad would scream and yell all the way to church, then he'd have us all walk in together and smile, like everything was perfect." She balled her fists. "I always felt like I was putting on a show."

Saba smiled gently. "I think every faith has those who try to twist a belief to their liking. This is a book of psalms. When I watched you tonight, this verse came to mind." She started to recite, her voice reverent. *"Blessed be the Lord, my rock, who trains my hands for war and my fingers for battle..."*

Rise stepped closer, took the thin book from Saba's hands and read the rest of the passage in silence. "Can I look at this for a while?"

Saba's face brightened. "Absolutely. As I said, everything I have is at your disposal." She motioned to various locations in the room. "Everything on these two shelves is about war and combat. Over there is religious studies. I have a section here on astrology and occult, history—"

"You've read all these?" Rise was awestruck; there were hundreds.

"Yes, many of them several times." Saba shrugged. "I'm still trying to figure out where someone like me fits into the grand design."

"How's that working out for you?"

"I have some ideas, but I don't know if I'm right." She laughed. "Right now, I simply maintain faith that I have a purpose. Are you staying here tonight?"

Rise looked at the clock on the wall and her face fell. "I'm supposed to be at work in four hours. I'm going to be a zombie."

"Do you get sick days? I know a doctor who could write you a note."

It was the best idea Rise heard in a long time.

Chapter Thirty-One
Dubious Motivations

Dominik parried the bamboo sticks whirling at him, and used his own weapons to bat them away. The sound of the wood cracked in the air, mingling with other noises in the large combat training arena. About one hundred of the Blue choir was gathered, the males dressed only in drawstring training pants, with the females adding tight-fitting tops to contain parts that would otherwise bounce. The effort wasn't working for several of them, much to the delight of their Blue brothers. The choir was close-knit, maintained good humor, and teasing remarks were bandied about without resentment.

The angels had split off into pairs, most choosing partners of comparable size and skill level. Dominik was larger and slightly more advanced than Carmen, but the two sparred well together. Neither was afraid to take a hit or give one. Both were bloodied and bruised, and had taken to keeping count of how many injuries they inflicted on the other.

Sweat beaded on Dominik's chest. His muscles were taut from getting a good workout for several hours. He spun and whipped his sticks at his opponent. He made contact and grinned.

"Sixteen."

"That was fifteen and a lucky blow." Carmen flexed his shoulder where the hit had landed. He recovered and attacked again. "She killed three minions? Even with help from the Returner, that's impressive."

"And unexpected." Dominik spun in a tight circle and brought his sticks down toward his opponents face. "I didn't think her presence would be detected for a while longer."

"You have your work cut out for you now, and so does she." Carmen fell to his knees and made a sweeping smack aimed for the legs. It was blocked and he jumped back to his feet, barely deflecting a counter-strike. "At least you know she doesn't have a problem dealing out death, but then again, none of them ever do." He leapt in the air, barely escaping a blow. "Do you think they planned to take her?"

"I think that's exactly what they intended. She won't be happy to hear what that might entail, but she'll need to be told."

One of the elders struck a large gong in the middle of the arena and called out to the Blue angels in a loud voice.

"Switch!"

Dominik and Carmen dropped the sticks and moved to the right, continuing the circuit. They picked up shields and broadsword, and took a moment to catch their breath. The elder struck the gong once more and Dominik went on the offense, swinging the weapon over his head.

Carmen raised his shield, blocking the blow. "Where does she stand in her trials?"

"She bears two marks," Dominik said, whipping his blade upward, "and she's learned to see into the soul." He swung his shield up as the sword came at him. "I suspect the rest of her powers will manifest in quick order." He lunged, and made contact on Carmen's shoulder.

"Bah! You have a longer reach." He recovered and closed the distance, ending up in a battle embrace with the larger angel. He gritted his teeth and he tried to push away. "How did she respond to the mission with Chi?"

"Better than expected." Dominik tossed his friend away. "She didn't argue as much as I had anticipated."

Carmen laughed and made another swing. "Is that pride in your voice? For a Herald?"

"Not pride." He jumped back, avoiding a strike. "A begrudging interest in her growth, perhaps." Dominik spun his sword in a move that would've been a killing strike in a real battle. "I'm learning more of her nature. It's troubling the way her mind works; she's quick to anger and demanding when she wants her own way. I see no other emotion in her eyes, but I think that disturbs her more than it does me. It's as though she wants to feel, but is unable to do so."

"I think you're fighting a losing battle trying to figure her out." Carmen flipped up his blade in a salute. "It's as useless as trying to understand the motivations of this weapon. Heralds are as hard as this steel, and just as cold. I wouldn't get too close, or you're liable to get cut."

The elder sounded the gong once more.

"Break!"

Dominik dropped the training gear and wiped sweat from his brow. He heard Carmen whisper a curse. He followed his friend's gaze and understood why.

A Herald circled above, his black armor and wings in stark contrast to the other angels. His presence created an immediate change; the atmosphere turned cold, charged with tension and fear.

He landed nearby, and turned up his nose as though smelling something foul. "So, this is where the lesser choirs train. Rudimentary. The arena in the castle is far more elaborate."

Carmen wiped his hands on his pants. "Then perhaps you should go back there and leave us in peace."

The Herald gave him a warning look. "From the looks of things, you've already sustained quite a beating today. Speak out of turn again, and I'll see you receive one far worse." He lowered his voice, infusing it with unmistakable power. "Step away and hold your tongue."

Carmen did as commanded, and the Herald turned his attention to Dominik. He studied him for a long while. He was openly critical, circling the Blue angel as though trying to decide on a steer for purchase. "And you're the advisor.

The depths the Scriptures have plunged to this time are astounding. You haven't held wings for a generation, yet they give you over as counsel to one of the nineteen. A travesty, but with any luck, you'll be dead or replaced soon, and we can get an upgrade."

Dominik forced his voice to remain steady under the insults. "I don't believe we've met."

"I'm called Rue." He squeezed Dominik's upper arms, testing the muscle strength. "Well, you're solid, I'll give you that." He grabbed the long ponytail and tugged a few times. "I don't care for this. The texture reminds me of horsehair."

Dominik bristled, trying to keep his aggravation in hand. "Perhaps you can take up the issue with the Great Architect."

"Perhaps I will." Rue continued to poke and prod, doing everything but checking Dominik's teeth.

Dominik tolerated the indignity, aware every eye in the arena was watching the encounter with apprehension. He clenched his fists when Ruse gave him a taunting smack on his backside, but said nothing.

"I'm surprised you don't challenge me," the Herald said, "and it's not from fear, I can see that."

"My choir is here to train, not to bear witness to a common brawl." He lowered his voice. "Plus, I know that's what you want, and I won't give you the satisfaction. Nor will I give you an excuse to exercise your power." Dominik knew what indignities the Black choir could administer, and though he was presently under protection from Herald commands, the rest of his choir was not. Rue could easily turn on another for no other reason than to punish Dominik. He'd once seen two Golds forced to fight naked until they were both so broken they were unable to stand.

Rue issued a chilly smile. "I assure you, my power needs no excuse to be exercised. I'd give you a demonstration, but I don't wish to endure the stench of your choir longer than necessary." He reached into the knapsack slung across his shoulder and brought forth a wooden case. "The Light Bringer commands you to present this gift to my new sister."

Dominik nodded and took the item, but the Herald made no move to depart. "Is there something else?"

Rue's face twisted into a mocking leer. "There is a rumor Tyre himself requested you be conscripted for this duty."

Dominik ignored the question that was insinuated and the Herald laughed.

"Oh, Tyre must have been mad with rage over being replaced. Either he wants the new Herald to fail, or he wants you killed. Maybe both." He leaned in close. "Tell me—is she of a pleasing form? None of us were happy with Tyre's punishment, but having a new female created was a small consolation. There are so few that hold the black wings. Is she supple and ripe, ready to be plucked?"

Dominik didn't miss the lust in the Heralds voice, nor the remarks about Tyre's dubious motivations. He ignored both. "I will make sure your *new sister* receives her gift."

Rue chuckled. "Feel free to break her, in all regards. She could enjoy your services now, and we can enjoy her proficiency later." He spread his wings and lofted, the anxiety in the room going with him.

"Their appetites are insatiable," Carmen said as he returned, "though, I admit, I'm curious about the new Herald, as well. What does she look like?"

"Dark hair, the green eyes. She's barely taller than a child, and I find her too thin." Dominik opened the box and heard his friend whistle at the sight of the contents. "Her physical appeal is not my concern."

"Ah, so she is appealing?" He laughed when Dominik scowled. "What of her demeanor? Does she already attempt to command you, or is she receptive to your counsel?"

Dominik closed up the box, his features still showing signs of frustration from the encounter. "So far she's been more interested in getting her hands on my wings than in taking my advice."

"Perhaps you should let her. It might relieve some tension for both of you." Carmen spread his arms wide as the gong was struck once more. "Come. Let's continue our rudimentary training in our unworthy arena! I think it's our turn for the pikes."

Dominik placed the gift with his personal belongings and grabbed up one of the staves. He tossed it back and forth in his hands, feeling a burn in his heart. The responsibility for the Herald was pressing on him, and mention of Tyre reminded him why he was in the predicament. He attacked with more vigor than was necessary, giving vent to his aggravation.

CHAPTER THIRTY-TWO
TARTARUS INFERI

Rise woke up on Saba's couch feeling rested. Someone had covered her with an afghan, and her shoes were off and placed neatly on the floor. The big white cat was curled up on her stomach, and tucked by her side was the book she'd fallen asleep reading. A familiar blue card poked up from the pages, marking her spot. Dominik sat in a chair a few feet away, watching her.

She groaned. That angel was the last person she wanted to see first thing in the morning. "What time is it?"

"Noon," he said. "I retrieved some clothes from your apartment." He gestured toward a stack of familiar items, carefully folded. "I also brought your phone."

She wasn't expecting that. "Okay, thanks…I think." The considerate gesture was surprising after the way he acted the previous night. She flipped through her missed calls, several from Danny and one from Emory. She also had a few text messages, but they'd already been read. She glared at the angel, remembering why she didn't like him. "Did you read my texts?"

"I did."

She wondered why she even bothered to ask. "That's an invasion of privacy." She scanned the messages; Danny was worried because she wasn't answering her phone and didn't go to work. He even called the clinic looking for her. "He needs to stop checking up on me," she muttered.

"You wouldn't need to worry about that, had you done as I instructed."

"Do I *have* to do what you say? Are you here to run my life for me?"

"I can only offer advice," Dominik said. "The decisions are yours, and the consequences that come with them."

"Good." She dropped the phone on the floor, peeved at having two males delving too deep in her business. She looked him right in the eye. "Stop spying on me. I'm not even close to kidding about that one. I don't like knowing I'm under surveillance from the great beyond."

Dominik remained silent and his lack of response fueled her irritation. "And stop telling me I can't be Danny's friend, because that's not going to happen."

"You're quite adamant." His eyes were hard, unflinching. "Why is this? What drives you toward the young man?"

Rise started to give a rote response, but the angel stopped her with a warning look.

"Don't tell me what you think I want to hear," he said. "And don't try to fool yourself, either."

She thought for a while. Dominik had been honest with her, even though he knew it would anger her. She figured he deserved the same treatment. Moreover, the angel might be a winged lie detector and she didn't want to look like a fool. She rummaged through her brain, visiting dark places she didn't like to go. She wanted desperately to say she was helping Danny because it was the right thing to do, or because she was worried about him, but neither of those were the truth.

"I owe him," she said. "He's done a lot for me, and there's something going on with his sister." She paused, not wanting to mention the angels all over the walls, especially the one that bore her name. "I don't know why, but I think it has something to do with me." She looked away, feeling ridiculous.

"I see. This is about you, more than your friend." Dominik stretched his long legs and adjusted his wings so they draped over the back of the chair, his expression unreadable. "Interesting."

Rise didn't appreciate his word choices. "You told me to tell the truth, and this is exactly why I didn't want to. You want me to think I'm selfish."

"I want you to own your thoughts and actions, and not be afraid of them. Accepting your limitations is every bit as important as embracing your strengths. Now then, moving on—Chi asked that I greet you on her behalf."

"Chi? You mean Keisha?" Rise closed her eyes tight. She almost forgot about that business from last night. Despite Dominik's assurance she wouldn't be caught, she expected armed men would be showing up any second to drag her off to prison. "Is she okay?"

"She has resumed her rightful position within the Scriptures," he said. "There was great celebration upon her return, and much relief. Your part in the matter did not go unnoticed. There was praise for your willingness to act."

Rise grunted. "I kill on command. Gold star for me." She ran a hand through her hair, wondering if her lack of guilt and remorse was the reason she'd been targeted by whoever was in charge upstairs. She didn't think many people would so willingly kill a child, even if an angel deemed it necessary. "Tell everyone up there I'm happy to do their dirty work."

Dominik leaned forward. "Chi was the first to offer words of gratitude."

Rise pulled her legs up and the cat scurried away. "I'm not sure I understand what you meant last night, when you said she was in danger from the minions. Were they going to come after her because she's so important?"

"They would come after her because she's a human soul, one they would see as vulnerable because she was adrift on her journey." Dominik steepled his fingers in front of him. "In every life, there are milestones put in place, certain events to guide the soul. We call them markers. It's much like taking a trip. If you have a map and plot the course, there is a better chance you'll reach your destination. If you leave without one, you can be enticed by signs along the road, tempting you to deviate."

"I guess minions are like advertisements." Rise pictured Zeb and Marcus on a big billboard, grinning and flashing a thumbs-up sign with the words 'exit here' written below their faces.

"That's their purpose," Dominik said. "They present temptations, challenges designed to test and strengthen the soul. Those who successfully overcome the challenge gain spiritual advancement. Those who fall, will not. If failure is great, or repeated, the soul is cast into the fires and becomes a minion; a tragic fate."

Rise leaned forward, enthralled by this new information and in finally getting some explanations. She wondered why the angel was suddenly so willing to talk. Maybe it was because she finally lost her temper and yelled at him. She would have to do that more often. "What if someone misses a marker?"

"Charting a journey is not an easy thing. It often takes many years of research and preparation. Angels assist in the process to ensure the soul has the best chance of success. But, as with any endeavor, there is risk. Some fall off course due to poor decisions, or failure to heed their instinct and intuition. Others miss markers through no fault of their own, such as what happened with Chi and Kafi."

"Kafi..." Rise looked around and lowered her voice. "Will he become a minion?"

Dominik spread his hands. "Not necessarily. Minions can sense that he has deviated, they view him as a weak link, one to be purged from the flock. They whisper seductions in his mind. He needs to remain diligent in order to defeat their influence. We can discuss these matters in greater detail at a later time. I have something for you."

Rise didn't like how the angel was always the one deciding what to discuss, and for how long. She felt handled, and her lack of control sparked a deep-rooted defiance. She watched as Dominik opened the knapsack that was his constant companion, and brought forth a box made of dark wood with intricate carvings. He held it out with both hands.

"A gift from the Light Bringer."

Rise wondered why the illustrious white dot was giving her a present. She took the case, shocked at its heft. Lying atop purple velvet was an object resembling an enormous nail or a small stake, but more elaborate than either. Perhaps eight inches in length, it was polished to a high shine.

"Is this real gold?" she asked.

"Yes."

That explained the weight. One end tapered to a dull point and the other was topped with a large chiseled ruby, surrounded by smaller jewels of every color. She assumed those were real, too.

"What is it?" The tapered end was hollow, and she held it close to her eye to see if something was inside. Dominik cleared his throat.

"I wouldn't do that," he said. "Point it in this direction and touch the red gem."

Rise moved the item to her right hand and held it as she would a baton, as far as her arm would allow. She pressed her thumb to the ruby, having to exert considerable pressure to make it move. It clicked down and a cone of blue-white fire shot forth with a great noise, reminding her of a faucet turned on full blast. She was so startled she nearly dropped the thing. The flames subsided as soon a she released pressure on the gem, but a smell like sulfur permeated the air. She looked at the angel in shock.

"Tartarus Inferi," Dominik said. "Hellfire. It will consume a minion, and they are loathe to risk such a thing." He shrugged. "If the flames fail to deter, it can also be quite effective as a blunt force weapon."

"Comforting." She placed the strange device back in the case.

"Take heart that minions work in small groups; two or three, sometimes up to five. Beyond that, power and ego take hold and they turn on one another."

"How do they keep finding me?"

"Everyone has a unique spiritual resonance. You can liken it to a fingerprint. The minions are drawn to yours as a river to the sea." He pointed to the bracelet on his wrist; he'd obviously gotten a replacement after he relinquished his old one. "Among other things, this glow allows us to keep track of own signatures so we can gauge our vulnerability."

"They come after you, too?"

"Oh, yes. Minions hunt angels and would kill me for no greater reason than to add my wing to their collection.

Rise wrinkled up her nose. "They would rip off your wings?"

"Only one, usually."

"That's...."—Rise shook her head—"really gross."

Dominik actually laughed. It was a rich sound, like his singing voice. "I agree. It's a reason angels don't remain in this realms apart from performing necessary duties."

"And what is your duty, other than driving me crazy?"

"As your advisor, I relay pertinent information and attempt to guide you on a course that will bring you to understanding of your purpose."

Rise thought about that. "You work for me, then?"

His expression lost all trace of humor. "I do not. I am under obligation to my oath, not to you. This duty was requested of me, and unlike some, I don't question tasks given me by higher authority."

She smirked. That explained a ton. "I get it, now. You don't even want this job." She thought it was poetic justice; he put a big kink in her life, too. "Saba said you're a new angel. Is that true?"

"Time in the human realm and the spiritual realm is quite different."

"Does that mean 'yes'?" She could be condescending, too.

"I've held wings for a short time, compared to most. Why do you ask?"

She crossed her arms over her chest and rocked back on her heels. "Because I get the impression I must be something pretty special—I can see the light of the soul, I have minions trying to grab me, I even have the Scriptures asking me for favors."

"They asked you to perform a duty, not a favor."

"Whatever, you know what I mean."

"I don't think I do." He eyed her with suspicion. "What are you trying to gain with this line of questioning?"

"I'm wondering why they sent *you*; a rookie angel that doesn't even want to be here." She watched him carefully and didn't miss the way his muscles tensed. She was onto something. "You just said your job was to give me information, and so far you suck at that part." She snapped her fingers and raised her eyebrows. "Spit it out, *advisor*. Tell me everything you're hiding, starting with why minions are gunning for me."

"I will not be commanded by you." Dominik's eyes blazed and he took a step forward. "Don't dare to use that tone with me again. I won't tolerate disrespect, not from you."

She backed off a little when his wings started to expand; the things could be intimidating, and she suspected that was part of the design. "You're not exactly polite to me, either. And it's a legitimate question. You explained how the minions find me, but you haven't told me what they want."

"They want your surrender. We've discussed this, and it would be useful if you listened to information the first time."

"That is not telling me anything." She tried to keep her voice down because Saba was still asleep. It didn't work. "They just want me to wave a white flag and say I give up?"

"There's far more to your surrender than just speaking the words," he said. "Any fool can recite a phrase or babble without thinking. Words hold power, but it comes from intent and understanding, and you lack both."

"What are you talking about?" She wanted to kick something, but didn't want to be accused of another tantrum. "I don't understand!"

"Which is precisely why I'm not going to explain it to you." Dominik pointed to the door. "You could walk outside at this moment and scream your surrender to every minion crossing your path, and it would have no more effect than if you offered it to a tree."

"Then why do they keep coming after me?" She was getting angry again. "If I can't give them what they want, what's the point?"

"Because they know one day you *will* understand. Your growth is inevitable." He shrugged. "I believe the ones that came for you last night intended to capture and hold you for this purpose."

"Hold me where?"

"In the midrealm, a place where angels such as myself cannot tread. You could be locked away indefinitely, primed for the moment when they could seize your surrender. I imagine the tortures inflicted upon you would be horrific."

Her eyes flew open wide. "They can do that?" She felt light-headed and couldn't believe he was so calm. "Let me get this straight: I might get kidnapped and tortured because of something I *don't* understand, and you're still not going to explain?"

"For now, your ignorance works in our favor."

Rise paced the room. "I am sick of people telling me what I can and can't know." She thought of her conversations with the Sister at the adoption agency, and the Priest at the church. "How am I supposed to protect myself? Those minions last night were on us before we even knew what was happening, and they were strong." She waved an accusing hand at him. "You weren't any help. Why didn't you rain down some fire and brimstone and smite something?"

Dominik snapped his wings. The sound was like a whip, the intent to grab her attention. It worked. "I am not here as your guardian. I cannot and will not fight your battles, and from what I witnessed, you didn't require my assistance." He peered at her through narrowed eyes. "Saba gave a detailed account of the battle. She said you fought as a warrior and described combat proficiency far beyond anything you should be capable of achieving. How did you learn such skill?"

"I don't know. I guess I got lucky." She didn't care. She was busy compiling a mental list of known torture techniques.

"I'm pleased you've started to read something other than fiction." Dominik glanced at the book on the sofa. "If you're interested in warfare, I'd suggest you study Sun Tzu. I had the honor of meeting him long ago during one of my journeys. He's an advanced soul. His writings are nothing short of inspired."

"I'll get right on that." She was unwilling to concede anything to the angel at that moment. She continued to pace until realization of what he said seeped through her anger. "Hold up. You met Sun Tzu? That was over 2500 years ago." He looked stunned at her knowledge and she smirked. "I have the History channel. How many lifetimes did you have?"

"Many. They served to advance my knowledge and experience."

He tensed up again and she understood why this time; he didn't like her asking questions. None that concerned him, anyway. "In those *many* lifetimes, how often did you screw up and go off path?" He was taken aback at the question. She would've killed for a camera to grab the look on his face.

"Why would you ask?"

His tone was a touch of warning, a touch of defense. She loved it. "Just curious. The way you dress, the way you talk. You're really self-righteous, and, in my experience, that means you're either so perfect you're above reproach – and I guarantee that isn't the case – or you're busting your ass trying to make up for something." She hoped to God she was irritating him. "I was wondering what that might be."

"I see." Dominik went silent, either considering his answer or considering if he was going to answer at all.

"Touchy subject?" Rise knew she hit a button and tossed him a challenging look.

"I went from my path several times," he said. "On a few occasions, I missed my final marker, my exit point from life."

"You mean you didn't die on time?" She snickered. This was getting better by the second. "Did someone have to come save you, the way we saved Chi?"

"Those events are called interceptions."

"I don't care what they're called. You still didn't answer me." She knew she was pushing things, but couldn't bring herself to back down. It was nice being on the offense with him for a change.

"Someone did...come to my aid." He didn't look happy about that admission one bit. His fists clenched and he stiffened. Rise almost licked her lips. She was close to something he didn't want her to know.

"Who was it?"

Dominik remained silent. A vein pulsed in his neck, betraying the effort involved.

"Fine, don't tell me." She shrugged, just like he did when he spoke about her being tortured by minions. It stunned her when he spoke.

"His name was Tyre," Dominik said. "He could alter paths that had gone off course. Few have such abilities."

"Jealous?" Rise knew she crossed the line; the angel's wings exploded to full range and he closed the distance between them in a heartbeat. He was so close she had to look straight up to see his eyes. They were enraged.

"I was not envious of him," Dominik said. "Tyre abused his power, made a mockery of his title and violated the oath of angels. He was stripped of his wings and banished for his crimes."

"Harsh." She barely whispered the word. "I'm sorry I said anything." She wasn't, but he was starting to scare her.

Rise took a step back, but he grabbed her around the waist with one arm, jerked her forward, and locked her in place against his body. His hold on her was like steel, and he was so much larger she could only stare at his chest. He slid his hand up her back, under her shirt. She shuddered, frightened and angry by the sudden contact. She moved her gaze upward until she was looking into intense blue eyes.

Rise opened her mouth, but couldn't say a word. She could smell the strange scent on the angel, feel the heat from his proximity. She noticed for the first time the fullness of his lips, the way his hair curled in little rings around his face. An unfamiliar feeling bubbled up, and a stray thought snaked its way into the fringes of her mind. She wanted to step back, to put some distance between them, but she also didn't want to move. She completely forgot why she was angry with him.

Dominik leaned down, and Rise held her breath. She focused on his lips as they came closer, almost touching hers before they moved along her cheek and came to rest by her ear.

"There's a reason for your longing," he whispered, "the knot that now forms in your stomach, the warmth in your chest." His free hand moved to her neck and she trembled. "Angels can be seductive, can we not? We can reach into your soul and find desires most deeply concealed. We can offer fulfillment as no other."

His words lit a fire under her skin, burning away all thoughts except the desire to have him closer. Her hands found his hips and a pulsing ache consumed her, growing stronger with every heartbeat. His lips brushed her skin as he spoke, drawing her into a spell.

"We can weaken even the strongest will, with words, or a touch." He pressed against her and she felt his chest moving as he breathed. "I could have you now, if I wished." He slid his hands down the length of her back. She closed her eyes, sighing with pleasure. "If I were you," he whispered, "I would commit this moment to memory."

He pushed her away with both hands, so hard she almost fell. He stepped back, smirking.

Rise was still tingling from excitement when she realized what he'd done. She was humiliated, but tried to appear angry. She felt betrayed, more from herself than Dominik's easy manipulation. She turned away, unable to meet his eyes.

"The fault is not your own," Dominik said without a trace of humor. "You're but a slave to your lesser impulses, aren't you?"

The words switched her outage from feigned to real. She spun around, a soliloquy of profanity positioned on her tongue she never had opportunity to voice.

"Good morning!" Saba bounced into the room wearing a long robe and fuzzy slippers. Her hair was down, falling in unruly tangles past her shoulders. She gave Rise a light kiss on each cheek. "Are you going already?" She pouted.

"No, she's not," Dominik answered, though the question wasn't directed at him. He continued to stare at Rise. "She can stay here today."

"You don't tell me what to do," she snapped. "I'm going home." She picked up her things and headed toward the door before remembering she didn't have her car. She stopped and her shoulders fell.

The angel chuckled. "A dramatic exit sadly averted."

"Are you going to fly her home?" Saba was excited about the prospect. "Can I watch?"

"He is not taking me anywhere." Rise stared him down. "I'd rather be carried off by a giant vulture."

Saba looked back and forth between the two. "Is there a problem?"

"A misunderstanding," Dominik said, "one caused by reckless words, deeply regretted." He placed a hand on his chest and bowed.

Rise wasn't sure if he was mocking her. She could still feel the effects of his touches and had to shift her stance.

Saba ignored whatever was going on between her guests. "Oh, Rise, you have such lovely feet." She leaned over to get a better look. "Would you allow me to decorate them? I do my own." She kicked off one of her slippers and pointed her toes like a ballerina. Intricate swirls and dots and other designs covered her foot.

Rise was impressed with the work. "That's amazing."

"I haven't been able to do anyone else for so long, it would be such a treat." Saba's eyes were hopeful. "Kafi can take you home later, I'm sure he won't mind." She looked at Dominik. "That's okay, isn't it?"

"I wouldn't dare presume to speak for her." His sardonic tone had returned.

Rise hated the idea of sticking around, mainly because that was exactly what the angel wanted, but she couldn't say no. Saba was a prisoner to whatever mysterious spiritual mess was transpiring and deserved a break. Plus, she did like the idea of having her feet decorated and she didn't have another way home. She forced a smile. "I'm staying."

Saba squealed in delight and clapped her hands. "You go get showered up and I'll get the paints ready." She almost skipped from the room.

Rise dreaded being alone again with Dominik, but the angel gathered up his bag and grabbed his jacket.

"I'll take my leave," he said. "Keep the Inferi close and don't think to lower your guard, even in the midst of"—he waved a hand at her bare feet—"feminine rituals." He was out the door without another word.

"I guess I'll see you later," Rise spoke into the empty room. That she wasn't completely adverse to the idea bothered her immensely.

CHAPTER THIRTY-THREE
Instincts

Rise decided she would have to own a convertible some day. Kafi's Jeep Wrangler, Betty, was amazing; all black and chrome, every piece polished to a high shine, and without a mark inside or out. Kafi made the girls hold their shoes in their lap so the flooring would stay immaculate. He drove in sandals kept on hand for that purpose. Saba was merciless, touching her finger here and there on the dash and front window just so her brother would bat her hand away and rub a fist over the tiny smudges she created.

"You see this?" Kafi turned his head toward Rise in the backseat. "And she complains I don't take her for drives more often." The comment elicited giggles from Saba.

Rise discovered Kafi took his sister on short outings sometimes, so she could get away for a few minutes. She wasn't supposed to tell Dominik, and had no problem keeping that secret. His little seduction episode still had her seething.

She spent most of the trip adjusting to the lights coming from people. It wasn't so obvious in the daytime, but still distracting. Saba didn't have one, but Kafi was a Purple, and so bright he looked like a disco ball. She tried to ignore it, and focused on the wind in her face, reminding her, in a small way, of her flight with the angel. Thinking of him put her back in a sour mood, so she turned attention to the artwork on her feet. It was nothing less of a masterpiece.

"Did you see what Saba did for me?" Rise stuck a leg between the bucket seats and rested her heel on the armrest.

"Nah!" Kafi swatted at her foot.

"Leave her alone," Saba said, as she inspected the designs. "I think this might be my best work."

"This detailing is *my* best work." He brushed off the armrest while the girls exchanged winks.

They pulled into the apartments and Rise saw a familiar truck parked in front of her building. Danny was leaning against the tailgate and she gasped; he was a Gold. Emory stood beside him, emanating a faint blue hue.

Saba turned to her. "Isn't that your friend?"

"Yeah, and he's going to ask where I've been." She had no idea what to say, it wasn't like she could simply tell the truth. Maybe Dominik was right; a friendship with Danny would be a problem if she had to lie all the time.

Kafi shifted the Jeep into neutral, but didn't turn off the engine. Danny strolled over and gave him a wave. "Hey, Doc." He smiled at Saba and she tucked her head and readjusted her scarf.

Kafi nodded. "How's the head?"

Danny touched the bandage with a finger. "Better."

"Rise needed some follow-up care," Kafi said smoothly. "If you have any problems, let me know. She has my number."

"Will do."

"Thank you," Rise said, hoping Kafi understood the double meaning. He saved her from having to make up an excuse, and it wasn't even a lie, strictly speaking. He checked her wounds, and gave her some antibiotic cream.

Saba squeezed her hand. "We'll talk later."

"That must've been the Muslim girl," Emory said as they walked into the apartment. "Danny said she was pretty."

"Did he?" Rise looked to Danny. He looked away.

"I said she had pretty eyes." He switched gears. "Hey man, did you get a good look at Doc's ride?"

Her friends plopped down on the loveseat while Rise poured some food for Oliver. She sat cross-legged on the floor, her face resting on her hand, while the guys made a fuss about Betty, discussing the benefits of manual transmission and other things equally boring.

"What's this?" Danny asked.

It took Rise a second to realize he was addressing her; she'd zoned out. He was scanning the papers from the adoption agency. She explained her encounters with Mother Mae and the Priest.

"Interesting," Emory said. He took the paper from Danny and held it toward the light so he could read. "Irish, German, English—damn, you're white. I guess I was wrong about the soul."

Rise laughed. "The *alleged* father's information isn't listed, so you still might be right." She'd tossed the idea around herself. Her hair was darker than anyone she'd ever met, she tanned like crazy in the sun, and recently one horny jackass with a bulldog tried to compliment his way into her panties by lavishing praise on her *exotic features*—whatever the hell that meant. "I doubt I'll ever know for sure, unless Indiana eases off the privacy laws."

Danny studied her face. "This is more important than you're letting on, isn't it?"

Rise shrugged. Now that she was some kind of player in the cosmic scheme, she was more curious about her heritage. She wondered if it would hold some clues since Dominik wasn't being forthcoming.

Emory leaned forward. "If you think your mom was a student at that school, you should check out the old yearbooks. And that priest, he said the family were still members, right? Lots of churches keep directories of parishioners. You can go back and cross-reference names."

"That's a good idea," Danny said. "That's a really good idea."

Rise's hopes soared. "Wonder where I could find yearbooks that far back."

"Library," Emory said. "I've got class tomorrow morning, and the downtown branch isn't too far from campus. I'll pop in and poke around." He held up the papers. "Can I keep this?"

"It's yours." Rise knew if anyone would be able to scrounge up information, it was Emory. He'd been researching his eye disease for years—he was thorough and organized. "I owe you for this."

"Damn right you do." He folded the paper and stuck it in his pocket. "It's not easy being the smartest guy in the room all the time."

She grinned. "Hey, why were you here, anyway?" The two exchanged a look she couldn't identify.

"Moral support," Danny said. "We thought maybe you weren't sick, that you'd heard the news about Keisha Williams."

"Keisha?" Her fake illness threatened to become a reality.

Danny got up from the couch and knelt in front of her. She knew what he was going to say and prepared to look shocked.

"She died," he said. "There was a news report, since people are still talking about the kidnapping. You saved her life and now…well, we thought it might've messed with your head."

It was absolutely messing with her head, in more ways than he knew. She tried to look suitably distraught. "Does anyone know what happened?" She held her breath.

"Preliminary reports say it was something like crib death," Emory said. "I guess that can happen to older kids sometimes, not just babies."

Rise sighed in relief; one felony murder conviction avoided.

"She's in a better place." Danny cringed. "Christ, I can't believe I just said that. I hated hearing that stuff after my mom and dad died."

"It's okay. I totally believe she's very happy right now." She didn't mention she knew it for a fact. "I appreciate you both coming over to tell me."

The guys left a little after dark. Rise wondered if Dominik would make an appearance and, if he did, how she'd respond. Her thoughts kept sneaking back to the way she felt in his arms, how he smelled and the blue of his eyes. She tried to focus on the part where he pushed her away, humiliating her on purpose, but it wasn't working. She had an uncomfortable yearning, unwelcome and persistent.

She never felt like much of a sexual person and knew that wasn't normal, especially for someone her age. Lack of libido was a common side effect from the meds she'd taken, and it looked like natural instincts had finally kicked in and planned to make up for lost time. The more she thought about Dominik, the worse it got. The ache threatened to overwhelm her. She considered ways to relieve the tension, but remembered the nosy angel was probably watching. Right then, despite the attraction, she loathed him.

"You can have him, you know."

Rise almost jumped out of her skin at the mental intrusion. She whipped her head back and forth, trying to shake off the tingle in her mind. This time she knew she wasn't hallucinating.

"Go away," she ordered. "Get the hell out of my head!"

Whoever, or whatever, ignored her demand. "The angel is handsome, is he not? Make him serve you. He's yours to command."

"Yeah, right." As perversely intriguing as the words sounded, she didn't believe them for a second. "Are you Lucifer?"

"Hardly."

"Then who are you? Actually, don't even answer that. My head is not a public chat room, so go away." She whirled around and shouted at the ceiling. "Do you hear me? Leave me alone!"

"For now, but I'll return soon." The voice was infuriatingly unperturbed. "I wish you a *pleasurable* evening."

Rise didn't miss the little jab at her current state, and after the voice faded, she couldn't help but laugh at the absurdity of it all. She had a brief moment of regret, wondering if she lost her temper with God, then decided she simply didn't care. So far, the only spiritual being she knew hadn't been particularly endearing, and if there was an Almighty, she planned to let Him know that at some point in the future.

She went to bed early, but couldn't sleep. She left the lights on, held the Inferi tight to her chest, and lay there feeling like a toddler scared of monsters in the closet. Her one comfort, if she could call it that, was the knowledge that minions didn't intend to kill her. Then again, death might be preferable to kidnap and torture.

She was starting to relax when the unmistakable stench hit her. She bolted up, backed against the wall and held the Inferi at the ready. She waited, but no minions appeared. She moved toward the bedroom door, taking large, deliberate steps. She placed her hand on the knob and rallied her courage. Whoever was out there was about to get a face-full of hellfire. She flung open the door, jumped out screaming and waving the Inferi, trying to look as intimidating as possible in a Tinkerbell nightshirt.

The room was empty, except for Oliver. The cat sat on the coffee table, grooming. He peeked up, stretched, and almost struck a pose. Rise thought he looked downright proud of himself. The stench was stronger in this room, and she had no doubt at least one minion had been there. She thought back to Dominik's words, telling her she had a protector in her home.

"You've got to be kidding me," she said, and dropped her arms.

Oliver hopped from the table, curled around her ankles a few times, and strolled into the bedroom. He took up position in the middle of the blankets, flopped to his back and fell asleep. Rise decided if she did get another life after this one, she wanted to come back as a cat.

Chapter Thirty-Four
Test of Will

Shay wrapped a small blue band around a piece of Dominik's hair. She picked up another section and started braiding. Her fingers worked quickly. She was getting good at this, thanks to Dominik allowing her to practice on him. He sat on the floor in front of her, researching while she worked.

"I can't believe she actually snapped her fingers at me." He tossed away the scroll he'd been reading and grabbed another from the pile beside him. "And I can't believe I lost my temper so easily."

Shay rolled her eyes, unhappy the conversation was back to the Herald. "I'm not surprised on either count. She's beginning to think she's in charge. If you don't put her in place, she'll start trying to command you. What you did today was an appropriate response to her attitude." She would've preferred he throw her in front of a large, moving object.

Dominik looked up from the scroll. "I'm sorry you witnessed that exchange."

"I found it amusing." She was lying and glad he couldn't see her face. A duty of the Purple choir was to keep track of angels in the human realm. Shay checked in on Dominik from a viewing room, but didn't tell him she switched shifts with a choirmate so she could do so. "I didn't like the way she was looking at you, though. She's probably dreaming of you at this very moment."

"She's probably dreaming of ways to be rid of me."

"I wish you would do the same. Why are you dwelling on this?"

"I don't like the way she's able to seize on my emotions." He shook his head. "I wanted to humiliate her. It was a disgraceful act of petty retribution, made worse because it was motivated by the offenses of others more than anything she had done."

"There are many who would love to have such an opportunity with a Herald," she said, "and, no matter the reason, it was good for her to be taken down a notch. This entire situation might've been avoided had Tyre been given a firmer hand by his advisors."

"That Herald still haunts me from the nether." Dominik continued reading the scroll. "Have you ever been to the training areas of the castle?"

"Never." She continued her work, tugging his hair a little harder than necessary. Despite what she said, the way he put his hands on that cursed Herald infuriated her. She knew it was a calculated ruse, but still painful to watch. It had been far too long since she'd felt Dominik's touch in such a way. "Did I ever tell you that Tyre invited me to his chamber once?"

Dominik's head jerked up and his wings shook in outrage.

Shay smiled; that was the reaction she wanted. "It still makes my stomach churn. He was a horrid creature, incapable of feeling. It was his nature." She hoped he understood the unspoken warning.

Dominik went silent for a time, deep in thought. "I'm starting to believe it might have been in Tyre's nature to desire what he couldn't have. A tragic condition, I imagine."

"And a fitting punishment," Shay said, "though being sent to the nether is a better one. I warned him it would happen if he continued his reckless behavior."

"A kind gesture that obviously went unacknowledged."

"I only bothered because I felt a certain obligation to him." She kissed his cheek, trying to calm down. "After all, he did bring you back to me."

"A fact of which I am constantly reminded. Even Rise questioned me about my human lives."

"That's the fourth time you've mentioned her tonight." She noted he switched to using her given name instead of her title, and tried to change the subject. "Why do you ask about the castle? Haven't you been there a few times?"

"Only for specific duties. I never took the tour." Dominik looked through the scroll. "I'm curious about their combat training. Rise has shown unusual skill in that area."

"Probably one of her powers starting to flourish. Can we talk about something else? I'm tired of hearing about her."

"I expected the next one to be influence," he said, still reading. "It concerns me."

She resisted the urge to hit him over the head with something heavy. "She's the first created in over two millennia. I'm sure there will be some variation in her growth to fit the needs of the new era." She sat back and looked at her work. Dominik's hair trailed past his shoulders in dozens of braids. "All done. Would you like to see?"

"I'm sure it's perfect, as always." He pulled her off the stool and into his lap so she straddled him. "You're good to me."

"Because I'm in love you," she said, and placed a hand over his mouth before he could speak. "I know you don't feel the same yet, and I don't want you to think you have to explain." She smiled when he kissed her palm. "I waited a long time for you to take up wings." She stroked a few of his long blue-silver feathers and then growled, pretending to be mad. "Then you made me wait even longer while you forged a reputation among the choirs."

"I never knew of your desire," he said, and then his eyes turned playful. "I admit I went a little too far there for a while. Becoming an angel had some…stimulating perks I wasn't expecting."

"Dominik of the Blue!" She swatted him while he grinned. "I gave you plenty of hints, but I wasn't about to throw myself at your feet. I remembered what it was like to take up wings, and I knew the reason for your folly."

"Did you?" He sounded curious.

"I know the look you get when you're in contemplation, trying to figure out one of the spiritual mysteries." She put her arms around his neck. "I saw that same look when you worked your charm on others. I think you were searching for something." She gave him a gentle kiss. "I hope it's been found."

He touched one of her long, spiral curls, gave it a little tug and smiled as it bounced back into place. "You wore a similar style the first time we met. Do you remember?"

"I'll never forget." She tilted her head and sighed. "I was such a spoiled young girl in that lifetime. My handmaidens did everything from arranging my hair to changing my linens. I didn't know what to make of you, this tattered old man who dared to chastise me for striking a servant." She lost herself in his eyes. "You saved my soul long before you were an angel. I always thought you would take up wings before me."

"I denied the call for a long time," he said. "I felt I had more work to do, more journeys to complete, before I was ready."

"If not for the oath, I would've approached you long ago. It's so ridiculous. That part should only apply to Heralds."

"Angels are in service to humans. It would create too many complications if romantic adoration was allowed."

"Bah, you can quote chapter and verse from every one of the edicts. You'll end up as one of the Scriptures some day and then I'll never see you." She wiggled her hips, pressing against him. "At least you're not going to the viewing rooms tonight."

He chuckled. "No, Rise made it quite clear she doesn't want me 'spying' on her anymore. I'm going to spend time in meditation—"

"No!"

"What's the matter?" He adjusted her a little on his lap. "Why are you upset?"

"You're talking about her again."

"Shay, there are things about her I need to understand, things that may help me guide her to success." He stroked her arms. "Her light has increased to a point I might be able to connect with her across the realms if I concentrate. It's a necessary part of my role as advisor. You know this."

"You should stay here and connect with me." She pushed herself up and crossed the room. "When is this going to stop?"

"When she completes her trials, however long that will—" He stopped when he glimpsed his reflection in the wall mirror. He turned his head in a few directions to get a better look at the braids. "What is this you've done to me?"

"The common term is 'cornrows'. You don't like it, do you?"

"No, it's very…skillfully done."

She vowed to shave his entire head next time. "Dominik, I'm trying to have a serious conversation with you. You're too wrapped up with this Herald. I don't like the way she's taken over your life."

"I have a duty. You know its importance."

"I have duties as well, but I always make time for you. You spent eighteen human years buried in research, and now you're completely preoccupied. Have you considered asking to be replaced?"

He crossed his arms over his chest. "Why would I request such a thing?"

"Why wouldn't you? I know you hold no love for the Black choir, and this Herald has started to show her true nature. She angers you beyond reason, and it will only get worse."

"I admit I wasn't happy when given this task, but I won't abandon it, and I will be damned before I admit defeat."

"Defeat to whom?"

"To the one who placed me in this position!" His volume escalated with every word and he must've realized he was proving Shay's point. He took a calming breath and raised a hand in a gesture of peace.

"This is more than allegiance to the oath, isn't it?" She took a step forward. "Do you consider this a challenge, a test of will between you and Tyre? He's long gone, Dominik."

"Is he? His shadow looms over every part of this assignment, his presence permeating the very air I breathe." He began to pace the floor. "Rise mentioned hearing a voice, and I can't help but wonder…" The angel halted, flicked his hand. "It doesn't matter. You're right. There's more to this than just duty. I'm learning from this Herald. Watching her development has given me a certain perspective, one I don't think could be achieved through study."

"You and your constant need for knowledge!" Shay felt like slamming her fist into a wall. "You have the most infuriating academic vanity I've ever witnessed."

He reached for her. "I didn't mean to upset you. I'll remain here tonight."

Shay pushed him away. "No, I don't want you to placate me. Go and meditate. Find the Herald's over-powered light. In truth, I hope it's soon extinguished."

Dominik frowned. "You would wish failure on her?"

"So you could be free, yes." Shay shook her head. "If she fails she'll go to the nether, another will be created, and that one can be someone else's problem."

"It's not just failing the trials. There's the risk of surrender. She's on the verge of understanding—it's a vulnerable time for her."

"I don't care about *her*," she said. "My only concern is with you. Besides the rage she inspires, you've been attacked almost every time you cross into that realm."

"And I've come away unscathed." He looked at the fresh wound on his arm. "Nearly unscathed, anyway."

"But the attacks are too frequent to be a coincidence. It has something to do with that Herald, and if any harm comes to you, I will hand her over to the minions myself."

He smiled, probably thinking she wasn't serious, but Shay meant every single word.

CHAPTER THIRTY-FIVE
No Faith Left

By lunchtime the next day, Rise concluded that purple was spiritual code for 'snarky bitch'.

"Here's some more." Tammy piled more paperwork in the already enormous stack in front of Rise. "You're putting these in order by date, right? January comes first, then February, March…just like a calendar."

"Yes, I know." Rise wanted to hold her down and give her paper cuts. Dr. Mark had given her the job of filing. The work had been piling up for months; everyone had been waiting for someone else to do the tedious job. Rise sat up front in a corner, trying to be invisible. The receptionists were in their seats, surfing the Internet and gossiping between clients.

The bells above the front door jingled. Rise glanced up. A big man lumbered up to the front desk carrying two Chihuahua puppies, one under each arm.

"Jose and Cuervo are here for shots," he said. The puppies wiggled and licked his face. The guy did everything but lick them back.

Rise smiled, and added another yellow to the mental list she was compiling. She was already accustomed to the little lights. Now she wanted to decipher what they meant. She started taking notes, trying to come up with a plausible explanation. So far, she'd counted eight different colors. The intensity of the glows varied, and there was a fairly even distribution. Except for gold—she only saw two of those so far, one being Danny. That bugged her, since the other was Keisha/Chi and she was off in the great unknown, happily controlling her side of the universe.

Rise peeked at the bracelet. The glow was the same as yesterday. She focused on the white dot and wondered if she should send a thank-you card to Lucifer for his gift. She had the Inferi strapped to her calf under her loose work pants. She used packing tape to keep it in place and it was going to hurt like crazy if she had to rip it off fast. Rise knew minions wouldn't come for her around innocents, but she didn't know how far that protection went. It was on the mounting list of questions for the angel, whenever he decided to grace her with his presence again.

The bells jingled. This time it was the delivery guy coming in with a load of boxes. He greeted everyone with a big smile as he always did, even when it was raining and he had to make two trips. Rise sighed. He was a purple, too, so personality was definitely not the key to the color-coding.

Dr. Mark came up front and patted her on the shoulder. "Rise, do you want to take off early today?"

He didn't need to ask twice. She thanked him, clocked out, and took a few minutes in the car to peel the tape from her leg. She held the Inferi in her lap while she drove, and was halfway home when her phone rang.

"I went to the library and I've got a few names for you," Emory said.

"Can you text them to me? I'm driving."

"Hell no, there's about twenty. I'll send an E-mail, I'm typing it up right now." He had her on speakerphone, she could hear the keys clicking.

"I went back eighteen years," he said. "I figured your mom was either a junior or senior when she had you, but I checked sophomores, just in case. I wrote down every Aryan-looking female I saw."

"Did any of them look like me?' She was more excited now the wheels were in motion.

"I didn't think so, but it's hard to tell in yearbook pictures. Oh, I called that church. They do have a member directory, but you have to pick it up, and you only get one if you register as a parishioner. I love you and all, but I don't love you that much. Okay, it's sent. Let me know if it helps."

Rise assured him she would, and she found the E-mail waiting when she got home. The whole thing was in pure Emory-style; the subject line read 'Potential Baby Mommas' and the names were listed in alphabetical order with the class year included in parentheses. She read the names aloud, hoping one might trigger something in her brain. None of them did.

She printed off the page and checked the clock. If she hurried she could make it to the church office before it closed. She tore off her work clothes, did a quick touch-up on her hair, and wore sandals to show off Saba's work, if anyone cared to look at her feet.

She made it with fifteen minutes to spare. The woman behind the desk at the church office was engaged in a phone call. Rise recognized her as the front pew winner-sinner who spent considerable time with her penance prayers. Her glow was pale green—a perfect match to the label on the bottle of water she held, proclaiming it was made from recycled plastic. Rise snickered at the joke no one else would get.

She leaned against the desk, waiting, and almost fell over when she saw the woman's name on a placard—Lillian Rizzo. She was on the list Emory sent. Part of her wanted to run out the door, but a bigger part kept her in place. Thanks to the phone call, Rise had a chance to give the woman a thorough once-over. Lillian was the right age, looked to be of the right ancestry, but was significantly taller than average height, even without heels.

"Sorry about that," Lillian said when she hung up. "What can I do for you, honey?"

"I was thinking of joining the church."

Lillian asked her a few questions; if she currently attended church, if she was a baptized Catholic, then slid a form across the desk. It was a simple information sheet and at the bottom there was an option to be included in the member directory. Rise checked yes.

Lillian handed over a thick folder. "Our latest bulletin is in there, along with mass schedules. We have three Sunday services, including one in Spanish and one in Latin." She beamed. "We're the only church in Indianapolis that still offers the Latin Mass. If you've never gone, I recommend you do. It's a beautiful way to connect with the church's history."

Rise grunted. "I might do that. I've been studying Latin." She didn't mention it was at the behest of a pushy angel. She flipped open the folder and right in front was the directory. Bingo. She rattled off a quick thank you and made a break for the door. Lillian stopped her.

"I'll walk out with you so I can give the tour." She grabbed her purse and flipped off the lights.

Rise wanted to start cross-referencing names, not go sight-seeing, but she didn't know a polite way to refuse. She didn't want to burn bridges in case she needed something else in the future. She followed the woman down the walkway, nodding in feigned interest at various entrances and buildings. A familiar gentleman emerged from the church and gave a little wave. His red glow was the faintest she'd seen so far.

"I saw him last time I was here."

"That's where I know you," Lillian exclaimed like she'd solved a riddle. "That's John. He lives on the next block and comes in several times a week. The prayers are for his wife and daughter. He lost them both within a few years. Such a tragedy."

Rise recalled the man lit three candles, but didn't mention that. She tried to formulate a plan to escape her chatty new gal-pal.

Lillian continued, "John reminds me how grateful we should be for our blessings and the power of prayer and forgiveness. That man doesn't have an ounce of anger in his heart, even after all he's suffered."

Rise spouted a few words of sympathy for the guy's plight, then made a show of checking the time. Lillian took the hint, wrapped up the tour and Rise dashed to her car with electricity in her steps. She cracked the window to get some air, flipped open the directory and started checking names against the list Emory compiled. She crossed off Lillian Rizzo; too tall. She eliminated a couple more before loud voices intruded on her concentration.

The man she'd just seen, John, stood on the sidewalk, while a woman screeched at him through the window of her gold Lexus. She was in her mid-thirties, hair cut and styled in the latest fashion, and she wore a sleek business suit. Rise saw the whole, impressive ensemble when the woman slid out her car and slammed the door. She was a blue and Rise was surprised; she'd have pegged her for a red.

Rise didn't intend to eavesdrop, but as the argument went on, the louder it got. She heard the woman call John 'dad' and that piqued her interest. Looked like she wasn't the only one around with daddy issues.

"I'm not going in there to help with this charade," the woman said. Her voice was intimidating, far different from her father's.

"It's two days a year that I ask you, Deb," John said. "You already missed your mama's birthday. You can honor your sister on hers."

"I haven't stepped foot inside that church since the day I graduated. It still makes me sick you forced me to go to school here after what happened."

Rise's ears perked up when she heard that tidbit, and she checked the names on Emory's list. The woman was about the right age, but there wasn't a Deb listed. She rolled down the window a bit more, now invested in the family argument. John's red glow was a tad brighter. Rise was pretty sure she knew what that meant. It didn't take any mystical skills to know he was getting upset. Deb was still ranting.

"I have no faith left, Daddy! What they did to my sister was wrong. I'm never going to believe otherwise."

"You should keep your voice down," John said, looking around. "We don't need a donnybrook on church grounds."

Deb laughed without humor and tossed her arms up. "Here we go. Let's keep it quiet. Let's keep all of our family business quiet! We can't let anyone know—"

"Deb..."

"Daddy, I'm sorry." The woman started wearing down. "I didn't come to argue, I came because I thought Scotty would be here. He doesn't know where he is half the time, but he always remembers Katie's birthday." She dabbed a tear from under eye before it could spoil her make-up. "I don't even know where to look for him anymore."

John removed his hat, revealing balding white hair. "I keep calling the police, to see if they might've picked him up for stealing again, or vagrancy." He shook his head. "I don't want to bury another child. I keep the door unlocked every night, hoping Scotty will come back home."

The conversation returned to normal volume. Rise couldn't hear the rest, though she tried. John walked away after a few minutes and Deb leaned against her car rubbing her temples.

Rise didn't want to butt into family business, but she couldn't help but wonder if the two were talking about the Scotty that wandered her neighborhood. She considered it might be another sign, and she hopped out of the car and waved her arms. She caught Deb just as she was about to drive away.

"Ma'am!" she called, and the woman looked at her, untrusting, and rolled down the window a crack. Rise picked up the scent of high-end perfume. "I was in my car over there," she said, pointing. "I heard some of that, uh, discussion you had with your dad."

"I'm sorry about that," Deb said. "I generally try for more discretion."

"I heard you talking about a person named Scotty. Does he have blonde hair, kind of choppy, and a goatee? He wears a Bears jacket?"

Deb's eyes lit up and she got out of the car. "You know my brother?"

"If it's the same person, he lives near my building on the east side. I don't know where, but he hangs out at the laundromat." She didn't mention he was usually asking strangers for money.

"That's his spot now? Last time it was a gas station. Can you show me?"

"You can follow me? Or I can give you the address—"

"I'll follow you now."

Rise took off, ready to do her good deed for the night. It wouldn't take long, and she could get back to looking at the directory. She took a peek at the bracelet and was amazed to see the glow was a little brighter. She pumped her arm, happy to make some progress. She also made sure the Inferi was within reach.

Rise pulled into the laundromat parking lot. Deb pulled up in the opposite direction so they could speak through the windows.

"This is the place," Rise said. "I don't see him. He might've gone home already."

"If he has one," Deb said. "Where do the homeless stay around here?"

"I don't know of any shelters, but we have a few that hang out in the park on the other side of the building. We'll have to walk."

It was still light out, and kids and parents were still enjoying the park. Rise scanned the area and saw a figure on a bench near the back. She couldn't see him well at her distance and there were several kids getting in the way, but it might have been Scotty. She pointed, but Deb was already heading that way at a trot. Her high heels sunk into the ground, so she pulled them off and carried them. Rise followed. It was indeed Scotty, and the kids surrounding him were throwing taunts and laughing.

"Sing one about Santa Claus," a little boy said. He poked Scotty with a small branch and the frightened man backed away in fear despite his larger size.

A little girl giggled. "I like his hat." She snatched it off his head and danced around, easily avoiding the half-hearted attempts Scotty made to retrieve his property.

"I want to hear Jingle Bells again," another boy said. "Sing for me!" He smacked Scotty on the back of his head.

Deb saw what was happening. She fell into a dead run and hollered at the kids. "Get away from him! Now!" She grabbed the branch from the boy and heaved it away. She went for the girl, but she dropped the hat and ran.

The two boys looked like they were about to say something, but then their eyes widened. They were looking past Deb, staring at a thick woman coming across the park, with two smaller children trying to keep up with her angry strides.

"Get back here!" the big woman demanded and waved her hand. Her eyes said she meant business. "I already told you to leave that poor man alone!"

The two boys looked at one another, and then ran to the woman, both insisting the other was at fault. The woman pulled them by the ears out of the park. She was a yellow, and Rise decided that was going to be her favorite color for a while.

"Scotty?" Deb bent over the haggard looking man, who was holding his head and singing. "It's Deb. I'm here to take you home, honey." She placed her hands on his face and tried to get him to look at her.

Scotty was in terrible shape. Rise had never seen him up close before. His hair was thin, and his arms were littered with scratches. He smelled like he hadn't bathed in a week, and from the gaunt look to his face, it might have been as long since he'd eaten. He kept singing, rocking back and forth.

"Peace on earth and mercy mild, God and sinners reconciled..." He tried to put his head back down, but Deb held him firmly.

"Scotty, look at me." Deb used a tone that must have been well practiced. It got his attention. He fell silent, and his eyes lost a little of the glassiness.

"It's Katie's day," he said. "I missed it. Dad's going to be mad at me."

"No, honey," Deb said, then smiled in relief. "I saw dad, and he's not mad at all. He's worried. Can I call him and tell him you're coming home with me?" She didn't get a response, so she changed tactics, and her voice turned light. "I haven't made dinner yet. I was thinking of getting something from a burger place. You'd like that, right?"

"With a toy," Scotty said, and almost smiled.

"We can get that, no problem. Can you walk to the car?"

Scotty stood up, a little shaky. He shuffled like an old man. He had well worn flip-flop sandals on his feet, and the bottom of his jeans were worn, damp, and dragging on the grass.

Rise walked with them back to Deb's car, all the while Scotty softly singing. Rise felt awkward. She wasn't sure if she should leave now, or if she should have already left. She was hoping for at least a thank-you, though.

Once her brother was buckled in, Deb turned to Rise.

"What's your name?" she asked.

"Rise."

"I like that," Deb said. "I appreciate you eavesdropping on my conversation earlier." She smiled to take the sting from the crack.

"I do what I can. I hope your brother gets better."

"Now, I want to do something for you." Deb pulled out her wallet with lots of big bills sticking out. Rise didn't necessarily want anything, she was actually feeling pretty good about herself right now, but had to admit some extra cash would be useful. That wasn't Deb's plan, though; she parceled out a business card.

"I'm an attorney up in Carmel. I typically work cases involving rights of the disabled, women's issues, that sort of thing. I have a blog—look it up sometime." She pointed to the card. "But if you ever need help with anything involving the law, give me a call. Pro bono, unless it's going to be a big one." She winked. "I *am* still a lawyer."

"Thanks," Rise said and held up the card. "No offense, but I hope I never have to use this. It's nice what you do. It sounds real...ethical." She cringed, wishing she had thought of a better word.

"After what happened to our sister, I knew I had to do something." She adjusted the purse on her arm.

"I heard she died.

"And I can guess from who," Deb said, her voice turning fiery. "Lillian has a big mouth and selective memory. My sister didn't just *die*. She was abducted and raped, and then left on the side of a road when she was only seventeen."

Rise had no idea what to say.

Deb calmed a little. "Do you go to that church?"

"I joined today." She was getting good at the little falsehoods.

"I'm not going to preach to you, but I'd recommend you un-joining."

"You don't like Holy Trinity?" Stupid question; the answer was obvious.

"I don't like any church that would destroy a family the way they destroyed mine." She breathed in and out through her nose. "They convinced my father to keep my sister on life support for seven months, just so she could carry the baby of the piece of garbage that raped her." The words sounded like they had been festering a long time.

Rise's mouth dropped open and a noise like rushing water filled her ears. "Did your sister go to school there?"

"Until she died, about eighteen years ago."

"She had a baby?" Rise's voice cracked a little.

"I never saw it, thank God. My father signed it over to catholic charities." Her face twisted in disgust. "The old

Priest up there promised he'd find a good, catholic family to raise the little bastard." She shook her head. "I guess the people had money since they paid most of the medical bills, probably fifty grand." She snorted. "At least it saved my dad from going bankrupt, but that doesn't make up for what happened."

Rise thought she was going to fall over. Her head was floating away.

"Makes me sick," Deb said. "My sister deserved to die with dignity, like God intended." Another tear came and this time she didn't bother to dab; she wiped it away, taking some mascara with it that streaked across her face. "Anyway, thank you for telling me about my brother. I've got to get some food into him."

She slid into her car, and Rise just stood there for a long, long while.

She had no doubt at all that she'd just met the first blood-family she'd ever known. She sat on the curb, her thoughts in turmoil. She couldn't move and had to concentrate to keep from vomiting. She remembered what the Sister at St. Anne's had asked her—if she was prepared for what she might find in her search. Rise knew now she wasn't. She wasn't prepared at all.

Chapter Thirty-Six
Revelations

Night had fallen by the time Rise got back home. She'd sat on that curb for hours and hadn't even noticed. She wandered from room to room, fed Oliver, showered—all without conscious thought. Danny sent her a text, she didn't even read it. She stared at her reflection in the mirror and wondered if her father, the rapist, had green eyes like hers.

Deb, the rich attorney with the fabulous suit, was her *aunt*. Rise was having trouble reconciling that with her own life. She looked around her apartment with the second-hand furniture and chipping paint, for the first time feeling ashamed.

She sat at her computer and watched as the blog page Aunty Deb mentioned loaded on the screen. Professionally made, it had links to horrendous human rights crimes all over the world. Deb had some daily personal entries, as well; most concerned cases in which she was involved. Right up top was a link to the Katie Connors Memorial Page. Rise clicked it.

A website popped up, much different from the blog. Photos covered the page and she regarded the face of her birth mother. Katie had been a pretty girl, but Rise didn't see any resemblance. Her father, the rapist, obviously held the dominant genes.

Tabs along the side linked to separate pages; one told of Katie's young life, another detailed her death. The event was transcribed in a detached, forensic style, probably copied right from the police report. Rise read everything without emotion. She felt dead inside.

Katie was killed while on a senior trip, Deb had written. She was taken from a hotel, assaulted, and suffered fatal injuries in a crash. Horribly, a photo of the wrecked car was included. Rise had never seen one so mangled. The driver, the person wanted for 'questioning' in the crime, fled the scene. She couldn't imagine how he'd survived.

Rise moved the curser to a link that would display a sketch of the driver, but didn't click right away. She was terrified to see the face of the man who sired her, the man who forced her into existence. She took a deep breath and clicked. Her old computer took a long time to load large files. She couldn't stand to watch the photo appear inch-by-inch, so she clicked a few more links that went to news articles about the crime. Some of Katie's classmates were interviewed and Rise found it amusing her mother had been in the choir; she could barely hum. Most of the articles had the same information in different words, but the final one contained a few unique lines at the end from one of the witnesses to the crash.

"I hope the girl lives. I hope the doctors can save her." The name given for the quote was Kafi al Alzeen, age eleven.

Rise leapt up, knocked over the chair and scared poor Oliver. It had to be the same person. She *knew* it was the same person. She was done believing in coincidences. Her hand shook as she clicked back to the photo. There, staring out from her computer screen was the face of the man that attacked her mother. It was a face Rise recognized instantly. It was the face of an angel.

"Dominik," she whispered.

"Rise?"

She whirled toward sound of the voice, bashed against the desk and the monitor crashed to the floor. "Speak of the devil." She whipped her head around, spotted the Inferi on the counter and snatched it up. She held it tight with both hands. "Why are you here?"

"You left the door unlocked." Dominik stared at her like she'd lost her mind. He moved forward. "Give me that before you—"

"One more step and I swear I'll kill you." She didn't know if hellfire could harm an angel, but either the threat or her tone was taken seriously. Dominik froze.

"Tell me what's happened." He had the nerve to sound demanding.

"Katie Connors!" She saw his eyes go wide at mention of the name. "That's right. You remember her, don't you?"

"I do." Dominik's expression was odd. "How do you know of her?"

"The church needs to train its priests a little better if they want to keep their secrets. And adoption agencies need to keep a leash on their employees."

"You're quite resourceful."

Dominik's little smile infuriated her. She took a step toward him, brandishing the weapon. "She was my mother," Rise said, her voice trembling with rage. "You knew that, too, didn't you?"

"She was a vessel."

"She was a human being!" Rise knew her neighbors could probably hear her through the walls, but didn't care. "She was raped and murdered!"

Dominik looked at her with open confusion. "This is what you believe? Where are you getting this information?"

"I saw the police report," she said, taking another step, "and I talked to Deb, *my aunt*. She told me what happened."

"There was no force involved." Dominik placed his hands up in a gesture of peace. "You must let me—"

"No force?" Rise barked out a laugh. "What did you do, then? Did you pull your angel seduction act, like you did to me?"

In response, he bolted forward and grabbed her, spinning her around so her back pressed against him. He clamped one hand around her neck, keeping her head in place in a steel grip, with the other, he squeezed her wrist.

"Drop the Inferi." His voice was right in her ear, filled with authority. He squeezed harder when she didn't comply. She struggled and pressed the red gem. Flame erupted and sulfur flooded the air until his hold became so tight Rise thought her wrist would break. She dropped the weapon, but kept battling.

"Let me go!" She kicked hard. Her heel connected with his shin, but she thought she hurt herself more than the angel. He jerked her up so her feet dangled in the air, and shook her while she bucked and tried to bite.

"Stop fighting me." He pressed his thumb into the underside of her chin. "I don't want to hurt you, but I will if that's what it takes to make you listen."

Rise didn't care if he beat her half to death, she refused to concede. She fought with all she had, until every drop of energy depleted. She sagged in his hold like a water balloon, barely able to breathe. A single tear borne of defeat and frustration slid down her face. She despised the show of weakness even more than she despised the angel.

Once she was still, Dominik loosened his grip, but didn't let her go. "Tell me what you think you know."

She summoned all her fury and spewed words like a volcano. "I think you're my father and a twisted freak." He didn't respond so she kept going. "They kept her alive until I was born, did you know that? This is why the minions want me, right? Why you never wanted to tell me? Because I'm the product of some unholy union."

"That's not why they want you." His voice remained hard, but the edge dulled a small amount. "And yes, I do know what happened to Katie."

"It makes me sick. What kind of angel does that?"

"The kind that is stripped of his wings and banished for his crime." Dominik allowed her feet to touch the ground, but kept her in a solid hold. "The one that created you was Tyre."

"I saw the picture," Rise said, trying to twist her head so she could see him. "There were witnesses. It was your face!"

"Tyre was a Herald who was granted many powers, including the ability to alter his physical appearance. He chose mine, out of a perverse desire to taunt me." He paused, and took a ragged breath. "He would no doubt find my current situation most amusing."

"A Herald?" Rise remembered the two minions in the alleyway kept calling her by that name. "Is that what I am?"

"Yes." He turned her around to face him. "I was not to divulge the specifics of your creation, or your title, until you achieved better understanding in other areas. You've placed me in a difficult position."

"I'm so sorry to have inconvenienced you," she snapped. "What's a Herald? Don't give me one of those evasive answers. Tell me exactly what that means."

Dominik looked her in the eyes. "Heralds are the rarest of all angels, the only creatures born as such, and granted powers beyond the scope of understanding for most."

Rise stepped back and glanced at a mirror on the wall. She'd been looking at herself for eighteen years and was sure she would've noticed if she was an angel.

"You were born into flesh, to be forged by trials," Dominik said. "If you succeed, you will earn the black wings and take your place among the choir of Heralds."

"Oh, my God." Rise could barely believe the words, but it made a crazy kind of sense, all things considered. "What do you mean by trials?"

"Challenges that must be overcome." He stopped her before she could say anything else. "I can't tell you what they—"

"You can't, or you won't?" Her tone was sharp, but the angel only smiled.

"They are unique for each Herald, though the results are the same. Each trial is designed to test and strengthen you, and each will leave its mark both spiritually and physically."

Rise felt like an elusive puzzle piece had just fallen into place, but there was another one still missing. "What about my mother? Was she an angel, too?"

"No. She was a human soul on a journey of sacrifice, and didn't know she was engaging in relations with a Herald." He looked away. "Not at the time, anyway."

"But you said she wasn't attacked?" She prayed he was telling the truth about that.

"I swear it," Dominik said. "Tyre took advantage of his position and broke his oath, but he did not force himself on young Katie."

There was something in his voice she couldn't place, and he looked as uncomfortable as she'd ever seen him. That made two of them, so she wasn't about to let him off the hook. "How do you know all this?"

"Sit down."

"I'm fine where I am." She crossed her arms.

"Very well." Dominik started to pace the room. "As I told you, I had many lifetimes before I took up the wings. I treasured each one, none more than Katie Theresa Connors. She was my final journey."

Rise never knew her eyes could open so wide. She thought they might pop from her skull, so she closed them up tight to make sure they stayed put.

"I need to sit down." She was already heading in that direction, and would've fallen had Dominik not whipped the desk chair around under her bottom. She stared straight ahead, unable to meet the angel's gaze just yet.

"You...were...Katie?" She thought saying it out loud would help, but it only made it worse.

"Yes."

"And Katie was my mother."

He started to answer, but furious pounding at the door interrupted. Rise knew who it was, even before she answered.

"You okay in there?" Mr. Crawford tried to look past her, his face deeply suspicious. "I just got home. My wife told me she heard a ruckus a little bit ago."

Rise assured him she was okay, and hoped if Dominik was in view, he'd at least stashed his wings. She stammered out an excuse about arguing with a friend on the phone.

He wrinkled up his nose and took a sniff. "What's that smell?" He looked at her with hard eyes. "You smoking something in there?"

The sulfur still hung in the air, and she scrambled for an explanation. "I was...cooking something on the stove and forgot. It burned." She hoped he was buying into her mess of a lie. "I'll open the windows."

"Don't worry about it. I'm just glad everything's okay." Mr. Crawford started back down the hall, then glanced back and focused on her slim waist. "I'm glad you're eating something, too."

Rise went back to sit, this time on the loveseat. She stared up at Dominik. "My mother has facial hair," she said in a flat voice, "and cornrows."

"Katie was a vessel," Dominik repeated his earlier words. "My soul released before the body was even extricated from the vehicle, before the seeds of creation had even taken hold."

"Okay, ick." She didn't want to think too hard on the details. "So, you're saying my father was a disgraced angel and my mother didn't have a soul. That's much better, a real self-esteem booster." She fell silent and stayed that way.

"Rise?"

She held up a finger. "I'm trying to organize my thoughts into a hierarchy of disconcert. It might take a while."

It did. The hours ticked by, the stench of sulfur dispersed, and at some point - though Rise couldn't have said when - her survival instinct kicked in and, mercifully, she fell asleep.

Chapter Thirty-Seven
Almost Sorry

Rise awoke at first light to the sound of soft singing. She opened her eyes and saw Dominik looking out the window at the rising sun. His wings were on display, and he held his hands as if making an offering. His voice was every bit as glorious as she remembered, almost hypnotic. She had no idea what he was saying; the words were lost on her, in a language as beautiful as it was unknown. Even so, there was an odd familiarity about the song and she felt a pang of loss when it was over.

"I can probably deal with the fact you're technically my mommy," she said after he finished. "But if you're going to start singing me lullabies, that might change."

His wings quivered in amusement. "I love this," he said, still staring out the window. "The first rays of light in harmony with the dark, the realm in perfect balance."

"I'm not really a morning person." Rise sat, and pulled her legs in close so she faced the angel. "You have an amazing voice." Her emotions smoothed out during the night. She owed Dominik a little courtesy after her misdirected verbal lashing. "I've always envied people that could sing. I definitely didn't inherit that from you."

"Nor anything else," he said. "There is nothing of me within you, or of Katie Connors."

"What?" Her voice rose awkwardly. "I passed science. I know how genetics work."

"You know of natural laws, not those that govern the divine." Dominik turned to face her. "Heralds are granted supremacy over all life. Tyre had authority to take it away, and he possessed the power to create it, without assistance."

Rise processed that as best she could, which wasn't much.

Dominik watched her reaction closely. "This is why intimacy with humans is a violation of the oath, and why the consequences for breaking that vow are so severe. Tyre chose to sate his curiosity with a human soul about to ascend, believing it would have no consequence."

Rise ran a hand through her hair as she tried to understand. "He didn't intend for this to happen? He didn't create me on purpose?" She was a little offended, but also found it funny. "So, I'm here because the spiritual condom broke." She could live with that.

Dominik offered a little smile. "Tyre spent many long years dealing in death and suffering, as his duties required. Perhaps it rendered him unable, or unwilling, to see the importance in anything else. He underestimated humanity's desire and increasing ability to preserve life." He looked down. "Sometimes the methods are misguided, but the intent is pure."

Rise considered that and deemed it logical. "What was he like?" She played with her nails, embarrassed at how vulnerable she felt right then in her desire to know. "I guess it doesn't matter."

"Your curiosity is natural." Dominik knelt beside her so his eyes were level with hers. He touched a wisp of her tousled hair, moving it between his fingers with unusual tenderness. "His hair was as yours—black as pitch. It matched his wings."

"Did he have green eyes?"

"All Heralds share those, as well as the scars."

Rise's touched the mark on her face. "I wasn't born with this."

"It's a badge of completion from one of your trials. There will be more."

She wondered what awesome trial she'd overcome when James Hawke planted her face into the side of that table. She didn't like hearing more scars were in her future, and hoped they wouldn't be too ugly. She realized that should be the last of her concerns.

"This is why the minions want me," she said. "They want to add me to their collection, the same reason they hunt you."

"Yes, though a Herald is much harder to claim. There are only nineteen in existence, including you. And Heralds are eternal, the only choir of pure angels. They cannot be killed, as others."

Rise readjusted her position, feeling overwhelmed. "You mean I can't die?"

"No, but you can be made to wish otherwise." Dominik's tone made it clear he wanted her full attention. "To be collected, a Herald must speak words of surrender in full understanding of the consequences. Minions will go to great lengths to achieve that goal."

"You're still not going to explain what surrender means, are you?"

"No, I am not. I've already broken my oath by revealing the details of your creation. I won't do so again."

"Didn't think so." She wasn't going to press the issue. She was more interested in why all this angelic power hadn't shown up yet. "I don't feel any different, and I should, right? When will I get to do all the cool stuff, like change my appearance and—"

"It will manifest in time." Dominik was in full advisor mode again. "Concentrate on what you would call the 'boring stuff' for the time being. Learn to use and understand the skills you already possess, instead of reaching for those not yet in your grasp."

"I am!" Rise hopped up and rifled through her handbag. She pulled out a small notepad and flipped it open. "I've been trying to figure out the light of the soul. I'm keeping track and I've counted seven different colors, not including the gold, and you said that symbolized a mission of sacrifice."

"You listened to me?" He moved toward her with suspicion. "And you're researching?"

"Yeah, I'm not an idiot." Rise flipped through a few pages, scanning her notes. "Okay, so the red glow is kind of a no-brainer. Anger, right?"

"Wrath." Dominik stood over her shoulder, looking down at the notepad. "When a soul is susceptible, the light will increase. It attracts the attention of minions and they will present challenges."

"That's what I thought." For once, the angel didn't seem irritable with her—probably a sign she was on the right track. "Then two days ago I saw a woman with a yellow glow. She won fifty dollars on a scratch off lottery ticket, but when she got the cash, she became brighter. Does that have something to do with money?" She already knew the answer.

"Greed," he confirmed. "Many times that one will feed on itself. It's a difficult challenge to master."

"And wrath and greed are two of the seven deadly sins. That's what the colors mean. I knew it!"

He nodded. "I'm impressed. You've caught on faster than most."

She tried not to show how much the words meant to her. "See, I'm not all bad. I might even make a good angel someday."

"You're already an angel." Dominik gave her shoulder a gentle squeeze. "The flesh is simply a tool, a way to help you grow."

Rise pulled away from him and snorted. "It's a way to keep me weak and able to get my butt kicked; totally unfair since I have a big target on my head."

He gave her a teasing look. "We've discussed your concept of 'fairness' before. Everything you've been given, even those you might view as a detriment, serves a great purpose."

"Does that include the big detriment known as Dominik, too?"

"It does." He put some distance between them and checked his bracelet. "Learn as much as you can. Embrace your divine nature, but never forget to maintain respect for humanity and all others. If I teach you nothing else, that will suffice. I would not see you follow Tyre into banishment."

"He was a jerk, huh?" Rise smiled. It figured.

"Tyre had many fine qualities, but he believed his position set him apart." He looked to the window, focusing on something far away. "In the end, the mighty Herald discovered he was not so unlike humanity. He created his own problems, and ultimately his own destruction. He created you."

"What a kick in the butt." She played with the notebook in her hand. "Is that why you don't like me? Because of Tyre?" She hated to ask but wanted to know. "I guess can't blame you after what happened."

Dominik didn't speak for a time. "Heralds are very different from other angels. There is a great deal I don't understand about them, and that includes you." He looked to have an internal argument. "Suffice it to say, I've found it difficult to be your advisor for many reasons, the circumstances surrounding your creation among them."

He didn't disagree about not liking her. She didn't know why that bothered her so much. "You shouldn't hold that against me. What happened wasn't my fault, and just because I'm a Herald doesn't mean I'm going to end up like Tyre." She wasn't as confident in her declaration as she tried to sound.

Dominik studied her, as though trying to see right through her skin. "In the future, I will endeavor to remember that." The words sounded wrapped in sincerity and he even bowed at the neck when he said them.

Rise shuffled on her feet, uncomfortable with the touchy-feely turn in the conversation. "Well, since you *almost* apologized, I'll say I'm *almost* sorry for trying to kill you last night."

He laughed, his blue eyes filling with warmth for a moment. "Now that I know the mistaken assumptions you held, I think I would've been disappointed in you if you hadn't." He moved toward the porch, becoming serious once more. "I must report to the Scriptures and make them aware of your newfound knowledge."

"Will you get in trouble?" Not that she particularly cared. She thought she had a right to know.

"Possibly," he said, "but considering the unusual circumstances - your curiosity run amok - I suspect they'll be lenient. I'll return soon. We have lots of work to do." He cocked a finger. "Continue to observe, read three more chapters in the book I gave you, and keep the Inferi close." He pointed. Her bracelet glowed brighter than ever. "As your understanding increases, so does the risk."

Rise watched him fly away, then hopped in the shower, her mind whirling with new information. She still had a thousand questions and she considered writing them down so she wouldn't forget. She was in the middle of washing her hair when she felt the telltale tingle.

"You should have given him a blast of hellfire," the all-too-familiar voice said. "I think we both would've enjoyed that."

"Do you mind?" Rise fumbled around, trying to pull the plastic shower curtain around her while she wiped shampoo from her face. "A little privacy here, asshole!"

"Tsk tsk...not very becoming language for an angel. Am I interrupting something?"

"I'm in the shower." She really hoped the disembodied voice couldn't see her, but she didn't trust the entity, whatever he was. "I thought I told you to leave me alone."

"And I told you I'd be back. I do try to keep my promises."

Rise cursed and tried to wash off the soap while still keeping covered by the shower curtain. "I'm getting sick of this mental ninja crap you're pulling." She blinked water out of her eyes.

"I find it distasteful, as well. My hope is that we will soon meet in a more personal setting. Farewell, little Herald."

As quickly as it had come, the disembodied voice departed. Rise bolted from the shower and ran through the apartment, leaving wet footprints on the carpet while she searched for the card Dominik gave her a while back. She dialed the number listed. It rang once and went to voicemail. She held the phone away and stared at it, disbelieving.

"You've got to be kidding me." She hoped Dominik was true to his word and returned soon. He needed to bring some more answers with him, including a way to get rid of the irritating mental buddy who seemed to know far too much about her.

She got dressed for work and wondered if being an angel could get her out of filing.

Chapter Thirty-Eight
Trust

Dominik released the final braid and ran fingers through his hair. He hoped Shay wouldn't be offended, but that particular style hadn't suited him. He peered into the small mirror atop his dresser, frowning at the kinked mess he created. He'd deal with it later. He had more important things to worry about, not the least of which was the decision from the Scriptures regarding his breach of oath.

He reported to the council immediately after returning from the human realm. He advised them Rise had gained knowledge of her creation, and a rudimentary understanding of her title. Several members questioned him, then Chi ordered him to leave so they could discuss the matter in private.

Dominik checked the time; he'd been waiting longer than usual. Most likely, the Scriptures were reviewing the encounter using their private reflection pool. He paced the room, anxious to return to his duties with Rise. He smiled, recalling the look on her face when he told her the truth about her heritage. She handled it far better than he'd anticipated, and he was relieved he wouldn't need to deflect certain questions any longer. The Herald was a curious creature, and determined; putting her off had become quite a chore.

A soft chime sounded at his door and he was surprised to find Chi standing outside. He stood back so she could pass into the room.

"We've reviewed the events," she said. "Strictly speaking, you were in violation of the oath, but we believe the situation was unavoidable. We find you free of culpability in the matter."

Dominik bowed. "Thank you for your leniency, and for taking the time to deliver the news personally."

"I wished to speak with you privately." She bunched her gown as if expecting to sit, but there was no chair. "I see you maintain your love of simplicity."

"I apologize," he said. "I'm conserving space. The common area down the hall is rarely in use—"

"Not necessary. I won't take up much of your time." She moved about the room, nodding in approval. "You have a true appreciation of refinement. You don't maintain many possessions, but what few you choose are of the highest quality." She knelt to touch the circular rug in front of the altar. "Did the master weavers design this?"

"Yes. I use it for meditation."

"It's perfection." She ran her hand along the soft material, then stood. "This is such a small area. I know the Blue choir was trying to woo you. I'm surprised the elders didn't offer something larger in gratitude for your petition, a chamber more befitting your reputation." She smiled at him. "And your size."

Dominik laughed. "They did, but I declined. This chamber suits my needs, I have room enough to stretch my wings and look up there." He pointed at the flickering lights streaming through the high, glass ceiling. "A view of the stars every night."

Chi tilted her head and placed an eye against the telescope Dominik kept pointed at the sky. "You're perfectly positioned to see the constellation of Aries. Fascinating." She stepped away. "I wanted to mention something that concerned me."

"I'm always appreciative of your advice."

"The altercation between you and the Herald, it became physical, even violent. She threatened you, and you responded in kind. It was rather surprising. Thus far, you've been considerably more forgiving of her Herald...energy...than advisors of the past."

"I've implemented various strategies with her, but last night I believed force was required to maintain control of the situation. She refused to hear reason or explanation, and I don't trust her impulsive nature. She has great passion, but not properly channeled, it can be a liability."

"Great passion," Chi mused. "Interesting choice of words."

Dominik's lip curled into a half-smile. "She was fully prepared to use the Inferi on me—I have no doubt."

"I'm not disputing that. I saw the fire in her eyes." She moved toward the door, paused, and placed a delicate hand on his arm. "I've discovered that trust between two souls is a precious thing, not easily attained and best forged mutually." She gave his arm a little pat. "That's all I wanted to say. I'll leave you in peace to resume your work."

Dominik considered her words. As one of the Scriptures, Chi was guardian to many mysteries and did not reveal secrets directly. She instead chose to guide, to help others come to understanding in their own way.

He decided to shower before departing. Rise enjoyed her little taunts almost as much as her predecessor; the state of his hair would give her far too much ammunition. He stripped off his shirt, glanced in the mirror and caught sight of the glowing pendant hovering below his collarbone. He hadn't taken it off since the day it was presented, but tonight he unclasped the chain and placed it atop his dresser.

Dominik felt an immediate sense of vulnerability and almost changed his mind. The Herald didn't know the power of the object her advisor wore, that it prevented him from being susceptible to any commands she might try to issue. He decided it didn't matter. He would look on the sacrifice as a show of trust. He hoped it wasn't misplaced.

After he freshened up, Dominik made his way through the Expanse and, as required, placed his hand on one of the many purple globes near the river Lethe. The action allowed his exit to be noted, his movements tracked. He chose an isolated entry location for his transition to the human realm.

He still had time before Rise would return from her clinic job. He walked the area, keeping a lookout for souls in turmoil, vulnerable to spiritual attack. He found a few and offered assistance—nothing dramatic, or even angelic. Just gestures of kindness borne from keen observation and a willingness to act.

He was less than a block from Rise's home when he smelled the stench of decay. He was between two buildings, out of sight from innocents and fair game. He whipped off his jacket and moved into a battle stance seconds before two minions came for him; male and female, both brandishing blades. They attacked in unison and he leapt into the air to avoid powerful blows. One struck his leg, only his heavy boot protecting him from injury. Dominik shrugged off the close call; he'd gotten used to the blitz attacks.

"I get the wing this time," the female said and looked up. "Get down here, dog!"

He granted her wish, landing right on top of her. She fell, stabbing upward in frenzy. Dominik controlled her weapon hand, pinned her to the ground and punched her in the face several times. The second minion attacked from the rear. Dominik kicked his leg up. The blow hit hard and the minion sprawled.

Dominik grabbed the blade from the female and turned to her accomplice. They engaged in a brief exchange, blades clashing. He disarmed the minion without difficulty and tossed the weapon away.

The female staggered to her feet, turned to run, and Dominik threw her own blade at her. It carved into her back. She fell with a scream and was shattered glass within moments.

The second minion wasn't going to run. His eyes were wild and he turned out to be a better pugilist than a knife fighter; he held his ground for several minutes, but then

Dominik got him in a tight hold and slammed him against the brick wall. The minion spewed curses, even as Dominik stabbed him through the gut.

"I'll be avenged." The minion laughed as much as his injury allowed. "You're as good as dead."

"But not by you." Dominik allowed himself a moment of satisfaction at the victory. He took no pleasure from killing, but minions who hunted were too dangerous to be spared. Most angels didn't have the arsenal of skills Dominik acquired over his many lifetimes and would be easier prey.

He picked up the minion weapons and his jacket. He didn't have one arm in a sleeve before another attack came, this time a group of three. They circled him while he whipped his head between all of them, trying to decide what to do. He wasn't one to abandon a challenge but this time he was out-numbered to an extent exceeding the mandate of his choir. Angels weren't permitted to risk themselves without necessity, and rules dictated he disengage if possible. He spread his wings and launched into the air, ignoring the taunts at his cowardice.

He transitioned back to the spiritual realm and took a moment to think about the situation. Another angel came into view beside him. It was Euriki from his own choir, returning from a duty.

"What happened?" she asked. "Were you attacked again?"

Dominik touched his lip where the minion landed a blow. "Twice, in rapid succession. There were three the second time."

"That's unusual." Eureki's voice was concerned. "Have you made notification yet?"

"I'm about to do so."

He found a purple globe and made report of the minion attacks, as was required. He noted the time, location and the numbers involved. He scrolled through other attacks; there had been many scattered throughout the human realm. His heart sank when he saw seven more angels had been killed, including a Gold in Denmark. That meant another Free Spirit had been unleashed.

He checked his timepiece. Rise was surely home by now, and he felt an urgency to be at her side. He would be safe in her apartment, but getting there would be a problem if minions were monitoring entry points. He decided to wait a while and try another location. In the meantime, he hoped Rise stayed put and kept the Inferi close.

Chapter Thirty-Nine
Choice

Rise stood by her car and searched for her keys, praying she didn't leave them in the clinic. She and Tammy were the last ones out the door and the tech just drove away. She was in a foul mood, thanks to another day of tedious busy-work, and didn't want to get stuck walking home.

A bigger irritant was Dominik. Despite his promise to return, the angel hadn't shown up in days and her patience was on shaky ground. Now that she finally had some real answers, she was ready to get to work and earn those wings. She didn't have a clue what being a Herald entailed, but it had to be better than filing.

She dumped her bag on the hood of her car and barely caught the Inferi before it rolled off. She found her keys, but a gust of wind grabbed a loose twenty-dollar bill and carried it across the parking lot.

"Great." She scooped everything back into her bag, bent to retrieve the bill and off it flew again. Looking ridiculous, Rise kept up the chase for a good while, happy no one was around to witness it. Finally, the errant bill hit the trunk of an enormous tree in the field behind the clinic. Rise stuffed it in her pocket, turned around and almost jumped out her skin. A man blocked her path. He'd come from nowhere.

"Hello there," he said. "What are you doing out here, all alone?"

Rise placed her hand on the Inferi in her bag and sniffed the air. There was no trace of the minion smell, but not all predators were of the supernatural variety. A warning tingle shot up her back as she realized the man didn't have a colorful glow. She backed away, whipped out the Inferi, and held it in front of her.

"What an interesting device you have there," the man said. "I haven't seen one of those in a while. Lucifer doesn't part with his toys often."

"Who are you?" She studied the man's face. He looked familiar, but she couldn't say how. He had a medium build, short blonde hair and a terrible complexion riddled with pockmarks.

"I'm hurt you don't recognize me," he said. "Do you forget all men whose lives you disrupt, or am I a special case?" He showed mangled teeth when he smiled.

Recognition hit Rise like a sucker-punch; this was the man who abducted little Keisha.

"Kevin Nichols." She remembered thinking his teeth were demonic. Maybe he *was* a demon. She knew a guard killed the guy. "How did that beating in jail work out for you?" She hoped it was slow and painful.

"Quite well. Thank you for asking." He placed a finger to his lip. "It's amazing how angry people get – especially fathers - when someone like me gives detailed descriptions of certain exploits." He shrugged. "I just had to wait for the right one. Wrath can be such a hard challenge for some."

"You're saying you wanted to die?" She kept her finger on the red gem, nervous he didn't appear at all concerned.

"Of course, I wanted to die," he said, as if it was the most obvious thing in the world. "I have far more power now." He looked down and shook his head. "The one drawback is I'm stuck in this repulsive form for the time being. Mr. Nichols didn't take his hygiene seriously, especially in the dental area. I'll choose wiser next time."

"What do you want?" Rise moved around, never taking her eyes off the man. "My surrender, right?" She still had no idea what that meant, but didn't say so.

He waggled a finger at her. "You and I both know you can't do that yet, but we'll discuss that in a moment. In the meantime, I thought we could get to know one another."

Rise tried not to show the fear building up fast. She had no idea what this man might be or what he could do. She wondered if his was the voice that had been talking to her. The thought made her sick and she whipped her eyes over the sky.

"What are you looking for up there?" Kevin followed her gaze. "Ah! You think that blue-winged hound is going to descend and save you." He waved a hand. "I'd put that notion out of your head, the minions are keeping him busy for me. I do hope he hasn't been killed quite yet, that would put a wrinkle in my plans. Let's hope for the best, shall we? Now, back to you."

Rise felt her stomach clench at what might be happening to Dominik. She pushed the thought aside. She had a bigger problem at the moment, and he started to circle her as he spoke.

"I think you should surrender to me." His tone was conversational. "What do you say to that?"

"I think you're insane," Rise said. "If you try to lay a hand on me, I will light you up." She considered doing that anyway, and she tightened her grip on the Inferi.

"I see we have a little problem." He clasped his hands in front of him and nodded to the weapon. "Go ahead. Please."

Rise didn't need to be asked twice. If hellfire couldn't hurt this creature, whatever he was, then she needed to know. She pressed the gem and flames shot forth.

"Over here, Herald."

Rise whipped around at the voice coming from behind her. He'd moved before the flames touched him. She had a moment of sheer terror, but didn't let it show.

"I can do that every time," Kevin said, smiling. "It's one of the little perks of being a Free Spirit. I can avoid the fires of Hell, when I know it's coming. Now that you have a clear understanding of your situation, we can get down to business." He started to circle her again, like the predator he was. "Will you agree to surrender?"

"No way." Rise was getting more confused by the second. "If you're planning to snatch me, then go ahead and try. I bet I can get in at least one shot." She prayed the bluff would work.

He clicked his tongue in regret. "I have no intention of taking you, until you can give me what I want. The minions might be content to hold you for years upon years until you gain understanding, but I'm not that patient."

Rise decided it was her turn to laugh. She wasn't about to give him anything, even if she could. "Then you really *are* insane."

"That is a possibility. It's a side-effect of being a Free Spirit. We tend to lose our focus after a while."

"A what?" Rise shook her head. "Don't even answer. I don't care, and I'm leaving." She started to back away. If he wasn't going to abduct her, she didn't think he was much of a threat.

"But you haven't heard my proposition yet," Kevin said. "Stay for that, at least."

"I'll see you later." Rise kept walking backwards and hoped she was still going in the general direction of the parking lot.

Kevin moved toward her, his steps matching hers, slow and deliberate. "It's amazing how many truly wicked people there are on the world. In my life, I've come across some that would make me look like an angel."

"Shut up." She risked a glance over her shoulder. She followed that stupid twenty-dollar bill a long way. She was going to rip it to shreds as soon as she got home.

"Mr. Nichols was a convenient soul, a man fresh out of prison with no friends or family still willing to embrace him." He sighed. "I do think he might have been trying to get his life back on track when I took him. You know I can do that, don't you? Destroy the soul within a body and take possession of the flesh? It's a special talent my kind are allowed." He grinned wickedly. "Among others."

"I don't care what you can do." Not true. She did want to know what she was dealing with, but wasn't about to let the guy have the satisfaction.

"I'm eager to find a new vessel. As I told you, this one has become tiresome." He tilted his head, as though he were in deep thought. "The problem is deciding the right one. It's not just a matter of physical appearance. When I consume the flesh I'm also stuck with the life, so certain factors must be considered. Location, for instance, is a big one."

Rise felt concrete under her feet. She was almost to the car.

"I've grown bored with large cities," the man continued. "Too much crime, don't you agree? I was thinking of going someplace smaller, someplace like...Nineveh."

Rise froze.

"Your friend, what's his name? Daniel?" He saw her reaction and almost salivated. "That's a fine-looking young man. A tad young. I prefer to destroy the soul of someone older, so I don't have to spend as long in the same body." He placed a finger across his lips and raised his eyebrows. "But his life does come with certain advantages. He also has a sister, does he not? As you know, I do love children."

"You can't touch them," Rise said. "They're innocents. But go ahead and try. I'd love to see Miri and Piri carve you into pieces."

"There you go, mistaking me for a minion again. Unlike those pitiful creatures with their horrid scent, I did not deserve my fate. Thus, I am not bound by certain laws, as they are. The guardians will not interfere."

Rise started to shake, and she blasted the Inferi again. As before, the Free Spirit dodged the fire.

"Here is my proposition to you," he said. "I'm going to call off the minions so your Blue angel can talk to you. You will convince him, by whatever means necessary, to reveal the secret of surrender." He waved a hand. "I'd tell you myself, but that's one law that does apply to me. It's terribly inconvenient."

"Dominik won't tell me," Rise said, "and if you come near Danny or his sister I will—"

"What? Kill me?" He laughed again. "Then I will release from that body and take another. I can destroy the soul of every single person you know if I choose."

Rise swallowed hard, her mind working to come up with a solution.

"But I don't want to do that," he said. "You're a smart Herald, I've been watching you. You will be able to get the necessary information and then you will offer yourself to me. If not, things will get nasty." He looked at the sun beginning to set. "I'll give you until sunrise to make your decision. Meet me over there in that field, under the tree. We'll make an event of things—won't that be fun?"

Rise dropped her arms and her face twisted with fury and conflict. She didn't know how to proceed, or even how to respond. This creature, if he could do what he claimed, was capable of things she'd never imagined.

"I'll be off now," he said. "One more thing—make sure that Blue dog stays out of the way. I don't need him confusing the situation and babbling on about the greater good, as angels are prone to do. If I hear one wing, I'll bring a legion of minions down upon him and consider our arrangement void. And then the next time we meet, you'll be looking into the face of your friend, Daniel."

Rise tried to control the shake in her voice. "How am I supposed to keep Dominik away? He's an angel. He does what he wants."

"I suppose that's another thing he didn't mention, though I can understand why. If you command him to leave, he will leave. You're a Herald, haven't you figured out your very words hold power? Why do you think you need to *speak* the words of surrender? Why do you think you can command that pitiful creature, Saba?"

Rise had wondered about that, but chalked it up to more spiritual craziness. The entire design was confusing and she suspected that was the point.

"I'll be off," he said. "Don't forget that I'll be watching you tonight. If you try to run—"

"Blah, blah, blah—you'll kill everyone I know. Yeah, I get that." She refused to let him know how much his words sickened her. "Enjoy the show when I take a shower."

"If you get rid of your furry companion, I'll be happy to oblige. Until then, you may keep your modesty. See you at sunrise." He disappeared into the air.

Rise sped home in a rage. She pounded her fist on the steering wheel, screamed curses, and hoped Dominik was still alive and hearing every word. That angel had some explaining to do and she wasn't tolerating any half-assed, cryptic answers any longer. She had enemies she didn't understand, with abilities she couldn't match, and the only weapon she had was useless.

She slammed the car door when she got home, and slammed the apartment door even harder when her she saw her so-called advisor was still absent. She paced back and forth, trying to find a way out of this mess. With such little information, her options were limited. She had no idea what to do, but she wasn't about to let minions or a Free Spirit, or even an angel, force her into a decision. James and Lynette Hawke taught her one thing, and did so by example; he was a bully and she was a coward. Rise vowed long ago she would never be either.

Shay was both worried and furious with Dominik. He'd been trying for three days to return to the human realm and minions had accosted him each time. She warned him to stop trying, but he wouldn't listen. He was determined to get back to that Herald, and now he'd been attacked again.

She flew through the Expanse with her heart and wings both pounding. She scanned the area below and her eyes fell on a cluster of angels and humans gathered around a figure lying prone on the marble. From her vantage point, she could see the dark blue circle of blood trailing outward.

She landed, and pushed her way through the crowd until she got to Dominik. She looked in horror at his wounds. He had deep slices in his chest and arms, and a myriad of smaller cuts all over. She knew the injures were inflicted by minion blades, and she gasped when she saw a mighty gash at the base on his wing. His breathing was coming in rasps, and blood was flowing in spurts.

"Summon a shaman," she said, looking up to the group standing around. "Go now! Fly! Run!"

They dispersed in haste and Shay placed her hands over the worst of the wounds, trying to stop the flow of blood. Dominik attempted to stand, pushing himself up with one arm, his eyes clenched in pain.

"Don't move," she said. "A healer is on the way."

"I'll survive," he said, and tried to push her hands away. "I have to go back."

"You're not going anywhere." She looked into his eyes. "How many were there?"

"Four this time." He grimaced, but managed to get on his feet. He took a ragged breath and more blood spilled forth from the cut on his wing. "Someone is leading them, inspiring them to attack."

"To what end?"

"They try to keep me from the Herald," he said. "There's no other explanation. They might be planning a concerted attack on her. I have to warn her."

"No. Your injuries are too great and you need time to heal." She pulled open his shirt and frowned. "And you've lost your advisor pendant. You can't be around her without that protection. We'll notify the Scriptures. They can send someone else to deal with her."

"The duty is mine." Dominik's tone was firm. "I promised her I'd return. That was days ago. My injuries are nothing compared to what she'll endure if captured."

"Nothing? They nearly took your wing, and next time they might succeed. She's not worth your life."

He grabbed Shay's hand when she attempted to cover the wound on his chest. "I won't abandon her."

"But you would abandon me?"

"We must put personal desire aside for the greater good."

"I will not place a Herald above you," she said. "Those creatures already believe they're better than the rest of us, and I won't add timber to that arrogant fire. I refuse to see you ripped apart piece-by-piece." She took a deep breath. "I'll request an audience with the Scriptures myself and tell them you're in no condition to continue as advisor. You know better than I do it's a violation of the oath to deliberately place yourself in harm's way without—"

"I will not leave my Herald!"

Shay stepped back, astounded at his words. "*Your* Herald?" She studied his face in disbelief, not liking what she saw. "You can't possibly care for her." The thought was too appalling to consider.

"She has courage—a trait to be admired." He held his ribs while he struggled for breath.

Shay couldn't believe what she was hearing. "She is incapable of true feeling. They all are. She'll come to despise you some day, if she doesn't get you killed first."

"She won't," Dominik insisted. "You don't know her."

"I know Heralds!" She grabbed his arm and her eyes blazed. "I know them better than you ever will. Have you forgotten what they did to me, and why?"

Dominik didn't answer, but his eyes flashed with emotion.

Shay forged ahead. "I still remember the night Tyre killed me, all those long years ago. He crushed me to death with his own hands, looking into my face the whole time."

Shay knew he was aware of what happened to her, but apparently he needed a reminder. She hated to inflict more suffering, but he'd given her no choice. Hot tears streamed down her face, her body shaking as memories overwhelmed her.

"After my soul released, Tyre and the one called Alira hauled me off to the fires. I stood there at the mouth of the pit, smelling the sulfur and knowing what awaited me. They didn't throw me in right away, either. They enjoyed my fear, fear so terrible I couldn't stand. Tyre held me up by my right arm, Alira my left, and they chattered away, discussing…private moments they'd shared. They laughed while I stared into that horrible pit, feeling all hope ripped away."

Dominik stood ravaged at the words. His muscles tensed and his eyes filled with despair as Shay continued.

"The last thing Tyre said to me before I…" She choked, unable to say the words. "Those Heralds shoved me into the fire like they were tossing a piece of meat into a pool of sharks." She grabbed his face with both hands. "*This* is the kind of creature you're risking your life to save. Do you not see the futility and the waste?"

The Shaman arrived, cloaked in a long robe and wearing a myriad of beaded chains and bracelets. He wasted no time before offering prayers and administering healing touches.

Dominik's chest heaved with a quiet struggle. "Do only what is necessary." He was addressing the healer, but still looking at Shay. "I require only strength enough to fly, so I can return to my duties."

"What has she done to you?" Shay stepped back, shaking her head furiously. "You are a fool, but perhaps I'm far worse." She lofted into the air and didn't look back. She hoped Dominik was right about an imminent attack. That Herald had caused too much suffering and needed a bit of her own.

CHAPTER FORTY
TIRED OF WAITING

Rise spent hours traipsing around her apartment and checking the time every few minutes. Dominik still hadn't made an appearance, and she was well past the point of anger. She only had one night to make a decision, and didn't have time for the angel's finicky sense of urgency. Danny was another problem. He wasn't answering her calls or texts. Around midnight, she grew tired of waiting on males of all varieties and headed to Nineveh.

Late as it was, Rise wasn't the least bit tired. Her head was ready to implode as she went over and over the conversation with the free spirit, trying to find a loophole. The way she saw it, she had two choices, and both were terrible. She could either save herself, or save people she cared about. She was leaning toward the first one, but she thought an angel ought to be a little less selfish. Either way, she was going to make sure her friend had a fighting chance.

Rise pulled into Danny's driveway without any kind of plan in mind. She had no idea what to say. Tell him to take his sister and get out of town? Go into hiding? Was there anywhere he could hide from a Free Spirit? She guessed not. She knocked on the back door, figuring she'd just 'wing it'. Her private joke gave a millisecond of joy.

Danny answered with disheveled hair and wearing nothing except loose-fitting sleeping pants that hung to his hips. Rise concentrated to look him in the face.

"What are you doing here?" He held the door close to his body and didn't invite her inside. He looked past her, scanning the area.

"I tried to call, but you didn't answer." She hoped she didn't sound too accusing. "Do you still have all your dad's guns?" That was a question of double-stupidity. She knew Danny hadn't parted with the weapons, and also knew they wouldn't do a bit of good against the spirit guy.

Danny blinked and shook his head. "Yeah, I have them," he said, then flipped to serious. "What's going on, are you okay? Did someone break into your apartment again?" He relaxed his hold on the door, and it swung open a little.

"No, I'm fine. You have a security system, right?"

"I turned it off last week. I'm trying to cut expenses. You came all the way down here at one in the morning for this?"

"Is something wrong?" a female voice asked.

Rise looked past her friend and saw a young woman with long, brown hair standing a few feet away. She was slim, and wearing a ribbed tee shirt that didn't quite cover her lacey black panties. Rise looked her up and down, and recognition hit her like a punch to the stomach.

"Michelle."

"Rise?" Michelle came closer and looked even better when she came into the porch light; she had flawless skin. "Wow, Danny told me you looked different. You do, you look great. I love your hair like that." She seemed to be sincere and leaned against Danny's shoulder. She was a blue.

Rise felt like a person who had just walked over someone's new carpet with muddy shoes. She backed away. "I didn't know you had company." Without another word, she turned and headed back to her car. Danny followed her.

"Hey, hold up!"

Rise ignored him. She opened the car door, but Danny slammed it shut. Rise didn't look at him. She just stared at her feet.

"I'm sorry I didn't call you back," he said. "I wish you hadn't driven all the way out here."

"Me, too." She wanted to cry or scream, and not from any sort of jealousy. The utter helplessness of the whole situation infuriated her, but she wasn't breaking down in front of Danny for any reason.

He let out a long breath. "We met up for dinner and decided to watch a movie. The rest just happened. I wasn't planning it."

"You don't have to explain anything to me." Her toenail polish was chipping, but Saba's art still looked great. She kicked a small rock and it bounced down the drive. She didn't have time for this drama.

"Talk to me." Danny leaned against the car. "What's so important you came down here in the middle of the night?"

"I was worried about you." She traced her finger on the window of the car and it left a trail. She was overdue on a carwash. "I have a bad feeling, like someone is going to try to hurt you, or hurt Emily." That was the truth, minus a few important parts.

"What are you talking about? Rise, look at me." He touched her chin and forced her eyes to meet his. "Where is this coming from? Are you still upset about those guys that grabbed us in the alley?"

"Sort of." Another half-truth. "They aren't the only bad guys around."

"Why do you think I still have those guns?" He grinned, then gave a shrug. "But if someone is determined to hurt you or me or, God forbid, even Emily, they'll find a way. Our best shot is to make damn sure we don't make it easy for them. I refuse to live my life in fear of what might happen."

"Yeah, I know." Rise knew there was no way Danny was going to run, no matter what she told him. She also knew he would never be truly safe and wondered if this was the reason Dominik told her to cut ties with him. He was in danger now, because of her.

"You've always been a good friend to me," she said. "More than I've ever deserved." She saw the blinds move in the front widow and realized they had an audience. Despite the dire situation, she almost smiled. During their freshman year of High School, Michelle started a rumor, saying Rise had an eating disorder because she always skipped lunch. Michelle probably forgot all about that. Rise didn't.

She grabbed Danny's face with both hands, pulled him down and kissed him with so much force she thought her lips might bruise. She ignored the sensation of wrongness creeping up her spine and enjoyed the moment of sweet, petty revenge.

Danny tried to keep hold of her when she started to pull back. "Took you long enough," he said, smiling. "It was worth the wait, though." He tried to kiss her again, but she pushed away.

"I've got to go." She drove off without another word, leaving Danny standing in the driveway, watching her.

Dominik was waiting for Rise when she returned home.

"Nice of you to show up." Her irritation with him diminished when she flipped on the light. He looked terrible; his clothes were ripped and filthy, he was covered in a blue substance she assumed was blood and there were multiple injuries covering his body. His entire appearance was that of a man returning from battle.

"What happened to you?"

"Minions," Dominik said. "They've been coming for me without mercy for days. They're trying to keep me from you, but I can't discern the reason."

"I can," she said. "Kevin Nichols, that man who snatched Keisha. He's something called a Free Spirit, and he said he was keeping you busy."

"You spoke with him?" His voice was coated in apprehension. "What did he say to you?"

"He threatened to destroy Danny's soul, unless I surrendered to him. Can he do that?" Any hope it was an empty threat evaporated when she saw the angel's face.

"Free Spirits are dangerous creatures," he said. "They aren't bound by the same laws as minions and angels. They were good souls once, but tragic events kept them from taking their rightful place within the light. Most spiral into darkness and commit unspeakable acts."

"That's an understatement. What would happen to Danny? Would be go to Heaven, or wherever?"

Dominik looked pained. "If his soul was destroyed, he would cease to be."

All hesitation Rise felt in regards to her decision flew away. "I won't let that happen." She started emptying drawers and sorting things into piles. "I have until sunrise to make up my mind."

"Surrender is not an option."

"Oh, surrender is most definitely an option, and that's exactly what I'm going to do. Can you take care of Oliver for me? No, forget that. I'll ask my neighbor." She called to the cat and loaded him into his carrier.

Dominik whipped her around and held her by the arms. "Rise, come to your senses."

"I'm tired of you grabbing me all the time," she said, pulling away. "You told me to respect humanity, so that's what I'm doing, starting with my friend."

"You have no idea of the consequences." He was upset, but a gleam of victory sparked in his eyes. "Besides that, you're not yet able to give him your surrender."

"I do know the consequences; he'll leave Danny alone. And it's true I can't give him what he wants right now, but I can later on. I'll offer to leave with him and I bet he'll agree to that." She winced. "I hope he doesn't torture me for too long, though."

Dominik turned away, fighting a losing war with his anger. "I will not allow this."

"You don't have a choice," she said. "You can't control me; you're nothing but an advisor. This is my decision and I've made it."

His eyes fumed. "You have no idea what you're saying." He tightened his fist, and followed her while she continued to work. "You're a Herald, the last piece in their profane collection. You cannot give yourself over."

"Why not?" She tossed a book across the room and planted herself in front of him. "Why am I so special? What's the big deal about my surrender? Whatever it is, it's not worth risking Danny and everyone else I know."

"Redemption is what they desire." His volume escalated with each word. "This is why angels are hunted. If minions can collect our wings, one of each choir, and then gain the surrender of a Herald, the gates of redemption open for them. Minions will be free from chains of servitude, and Free Spirits will gain the peace stolen from them."

Rise laughed and tossed her arms out. "That's it? *That's* the big secret? If I surrender, the bad guys go back to the happy place and dance on clouds and play with unicorns?"

Dominik was apoplectic and looked to be fighting the urge to slam her into a wall. She'd never seen anyone so enraged in her life.

"There can be no light without darkness," he said. "Every soul that takes on a journey does so in the hope of achieving advancement. There is always a chance they will fail and become a minion of darkness. Few of those will ever earn a chance at redemption, but the risk is one of necessity."

Rise crossed her arms and plastered an apathetic look on her face. It riled the angel further. He moved close to her, threatening in his proximity. His wings fully expanded and blocked out the light in the room. A shadow crossed his features, giving him a terrifying appearance that was more demon than angel. His voice held layers of warning when he spoke.

"Those who have fallen, damned as they are, still serve a great purpose. If they gain redemption and return to the light, no trials will be left within this realm. Minions and Free Spirits are vital components in a carefully woven tapestry. To rip those pieces away would be the greatest of abominations. It would destroy the cycle of growth human souls require to survive. Within a generation, they would all begin to deteriorate and eventually cease to exist."

"That doesn't make any sense," Rise said. "Why do they want something that will only eventually destroy them?"

"The fires and madness have burned away all reason. They can't see past their own suffering, and even if they could, their choice would be the same. Which would you choose—death, or an eternity of torment?"

"I can't just stand by and watch while Danny and everyone else I care about is picked off, one–by-one. That would be *my* torment."

"This is exactly why Heralds do not form attachments," Dominik said, each word getting louder, "and why I warned you to distance yourself from the boy. You ignored my counsel and now the very thing you hold dear has been used as a weapon against you."

"I don't care." Rise took a deep breath, squared her shoulders, and prepared to see if she really did have some power. "I want you to leave." Something deep inside began to swirl, filling her with a sense of invincibility. She was in control and knew, somehow, the angel would do exactly as she said.

Dominik looked like he'd been shot in the heart. He took one step back, then halted. "After what I've told you, you would still offer yourself?"

"Didn't I make myself clear?" She pointed at the door, irritated he wasn't moving fast enough. "I *command* you to leave. Now."

The angel's face was a mixture of outrage and despair as he backed away. "And the Herald appears." He looked to be in horrible conflict. "I've failed in my obligation, and you've failed in yours."

Dominik went to the porch and lofted into the sky, leaving a few drops of blood behind. Rise watched him go with a knot of uncertainty in her stomach. She shoved all stray thoughts aside and focused on gathering her worldly belongings. She filled trash bags with books, candles, clothes and everything else that would fit. She put a few specific items in a backpack, tossed it over her shoulder, and headed for the dumpster. She heaved everything into the trash and brushed off her hands. She knew the Free Spirit was out there in the dark somewhere, keeping track of her every move. She gave him the one-finger-wave as she walked back inside and hoped he was paying attention.

Rise flopped down on the floor and stared at the decorations on her feet. Her heart hammered in her chest, but not from fear. She was resolute in her decision and prepared to accept whatever consequences it might entail. She picked up her phone and dialed Saba's number, ready to issue her first, and possibly last, command to the young woman.

Chapter Forty-One
Reprimand

Dominik knelt in front of the altar in his personal chamber, his legs tucked underneath him, his wings in array. He kept his eyes closed, his hands open in front of him. The smell of incense was in the air, and a trail of smoke trickled upward to the high ceiling. He ignored the pounding at the door. It wasn't locked, and anyone that required his service could enter. He heard hard footfalls come to stand behind him and recognized the distinctive sound of the armored boots.

"Dominik."

He knew the voice echoing in the room. It was the Herald, Alira.

"We're here to escort you to the castle," she said.

Dominik opened his eyes. The white scroll with the black tie was lying beside him. He had no intention of ignoring the summons, and was offended Lucifer sent Heralds to fetch him. He stood in one graceful move, then turned to face Alira and the other with her, the broad shouldered brute known as Ikizo.

"Does the Light Bringer think me a coward?" Dominik regarded the manacles they carried. "That I would need to be dragged before him in chains?"

"No," Alira said, looking him up and down with open approval. "But he loves to make examples."

"And so do we," Ikizo said. "I've been waiting a long time for this moment."

Dominik held out his hands and the Heralds bound him, locking thick metal bands around his wrists and securing chains around his waist. They took hold of his arms and escorted him through the expanse, taking the longest route possible to the portals.

Many eyes fell on him, some with compassion, others with contempt. Dominik didn't blame those who held him in disdain; he felt much the same. He'd broken his oath by revealing the secret of surrender, and knew he deserved the reprimand that was coming. The Scriptures had been forgiving once, but this last breach was too great and now Lucifer was involved. He saw Shay standing with a few others from her choir. She caught his eye and a flutter of sadness fell across her features, then she lifted her chin and turned away.

Once at the castle, Dominik was taken to stand before the throne of the Light Bringer. The rest of the Heralds awaited and held varying expressions; some appeared eager, others infuriated. Lucifer sat, his silver eyes boring down from his position above.

"Dominik of the Blue choir," he said. "You are charged with violating the oath of angels. You have disobeyed orders given to you by lawful authority, and revealed information that was not to be disclosed. How do you respond?"

Dominik held his gaze steady. "I admit to the charges and accept whatever punishment is required."

Lucifer snapped his fingers and several Heralds descended, preparing Dominik for reprimand. Two brought chains down from the ceiling and latched them to the manacles on Dominik's wrist. Another grabbed his shirt and ripped it open down the center of his chest. He was hoisted into the air, his arms spread and stretched tight, almost to the point of breaking. It was excruciating, but he allowed no trace of pain to show on his face.

"Begin." Lucifer motioned, and the largest Herald came forward, holding a scourge that showed signs of heavy use. Bloodstains of every color tarnished the weapon, and the tips of the flails glowed with fire. The Herald reared back and released the first blow. The sound of breaking flesh cracked in the air like an explosion.

Dominik felt the skin on his chest rip away and scorch beneath the assault. He clenched his fists and gritted his teeth, knowing he deserved every stripe. He allowed his emotions, his fury, to take control of his wits and he spilled secrets that weren't his to give. In doing so, he placed everything at risk.

The blows kept coming, one after another, and Dominik saw his blood pooling on the floor below his feet. The physical agony was nothing compared to the tortures in his mind. He thought of the young Herald, and wondered at her fate. It was nearly sunrise in the human realm. He still retained a sliver of hope that she would reconsider her actions. If she did not, humanity was doomed, and the sacrifices of every angel would have been in vain.

He made no sound of protest as the strikes continued. He embraced the pain.

Dominik returned to his chamber under the same escort that procured him. His strength was gone, left in puddles of blood and sweat on the floor of the throne room. Ikizo and Alira shoved him into the room and he landed hard on hands and knees. He struggled to stand, but a heavy boot kicked his arm from underneath him and he fell once more.

"Stay down, dog." Ikizo said. "Kneel before your betters."

"Return to the castle," Alira said, moving her eyes over the blue angel. "I'd like to chat with him for a little while. Alone."

"Is that what you're calling it?" He laughed. "I don't think he's going to be up for anything too physical for a while, but enjoy yourself."

Alira knelt by Dominik as he lay on the floor. His shirt was in tatters, and he was sticky from blood loss. She played with a piece of his hair, wet with perspiration.

"Leave me," he said, and batted her hand away. "I have no desire for games."

"I'm not going to abuse you." She stood and took inventory of his chamber while she spoke. "I'm impressed by you, Dominik. It's rare that an angel endures such a strong reprimand without begging for mercy. I think Tyre might have been the last one." She clicked her tongue. "Of course, he'd gotten used to the lashes after a while."

Dominik didn't respond. He couldn't afford to waste what little energy he still retained in trying to hold a conversation. He needed to concentrate, to find the tenuous connection he forged with Rise.

Alira ran her hand across his dresser and moaned. "We do need to work on your decorating skills. Why do you insist upon such an austere lifestyle? Not even a proper bed." She nudged the corner of his resting pallet with her toe, and her voice turned sultry. "You should come visit my chamber some night. You might enjoy the feel of something warmer."

"If you have something to say, speak, and then go." Dominik closed his eyes and held out his hands, returning to his preferred meditation position. "I need to focus."

"You expect her to rescind her words, call you back?"

"If she does, I will return to her side."

"I'm sure you will." She picked up the chain atop his dresser and made the glowing pendant swing back and forth. "Did you think you were being noble by allowing yourself to be open to her commands?"

"It was a gesture…of trust."

"That worked out well, didn't it?" Alira laughed and tossed the chain away. "I'll give you credit for trying a unique method. I've never known of an advisor to abandon his protection."

"I wanted her to learn control," he said. "There is a far greater power in mercy than in a display of strength."

"Oh, you spew platitudes like a sallow-faced monk." Alira moved in front of him and stared down. "I'm surprised you've lasted this long. I went through six advisors during my period of trials, three of them before I even earned two marks. Most were killed, but a few were replaced. Tyre went through twice as many, if the stories are true."

"I don't care of the risks to myself," he said, breathing through waves of pain still coming for him, "and I don't want to hear about Tyre, or any of his exploits— good or ill."

"Still harboring a grudge, are you? So am I, but against you." She touched his wing and slid her hand up a long feather. "I miss him, you know. He offered amusement from time to time. He had skills, in many areas." She bent down and spoke into his ear, her breath hot on his skin. "But you know all about that, don't you? Did he make that pretty little girl cry out in pleasure when he took her? When he took *you*?"

"Get your hands off me and leave," Dominik said, shaking his wings violently, "or I will throw you out."

She nipped at his earlobe and he whirled on her, grabbing her wrist while she laughed.

"You're quite a beast, threatening a helpless female." Her green eyes blazed. She was far from helpless and they both knew it. "I think I like you, Dominik. If your Herald fails, humanity will be lost, but we angels will survive." She pulled her hand away. "You will be despised for your part in the downfall. Friends will be scarce. I wouldn't be too quick to burn bridges if I were you." She turned on her heel and left.

Dominik fell back to his knees and focused on the tiny beacon of energy within the human realm who he knew to be Rise. Due to her command, his connection to her was broken in an infuriating manner, as though she was standing behind a wall of glass, within view, but out of reach. He didn't know how she'd learned of that power, but hoped she knew the command could be retracted. He would wait, and pray for the barrier to lift.

"Call to me," he whispered.

There was nothing he could do about the Free Spirit; he didn't have authority to kill such a creature. But if Rise surrendered, Dominik wanted to stand with her, to take his own responsibility in her fall.

Chapter Forty-Two
Surrender

Rise got to the designated place early. She sat beneath the large Oak tree, relieved the morning wasn't terribly cold. She didn't wear a jacket, bring her handbag, or anything else, and she came alone as Kevin instructed. She looked at the stars still littering the sky, finding them particularly beautiful. She let her mind wander, and thought about her family for the first time without any resentment. She wondered what their colors might be.

Rise patted the lump of earth under her hand, and smiled. She dug her fingers into the dirt, and ran her hand across wet blades of grass. She gazed at the wildflowers nearby, and could smell something else all around her, something distinctly chemical. She wondered if she would ever see this world again, after today. She didn't know what would happen at sunrise, but she was prepared for the worst.

Right on schedule, Rise saw a dark form strolling across the field, at first a dark shadow, but then taking form. The Free Spirit saw her and held out his arms in greeting.

"Hark! The Herald angel!" He laughed at his own cleverness.

"Like I'll never hear that one again." Rise stood and felt a shiver of fear run down her spine. She almost wished Dominik would appear and bring a dozen friends, but she knew he wouldn't, and not just because she sent him away.

She knew, somehow, that this moment was hers and hers alone. She crushed her anxiety and tried to stay focused.

"Are you prepared to offer your surrender?" Kevin clasped his hands in front of him, a cocky smile on his face.

"You promised me you'd leave Danny alone, right?" She kicked at a little mound of dirt, and moved further to her left, looking at the ground.

"I did indeed," he said, "but let's not pretend your decision is not already made. I observed you last night; the touching good-bye with your dear friend, and the note you left for your neighbor. It was a nice gesture, asking him to care for your pet in your absence, and even cleaning out your apartment. How considerate."

Rise grunted. It was exactly as she assumed; the minion had observed her every move during the night, just as he promised.

"Shall we get on with it, then? I will take your surrender. You only need to say the words."

"Do you care if I say a prayer first?"

Kevin chuckled. "As you wish, Herald. I grew tired of the practice long ago, but by all means…" He waved a hand.

Rise closed her eyes, knelt and bowed her head. She heard Kevin sigh heavily.

"Our Father, who art in heaven, hallowed be thy name, thy Kingdom come, thy will be done…" Rise continued reciting the prayer she learned when she was just a toddler. It gave her strength, gaining confidence with every word, and by the time she got to the end, she felt like water behind a dam, ready to burst. *"And lead us not into temptation…but deliver us from evil."*

She whispered the final words and her eyes flashed. She grabbed at the dirt pile below her right knee, finding what was hidden. She whipped out the Star of David, the one she found many months before, now sporting a brand new silver chain. She spun it a few times and hurled it with all her strength. It hit, making a deep slice on Kevin's upper arm.

The Free Spirit bellowed as dark blood poured from the wound. The turn of events stunned him, and before he could regroup, Rise sprinted forward. She tackled him and they both went down hard. She thought of the times Danny teased her about being too small for football. He'd be proud of her now. She'd learned a few things watching his games.

Kevin was on his back, still in shock at the unexpected attack. Rise took advantage of his confusion. She straddled him, throwing frenzied, but damaging, punches to his face and neck. She put all her weight behind one strike and broke his nose, and that's when the Free Spirit started to fight back.

He flung up his arms and knocked Rise from atop him. She flipped around and managed to stand, but he landed a kick in her midsection and she flew back and hit hard. The Free Spirit came for her again, and only a burst of instinctive skill enabled her to roll out of the way before his foot impacted with her face.

Rise scrambled away and moved into a squat near another pile of dirt. They were obvious now that she knew what to look for. She reached in and pulled out the baton Mr. Daly gave her when she moved into her apartment. She flipped her wrist, the baton extended, and she held it in front of her with both hands like a sword.

"You're making this harder than it needs to be, Herald." Kevin spit out some black sludge, and wiped his mouth. "For every second you delay, you will scream a hundred times. I had no intention of harming you, but now I've changed my mind!"

Rise backed up when he charged. She remembered the trick Dominik used on the minions in the alley. She allowed the Free Spirit to come close, then sidestepped his assault and smashed the baton into his neck. He was back on the ground and she struck him in the stomach and legs. He cursed, grabbed the baton and ripped it from her hands. He stood, she ran.

One spot remained where the earth had been disturbed. Rise fell to her knees, digging with her hands until she felt metal. She smiled with relief, and silently thanked Saba for a job well done. She hated to command the always-immaculate young woman to retrieve the backpack from the dumpster, and hoped Saba hadn't gotten too filthy. Rise pulled the Inferi from the dirt and ignited it.

"I thought we already went through this," Kevin said. "That will do you no good."

"You don't think so?" Rise pointed the weapon at the ground, toward the now distinct smell of gasoline. The fire ignited the flammable liquid Saba poured during the night and within a heartbeat, a great burst of flame shot up and traveled in a tight circle, trapping Rise and the Free Spirit in the middle.

"You didn't see that coming, did you?" She pointed the Inferi at his face. "Welcome to your personal circle of Hell."

He whipped his head around, saw he had no retreat, and his face twisted in rage.

"So, you think you can fight me?" He raised the baton. "You have some courage in you, but that won't save you. I want your surrender and I will take it, even if I have to rip it from your throat!" He charged.

Rise didn't move. She kept the Inferi raised and prepared to consume him with fire, but at the last possible second, he dove to the ground like a baseball player sliding into home. His momentum propelled him forward and he knocked her off her feet. The Inferi tumbled from her grasp.

She landed inches away from the fire and felt embers landing on her face. The Free Spirit stood over her and swung the baton in a move that would've crushed her skull if she hadn't move when she had. Instead, it impacted with her shoulder and it felt like her bones exploded.

Rise screamed in agony, the pain almost unbearable. Kevin hit her again and again, more times than she could count. When he tired of that, he straddled her and pressed the baton to her neck using both his hands, cutting off her oxygen. Rise thrashed on the ground, trying to free herself and felt a horrible burn under her right shoulder. Something was searing into her skin and it was worse than all the other pains combined. She tried to move away, but she was pinned tight to the ground.

"We can do this for a long time," Kevin said. "Surrender to me and it will be over." He pressed harder, and smiled down at her. "You are no more a challenge than a child."

The words enraged her. She remembered how it felt when she was small and helpless, with her own father humiliating and debasing her. She rallied her last drop of strength and brought her knee up as hard as she could. She caught the Free Spirit in a place that would take down any man, human or otherwise.

He gasped, and he fell to the side. Rise rolled away and grabbed up the Inferi. Her hands shook as she pummeled him in the face until he was almost unrecognizable. Dominik had been right; it was a great blunt force weapon. When he finally lay still, gasping for breath, she stood and brought her foot down as hard as she could, right between his legs. Poetic justice for all the innocence his miserable existence had stolen.

She placed her knee on his chest and shoved the Inferi into his mouth. "You will never, ever, harm another soul again." She looked him right in the eyes when she clicked the red gem. Flames engulfed the Free Spirit, and he wailed and kicked as he burned. Rise kept up the assault until the body turned black and shattered into glass.

She fell limp to her back, and the Inferi rolled from her palm. As her adrenaline diminished, her pain increased. Her stomach was bloated, her shoulder in agony both from the baton strikes and the burn, and she didn't want to imagine what other injuries she'd sustained. She tasted blood in her mouth, something warm streaked from one ear, and her head started to spin. Her eyes were heavy, and she struggled to remain conscious.

"Dominik," she whispered. She wanted to tell the angel she was sorry for what she'd done, for tricking him into believing she was planning to surrender. She wanted him to know she hadn't failed.

Rise heard the sound of a vehicle coming across the field, and then slamming doors. She heard Saba calling her name and Kafi ordering his sister to stand back. There was the sound of a fire extinguisher, and then someone was at her side

"Rise, I'm here," Saba said, taking her hand.

"Right on time." She thought about smiling, but decided it would take too much effort. She was struggling to even breathe.

"Kafi, come quickly!"

"We have to stop meeting like this," Rise said as she watched Kafi inspect her new injuries. "How bad do I look?"

"Terrible," he said, shaking his head. "What hit you? A truck?"

"I wish." She wanted to die and had no idea how she hadn't.

"Look!" Saba pointed skyward.

Rise heard the familiar sound of large wings. She looked up at Dominik and could tell he'd had a bad night. He had fresh injuries, and his shirt was little more than shreds.

"What happened?" She reached up with a finger to touch the angel's swollen face. "Minions again?"

"Let's concentrate on you." Dominik knelt beside her and took rapid inventory of her condition. The rising sun framed his wings and the tips sparkled in the light.

"I'm fine." She attempted to move, discovered more pain, and fell back. "I didn't surrender."

"I know." There was pride in his eyes. He placed his hands under her knees and shoulders and stood, cradling her to his chest. "Kafi, I'll meet you at your home."

Dominik launched into the air, and Rise grabbed onto what was left of his shirt. Her head rested against his chest, her eyes refusing to stay open.

"Don't drop me," she whispered

"I won't," he said, holding her tighter. "I've got you."

Rise relaxed in the angel's arms. In a moment of absolute trust, she allowed her body respite from the pain and fell into unconsciousness.

Chapter Forty-Three
Tyre

Rise awoke in what could only be Saba's bed. Big, fluffy pillows surrounded her on all sides and she was lying atop one of the thickest comforters she'd ever seen. Someone had changed her clothes; she was in one of those uncomfortable, high-necked nightgowns she hated. Kafi sat on the edge of the bed.

"Hello there," he said. "How do you feel?"

"I think I want to pass out again." She felt like one big bruise, and from what she could see, it was close to the truth. Even her hands were discolored, all purple and blue. "Where's Saba? I need to thank her. And Dominik…"

"They're waiting in the great room," Kafi said. "They were hovering—one of them literally. I made them leave so I could do my work. You've been unconscious for quite a while; it's nearly noon."

Rise moved a little, and a wave of pain shot through her shoulder. She saw the outline of a large bandage under the nightgown. "I think I got burned."

"Oh, you did. The rest of you will heal, but that's going to leave a scar." He had a gleam in his eye. "You want to see it?"

"I don't care." She didn't want to move, but Kafi was already lifting her into a sitting position. He unbuttoned the back on the gown, pulled away the bandage, and held up a mirror. Rise stared, and then started to laugh as much as she could. The Star of David was perfectly burned into her flesh.

"A piece of the *necklace of destiny* fell into the fire," Kafi said as he buttoned her back up. "It heated up the metal, including the medallion. Saba saved it for you."

"I'm turning into a walking religious emblem." Rise looked down at her palm. "I have a cross on my hand, a star on my back—"

"And a crescent moon on your face," Kafi said with a smile. "I'm glad my people are represented."

Rise shook her head. She never thought about that. "Can I ask you a question? It's kind of personal."

"I don't see why not."

"Why did you decide to become a doctor?" She thought she knew, but had to be certain.

"I witnessed something when I was very young. It affected me. Changed the course of my life, in fact."

"A car crash?"

"Dominik told you?" He grunted and shook his head. "So much for angels keeping secrets, and I thought dogs were loyal."

"He didn't tell me, I found out on my own." She gave a little grin. "There's not much you can't find on the internet. I saw your name in an old newspaper article." She adjusted a pillow under her head. "Hey, why does everyone keep calling him a dog? Is it because of the paw print on his business card?"

Kafi laughed. "Have you ever heard of a religious order called the Dominicans?"

Rise thought about that. "They were monks and had the little bald spot?" She made a circle over her head with her finger.

"That's right. The name became a joke. In Latin, *domini* means 'of the Lord' and *canes* means 'hounds' or 'dogs' so…"

"Hounds of the Lord." Rise remembered the minion, Zeb, used that term.

"Dominik started the order and his church named him a saint."

"Hold up," Rise said, pointing to the door. "That's *the* Saint Dominik?" She tried to remember all she learned during church history lesson. It wasn't much; she was never an attentive student.

"That's him, but I wouldn't mention anything. He doesn't think he's deserving of the veneration."

"Why not?" She tried to picture Dominik in a brown robe and chanting.

"He said he went off his path," Kafi pointed to his chest, "just like I have done. He probably told me the story to make feel better about my predicament. Anyway, there was an angel that helped him get back on track. Bah, I can't remember what he said the name was...one with black wings..."

"A Herald?" Rise leaned forward in interest.

"That's the term he used, yes." He stood and gathered up his medical supplies. "Dominik swears if not for this angel, he would've ended up a minion instead of a saint."

Rise bit her lip. If Kafi thought she wasn't going to mention this, he was crazy.

He headed for the door. "Maybe one of these black-winged Heralds will come and help me, too." He called down the hall. "Okay, she's awake now. One at a time, and only for a few minutes. I want her to rest."

Saba came bounding into the room and bounced onto the bed. The small movement of the mattress created a wave of hurt, and Rise grimaced.

"Sorry!" Saba pulled up a chair, looking ready to burst from excitement. "Dominik told us what you did. You're so brave."

"I couldn't have done it without your help. I owe you, especially for rummaging through that dumpster."

"I didn't mind at all, and I finally got to drive Kafi's Jeep." She squealed. "He was upset at first, but now he thinks

Betty helped save the world. I suspect an oil change and a thorough waxing is in her future."

"I hated to bring you into it," Rise said, "but I couldn't do it by myself. That Free Spirit was watching me all night."

"I don't want to hear another thing about it. I was sent back to help you, remember? I am going to need a side-kick name, though. Something like Robin or Tonto or Watson, but with more flash and style."

Rise giggled. "I'll think on it."

"Think later," Kafi said from the door. He tapped his watch.

Saba rolled her eyes and kissed her friend on the forehead.

Rise wasn't alone for long. Dominik strode in with his wings peeking out. He'd changed his shirt, washed off the blood, and was back to being the beautiful angel. Rise was envious; she got a glimpse at her face in the mirror and it wasn't pretty. She grinned up at him.

"Woof!"

"You enjoy your taunts, don't you?" He glared at Kafi and slammed the door in his face. He stood at the foot of the bed and watched Rise in silence.

"What?" Rise pushed into a sitting position and leaned against the headboard. "Say something. You're making me nervous."

"You were never going to surrender." It was not a question.

"No, but I knew if you believed I was going to, you'd have to tell me the reason why I shouldn't." She took a gamble that Dominik would have to explain things if she'd backed him into a corner. "I'm sorry I had to trick you."

He cocked an eyebrow.

"Okay, I'm not sorry. I wanted to find out why all these minions and Free Spirits are after me. I'm tired of being the last one to know everything, especially when I'm the one at risk." She looked down. "I hope you didn't get in trouble."

"The Light Bringer had some…choice words for me." Dominik moved to sit on the bed. "He threatened to have me replaced if it happens again."

"No way," Rise said. "Tell him I don't want another angel. I want you."

"You've grown so bold you think you can command even Lucifer now?" His eyes sparked with humor. "But, if you wish me to remain as your advisor, we'll have to work on our communication skills. Not everything has to be a battle. There's such a thing as compromise, even for a Herald." He smiled gently. "And for an advisor."

She pretended to pout.

"The Light Bringer also has a message for you. He wanted me to tell you, and this is a direct quote, 'Stop malingering and get back to work.'"

She puffed up, a little offended at the insinuation. "Why is this guy giving me gifts and sending messages?"

"Because one day, if you succeed in your trials, you will serve him in his castle."

"A real castle?" She liked that idea. "What will I get to do?"

"Earn the black wings and find out." His eyes narrowed. "And don't try to glean any more information from me. I'm onto you now. I won't fall for it again."

Kafi pounded on the door. "You better wrap it up in there, angel."

Rise laughed, but then a sharp pain hit her and she groaned. The burn was going to be a problem.

"Lay back." Dominik helped her and remained close, looking into her eyes as though searching for something.

His scrutiny became uncomfortable. She turned away, wincing at the large gash near the base of his wing. It looked to be in the early stages of healing. She reached out and touched the wound with her fingertips. "They almost killed you."

"It was a near thing," he said. "They were determined to keep me from you."

"You faced down minion blades to help me." She wasn't sure where the strange phrase came from, and wondered if Dominik was rubbing off on her. She touched one of the blue feathers, and this time he didn't admonish her. She ran her hand along it, fascinated. It was rigid, much stronger than it appeared.

"Rise."

"Hmmm?" She kept playing with the feathers, letting her palm swipe across the tips. She couldn't wait to have her own.

"Rise."

His tone got her attention. She looked into blue eyes swimming with conflicting emotions.

"The wings are an erogenous zone," he said. "That's why I keep telling you not to touch them."

He was probably trying to embarrass her, but two could play that game. She stroked another feather, slow and deliberate. "Why aren't you stopping me, then?"

His smile faded, and his eyes moved across her face. "That's an excellent question."

Rise thought she knew the answer from the way his gaze lingered on her lips. She was going to lose points for this, but didn't care. She placed a hand behind Dominik's neck, trying to coax him closer. His hair fell forward, but he planted his hand on the bed, preventing her from pulling him into the kiss she found she desperately wanted.

"This wouldn't be right," he said. "There are rules."

Rise groaned. "Again with the rules and the oath and the vows..."

Dominik smiled. "They are in place for a reason. I'm an angel, your advisor—"

"I'm an angel, too."

"You're a Herald." He touched her face, tracing the scar around her eye. "A courageous, beautiful, and infuriating Herald."

Despite his words, Dominik hadn't moved away from her. She exerted the smallest pressure on his neck, tempting him.

He didn't move, but his lips parted slightly in denial of his hesitation, so she stretched up to meet them. They were warm and soft, and the kiss felt anything but wrong. She closed her eyes and savored the contact, losing herself in a wave of unexpected longing.

Dominik started to pull back, but she refused to let him go. She intensified the kiss, driven by something beyond physical desire. It was a need for connection, a craving to unravel the mysteries laying inside her. The angel was her only link to that part of her life, and she held onto him as long as she could. When they finally broke apart, a devastating sense of loss consumed her, almost agonizing in its intensity.

Neither of them spoke a word, and Rise wondered if Dominik was angry with her, or perhaps angry with himself for overstepping the line between Herald and advisor. She tried to find the answer in his eyes, but only saw her reflection. She couldn't look away, and noticed their breathing was in perfect harmony. Then the visions came.

For a split second, she was no longer herself. It was surreal, frightening, but at the same time, strangely natural. She saw Dominik with new clarity, not limited by simple eyesight. She saw the angel and saw through him, as he was in many lifetimes. He was different in appearance, sometimes very much so, but she knew without a single doubt it was still Dominik.

She saw him as an old man in a brown robe, sleeping on a bare floor and surrounded by stacks of parchment. He was in a vineyard picking grapes, and in chains being loaded into a ship. She saw him in armor, sword in hand in the midst of battle. The images went on and on, flipping through her brain like a shuffling deck of cards. Finally, she saw him as a terrified girl with red hair. She locked onto that image and held it steady. She was seeing through the eyes of another, and the girl was looking right at her when she spoke.

"You need to slow down," the girl was saying. "I mean it Dominik, I'm getting scared!"

"That's not my name, by the way," Rise said, though the voice was not her own. "Tyre. Pleased to meet you."

She gasped, pushed Dominik away and sat up, ignoring the pain. "I know you." She could tell by the look on his face he understood what she meant. His wings made a peculiar sound, like a sigh.

"I think I'm Tyre. I don't know how, but..." She stopped when the angel didn't react with shock. If she had to guess, she'd say he looked relieved. "How long have you known?"

He released a long breath. "I didn't, for certain. Like you, I'm told only what I need to know, but I have suspected for some time there was the echo of Tyre in you." He sat tall, his gaze falling over her small form concealed under the nightgown. "I was still trying to decide if my suspicions were right. There's not a single incidence of such a thing in all my research, and I have spent a great deal of time in study and contemplation, trying to understand you."

Rise felt on the verge of a panic attack. "I'm not me?"

"Of course, you are," Dominik said, touching her face so she would look at him. "You will always be Rise. Your achievement and failures, your strengths and weaknesses—they are your own."

"Then what happened to Tyre?"

"I can't be sure, but I believe he is gone, his face never to be seen again, as was his punishment." He looked away, deep in thought. "He always swore he'd never allow another to take up his wings. Perhaps he found a way to keep that vow. He had his faults, but he saved many souls that otherwise would've been lost. Perhaps when he appealed to the Scriptures, they took mercy on him and offered him a choice."

"A choice of what? Banishment or...me?" She fell back on the pillow and stared at the ceiling. "So, I'm the lesser of two evils. I'm a punishment. That's great."

Dominik laughed, and the little lines around his eyes made him appear both older and younger at the same time. "I don't know if it was courage, foolishness or pride, but I can think of none other but Tyre who would agree to endure the trials a second time." He touched a piece of her hair and shook his head. "And he's the only one who could ever drive me to the brink of madness, until you."

"This is so messed up." Rise didn't know whether to laugh or cry, so she did both. "And no one even bothered to tell you?"

Dominik wiped a tear from her face with his thumb. "You will find that the Scriptures, the Light Bringer, and perhaps even the Great Architect of it all, have a sense of humor."

"Hysterical." She acclimated herself to all the new information, then took several deep breaths. It was time to address the big elephant in the room. "I probably shouldn't have kissed you."

"No, and I shouldn't have returned the affection." His tone made it clear it wouldn't happen again. "But, it wasn't the first time I've found myself at the whim of a Herald."

Rise groaned, rolled onto her side, and covered her reddening face with her arm. "Don't ever say that again, please." The bracelet on her wrist was brighter, but instead of excitement at her progress, she felt tremendous unease. She was a creature unlike any on earth, one to be hunted and hated, in possession of a power and title she'd only begun to comprehend. She was alone, a keeper of secrets—different, even from Dominik.

"You won't leave me, will you?" She craned her head to look at the angel. "Even though you know what...who...I am now?" The words trembled. She needed his help now more than ever.

"I will assist you until the end, if I can." He stroked her cheek with a comforting touch. "And one day, when you complete your trials..." He raised his eyebrows. "*If* you complete your trials, I will stand with you at the ceremony of wings, and see you take your position within the Black choir."

Kafi pounded on the door, harder than before. "Dominik, if you're not out of that room in the next sixty seconds, I will rip out your feathers and use them as stuffing for my pillow!"

"I think he means it," Rise whispered.

Dominik smiled. "As do I. Rest well, Herald." He pulled a blanket over her, kissed her forehead and headed for the door.

"See you later, *Saint* Dominik." She couldn't help herself.

He shook a finger. "Your taunts will stop."

She only smiled.

After he departed, Kafi returned to make another check of her injuries. He didn't want her moving, so he left the door open, instructing her to call out if she needed anything. Rise lay back and closed her eyes, hoping to sleep for a week. She could hear the television coming from the great room, and knew Kafi had chosen the station since it was a news program and not another martial arts flick.

She strained her ears and listened to the interview with a local woman celebrating her 100th birthday. She was a spry old bird from the sound of things. She talked about her long life in detail, saying every day had been a blessing, filled with joy, and insisted she was ready to go for another century.

"Amateur." Rise rolled onto her side, tucked the blankets around her chin, and was drifting away when she felt that annoying tingle. Her mental buddy was back, no doubt ready to issue more cryptic statements. It was going to be a one-sided conversation. She didn't have the energy to argue, even telepathically.

This time, something was different. Rise couldn't say how, but she knew there was more than a single presence with her. All had a slightly different feel, as though they were mental fingerprints—similar, but at the same time unique.

She began to count the entities as they arrived, wondering if this was some sort of spiritual conference call. By the time she got to seven, the pressure in her mind had expanded to the point it was uncomfortable. She had a moment of panic, like she was in a tiny elevator, being smothered as an entire football team tried to squeeze inside. She kept counting and the pressure kept coming. Ten, eleven, twelve…

Just when she thought she was about to be ripped apart from the inside out, a wave of absolute bliss coursed through her. She was flooded with a sensation of wholeness and completion, as though she regained a piece of herself lost for so long, she forgot it was even missing. She closed her eyes, every nerve in her body tingling with relief and joy and, above all, absolute recognition.

She smiled a tiny bit, getting the distinct impression her phantom friends were waiting for her to say something first. She let them wait, figuring they should be used to it by now.

"Admit it," she said at last. "You've missed me."

There was amusement on the other end of the mental connection, and Rise could hear rumbling laughter coming from what she knew to be other Heralds, her brothers and sisters, the absent pieces of her own soul. She was certain all eighteen were poking around in her head. Finally, one of them spoke.

"Welcome back."

The End

Crisis

Book two of the Fires of Providence Series

Coming soon

Dawn Jayne: A lifelong Hoosier, she attended Purdue University before enlisting in the United States Marine Corps. She met her husband, Todd, in Okinawa and enjoys reminding him she held a higher rank for a while.

When she's not writing, Dawn takes courses in religious and spiritual studies, rearranges furniture, and spends as much time as she can with her teenage kids. She loves midnight movies, hates wearing shoes, and is terrified of giant sunflowers. Her new favorite hobby is motorcycle rides with Todd.

Dawn lives with her family in Indianapolis.

www.dawnjayne.com